TRUTH UNEARTHED

A Novel

ERIC SPARKS

BEING THE FIRST BOOK IN THE SAGA

A FALSE DAWN

FOR THE SERIES

Tales of Lugon

Cover and map illustrated by Trey Waters.

Published by Swift and True Media, LLC
1138 N Germantown Pkwy
Ste 101 Box 210
Cordova, TN 38016
www.swiftandtrue.com

ISBN-13: 978-0-9961086-3-8
ISBN-10: 0-9961086-3-7

Official website for the Tales of Lugon series:

www.talesoflugon.com

DEDICATION

This book is dedicated to my Dad. Dad, thank you for teaching me that the treasures you find in the world of Faerie are not only real, but can be brought back to our own realm - if your heart is willing to carry them. I write of another world; you live in one. But we found the same bridge, and we'll meet again once I finish the crossing.

ACKNOWLEDGEMENTS

I would like to take a moment to thank first and foremost my father, Eric Sparks Sr. (to whom this book is dedicated), my mother, Regina Sparks, and all my friends and family for their support and encouragement and patience as I kept postponing publishing over the years until I finally felt this book was ready to be shared.

A special thank you to Winston, FHS, and Buddy (you know who you are) for reading the drafts and helping me ensure readers would be able to enjoy the story. Also, a special thank you to my editor, Max Dobson. This book would not have been possible without all of you.

TABLE OF CONTENTS

SECTIONAL MAP OF LUGON FOR TRUTH UNEARTHED

TRUTH UNEARTHED

A Novel

ERIC SPARKS

BEING THE FIRST BOOK IN THE SAGA:

A FALSE DAWN

FOR THE SERIES:

EXORDIUM

Assumptions

Twelve Years Ago...

Midnight had already passed, but Arun still couldn't sleep. Even though he was only five years old, the Watchers had declared him "Gifted." It was supposed to be an honor. He would be harvested from the Yeomanry, go to "school" (whatever that was), and given a chance to pursue a life in the Capital of Hilae. However, it also meant he would never see his family again. His father was quite proud. His mom was proud too, but Arun felt more like her: why should the reward for being Gifted be separation from his family?

Arun's chest jerked up and down as he choked back the sobs he was trying to keep quiet. Afraid he was about to wake everyone and get in trouble, he decided to sneak away to his favorite hiding spot down by the lake at the bottom of the valley—a place only he knew. Quietly, he put on his older brother's hand-me-down shoes. The soles were almost completely worn away, but that just made it easier to be quiet. He carefully dodged the creaky spots in the floorboards and made his way past his parents' and brother's beds in their one room hut. It took all his strength to keep his balance and avoid the groaning boards near the door as he removed the beam that locked the door and stepped out into the night. He hoped he wouldn't get caught so the last memory of his parents wouldn't include a beating.

Like a whisper into the night, Arun ran through the grass. The warm summer night had a cool breeze that gently brushed the tears from his face as he fled to the lake. He found his tree with the trunk hollowed out near the bottom. It was a small hole, and tall grass concealed it from those that were too big to enter. Arun had almost grown too large himself, and he had been afraid of having to find a new hiding spot. That wouldn't matter now.

He cried. Hard. There was nobody there to scold him, and he let the tears run freely and sobbed without fear of being heard. The loud cries worked themselves out after a short while, but the tears were still falling when he heard a soft, pleasant voice singing. He didn't understand the words, but they were beautiful, yet also sad. In his current mood, he found himself irresistibly drawn to it; the song was comforting in its beauty mingled with grief. Arun slowly ventured out of the hollow and followed the voice. It was coming from the other end of the lake on the same bank as he was. He crept closer, and soon he saw a beautiful woman lying down on a large rock, leaning over the water with her arms crossed under her. She looked young, but her hair was as white as the robe she wore.

Suddenly, she paused her singing and quickly turned in his direction. Arun tried to duck and hide in the weeds, but he slipped in the mud and fell. When he looked up, the woman had retreated some distance.

However, once she saw it was only a nervous child, she laughed and came back to him to help him up. She looked into his green eyes and saw the tear stains on his face.

"I'm sorry, little one. I didn't mean for my song to upset you," she said gently.

"Oh, no, miss …"Arun stammered, not sure what to say. "I … I was already crying, and I heard your song. It seemed sad too, but it made me feel better. It sounded so pretty. I didn't know sad could be pretty."

The lady laughed and picked the boy up, swinging him around. "Oh, little one, will you tell me your name?" She set him back down on more solid ground. "A friend once told me sorrow takes on the form of those it visits, so I thank you for the compliment," she said with a smile.

Arun didn't know what that meant, nor did he know what to do now that she had seen him. He wasn't even supposed to be there. As if she knew his thoughts, she said, "Don't worry, I won't tell anyone. I'm not supposed to be here either, but I can't help but come out and see the water and the stars at least a little."

"Arun," he finally said. "My name is Arun." There was a pause, and then Arun asked, "If you aren't supposed to be here, why not watch the stars from your hut?"

"Well, Arun, you ask very good questions," she said.

"That's why I was crying," Arun wailed miserably.

"Now why would you cry over something like that?" the Lady asked.

"I get told I ask good questions a lot, and now they say I'm Gifted. And that means they are going to take me away and make me go to school, and I'll never see my family again."

Poor child! the Elf thought to herself. For though Arun did not know it, or that even such creatures existed, that's what she was. Arun began to cry again.

"Shhh," she said. "Don't cry." She brought him back to her rock where she had been singing, swinging her legs over so that her feet touched the water. "Lay your head on my lap while I sing. I promise to sing about something happy this time." And she did, a slow, beautiful melody that matched the warm, sleepy summer night that surrounded them. As she sang, voices that Arun could not hear called back to the Elf maiden. Never stopping in her song, a new soft blue light radiated from her eyes as she heard the Sea calling to her from the water in the lake. The water likewise shone with the same light, though Arun would have seen neither even if his eyes had been open. In place of her reflection, visions of potential futures began to take shape in the water. She saw a great battle with their ancient enemy, Bälech. Though she could not see him clearly, the great warrior struck down their hated foe. Her people were free. Next, she saw a young man walking among her people on the surface, laughing and eagerly talking with Dwarves and Elves. Her singing paused as she saw the mature face of the young boy now in her lap. She looked away from the water and back to the boy. His face was calm as he neared sleep, unaware of the flushed face staring at him.

Could this be the one? Is this young boy the future hope we have long searched for? If I can just lead him to his proper place, it will be for the benefit of all peoples!

Truth Unearthea

The thought had barely formed in her mind when several voices in the Sea called out to her in a dark, foreboding voice.

> *Should this future you wish to see*
> *Forsaken by your own will you be*
> *A life in exile 'til you Fade into eternity;*
> *A drop of rain longing to return to the Sea.*

It was a warning, but of what she was unsure. Still, she could not let this chance slip by. She did not dare look back at the water lest she lose her nerve when the Sea showed her the price she would pay. *Whatever the cost, we must accept this chance!*

The light in the lake immediately extinguished, leaving her alone. The Sea had never so abruptly cut off a vision before, and the shock of it sent a tremor of fear through her body. At the sudden movement, Arun stirred, his drowsiness momentarily paused as he looked up at the Elf. Her eyes were dark blue, almost black, like the nighttime water in the moonlit lake beside them.

"Can I know your name?" he asked.

The Elf smiled at him. "Vera," she said. "I am called Vera."

"Vera …" Arun mumbled. "Vera … I think I'm going to miss you t —," Arun's voice trailed off as he fell asleep.

Vera smiled at the child on her lap. "No, sweet Arun, you won't. But I will miss you. I look forward to when our paths cross again." And with that she placed her hand over Arun's forehead and began other words that Arun would not have understood, but these words, beautiful in their own right, were powerful, unlike the soft like music she bad been singing before. Arun's lips contorted as images of his night thus far flashed in his mind: listening to the song, crying in the hollowed tree, running through the grass, and finally fleeing the hut. It lasted only for a moment, and then he smiled in his sleep. Now that Vera knew where he lived, she lifted the sleeping child in her arms and carried him back home. Placing him on his bed, she took off his shoes and went to the door, putting the locking beam in place. Then, pulling back the curtain on the high window, she leapt as quietly as a deer onto the window sill.

The Elf took one last look at Arun and vanished into the night.

"There you are!" The Lady Lyr's attempt at scolding was weakened by the relief of seeing Vera walking safely back in the camp. She had never felt fear coming from Vera before she lost her connection with her granddaughter over distance, but the surface was filled with dangers. Lady Lyr had been organizing a search party when she felt Vera's presence approaching, still some miles off, but filled with an excitement and happiness that assured her there was no danger.

"I had thought that so close to becoming of age, bringing you to meet our kin in the Makrin Mountains was prudent in case something should happen to me, but perhaps you are still too impetuous."

"Valima," Vera began, hoping the term of endearment would help settle her normally stern grandmother. "The Sea granted me a vision. I have seen the future savior of the Savanir that the prophecy foretold." Lady Lyr's eyebrows arched in skepticism. Vera had more natural prowess in communing with the Sea than anyone had since ... well, since Lyr herself had been a young Elf maiden, but the claim was still incredibly bold, even for her.

"Don't you mean *potentially seen*?" her grandmother corrected.

"Yes, yes," Vera said, annoyed at the reminder. "I know all visions are fluid and nothing is set in stone. But I saw *him*," she said. "And after Bälech was struck down, our people walked with this young boy, only now a grown man, laughing and rebuilding the world as it should have been."

A slight tingle in the back of Vera's mind made her shiver. Lady Lyr looked gravely at her granddaughter. "I sense doubt. Are you sure of what you saw?"

Vera shook her head and with it all reservations. She was convinced in her vision. "Yes, I just wasn't expecting a vision tonight, and the boy is still so young. It's hard for me to imagine him as a warrior, but that is years away."

The Lady Lyr paused. It was odd that the Sea had not shared this vision with her also. *Still,* she reasoned, *my time draws near its end, and I may well fade before this young boy battles our Enemy. Perhaps the Sea also believes Vera would be a fitting seer to lead our people when this body is washed away and I return to the Sea.*

Lady Lyr kept her emotions from her granddaughter. She must be sure of Vera's conviction. Refusing to let Vera see any hope or joy coming from her, she stared long and hard to see if her granddaughter would waver in her proclamation. But in place of doubt, a defiant gaze met hers, as if daring Lyr to challenge her again. The old seer smiled.

"Even while reckless, I acknowledge your ability to commune with the Sea bodes well for you ... and our people. But be careful. Visions are not to be chased."

"Yes, Valima," Vera replied.

Lyr smiled, knowing she had crossed into nagging. "Well, now that you've made my heart race, first with worry and now hope, I think it's time we tried to sleep. Goodnight, little one ... or not so little if the Sea has already entrusted you with such a vision."

Vera smiled at her grandmother's pride. "Goodnight!"

Twenty-Four Years Ago...

Athaz smiled as he looked around him. Even here, just outside Setenbor in the Northern Wilds, the camaraderie that surrounded him provided more warmth than the campfire they sat around. They were soldiers of The Dawn, meaning theirs was a bloody business. However, the battle was going smoothly, and already they had Setenbor under siege; their lookouts would let them know if any sortie was coming from the gates.

"Avid must be a bloody fool to try and rebel against the Son of Bälech," a nearby soldier said. "Did he honestly think that the Emperor would tolerate treason, even in this miserable territory?"

"I doubt he was that stupid," said another. "The snows are late; we would never have gotten through the pass to Lokin otherwise, and he would have had all winter to fortify this place. He already had quite a few mercs."

Athaz laughed quietly to himself at that remark. Half of them had fled in terror when they had seen how many Wardens were leading the force to quell the rebellion. Now it was just a matter of hoping the snows waited a little longer. If they assaulted the strongest city in the Northern Wilds, they would win. But the price in blood would be much greater than letting their resources deplete and the people rebel against Avid in hopes of a pardon from the Son of Bälech.

A horn blast from the south penetrated the darkness. It echoed all around them, save for the direction of the city, startling the entire camp. "For Xiarch!" came a fell cry in unison from locations south, east, and west of their position.

"Bewildered ambush!" Athaz yelled.

It was too late. War horses cried as The Bewildered charged the camp, spears pinning men still in their sleeping bags, which then became their death beds. Those who managed to get up quicker found swords sweeping for their necks long before they were oriented enough to fight. Everything was chaos.

Damn Bewildered! Athaz cursed as he ducked under a sword and spun behind him to levy his zweihänder across his attacker's chest, unseating him. Athaz was on him in an instant, quickly pulling out a dagger and stabbing the man in the throat before rolling away lest a spear find his back. *They must have heard of Avid's rebellion and are coming to his aid; any city no longer part of The Dawn is worth defending in their addled brains!*

The initial charge was over, and The Bewildered were gathering to the north near the city, turning around and preparing for another charge. "To the east! To the woods!" Athaz yelled to any that could hear as he began obeying his own advice. The nearby forest was dense, and The Bewildered's horses would become a liability instead of their biggest advantage.

On his way there, he found one of the Wardens gravely wounded. "I've got you, sir," Athaz said as he put the Warden's arm over his shoulder and called for help. Three other soldiers made their way toward them. The Warden was bleeding badly. They needed to get to a Healer quickly, but Athaz didn't know if they would find one in time.

"Damn Bewildered targeted the Wardens first to keep us from quickly shaving their numbers," he swore. "How they knew we would be holding council at that moment, I'll never know, but they couldn't have picked a better time to strike. Most are dead, and I won't be long."

At that moment, one of The Bewildered soldiers spotted them and sounded a cry for his fellow warriors to join him in chasing down the wounded Warden.

"Stop them!" Athaz shouted as he gently laid the Warden in the shallow snow and readied his zweihänder. Racing to the front, he led the charge, dodging under the swing of the first man's sword. Rising back up with his own, he caught the second Bewildered attacker under the arm and threw him backwards into the snowy ground. Most of Athaz's fellow soldiers had encircled their wounded commander and were trying to fend off the determined attack. A madness came upon Athaz as he saw his comrades falling. He leapt into the fray and slew his enemies. Too late did The Bewildered realize where the chief danger lay. After the final attacker fell, Athaz made his way to the man he wounded at the beginning of the fight, ready to finish him off.

"Hold!" wheezed the Warden. "Take him for questioning."

Most of The Bewildered had already established a wall and no longer pursued the army into the woods. Hailing a few more soldiers, Athaz carried the Warden to cover while two others pulled the wounded Bewildered fighter with them.

"Get him to tell you how long they have infiltrated Setenbor and how long they had the ear of Mayor Avid. I'm too weak to search his mind. Don't stop until you get answers."

Athaz's stomach did flips inside of him. He despised torture. He was glad it had always been the responsibility of the Watchers, not the military. But now he had just been given a direct order, so he beat the man. He broke every finger on one hand, but the man would not budge. "Start ... the next ... hand ..." Though the Warden was weak, Athaz was still under his authority.

"You will tell me something!" Athaz roared as he punched the prisoner, felling him to the snow. Bending down to grab the man's hair, he paused for just a brief instant. "Please tell me so I may stop!" he hoarsely whispered to his captive.

The prisoner looked into Athaz's eyes through his one eye that he could still open. Had he really just heard that? He cried out in pain as Athaz yanked him up by his hair. But those eyes were still staring back at him, silently pleading. A chance to sow doubt among a loyal soldier, end his own suffering, and keep the spies of the Savanir safe lay before him, if he could just work this chance correctly.

"Stop! I beg! There isn't much to tell, but I will share what I know. We heard rumors of the army on the move and were watching from afar. We have a camp on an island north of here." He was glad an uninitiated grunt was questioning him and not the Warden that would know it was a lie. "While you were laying siege, some of our men got close enough to hear this Warden and the others plan to burn the city with ev —"

Suddenly, the Warden faced the prisoner and yelled, "*Zol ete Bälech, a veryn fa Anpet falun cree, Shrik!*

The Bewildered's speech fell into a gurgled scream as an ice shard shot through his mouth, pinning his head to the tree behind him.

Athaz numbly turned to the Warden. The Divine Command the Warden had used had drained most of his remaining energy. "Nobody … lives … accusing … The Dawn of such atrocities."

Athaz couldn't believe what the captive was about to say. Was it true? Had that been the plan? Surely not …

"Look in my cloak pocket for the parchment and ink and find me something to write with," the Warden whispered weakly. "I don't have much time left."

Athaz carefully lifted the Warden from the tree he was leaning against and found the requested items. Quickly scanning around him, he found a small twig that would have to do for a pen. "Lie down. I must have something to write on."

Feeling awkward, Athaz obeyed. It was only a moment before the Warden spoke again. "Arise." Athaz stood at attention before the dying Warden. "Take this. You might as well try to read it, they won't believe you if you say no anyway." A fit of coughing overtook the Warden, and he spat blood into the snow. "You can't read it, but try to remember what it looks like; it will help during your questioning with the Watchers."

Athaz shivered at the thought of them. "May I ask what it is?"

The Warden had already closed his eyes, thinking never to open them, but at this he looked at the young man before him and coughed out a laugh. "Your recommendation to be made a Warden for … your service." Closing his eyes again, he took a few more breaths before his lungs stopped laboring.

* * * * * * * * * *

A familiar, lovely voice called to him. "Athaz, you're doing it again." Athaz's head shot up from the plate he had been staring at, lost in the memories of three months prior. He wasn't in Setenbor. He was home, in his humble but comfortable quarters. Lilleth was nursing their five-month-old son, Caedin, her soft brown eyes filled with worry as she looked at her husband. She had gone to feed Caedin after preparing Athaz's breakfast, which still remained untouched on his plate. He quickly scarfed it down before standing and putting the plate on the counter. Lilleth walked over to him with their son and leaned against his chest in an effort to calm him down. Athaz scolded himself for letting that night overwhelm him again. He stroked her long brown curls. Her life as a soldier's wife wasn't easy, but it was the price both had willingly agreed to pay to escape the poverty of the Yeomanry.

"I know you don't want to share what happened," Lilleth said as she laid her head on her husband's shoulder, "but this is tearing you apart. Please, don't keep me out."

Athaz put his arm around his wife, leaning his forehead against hers. Caedin grabbed at his father's shirt and squealed.

"You've always been there for me —"

BANG. BANG. BANG. "Open for the Son of Bälech!"

Athaz looked at Lilleth. "Later," he mouthed as he went to open the door.

The Tales of Lugon

A Healer was at the door. His hair, originally brown, was now mostly gray, but his face looked young, closer to thirty than forty. "Athaz of the House of Haedrin?" Athaz nodded, waiting for the man to explain himself. "My name is Palit. I am a Healer, as you can see," he motioned to his robes.

Athaz confirmed he had indeed noticed. "But why are you here? There is nobody needing treatment in my house; I did not send for you."

Palit looked surprised by the question. "Well, they said this was a rush, but I assumed you had at least been told. You are going to be made a Warden, and I have been tasked with preparing your body and overseeing its recovery."

"Preparation? Recovery? What is he talking about, Athaz?" Lilleth strained her voice, trying to hide as much of her apprehension as possible.

"I don't know," Athaz responded calmly to ease her concern. Turning to the Healer, he said, "I was aware I was up for consideration, but they hadn't even told me they had made a decision."

"Odd. The Son of Bälech was in a hurry, but I hadn't heard of anyone not receiving their notices." He looked up at the future Warden with some concern. "Are you ready? Then again … I guess that doesn't really matter now, does it?"

Athaz shrugged. "Since you seem to know more than we do, I guess you could at least tell us what's going on."

Palit then explained that the Son of Bälech was on his way; only he could perform the transformation process of Wardens, Watchers, and Healers. "It's not as bad for Healers," he admitted, "but bad enough. If not for having a Healer to help afterward, I'm not sure men would live through becoming a Warden." Palit paused for a moment before continuing. "I don't know if you could call a Watcher's existence living," he admitted with a shudder. "Let's not talk about them. I had to make sleeping potions for myself for a month after my first one." Lilleth's face went white. "Don't worry my dear, not nearly that bad for Wardens, though it's certainly an ordeal. And soon you and your little one will be in Hilae with all of the other Warden families, not stuck in this Light-forsaken village. You will have access to everything you and your child may need, including The Academy."

"But will my son have his father?" she muttered under her breath.

Palit did not hear her. "Alright, quickly now. The Son of Bälech doesn't like to be kept waiting. Normally you are told to prepare a bed for your transformation and recovery, but your main bed will have to do. And you ..."

"Lilleth," she responded curtly.

"Apologies, milady, but could you please peruse my drawings here? These are some symbols to choose from so you may identify your husband from the other Wardens."

Lilleth would have liked to stuff the papers down the Healer's throat, but she began looking through them while Palit led Athaz back to the bed and removed his clothing. "Hurry, my dear, the Son of Bälech may be here any minute!"

Lilleth returned with one of the sheets in her hand.

"Really? That was one from my first batch. I never thought it would be used. I was a fool for thinking Yeomanry symbols would be chosen. Those not from there find them insulting, and most like to forget about their past if they are from there."

"Please, Palit," Athaz said before Lilleth got any more upset. He could already read it in her eyes. She was terrified of losing him. "I will *always* remember where I came from," he said to her.

The Healer was already busy covering his chest, explaining how his skin would absorb the permanent tattoo during the transformation process, but Athaz wasn't listening to that. Lilleth had placed the infant in his crib and was near the bed, holding her husband's hand. He motioned for her to come closer, whispering into her ear, "... and where I'm returning."

A single *THUD* sounded from the front door.

"Dawn's Light! We barely got that done in time!" Palit said as he hurriedly put away his things. "That will be him! Quick," he said, handing Athaz a small vial. "Drink this. You'll be out before I get back in the room." Then, without waiting for permission, he ran to let in the Emperor and his personal guard of six Wardens. A Watcher also accompanied them, his face hidden in the depth of his hood. Palit shivered involuntarily.

"Not a good idea to keep his majesty waiting," the first Warden said darkly.

"A thousand apologies," Palit said, bowing deeply. "He is ready for you. Right this way."

Lilleth went prostrate as they entered the bedroom, as was customary in their Emperor's presence, but she couldn't help but look up at their ruler and the man that was going to change their lives forever. When she did, their eyes met, and she stared, transfixed. She had heard the Son of Bälech's eyes shone like the sun, but she hadn't expected the glowing orange irises that looked back at her. Then he spoke an unnaturally heavy, gravelly voice that hissed like lava cooling into stone. "Normally, it is death to gaze upon me without my bidding. But I am nothing if not merciful. And it would not do to spoil my newest Warden's baptism day by leaving him a widower with no one to raise his child." At this, he stared at the infant in his crib with an intensity and hunger that made Lilleth sick. But he finally turned his attention back to the bold woman before him. "No, that would not do at all," he said as he stepped up to the bed. "Leave us," he commanded.

Lilleth rose, but she did not leave her husband's side, though she couldn't bear the thought of looking into the Son of Bälech's eyes again. It was not fear of the consequences but the eyes themselves that were so unnerving.

The first Warden unsheathed his weapon, ready to kill the woman. "How dare you repay our lord's mercy with such insolence!"

"Stay your weapon, Warden!" the unnatural voice commanded. "Loyalty should be encouraged wherever it is shown. It's so hard to find these days, as we all know from recent events." His eyes glowed even fiercer as he said this. "She may stay. Watcher, stand with her. Prepare yourself, woman!"

Quickly, Lilleth made her way over to the crib. She pushed Caedin into the arms of the unexpecting, hitherto unwelcome,

Healer, who now felt like a dear friend compared to the other guests.

Palit rushed the infant out of the room. The poor woman! If she knew what she was about to witness, she wouldn't have stayed.

Suddenly, the Son of Bälech began speaking in a language Lilleth did not understand. For a long time, nothing happened. Athaz's breathing shallowed, and he seemed to be merely in a deeper sleep. But it was not peaceful. He began to moan. His back violently arched and he roared in his sleep — in agony that no lack of consciousness could dull. The Son of Bälech bent down and held Athaz down as an unnatural orange light enveloped the young man's body. It looked like a fire from within was burning him to death. Lilleth gasped and hid her eyes.

"Oh no, my dear, you wanted to see, and see you will!" another spine-chilling voice said. It was the Watcher's. But where the Emperor's voice was thick and heavy, this one was light and fragile. Speaking in the same tongue, Lilleth suddenly felt her hands go straight to her sides. Her eyes flew open, refusing to obey her mind's command to close. Unbidden and unstoppable tears began to flow as her husband screamed and his body contorted in protest. Her legs gave way, but still she found herself supported by an unseen force, her mouth agape in a silent, terrified scream.

* * * * * * * * * *

When it was over, The Son of Bälech summoned the Healer back to him. "Stay with him. You are now his personal Healer."

"Of course your majesty," Palit said with his head bowed.

"I mean permanently. The situation at Setenbor has revealed that The Bewildered were stronger than we realized, hasn't it?" At this he turned to the Watcher, who trembled violently in a memory that Palit couldn't even imagine. "We have lost far too many Wardens lately, and we must take steps to ensure their ranks stay filled. You are now at his command."

Palit was grateful that his bowed head hid the shock on his face. "Your wisdom is unquestioned, as always," he managed to reply correctly.

Walking past the Healer, he turned his gaze toward Lilleth, who sat in a heap, looking as far as she could in the opposite direction. "Remember what you have seen today, woman, and you will be wiser for it. I have taught you the nature of things, a gift many in Hilae must wait years to see. Use this wisely and you will find yourself in a place of power among the families in my capitol."

* * * * * * * * * *

Athaz awoke to the feeling of Lilleth wiping a moist cloth across his brow. He didn't have to ask to know he had a burning fever. "What time is it?"

"It's been a week since you became a Warden," she said without emotion. "Palit has gone to retrieve some more supplies."

Why wasn't she looking at him? "What's wrong?" he asked. "I have never seen you like this."

Lilleth laughed bitterly, handing him a mirror. "You're one to talk. Look at yourself."

Athaz gazed at his reflection. He looked like every other Warden, though he had to admit it was still a shock to not recognize the face staring back at him. "This can't be what's bothering you."

"How much do you remember?" she asked.

"Not much after Palit put the ink on my chest."

"Thought so."

"What's that supposed to mean?"

"I watched *him*, Athaz. I watched … what became of you."

"What became of me? I'm still me, no matter what I look like!"

"You are his now! You no longer belong to me … to us!" she screamed.

But now she could only sob. Athaz tried to hold her, but he was weak. She let him, though he might as well have been holding a cold wall; she couldn't have felt further if they were on opposite ends of the world. "Where is Caedin?" he finally asked. "Can I see him?"

"I don't think that's a good—"

Truth Unearthea

"Let me see our son," he demanded.

Lilleth finally looked him in the eyes. Pain like he had never seen stared back at him. "Fine, I'll get him."

When she brought him, Athaz reached out for his son, but to his surprise, Caedin began to scream and burrowed into his mother's bosom.

"What the ...?"

"He is remembering the first time he saw that figure. He sees only a Warden," Lilleth explained.

"And what do you see?"

Lilleth couldn't stop the tears from starting again. "I still see you, Athaz." She paused, but he could tell she wasn't finished. She put their son in his crib and crawled into the bed, lying next to him. Relief poured through Athaz as he hugged her tightly. "But I also see the man our son sees. I fear there is no stopping you from growing into this body... I fear that the Son of Bälech will not settle for transforming only your flesh." Lilleth's fingers clutched him, like he was something slipping through her grasp.

Athaz looked down at his chest. "You chose well. As I told you, I will *always* remember where to return."

"Then so much the worse for you," she said, trembling in his arms. "You will never be free of him."

CHAPTER I

The Graduates' Task

Arun checked the official seal of the headmaster three times before allowing himself to be convinced of its authenticity. His proposal for a Field Graduate Task had actually been approved! He would be studying a pre-Dawn historical site—well, at least that was how he saw it. He had phrased it as studying the First Light of the Dawn, where their first Emperor, Bälech, The One, had united the scattered human tribes. Bälech was of an old race, one with incredibly long life spans that preceded Men by several millennia. A disease had destroyed their population and Bälech, himself now slowly succumbing to the disease, wanted to unite the new noble and sentient race of Man to mirror his glorious society of old. Upon finding a human wife, his line, which had inherited his abilities in the Divine and the ability to imbue others with it, had ruled in an unbroken dynasty for 2700 years. Every emperor since their founder was addressed as "Son of Bälech."

Arun chose Chronicling as his specialization at The Academy, desiring to become a Keeper. The Keepers of the Chronicles, historians and sociologists of The Dawn, kept meticulous records of every society The Dawn's Light had reached, which was practically everywhere human civilization could be found. He had one class on pre-Dawn history and had learned very little other than what was generally known to everyone: Man was scattered, leaderless, and too busy fighting tribal wars to ever accomplish anything worthwhile. He saw pictures and even one exhibit of their crude weaponry, but he knew nothing of their culture. There must have been something for Bälech to unite, but no one seemed interested rediscovering what had been forgotten.

Arun knew he would never be granted a Field Task for pre-Dawn history, so he got as close as he could. Most of the tribes were united through diplomacy, eager for the benefits of The Dawn. A few had waged war, refusing to be led by anything stronger than themselves. Bälech despised war with Men; there were too many other enemies — Orcs, Goblins, and Giants — to spend time fighting with Men who could still redeem themselves. Some, becoming desperate, allied themselves with those vile creatures, and Bälech's hand had been forced. Unveiling his true Power, the Divine Tongue, he destroyed the tribes that had united to defy him at Lacris. The ruins of that city were all that remained of pre-Dawn history.

And so that was where Arun wanted to go. If there was anything left to find, it would be in the Ruins. About a two-month trip one way, it would delay his start with the Keepers, but the opportunity was more than worth it. It would also delay his roommate and project partner, Baran, from getting his military commission, but Baran wasn't about to complain about avoiding a thesis, no matter how much work getting out of it might require.

Arun was still reviewing the letter when he heard Baran's booming voice singing boisterously and off-key as he approached their dormitory. He guessed his friend had been at the Bard's Barrel again, where he spent a good bit of his time playing Six Stones or Courting the Deck with his allowance from their family. Baran had a lucky streak that didn't seem natural, Arun thought; he should always be broke, both games were pure chance, but Arun had yet to see him ask his parents for more money. Baran's family had adopted Arun from his original Court Family when they realized Arun was the only hope their son had of not being thrown out of the Court and becoming a Yeoman. Court members must graduate The Academy to maintain their position. Arun smiled, remembering how their odd friendship started when they were both eight years old. Compassion had forced him to help the struggling Son of the Court. Everyone knew who Baran was. As if the fiery red hair, blue eyes, and pale skin didn't make him stand out enough, at eight he was already the size of a youth of twelve. Their Instructors seemed to enjoy that they could intimidate him by reminding him of the disgrace that would befall his family, and the fate of Yeoman awaiting him personally, if he continued to fail.

Arun had always been sensitive to the splitting up of families. It might seem natural to everyone else in the nobility, but he still had a few happy memories of the family he had been forced to leave behind. And so, after overhearing the instructor berating Baran after class one day, Arun decided to tutor his struggling classmate, and in turn Baran protected Arun from the bullies that tormented him because of his heritage. The rest of the Court never let the Gifted forget their Yeoman roots, but in Arun's case, they at least stopped using it as an excuse to beat him. Over time, their mutual contract of survival developed into an incredibly strong, if odd, bond of friendship that had lasted up to this very year, when they would be graduating at age eighteen.

Baran's six-four frame barged through the doorway, still singing. Arun hid the envelope. He owed Baran for the dead snake under his sheets last week, and this was the perfect chance for revenge. He quickly gathered some study materials right as Baran entered the room.

"Glad to see you're in a good mood for another rehearsal," Arun said, leaning over a tome, furiously scribbling away on a piece of parchment.

"Oh, c'mon," Baran complained. "Now? I just got back from having three rounds of ale paid for by those unlucky bastards at the Barrel, and you want to ruin my mood with this?"

"Your mood will be a lot worse if you lose your commission by not graduating," Arun pointed out. "Start at The Ramifications of the 737 Rebellion."

Baran groaned as he began his part of the speech that had been planned should the Field Task not come through. Arun waited until Baran got to the part he always struggled with.

"It was at this point," Baran continued in his best imitation of an academic tone, "that the citizens —"

"Denizens," Arun corrected.

" — denizens..." Baran glared at Arun "...of Flur had the Light of the Dawn rekindled and Helite Katrina."

"Katina!" Arun blurted with feigned impatience.

"Katina ... aw hell ... you made me lose my place!" Baran

Truth Unearthed

complained.

"You're always lost." Arun laughed, fetching the paper as he continued. "But that's ok because I no longer need you to present anything."

"Please." Baran released a hearty laugh. "We both know you could do this better on your own, but we both know you won't."

"That thought had occurred to me," Arun said, walking with the envelope containing the prized sheet in his hand. "But it wouldn't be wise for me to do that just yet ..." he said, tossing the envelope into Baran's hands as he excused himself to the lavatory to relieve himself.

He almost didn't get the door shut in time. "YOU LITTLE—" *Clank*. The latch closed and Arun bolted the door just as Baran started yanking it open.

"I know I normally carry you," Arun called out from behind the safety of the door, "but you'll be carrying quite a bit for this grade. That brawn of yours will come in handy moving rocks ... other than the one between your shoulders for a change!"

Baran was fuming, and Arun thought about going ahead and bathing while he was in there to give his friend time to cool off. Then he realized that this would leave his peeved friend alone, in their room, with a sense of humor and vengeance that was a little more ... direct than his own.

Deciding the bath could wait, Arun stepped out and put on his most disarming grin. "I owed you for last week," he reminded Baran.

"Fair enough. At least that's over," his friend said, thumbing over to the scrolls and tomes they had poured over for the past month.

They looked over the approval sheet. There had been some stipulations to their trip. All artifacts must be turned over to the Keepers. Expected. All findings must be reviewed before being shared with The Academy. Also expected. One caught their attention though.

"A Warden?!" Baran exclaimed. Arun whistled.

"We're going into ruins. Why do we need such a powerful

chaperone?" Arun wondered aloud.

"Beats me, but I can't wait to ask him to train me," Baran responded.

They soon realized Baran would get his wish without having to ask. The Warden had been tasked with getting them ready for the potential hardships encountered on the trip, like confrontations with Orcs, Goblins, Giants, and Bewildered—small, nomadic groups of Men that refused to recognize the Son of Bälech.

"Too bad Bälech hasn't given me power in the Divine. My weapon skills are already pretty good," Baran said.

"Pretty good compared to me and the other future scholars," reminded Arun. "If you fare as well against a Warden, I'll volunteer as a footman."

The two friends continued reading the approval document, but nothing else really caught their eyes. One month of training, followed by five months allotted for their travel, survey of the site, and return, then one month to prepare a presentation of their findings. Arun knew he would be handling that final part.

The next morning, Arun and Baran excitedly talked about their upcoming expedition on their way to the Keeper's Tower. Light was just peeking over the high walls that guarded the capital, Hilae. The streets were paved with white large stones hewn out of the Briarthorn Mountains to the south, which was used to construct most of the buildings in the Court of Hilae. The colonnades adorned with drapes bearing family emblems of the Court gave a false sense of permanence—rarely did a family stay in favor with a Son of Bälech for more than a single generation, but everyone in the Court believed they would be the exception and spared no expense in presenting their best image to their emperor. But each one would be torn down as a family erred in service, one way or another. On more than one occasion, Baran had nearly been that error for his family, and he knew it. He looked at Arun as they crossed his family's gate. His family had never understood why Baran considered Arun a friend. They viewed him as a tool, nothing more. In their minds, it was Arun that should be grateful to Baran and the family for his relatively privileged life as a Gifted. Most Court families never thought to thank a Yeoman for anything, not even keeping them in the Son of Bälech's favor.

They entered the Keeper's Tower. A young Keeper, she couldn't be more than twenty-one, turned and formally greeted them. Her brown hair was kept in the fashion of female Keepers: two braids that started at her forehead circled around her head before joining into a single braid that went down her back. Her dark green eyes were shrewd and searching, quickly analyzing everything in front of her, and immediately dissolving any thought that the petite five-three frame housed a demure girl to match. Much to Arun's embarrassment, Baran felt the need to impress the young, attractive Keeper. "Baran of the House of Halew," he said, bowing deeper and with more flair than the Emperor's advisors. "Would you do me the honor of escorting me and my friend to Keeper Descia's study? Perhaps on the way, I could entertain you with my family history, and if that fascinates you, perhaps you would like to see our grounds sometime? Show you some of the treasures not visible from our gate?"

"Baran II, son of Taran. Chronicling Specialist to breeze into the military with the ambition…" the woman paused to eye him doubtfully with pursed lips "…of becoming a Warden. House of Halew, a Yeoman family until thirty-two years ago, when Taran, son of Baran I, sprinted five miles from his hut on the Green Path to warn a battalion of soldiers of an impending Bewildered ambush." Baran swallowed hard as she continued while Arun tried not to laugh. "Allow me to introduce myself. I am Descia, third-generation Keeper blessed to serve two Sons of Bälech. I will be attempting to instruct you, assuming you possess thought above your belt."

Arun's shoulders shook involuntarily at this point, and he feared opening his mouth. The Keeper looked at him as she waited for him to finish. "Forgive me, Keeper Descia," he said when he composed himself. "I didn't want to add to my foolish behavior by attempting to speak."

"At least Gifted are aware of their shortcomings," she said nonchalantly.

The Tales of Lugon

Arun tried to let the unintended insult slide off his back. To her it was a mere observation, he reminded himself. Baran started to come to his friend's defense, but Arun elbowed his ribs. Even if she had thought highly of the aspiring Warden, it wouldn't have done any good.

"Follow me to my study," she ordered and turned without seeing—possibly without caring—if they followed. They climbed up seven flights of stairs before she turned into a room. Baran felt a little less undignified as his friend tried to hide his shortness of breath.

The room had two bookshelves crammed full of tomes, scrolls, and parchments. Keepers, by rule, shared everything in the Chronicle Library and were only to have in their study items pertaining to their current research.

Without turning, she motioned to two plain chairs in front of her desk. Taking her place across from them, she put her hand on some pieces of parchment and two scrolls that lay on the desk. "These are copies made by our novices of all we have concerning the final battle before The Dawn was formally established."

Arun couldn't hide his disappointment. How did the Keepers know so little? He wondered if they were holding back. "Will we have access to the Library?" he asked.

Understanding his thought process, she answered him. "I can see to it, if you want to waste your time. If I wanted to hide something we had from you, I would not have bothered acting helpful."

Baran bit his tongue. *This is helpful? What do unhelpful Keepers act like?*

Arun bowed his head. "Thank you, Keeper Descia. I just had hoped for more information."

"And we want more information," she responded. "And that is why the Keepers will be joining your expedition when your training is complete," she announced.

Baran sat up as Arun stammered, "You'll be joining us?"

"Not just me," she corrected. "Geown, Sylphia, Nihl, and many novices will also be joining the company."

Stunned silence. The Keepers had every right to take over the expedition, but they had hardly anticipated it. "Do we still get credit for the Graduate Task when whichever Keeper claims the lead?" Arun finally asked.

"You are still the lead, at least for as long as your part in the dig lasts," Descia said, and for the first time smiled encouragingly. "Some of us have been waiting for generations to explore the Ruins of Lacris. And I will be your Chief Councilor."

Baran, tired of feeling like a mute fool, said, "Impressive for a young Keeper to have so much respect."

"Your flattery, while pleasing, isn't going to raise my assessment of you, Baran. Still, I thank you." For a moment, she dropped her commanding presence as she admitted, "They tell me it's because I am closest to you in age, only three years out of The Academy myself." Quickly regaining her former authority, she continued. "But in truth it's because I was the one who fought with the Watchers about allowing two students of your backgrounds an honor the Keepers had yet to be granted."

Arun's fears were put to rest, but he was also confused. The Keepers had not yet studied the Ruins? Not been allowed? But he had no time to ponder these things, as the young Keeper launched into what they did know of the battle and, much to Arun's excitement, pre-Dawn history.

The two hours flew by for Arun, but Baran kept glancing at the hour-candles to see how much time remained until he met the Warden. At last, Descia began collecting the scrolls and parchments for them to take back to their dormitory.

"Most of our meetings after today will be discussing plans and preparations for the expedition," she said. "There is much to teach you. You have never been on a dig, and now you will be leading one, if only in name and for a short while. You will study the scrolls in your own time, but feel free to ask any questions when you arrive the following morning."

Arun and Baran thanked her for her time and quickly departed. They had an hour to eat, take the pre-Dawn material back to the dorm, and present themselves to the Warden. As they ate, Arun started laughing at how the last introduction had gone.

"You can't help yourself can you?" Arun asked.

"What?" Baran asked.

"Trying to impress every girl you meet whose hair hasn't started turning gray," Arun explained.

"At least I try," he retorted and bit into a large piece of lamb to avoid having to talk.

Arun let it drop. Maybe the experience with Keeper Descia would keep his friend from acting overconfident in front of the Warden. That would be a much more grievous mistake.

They arrived five minutes early but found the Warden already waiting for them. He looked the same as all Wardens. Infused with the Divine, Wardens lost their previous appearance. Their bodies morphed into a muscular six-foot-six frame, and their eyes became black. They wore a full but neatly trimmed black beard and mustache. The only way to identify a Warden was a mark on their chest, which they kept hidden even while sleeping; only each one's family and the Watchers knew which mark belonged to which person. It was then the boys realized they had never thought about how to properly introduce themselves to a Warden. Most were busy fighting battles or living as the personal guard of the Son of Bälech. They had always bowed prostrate in front of Wardens, but it was to the Emperor, not his guard. Not knowing what else to do, they both bowed deeply and waited until he spoke.

"You finished yet?" the Warden asked when they stared at the floor for more than ten seconds.

"Yes, sir," Baran said.

"We weren't sure what to do," Arun explained.

"Salute, if anything, but only you need to practice that," said the Warden, turning his gaze toward Baran. "I understand you wish to become a Warden yourself, so you might as well get used to it."

"Yes, sir," Baran said again.

"Athaz," the Warden said.

"Sir?" Baran asked.

"Athaz. I'm going to get tired of hearing 'sir' as much as you say it," the Warden replied.

"Yes, s— Warden Athaz," Baran stammered.

Athaz shook his head. "Alright, let's get started. First things first, the Son of Bälech has graciously provided weapons for you to pick from. You will each select two weapons," he said, pointing to the racks on the wall behind him. "Go on."

Baran strode right up to a short, stout sword and a large rectangular shield. He fastened the sword's sheath to his belt and slung the shield over his back before going to a rack with all manner of bows. He chose a short bow and a quiver of arrows. Athaz looked at Arun and nodded toward the weapons racks. "You waiting for a golden-inked invitation?"

Arun took a deep breath. He had never wielded a real weapon before, and he didn't care for the thought of using one. He tentatively walked over. Finally, he picked up a quarterstaff from the melee weapons and a sling from the ranged.

The Warden sighed quietly and shook his head before going up and taking both away. "I may have let you pick one of those, but in picking both you are telling me your wish to avoid killing in a fight. The worst thing you can do is make your opponent angry by hurting him without disabling him. I could teach you to kill with both of those weapons, but this is more efficient," he said as he handed Arun a fauchard, a weapon much like the quarterstaff he had chosen, but with a large, curved blade at one end. "And," the Warden continued, "in trained hands, anyone can use any weapon without killing."

Arun stared at the fauchard, and he felt his stomach already churning in knots at the thought of striking another person with it. He had to remind himself odds were it wouldn't happen.

"I'll let you try again for your second weapon," the Athaz said.

Arun ventured to the rack again, trying to find something that would keep the Warden from changing his choice again but wouldn't make him sick every time he had to look at it. Spotting a vest of throwing knives, he chose it. *Won't be many mirrors on the road,* Arun thought to himself.

"The weapons of an assassin?" Athaz asked incredulously. Arun feared the Warden would change his weapon again, but he just shrugged. "Very well, I suppose just getting you to not kill yourself or us with just one weapon will be enough of a challenge in the time we have. I can give you some tips about how to throw these as we travel." Speaking to both young men, the Warden pointed to a squire and said, "Give your weapons to this boy." The squire bowed and left as soon as he had the weapons.

Turning to Baran, Athaz said, "Your friend needs some basic training you already possess. Go down this hallway, take the second right. First door on your left you will find Captain Muin. He will teach you some basic military tactics for the first week. Get used to him. He will be your commanding officer when you're commissioned." Baran saluted and with no small amount effort contained his excitement enough to not sprint down the hallway.

Athaz walked up to another rack with wooden training weapons. He grabbed the fauchard and tossed it to Arun. When caught, a splinter pierced his soft hands. Arun caught himself before he moved the hand all the way to his mouth, but not before it got close enough for Athaz to notice.

"We have a long way to go," was all the Warden said.

CHAPTER II

Still Got a Lot to Learn

Arun spent the first week learning basic stances, blocks, and forms — enough that he at least wouldn't kill himself when handling the fauchard. Two hours of weapons and combat training every day, during which Baran would be studying strategies and tactics with Captain Muin, followed by two hours of conditioning. After the first week, Baran joined him in weapons training.

"From here on out," Athaz began, "we will spar for half an hour a day to get you used to using your weapon in a more realistic scenario." He unsheathed his large zweihänder. Just as he finished drawing the sword out, he began speaking strange, terrible, and powerful words. A blinding light began radiating from the sword. Shielding their eyes, the two friends saw Athaz reach his other hand toward the light. Arun and Baran could barely make out him pulling his hands apart before the light vanished. When their eyes readjusted, Baran and Arun gasped. In place of his zweihänder was a perfect replica of Baran's short training sword and shield.

"How in The Dawn's Light ..." Baran began.

"A Divine weapon!" Arun exclaimed.

Athaz nodded. "A gift from the Son of Bälech for years of service faithfully rendered," he explained. "Very handy in combat ... and now for teaching." He pointed the blade at Baran and nodded toward the ring.

Baran entered and brought up his shield with his sword a little behind and outside of the shield. He cautiously advanced toward Athaz, who was still at ease. But when Baran closed in on him within fifteen paces, the Warden brought up his shield, lowered his shoulder, and charged in one quick motion. Caught off guard, Baran sidestepped a hair too late and was sent sprawling. He quickly got to one knee and brought the shield up again.

"You react slowly to the unexpected," Athaz pointed out. "Never a good thing, but even worse against the Savage Races. They're fighting style is chaotic, impulsive. They fight without thought of the consequences. You cannot assume they won't execute a certain maneuver simply because it leaves them exposed or gives away an advantage they already have."

Baran, eyes still focused on Athaz, nodded his understanding. The two then drew close together and began circling. Finally, Baran charged and sent a low thrust at the Warden's knees, below his shield. Athaz slammed down with his shield on the wooden blade and came over the top with his own. Baran blocked with his shield, exposing his torso, and Athaz quickly raised his shield back up and slammed it into the would-be Warden's gut and chest, sending him back as he dropped to a knee, gasping for breath. Athaz was on him instantly and brought the blade to his young charge's throat.

"Never, NEVER, never stop fighting until your opponent is down," Athaz said vehemently.

Baran, this time not looking him the eyes, again nodded his understanding; he was unable to speak. He suddenly fell backwards, away from the blade, and swept the Warden's feet out from under him.

The Warden was back up before Baran was, however, and this time he had his foot on Baran's throat, glaring. Then he suddenly smiled. "That was well done." Speaking a single Divine word, he placed his sword and shield back together into its original zweihänder form before extending a hand to help Baran up. "You learned the lesson quicker than I thought," he admitted to Baran.

"I thought I might die if I didn't learn soon," Baran said, still gasping from the shield-slam.

"Possibly, but you were never in any danger … this time," Athaz said with a laugh. It was the first time either of the boys had heard the sound escape from Athaz's lips since they had met him. "It wouldn't go well for me if I reported you dead before we ever left Hilae." He helped Baran to a bench. "Your turn," he said, turning to Arun.

Arun entered the ring with some trepidation. He detested violence. It might be a necessary evil, but necessary did not dismiss evil in his mind. He brought up his weapon as he heard the Warden begin speaking in the strange language again, which was followed by another bright light. Once finished, Athaz, with a newly formed fauchard, advanced toward Arun. At first the Warden put him through some familiar paces from their previous training sessions, and Arun handled his blocks well.

Athaz nodded his approval. "Now, go on the offensive."

Arun continued blocking the attacks, but the Warden was leaving intentional, gaping holes in his defenses. Each time, Arun would not attack; he knew he wouldn't really hurt the Warden, knew he couldn't land a strike that wasn't handed to him, but he made up his mind that he was taking a stand. Athaz began to get frustrated.

"Attack, boy!" he yelled, leaving himself open again. When Arun didn't, he spun furiously and with a flurry of attacks a seasoned veteran couldn't have stopped, walloping Arun on the forehead. The blow sent Arun staggering and falling backwards, his world spinning. Eventually he got up.

"Attack," Athaz repeated and again started going through a litany of poorly executed maneuvers. Arun still did not strike. Angrily, the Warden went into another offensive, put the butt of his fauchard in Arun's gut, and brought the flat of the blade on his back as he bent over from the blow.

"You have one more chance," the Warden threatened. Arun looked him in the eyes, unflinching while gasping for breath. "I'm guessing you still won't?" Arun shook his head. The Warden inhaled deeply before slowly letting it out. "You will regret this choice." He threw his fauchard to Baran before snatching Arun's and doing the same. The young scholar looked defiantly at the Warden. "Follow me," was all he said.

Willing to take whatever punishment the Warden dealt, Arun followed. They walked all the way out of the Court, passed the streets, and outside the gate. Arun saw the field in which the Yeomen labored, a life he had avoided. They continued until they were at a whipping post where a bailiff was whipping different Yeomen for their crimes. Theft, lack of production … it all meant the same thing. Arun prepared himself. The Warden tied one wrist to a post. Arun closed his eyes. He heard the Warden talking with the bailiff. When he turned, he saw the brute grinning wickedly as Athaz took the whip. Arun swallowed hard as he prepared himself. He unfastened his shirt to show his readiness.

But the Warden shook his head. "That would hardly solve our problem." Putting the next Yeoman on the whipping post adjacent to Arun, Athaz then put the whip in the young man's hand. Raising his voice for all to hear, the Warden declared, "Bailiff, you see before you a budding scholar who believes he is above violence. That others should have to protect him as he goes about digging in the earth for the story of our glorious empire. He must learn better. He is to whip each law-breaker you have today. If he refuses, or you believe he is not whipping them earnestly, you are to give him the lashes assigned…" the Warden paused and looked at Arun before finishing "…and then perform double on the Yeoman."

Arun stared at him in horror while the bailiff laughed with sadistic mirth. Athaz turned and walked back to the training grounds, eyes staring straight ahead and blood coming from the corner of his mouth as he attempted to ignore the pleading and then cursing assailing him.

* * * * * * * * * *

When Arun returned to the dorm that night, he wore no shirt. The stinging pain was too much. He whipped them, all of them. But one was a young boy — he could not have been more than ten. Whipping was a punishment for adults only, and the Dawn had set the age of accountability at fourteen. When Arun had pointed out the boy's youth, the bailiff mocked him. "Hey, Tenderheart, these Yeomen don't keep records of their brats' births, so I judge who is old enough, and I say he's fourteen."

The boy was trying not to cry, but he couldn't stop his shaking. Arun walked up to him. He couldn't bow his head lest he get caught, but he whispered. "I promise you'll make it, though it will hurt," he whispered. "In fact, I'll show you." Turning to the Bailiff he said, "While you may not have any pity in your heart, I bet you would love to let me have the boy's lashes," Arun said.

"You heard the Warden. He gets double if you refuse," the bailiff replied.

"I'll still whip him," Arun said. "But whip me first." The bailiff laughed. "Well, ain't this a grand joke! You can't take it for him, so you'll take it with him. Fine by me! Hand it over!"

It did hurt, more than he ever imagined, but Arun accomplished his goal: he didn't let a single tear fall, letting out angry yells rather than cries of fear. The boy couldn't help crying when his turn came, but he faced it with a trembling courage. The boy looked at Arun as he left. There was no anger in his eyes nor in any that followed that had watched the spectacle. In fact, in some there was pity, a feeling of kinship. It wasn't empty sentimentality. After being whipped, Arun felt claws in his back, further tearing his skin each time he raised his arm.

"What happened to you?!" asked Baran when Arun entered the dorm shirtless. Arun lay on top of his stomach on the bed.

"He whipped you?!" he asked incredulously.

Arun's answer was devoid of emotion. He needed to save all of it for the morning. "No, I had to whip the Yeomen or let them receive double from the bailiff, but I insisted on taking a young boy's with him."

Baran didn't know how to respond, so he stalled. "But it's illegal to whip people under the age of fourteen," Baran replied.

"Haven't you heard?" Arun asked, some of the bitterness surfacing in spite of himself. "Yeomen don't keep records of their children's births." Then, to himself, he added, "At least not on signed paper."

"What are you going to do?" Baran asked.

Arun looked him square in the eye. "The Warden will get what he wanted. I will fight. And tomorrow, I will lose. But one day he will feel every lash I inflicted on those people today. For now, let me be."

Baran respected his friend's wish. He went about his evening activities and took care of Arun's chores as well as his own. Eventually, he blew out the candles and got in his bed. Arun looked straight at the wall through it all. Sleep would not come that night, but he didn't want it anyway. He knew his anger would cool if he slept. And that was something he wouldn't let happen.

The next morning dawned with Arun still staring at the wall. When he got up, he cried out from the pain but also relished it. He might lose the fight today, but he swore to himself he would land at least one blow as he forced a shirt over his back. Baran got ready quietly, staying out of his friend's way.

Descia noticed the pain on her pupil's face. "What's wrong?" she asked.

"Don't worry about it." Arun breathed through his teeth but involuntarily arched his back when he tried to take the next step. Descia walked behind him and gasped. "Take that shirt off, you fool! It will get infected! You need a Healer. You needed one last night!"

"The Yeomen got no Healer! And they won't get one either!" Arun retorted in rage, remembering her insult from the first day.

"So you're going to refuse treatment you have access to? You truly are a fool! Refusing won't help them at all," Descia said hotly.

"No," Arun said calmly, reminding himself he was not angry at her. "I'll go to a Healer, but not until I face my 'chaperone' in training this morning," Arun said.

"I don't understand," Descia said, furrowing her brow. "Wardens don't use whipping as discipline." That was when Arun explained what had happened. She was about to excuse herself to personally talk to Athaz. She wasn't intimidated in the least by the Warden. Baran wasn't sure if she was completely sane, though Arun's opinion of her was rising quickly.

Still, he stopped her. "Not until I meet him," he said.

She argued at first but finally agreed. They went through their morning preparations for the expedition as usual, except Arun was standing the entire time.

"I was able to get the Keepers permission to go," she explained. "But The Dawn refused to provide funds. Still, we are given a small allowance. Each one of us going believes this to be well worth living on bread and water for the next six months. We'll still need some time to prepare and secure funds when you leave, but we'll be going on horseback while you all are on foot. We'll all meet where the Grigor River runs into the Argom, to the South. From there, we will all board boats and take a short ride down to Simpat, where we will all march east to The Ruins of Lacris."

Baran looked wistfully at the map, thinking how much easier the journey would be on horseback as opposed to walking. "I don't suppose we could wait a while and come on the horses with you?" he asked, hope filling his voice.

"Absolutely not," Descia replied. "There is no way we could afford three more horses in time. And you know as well as I do that your family isn't allowed to assist you in this task."

Arun's shirt scratched his itching back again, and he thought of something else. "Hope you all know how to wield weapons." Descia's face looked the same as Arun's when he first picked up the weapon. "Warden thinks we should all be fighters if we travel," he said bitterly.

"We've hired mercenaries for that," she said.

Baran laughed. "I think the Warden would rather defend you all alone than deal with those vagabonds. They were discharged from the military for a reason, you know."

"Well, if he wants to do so, he's more than welcome and save me the gold from their pay!" Descia snapped.

Baran shut his mouth and looked at the hour-candles. Thank The Dawn's Light, it was almost time!

When they arrived at the barracks, Arun looked at Baran and said, "He's mine first."

Baran nodded and slowed to let his friend take the lead. The yellow shirt Arun wore was almost completely orange now. Baran knew his friend didn't stand a chance against the Warden, but he would do his best to land one for him when his turn came.

Athaz was waiting for them. "I see you complied," the Warden said, seeing Arun's shirt. So it wouldn't add to the pain while fighting, Arun took his shirt off and tossed it to Baran as he fetched his training fauchard from the weapons rack. Without even realizing it, he found himself wishing for the real thing.

"Spoke too soon, I see," the Warden said grimly. By now Arun was in position. Athaz brought his weapon out and Divinely changed it to a replica of Arun's. The instant the flash died down, Arun charged.

He swung his weapon furiously, trying to remember all the techniques. He was doing well, but every time he thought he had an opening, the Warden always had an out, whether it was a parry, side step, or counter attack.

"*Hmph*," the Warden grunted. "A shame yesterday had to happen for this to come out of you. You're a damn good fighter when you want to be." Even as he said the words, the Warden grabbed Arun's fauchard and pulled Arun to him, stepping to the side and then hitting him on the back with the flat of his blade. The blow caused Arun to howl in agony. "That's for letting one of the Yeoman take double the lashes," he said.

If the rage in Arun had settled any since yesterday, it was now rekindled and multiplied many times over. With a savage yell, he sprung at the Warden. There was no technique now, just blind rage.

"Control your emotions!" the Warden warned. "It only makes you easier to defeat."

Arun continued swinging with all his might, deaf to everything except the echo of the cries of those he whipped yesterday, especially the young boy.

The Warden realized this was no normal frustration and was lost as to what could have caused it. Fearing Arun would soon hurt himself if he wasn't stopped, he quickly countered the next wild swing and grabbed Arun's leading wrist. Arun released the fauchard from that hand and tried to swing it with his other, but the Warden was too close for him to have a hope of landing a strike. The Warden grabbed his other wrist. When their eyes met, Athaz saw the tears of rage falling from his student's eyes.

Fearing he was probably throwing his future hopes down the

drain, but unable to watch the spectacle anymore, Baran yelled, "No Yeoman took double the lashes, you self-righteous tyrant!" The Warden turned to look at his other charge. "When the bailiff wouldn't let a young child go, Arun insisted on receiving every lash first."

The Warden looked at Arun. Exhaustion finally overcame Arun, and he fell to his knees, silent tears streaming down his face as Athaz still held his wrists. A short time later, the Warden gently put his hand under Arun's arm and lifted him up, calling Baran over to them.

"See that he makes it back your dorm. Come back for your training when he is in bed."

After the friends left, Athaz went into the Court. He scanned the houses until his eyes found a familiar family emblem, one of the few that had been there for almost a century. Seeing a servant watering the garden beside the gate, he said, "Tell your master Athaz is here to see him." With a bow the servant left.

Athaz began removing his armor to bear his chest to prove himself to the man of the house. After a couple of minutes, and elderly gentleman came out, making his way as fast as his crippled leg and would let him.

"Well met!" the elderly gentleman said hoarsely. "Time is not as friendly to decommissioned Healers as Wardens it would seem," he said with a laugh. The laugh turned into a coughing fit. He then stuck his hand out; Athaz had removed his shirt to show his identifier. "I don't need to see that," the man said with a chuckle. "No other Warden would take the time to visit an old friend."

Athaz shook his head and smiled. "You always have taken too many risks, Palit."

"Well, come on in!" said Palit. "It's always good to remember better times with old friends, even if some are fortunate enough to still be able to move about more easily than myself."

Athaz laughed. "I wish my body would let me rest," he said. "I'm afraid we can't talk long." He explained his current mission with the two students and the incident with the bailiff.

"I need you to tend to him," Athaz said. "Put all the charges to me."

"Pfff." The old Healer waved him off. "I have no family to leave my money to, but you should be saving yours for that wife and that boy of yours. They'll need it if something happens to you."

Athaz nodded. Hundreds of memories raced in both of their minds in a few short minutes, but neither said a word. Words were often superfluous between the old friends, nothing more than obstacles to trip over. "One last thing," Athaz said as he turned to leave, "He must not know I sent you."

"Of course," Palit replied. "Can't have you getting in any more trouble, unless I misunderstand why you were given an assignment more fit for a young sergeant." Athaz smiled with a raised brow. Palit hadn't exactly been one to unquestioningly follow orders either. "I'll do this, but you really should try to come for a visit before they chuck this old body out with all the others." Palit put his hand on Athaz's shoulders. "I would like you near when I march into the unknown."

"If I can, when I get back. You know our lives are not our own once we have been Augmented."

Palit released his friend. He knew that fact well. Athaz even coming by at all marked him different than all the other Wardens who had lived so long. "Farewell."

Palit turned back to his house to get his salves and ointments. He sighed, thinking of all of the vain campaigns he and Athaz had been on together. The Dawn was so paranoid of letting a single chink show in its impenetrability that it had crushed — most cruelly — any hint of rebellion. Palit lost count of how many men he had revived, only for them to be tortured to death again in a quest for their coconspirators. The Dawn itself needed a Healer, but that was beyond his skill. Still, perhaps one day something would come along to aid this troubled land, even if he wasn't around to see it.

* * * * * * * * * *

After completing the training session with Baran, Athaz went outside the gates and back to the whipping posts. The bailiff was happily at work again. His grin only grew when he saw the Warden approaching him. He stopped beating his current victim.

"Got another assistant for me today?" he asked with a grin.

Athaz smiled back and reached out for the whip, which the bailiff gave freely. "Not exactly," he said. He suddenly grabbed the bailiff by the throat. "What is the punishment for assaulting a young child of The Dawn?" he yelled, loud enough for all to hear.

"But, sir," the bailiff began, too shocked to be scared. "These Yeomen don't keep records of —"

The Warden squeezed his hand around the bailiff's throat to quiet him. "Where is the young child that was whipped yesterday?" he asked those near him. Unsure of what to do, the Yeomen simply stared. "Find him," Athaz commanded. Five minutes later, the boy stood before him, trembling. Rage glinted in the Warden's eyes. "Records or no, I trust you have eyes?" The bailiff stared with eyes wide open in fear. "I ask again: What is the punishment for assaulting a child of The Dawn?"

"Twenty lashes ..." the bailiff whimpered.

With one hand, the Warden ripped the bailiff's shirt off his back. After tying him to the post, he began, "You think these Yeomen can keep record of how many lashes you're receiving? 'Cause I might lose count!"

The Yeomen, finally understanding what was happening, cheered with each cry from the bailiff.

Athaz didn't lose count, nor did he pretend to. At twenty, he dropped the whip and untied the bailiff, who collapsed to the ground, gasping in pain.

"Why do you care?" the bailiff finally managed to say. "They're just Yeomen!"

The rage in Athaz's eyes had ignited into a full inferno. "Yes. One of your crimes was against a Yeomen." Athaz jerked the bailiff up by his hair to look him the eye, ignoring the cry of pain the object of his rage let out. "But I told you to only whip my charge if he refused to follow my orders." Terror flooded the bailiff's eyes. "I assume you know the punishment for abusing your office and whipping an innocent member of the Court?"

The Tales of Lugon

That night, every Yeomen in the nearby countryside couldn't stop talking about the Warden that whipped the bailiff before he dragged him off to the dungeons.

CHAPTER III

Unexpected Company

The last few weeks of training went by without Arun ever learning of Athaz's actions after he was sent home to nurse his wounds. The two maintained a formal, cold relationship. Arun was unsure how he was going to stand being with the man for six months but kept reminding himself how much of an honor getting to go was. And who knows? The Keepers may not have been allowed to go if he called off the Field Graduate Task. Plus, the due date for the paper and presentation had already come and gone. He was going to have to find a way to live with the Warden.

Baran's admiration of the Warden cooled, but he didn't share his friend's hostile feelings toward him. He had been raised in the Court, and his father and mother certainly hadn't kept in contact with the Yeomen. While he didn't like the method, he did agree with the Warden that Arun needed to learn to fight. Still, the first time he and Athaz shared a laugh after the incident, he guiltily looked over at his friend.

"Don't sweat it," Arun said on the way home that evening. "No sense in both of us hating him. He's done right by you, and you would be a fool to throw away this opportunity with your ambitions."

Finally, the day of departure arrived. It was now late spring, and the mornings were still pleasant. The Warden was waiting for them by the gate with two mules, one loaded with baggage, the other waiting for its load from the two students. In spite of himself, Arun couldn't help but smile now that things were really getting underway. They were able to travel light; the Keepers would be bringing most of the equipment needed for the dig.

"Couldn't ask for finer weather," Athaz said with a smile. "Let's get going and enjoy it while we can!"

The Tales of Lugon

He set a moderate pace. There was no rush, but this was still business, not a vacation. They made their way southwest, following the Grigor River to their left and walking just beyond the twenty-yard expanse of dirt that formed its near bank. The Briar Patch Mountains were on the far bank. Here, the river was about fifty yards wide, with tame currents and bends until it joined the much wilder Argom River. Mizcur, where the Keepers would catch up to them and would be their second stop, was founded where the two rivers met. To their right was the Mossy Plain named for the springy turf that grew in abundance instead of grass. The moss was green with the tiniest blue tint when the sunlight hit it just right. It looked as if a deep blue paint had been spilled and the stains, despite many scrubbings, could still be found to those with keen eyes.

The next day continued as the first, and Arun was beginning to wonder if his desire to become a Keeper and shut himself out from the world would be a decision he regretted. But the third day reminded him that being separate from the elements had its benefits as well. A storm whipped wind around them, drowning out their voices while penetrating needles of water found their way through all clothing and protection. No shelter on the plain could be found, and Baran and Arun looked longingly at the mountains across the river, wishing they could cross. Athaz kept pressing them on, and at last they found the most shelter they would find in this terrain: a small, pitted valley around twelve feet deep with a fairly steep slope. It bore the evidence of numerous floods. Athaz assured them that unless this kept up for several days, they were safe, but the two friends weren't so sure the rain wouldn't create a pool out of their shelter. They pitched their tent, but it had already been soaked during the march. With no hope of fire, dinner was cold and wet. It was at this point Arun realized being a Keeper wasn't a foolish idea at all—but maybe a sheltered scholar going on a field Graduate Task instead of sticking to a thesis was.

Fortunately, the rain let up shortly before dawn and the sun returned. They laid out all of their soaked belongings along the stony bank to absorb the warm rays and dry out, and did the same with themselves after a quick breakfast.

"I never knew a rock could be so gloriously comfortable," Arun said as the rock's warmth heated his back and the sun heated his front.

"Or a tent so miserable," Baran replied, equally enjoying the warmth.

Athaz was laughing quietly to himself. The aspiring Warden showed promise in skill, but Baran was still pampered and unprepared for a military lifestyle.

"It was amusing watching both of you last night. You looked as lost as orphaned fawns!" said Athaz, still chuckling to himself.

Arun sat up when he heard the expression. It was a Yeoman expression, one his father had used often, but he hadn't heard it since he was a young boy. Athaz stopped laughing and bit his tongue as he stared back up at the sky.

After a couple of hours, Athaz forced his charges to pack things up again. Arun and Baran slowly responded, wishing the whole day could be spent relaxing after the arduous trek the day before. Still, the journey was pleasant as it had been when they first started. Shortly before they were going to stop for lunch, the Warden spotted something across the river approximately two hundred yards ahead and instinctively held up his fist for them to halt.

"What is it?" Baran asked.

Athaz pointed at three crude canoes launching into the river, each with three passengers.

Arun came up behind the two. "Who are they? I didn't know there were any villages in the mountains."

"There aren't," Athaz replied. "At least not until you have traveled for weeks. There you'll find a few bandit hideouts, but none of them will come near Hilae. These are not bandits. Hopefully, if we wait, they won't even notice us."

By now the three vessels were halfway across the Grigor, and Baran could make out their talon-like hands. "Orcs!" he cried hoarsely. The Warden nodded. "What are Orcs doing so close to Hilae?"

"I would be finding that out myself, but I don't want to be worrying about you two in a fight."

Suddenly the Orcs starting yelling excitedly and swung their boats up current toward the three travelers.

"Looks like I won't have a choice," Athaz said with some annoyance. "We can't outrun them. Orcs do not tire easily, and we are heavily burdened by our supplies. Ready your weapons."

"Can't you strike them with the Divine?" Arun pleaded.

"I plan to, as soon as they finish crossing. But the Divine does exactly what you say. *Exactly*," he emphasized. "It's almost impossible to hit a moving target with it. And it takes time; I will only get off one attack before they are on us."

Baran already had his sword strapped to his waist with his shield on his back and was readying his bow. Trembling, Arun grabbed his fauchard and put on the vest of throwing knives.

"There are too many for me to protect you in close combat. But when they realize what I am, it will pull the majority of them to me, and I will separate myself from you. Hopefully, you won't have more than two or three to fight between the two of you. Your opponent is as reckless as he is evil, and that will play to your advantage, for I have trained you myself on how to deal with them. Now leave me; I must even the odds a little before we engage." Even as he spoke those words, the first Orc canoe docked on shore.

Athaz began to speak the powerful and strange words again, his eyes unflinchingly trained on one of the Orcs that had just gotten out of the leading canoe. The second canoe then the final canoe landed, and still Athaz's Divine command continued. Suddenly, he raised his hand and cried, "*Shrik!*" A bolt of lightning shot out of his hand and hit the Orc nearest to them in the chest, which sent him flying back into another behind him that was knocked unconscious. Seven Orcs remained. With a cry, Athaz unsheathed his zweihänder and ran a circuitous route toward their enemies.

The largest Orc in the back shouted commands in a short bark, and four of the Orcs sprinted toward the Warden, spreading out in case he tried another Divine attack. The Orc commander then grabbed two members of his squad and sprinted toward Baran and Arun. Taking a cue from Athaz, Baran sprinted away from the river and let loose his first arrow. It went wide, but it did what he intended. The Orc commander and one of his companions turned to chase him, leaving Arun to defend himself against one. Baran continued running as he let loose another arrow that also went wide. Finally, he stopped before pulling out his third arrow. The Orcs were only thirty paces from him now. Forcing out his breath slowly, he took aim at the smaller Orc and let the arrow fly. It went through the Orc's eye, and it fell with a shriek. Dropping his bow, Baran pulled out his sword and readied his shield for the commander.

Arun was already busy with his opponent, who swung a large two-handed axe. Arun was forced to keep retreating, just barely staying out of range with each strike, trying to wait for a gap large enough in time where he felt he could counter. Finally he charged and attempted a thrust, but the Orc simply sidestepped and brought his axe overhead. Arun barely got the shaft of his fauchard up in time. He managed to slide it under the axe's head, but the force of the hit still knocked him to the ground. Dazed, he lost his grip on the fauchard but got his wits about him just in time to roll away from the second swing. Arun scrambled to his feet and frantically looked for his weapon. The Orc made a strange gurgling noise. Arun's knees went weak as he realized it was laughter — and the reason for it. The Orc was standing over the fauchard. Realizing it wouldn't take the Orc long to finish him, Arun did the first thing that popped in his head. Reaching in his vest, he grabbed as many knives as he could and hurled them at his foe. The Orc swung his axe to try to bat them away, but one knife got through and cut his forearm, causing him to drop the axe. Reacting purely on instinct, Arun hurled himself into the Orc, hoping to get back his weapon. It almost worked. The Orc was knocked off the fauchard, but he grabbed Arun's arm as he fell. They tumbled over each other, the beginning of a life-or-death wrestling match.

Baran, meanwhile, had been busy with the Orc commander, who was wielding two spiked maces. The Orc's attacks had been reckless, as Athaz had predicted, but they were so furiously paced that Baran was rarely able to counter with a thrust or swing of his sword. When he did, the Orc easily dodged or batted the blade away. Baran could feel weariness overtaking him, and he feared any second he would drop his guard. Suddenly, his first sparring match with Athaz came to his mind. He smiled, knowing it would be the last thing the Orc expected after having fought so cautiously. He feigned a weak swing from his sword. The Orc batted the sword away with the mace nearest and, as expected, raised the other for an attack. But instead of raising his shield, Baran leveled it with his shoulder and charged. The Orc commander was knocked backwards several feet, landing on his stomach with his feet closest to Baran. Though his opponent was down, Baran continued his charge. When the commander tried to get to his feet, the last sensation he felt was cold steel going into his back and penetrating his heart.

Baran's joy was short lived as he heard Arun cry out in pain. Turning, he saw the Orc throw his friend across the ground. Arun's left arm rested at a grotesque angle. The Orc went back to where he had dropped his axe, picked it up, and began walking toward Arun who hadn't moved since landing on the ground.

"Arun!" cried Baran as he sprinted toward his friend. But there was no hope. He wouldn't make it in time, and he knew it. He hurled every curse and insult he could think of at the Orc, hoping to distract it, but he didn't even know if the Orc understood human speech. With only ten paces let to go before he slaughtered his target, Arun suddenly raised himself with a cry and swung his right arm toward the Orc. Despair filled Baran's chest, thinking his friend was swinging blindly. But the Orc stopped. It dropped the axe, fell to a knee, and began raising its hand up before it completely collapsed. Baran still hadn't stop sprinting. When he got there, the Orc was dead, one of Arun's throwing knives lodged in its throat.

"Arun!" Baran said, and tried to gently lift up his friend. With his good hand, Arun held Baran back. "Help Athaz," he said wearily. Baran felt like a fool. He had forgotten about the Warden. But even as he turned, he saw Athaz kill the second of his four opponents. Baran ran as fast as his exhausted legs could carry him, calling out as he did. One of the Orcs began to turn its head, but the act allowed Athaz to remove that head from the Orc's shoulders. The final Orc, realizing death was upon him, turned in a desperate attempt to flee. Athaz began speaking in the Divine again, but this time it was to his weapon. In much less time than it took to fire the lightning bolt at the beginning, he suddenly finished with the command "*Shrik!*" A blinding flash of light appeared around his sword, and Baran looked to see the Warden raising a bow with an arrow already notched. He let it fly, and the battle was over.

Athaz began walking toward the unconscious Orc and then stopped. "Where's Arun," he said, the concern audible in his voice.

"He made it," said Baran breathlessly, pointing toward his friend. "But he's definitely hurt."

"Bind our captive," Athaz ordered and began jogging toward the wounded scholar. "But whatever you do, do not kill him!" He shouted over his shoulder.

By the time he made his way to Arun, his charge had managed to work his way into a sitting position. After seeing the vomit, Athaz became alarmed that Arun was in danger. But Arun explained, "My arm's the only thing hurt. But ..." Athaz nodded in understanding. "Let me help you up."

Arun put up his good hand and looked down at his pants, embarrassed. "Can you fetch me a change of clothes first?"

Athaz gave him a sympathetic smile. "That's more common than you would think for people in their first real fight. Nothing to be ashamed of. Come on, up we go." In spite of Athaz's best attempt to be gentle, Arun cried out in pain as the Warden lifted him up.

"Can you heal it?" Arun asked as they slowly walked toward the river.

"Not with the Divine," Athaz responded, knowing what he meant. "But I can and will set it." The pain in Arun's arm seemed to double just at the thought. "I don't know the words for bones," the Warden continued, "tendons, or a host of other things I would need to know for the Divine to mend it. I'm not aware of any Warden that does. But even if I did, that's not where the Power given to us lies."

By now they had made it to the river, and Arun sat in the shallows. Athaz carefully removed the vest. "I'll go collect your knives," he said. Then he cut off Arun's tunic and left him to bathe in the river and change his soiled clothes. "I'll be back in a minute to set your arm and dress your wounds," he said. "But first I have to check on our prisoner."

Baran, as ordered, had bound the Orc who was just beginning to come around. Athaz grabbed him roughly by the throat, dragged him to the river, and held his head underwater for a few seconds. When he began to struggle, Athaz knew he was fully alert again and pulled him out.

"Good, that concussion didn't leave you permanently incapacitated; you have some information I need," he said to the Orc. The Orc cursed in its crude, foul language. Athaz laughed grimly. "All the same. Blinding hatred overriding even fear if there is no hope for escape." Dragging the Orc back to Baran, he threw him to the ground. "Watch him while I attend to Arun." Baran nodded and sat a few yards away, watching the Orc as warily as if it were free.

Athaz rummaged through his baggage and grabbed a vial of dark liquid before walking over to Arun, who by now was in clean pants and trying to wash the cuts he had received from the Orc's long nails and teeth. "I'll get those," Athaz said. "But first I'm going to have to see to your arm." Arun nearly swooned at the mere thought of someone touching the broken bone. "Drink this," he said, handing the vial to Arun.

"What is it?" he asked.

"A concoction we normally use for unruly prisoners," Athaz said. "Tastes nasty, and you'll wake with a horrible headache, but you'll be out while I work on that arm."

Arun didn't have to be convinced it was a good idea. He took the vial. "Where do you need me to be?" he asked.

They walked back toward the mules, and Athaz had Arun sit about ten feet from the river bank, so he could easily fetch water for cleansing the wounds. "Lie down quickly once you drink it,"

Athaz said, "or you'll have an even worse headache."

Arun nodded and tossed back the vial. It did taste horrid, and Arun had to stop himself from gagging and choking on it. As soon as he swallowed it though, he could feel the effects beginning and quickly lay down to avoid falling over. In less than a minute, he was out.

Athaz Divinely changed his weapon into a small knife and went to work on Arun's arm. It took him well over an hour, and then he began dressing the wounds. When he finished, he went over to Baran and the Orc and explained to Baran what he had been doing. "Now I'm ready to deal with our captive; I'm sure you're tired of his company anyway."

Baran wholeheartedly agreed. "What are you going to do with him?" he asked.

"Search his mind for answers," Athaz replied with a disgusted look on his face. "Rarely do we do it for Orcs, and I'm not nearly as effective as a Watcher, but I have to try; there shouldn't have been any of this filth near Hilae, and I need to know why. I will bring him over near Arun first. You will have to guard both of us. I will be completely unaware of my surroundings as I do this."

With that, he dragged the Orc toward his unconscious charge with Baran following. As Athaz began speaking the Divine with closed eyes, he grabbed the Orc's head, who began to struggle. As soon as Athaz opened his eyes with the command *Shrik!*, their eyes locked, and both became as still as statues.

In spite of the day's events, Baran grew bored after the first half hour — partially because he realized the Warden had not said how long this process would take, but also, as his nerves calmed down from his first fight, his stomach remembered they had been about to stop for lunch before this unexpected encounter. Picking up dry, discarded wood that had been left on the bank when the river had been higher, Baran soon had a fire and cooked what could either be a very late lunch or an early dinner.

Three hours passed. The sun was now getting very low across the Mossy Plain, and Arun began to stir much sooner than expected.

He suddenly sat up with a start and yelped in pain as he tried to move the arm that was bound to his torso in a cast Athaz had made for him. Baran ran to his side immediately to check on him. Arun saw him but lay back down. "No talking," he said weekly. "My head feels like that Orc's axe found my skull, even though I distinctly remember blocking it."

Baran chuckled. His friend may be in pain, but at least he was keeping his spirits up.

"Fine," Baran said. "I'll keep quiet like I have been for the past three hours, but I thought you might like it if I cooked something for you."

At first Arun said no. Then he remembered there was a river next to them. "Maybe make some broth," he finally said. "My stomach and head need a compromise." Baran willingly fetched a pail of water, gathered some more firewood, and put some of the salted mutton along with some of their vegetables in the water. When it had come to a boil, he set aside to cool for a few minutes before nudging Arun.

"Thanks," Arun said, opening his eyes. He looked and saw Athaz for the first time, still locked in a staring contest with the Orc. "What in The Dawn's Light is he doing?" Arun asked.

"Reading the Orc's mind with the Divine, I think," Baran answered. "But at this point I am beginning to wonder if he's lost in there."

Arun sipped the broth in silence, and the sun sank beyond the horizon. About the time he finished eating, Athaz stirred, and the Orc fell back. Suddenly, Athaz roared, grabbed his zweihänder, and began to hack at the Orc. It was dead after the first blow, but Athaz cut through it thirteen more times before he threw sword into the ground and fell on his hands and knees, panting. Arun's head pounded, but he never thought to complain. Both he and Baran were so shocked at the sudden violent rage of their chaperone, they didn't even realize they had prepared themselves to run for their lives. When the Warden finally stood again, he dragged the Orc's broken corpse and hurled it into the river. Baran and Arun remained silent as he came and sat by the fire with them. No one spoke for a full five minutes when the Warden finally offered some explanation.

"Orcs," he said, slowly, "like men, love inventions. But the Orcs only invent things that are cruel and painful. I am sorry you saw that outburst, but I could not control myself after I saw what that filth had done to his victims. I have read minds before, but never one of the Savage Races. I fear I will not find a restful night's sleep for weeks. And until the day I die, I will still wake with a start from what I saw tonight."

"Did you learn why they were so close to Hilae?" Baran asked.

Athaz scowled at the question. "Not exactly, but we must continue to move, and we must move quickly. We need to get to Mizcur with as much speed as possible." He looked at Arun and sighed. "Baran, I'm afraid we will have to shoulder one of the mule's burdens, at least for a couple of days."

Arun insisted he was fine, but Athaz interrupted him. "If you can stand up without staggering and jog without crying out in pain, show me." Much to everyone's surprise, Arun did stand, a little wobbly — a combination of the lingering effects of the elixir and not having his left arm for balance. In one of his off-balance moments, he instinctively tried to move his broken arm and yelped in pain.

"Thought so," Athaz said.

"Sir," Arun said, "If there is trouble, why not just turn around? I'm sure when The Academy hears of this, they'll allow us to give a late presentation."

Athaz looked hard at Arun with weary eyes. "I'm not sure that's an option," he said at last.

Baran and Arun both tensed, alarmed. Can't turn back? Not an option?

"What do you mean we can't go back? Why is that not the first course of action if you believe we are in danger?" Baran finally asked.

The same eyes now turned to Baran. "I cannot say," he finally answered him.

Arun squinted. "Can't..." he paused "...or won't?"

"Both." Anger replaced some of the sadness, but it immediately evaporated. "I have … concerns," he said, carefully picking his words, "but I can't account for what I learned, and I dare not speculate. Now, leave me be. You both need rest, and I need to think. We leave at dawn. I'll keep first watch, then Baran, and finally Arun."

With that he turned his back to the fire and to them. As if the cryptic answers weren't unnerving enough, he was now setting a watch inside the shadow of Hilae? What he had seen in the Orc's mind, the two friends could not guess, but neither of them rested well that night.

* * * * * * * * * *

Six hours had gone by, and Athaz still had not woken either of the students to take their watch. He couldn't sleep until he could think of something to account for what he had seen in the Orc's mind. The Orc had come from The Tennebron, the great prison of The Dawn. But it hadn't been living there as a captive; it had been a guard. From the same commander that led them in this attack, the Orc had received orders to track two young men that were setting out from Hilae, and it was given a drawing of each of them.

"Make sure you don't get too close," the commander had said, "until they make it to the ambush point. They have a Warden with them. Though he has fallen out of favor with the Emperor, he is still quite formidable. You may kill the Warden if you wish, but there is no need. His fate will be sealed by simply killing the two youths with him."

The Orc whose mind Athaz was searching spoke up. "I don't like this. Those sheltered in Hilae have betrayed us before, safe behind their walls. How do we know we ain't gonna be left high 'n dry? How we know we gonna get paid?"

"Easy, lad," the commander answered. "I secured a sizable upfront payment that all living parties will distribute equally. But here is the best part…" he paused to soak in the hungry looks of his men "…that Warden has a nice woman and boy. We do this job proper, and we go to the front of the line to welcome them when they are sent here for the treachery of that Warden. What do you say to that, lads?"

Memories of the Orc the last time he had free rein with men, women, and children made Athaz lose his grip on the Orc's mind. Their love of torture knew no bounds, and the next thing he knew, he was back in the present world, hacking the Orc to death for desiring to bring such things to his family.

They had been fortunate of the Orc's miscalculation. But now Athaz was met with a horrible dilemma. How far did this go? The fact that Orcs now ran The Tennebron was news to him, and it couldn't have happened without the Son of Bälech's knowledge. Athaz wondered who was pulling the strings in trying to ambush Arun, Baran, and himself. Was it his commander? A Watcher?

Pushing those thoughts to the side, he focused on his problem at hand. What should he do now? That depended on who was directing this operation. He doubted the Emperor himself was involved in this particular plot. If the Son of Bälech actively wanted him dead, he never would have left Hilae alive. He was formally "out of favor." It was the last step before a slow, painful death. He could still work his way back into favor; but the Emperor had officially removed his royal protection from Athaz.

Knowing what he knew of the Dig, and what he had seen thus far, the best Athaz could come up with was that Arun was an embarrassment on the Headmaster of The Academy. With a sizable payment, he could probably pull some strings to get prisoners placed where he wanted them. Baran? Athaz wasn't sure, but he knew Baran and himself (being out of favor) could be spared as casualties even if Arun was the only target.

And so, Arun and Baran could not return, especially not Arun. It was apparent that someone with serious clout wanted the young scholar dead, and immediately returning would likely cause that person to kill him outright in a panic. *But what about Lilleth? Caedin?* It was tortuous to think about how he could save them. Go back and send Arun on his way? That probably wouldn't work. The Watchers would see the Warden returning, and if he failed in this mission, it would be the end for him and his family. Could he get a message to them? That might be the worst idea of all. Surely any communications he sent would be monitored.

Dawn was climbing over the horizon, and still he hadn't thought of a course of action he was happy with. Perhaps he would think of something as they journeyed to Desip. That would be the first time he would be able to get any message out anyway. And with that in mind, he went over to wake the two friends. No time to rest. They had to move.

CHAPTER IV

A Choice to Make

Baran and Arun awoke with a start when Athaz nudged them. With the morning light just beginning to cover the Mossy Plain, they realized the Warden had let them sleep all night. Had he not rested at all? Or had he decided he overreacted and a watch hadn't been necessary?

The Warden took most of the burden from the mule, but Baran did have to shoulder some of it. They marched until lunch, when they stopped for a brief bite to eat. Baran finally got the nerve to ask what they had been wondering and whispering among themselves all morning.

"Did you decide a watch wasn't needed after all?"

Athaz never looked up from his food. "I decided if I couldn't sleep, I might as well watch. I was thinking. I'm still thinking. And don't ask me about what right now."

The next five days were uncomfortable for all of them, in spite of the beautiful late spring weather. Baran and Arun talked in quiet whispers and were continually looking over their shoulders at every sound. Athaz remained mute, deep in thought. In the evenings, Athaz began sparring with Baran, and it was far more rigorous than anything he had tested the aspiring Warden with back in Hilae. He pointed out every flaw with as much grace and patience as he could muster. Baran still became frustrated, but any time he thought of saying something, he only had to remember the helpless sensation he had when he felt Arun's death was near. He kept silent and absorbed everything he could from the Warden.

On the sixth day after the battle, and the tenth since they had set out from Hilae, they could finally just make Desip out in the distance when they paused for lunch. It was a sight welcomed by all three, and for the first time since the Orc attack, they were all eating and smiling. Tonight, their tent would be traded for an inn and their sleeping bags for feather beds.

Athaz was still concerned. It had taken them ten days what they should have been able to accomplish in a week. Originally the plan was to rest in Desip for a few days, but he feared that course of action now. Walking by the Grigor River, he could see any threat coming long before it reached them, but in a city, enemies could hide in the shadows and wait for them to stray into their path. He knew they wouldn't like it, but already the Warden had made up his mind there would be a watch tonight. The walls of Desip could provide comfort, but not safety. Athaz knew that his young charges would be tempted to lower their guard within the perceived safe confines of the inn.

They still had about two and half miles to go. Athaz took what remained of the march to warn them of becoming too lax in the city.

"We are not safe here," he told them.

Arun's voice quaked from trying to contain his frustration. "Safe from what? Orcs? I would think we are much safer from any of the Savage Races in any town than traveling alone."

Baran also chimed in. "Can you please give us something more than 'be cautious'? Danger is easier to avoid if you know what it is or at least where it might come from."

"Not yet," Athaz said wearily. "Just stick with me when we enter the town. I know a quiet inn that will be safer than most, and I need you two to stay put while I go restock our supplies."

Arun gave a cry of exasperation, and Baran fell quiet. The only good thing was at least the two friends would get a chance to have a private conversation, their first since they departed Hilae, and they sorely needed it. Why were they trusting the Warden anyway?

Desip was a small town, built on the trade between Hilae and Mizcur. Being on the river, it was fertile with crops and also had good fishing, able to sustain itself. This allowed most of the citizens to live comfortably but not extravagantly. Houses were often passed down for generations. Occasionally, additions were made

Truth Unearthed

with the popular tastes of the day, attempting to meld with the older features, making each house unique and almost like a history book for each family. However, unlike Hilae, which had the wealth to bring in stones hewn from the mountain, these homes were built of wood from the trees at the foot of the mountains across the river. Their beauty combined with humility struck Arun as more magnificent than the finest homes in Hilae.

The inn they were staying at was old and plain but well kept. The furniture was at one time beautiful, hand carved with ornate, fluid designs. They were made of a dark wood, maybe cherry, but both the color of the wood and upholstery had been sun-bleached. The only people old enough to remember the color were also old enough to have forgotten it. Still, they were sturdy and comfortable. One felt that the inn at one point was immensely popular but was now left to a few who reminisced about times passed.

When Athaz had left for their supplies, the friends had their first relaxed conversation in over a week. At first they kept it light, but they both knew a serious discussion loomed. It was actually Baran who brought it up.

"Why on earth are we not turning back to Hilae?" he asked. "There's three of us, only one with any significant fighting experience, and you have a broken arm. Even when we get to Mizcur, most of our company will be scholars!"

"I was thinking the same thing," Arun said as he reclined on the bed. If his brain had to work, at least his body could rest. "I have no doubt Athaz is being sincere. I've never heard of Orcs so close to Hilae before. Certainly the Son of Bälech would want to know about this? What if they are building some sort of fortification in the mountains just south of the capital?"

"I have an idea," Baran said. Arun turned his head and cocked his eye. "I don't know what the danger is, but I suspect the Warden is out of favor with the Son of Bälech. I mean, we both know this task is way below him. He wields a Divine weapon! Even for a Warden, that's impressive. But he's done something, and he's afraid of turning back without fulfilling whatever command he's been given to redeem himself."

Arun considered the possibility but dismissed it eventually. "I don't think Athaz would do that," he said finally.

"Well, you're the last person I would have expected to come to the defense of his character," Baran commented.

Arun gave a small laugh. "I don't mean it as a defense. More as a conclusion drawn from observation. Everything the Warden does, he believes he is in the right. I think he is wrong a lot, and the night at the pillory I will never forgive him for, but even that he thought was necessary—not for his benefit, but mine." He sat silent for a while before he finished. "No, I think Athaz believes we are in as much danger as himself if we return to Hilae. But we must find out why he believes that. He must tell us so we can decide for ourselves."

"Must he?" said a voice from outside the door, which was beginning to open. In an instant Baran had pulled out his sword but quickly let the blade down when he saw the Warden, a weary grin on his face.

"Or maybe I was wrong," Arun said hotly. "Eavesdropping is hardly—"

"I wasn't spying," said the Warden, placing the supplies down beside the coat tree. "I came up at just that point and heard nothing but the last bit as I happened to come up to the door, which, by the way, you should be more cautious about. Granted, I can guess a lot from that last sentence." He sat on the bed nearest the door and slowly lay down with a groan. "I was thinking I was probably going to have to tell you tonight anyway. I would not be able to blame you for demanding an explanation when I setup a watch while staying at an inn. Not to mention you'll see the horses in the morning; we're changing our route. Yes, you were about to learn what I think anyway."

Baran and Arun waited patiently as the Warden collected his thoughts, trying to think of how to separate what he knew from what he suspected. Then he told Baran to check for any ears near the door before he began:

"I actually know very little. When I read the Orc's mind, I confirmed my suspicion that it was not some raiding party that had strayed too close to Hilae. It was a tracking party. But what they were pursuing startled me, for it was not a Hilaean noble or the armies of The Dawn they were looking for. It was us."

The two friends were so surprised, they could not speak for a few seconds. Finally, Baran asked, "But how in The Dawn's light could Orcs know of our quest at all? Especially when we had just started a few days ago, and their journey must have taken weeks? And how —"

Athaz held up his hand for silence. "We have reached the end of what I *know*. From here on out, it is speculation. But I do have a theory." At this point he sat up so he could look his charges in the eyes. He knew what he was about to say would shock them.

"The Dawn is not what you imagine it to be. Only to the masses does it appear as a good beacon of light in a world of darkness. And maybe one day it was, but that has not been the case for generations. No, the Sons of Bälech are absolute rulers with iron fists. As you grow in power and prestige within The Dawn, you learn little things that cause you some discomfort. But they pale in comparison to the benefits The Dawn brings. So you let it slide. Soon, discomforts lead to genuine concerns, and the concerns to compromises. By the time you have learned enough to want out, you can't escape. You are too deeply woven into the web of lies that surrounds The Dawn. For myself, my family is held hostage. They are not even aware of the extent of it, that their every move is followed by Watchers or spies. If an agent is spotted, it's passed off as being 'for their safety' with some threat made against them as the reason. And until I fell out of favor, that might have even been true, but I now know beyond a shadow of a doubt if I were to stray too far, my family would be slaughtered like Yeomen cattle.

"In the Court, people are always trying to advance their position with Son of Bälech. The further up you go, people like the Headmaster of The Academy for instance, the stakes and gambits get even higher. Your project no doubt got his attention. Searches into pre-Dawn history have always been forbidden. But, as the war with Bewildered worsens, more and more people are beginning to ask questions. You, undoubtedly, are unaware that The

Bewildered now have strongholds, locations unknown, and they are routinely striking out from them and retreating before a large force can confront them. I have seen constant bloodshed my whole life, and honestly I am tired. I had hoped that my past laurels with The Dawn would buy me some grace, but I was wrong. I hinted, indirectly, maybe it was time to seek peace with The Bewildered. And, well, now you see where I am."

Athaz looked at them directly. "And now to where this affects you … You, Arun, I suspect have been fascinated with the pre-Dawn world for years. You are a stain for the headmaster, and one he needed to make an example of. What better way to subconsciously curb curiosity than having you butchered by Orcs? The Savage Races, while rarely used, can be hired as cheap mercenaries, especially Orcs. Goblins are too stupid and Giants don't like being led around by Men. But all of the Savage Races are unreliable, as our encounter proved. Still, they can be a great way to set up a 'tragic event' that gets rid of problems and leaves the real perpetrators unsoiled. Of course, if you get caught, it's pretty much an automatic, painful, and slow death sentence. I imagine your headmaster will soon be very ill once he hears we survived our encounter with the Orcs."

"But surely he didn't think nine Orcs could take on a Warden?" Baran asked. "If not for us, you could have handled them with ease."

Athaz laughed. "Not with ease. We Wardens are greatly skilled in combat … and fused with the Divine. All of that is true. But without numbers, our name carries more fear than our teeth can support. I *might* have survived that encounter. But your suspicion is in the right direction, for the headmaster would not have risked such dicey odds. Those Orcs were not meant to engage us. They were supposed to be tracking us, sending intel back to others for an ambush later down the road, for which they would act as the back gate. But once they spotted us and knew they were made, they were forced to attack. I'm guessing they overestimated our progress in the rain; they probably were thinking of how far they could travel or how far I could have pulled two soldiers, but not two tender-footed scholars. They paid dearly for that mistake."

Everyone sat in silence for some time. Finally Arun spoke. "I don't know what to think. But let's assume you are both telling the truth and are accurate. I can understand now why you didn't want to turn back to Hilae. But if there was to be an ambush later, isn't going forward just as dangerous? Won't we be walking into a trap?"

Athaz sighed as he lay back down on the bed. "That is why I asked for time to think before I spoke to you," he said wearily. "Or at least one reason. The other is that if either of you breathes a word of this to anyone, not only is my life in jeopardy, which apparently is already the case, but so is my family's. But here is my hope, slim though it is, the Orcs may abandon the quest now that it has already run foul. In case they don't, we will be taking a different route now, for they must catch us before we reach Mizcur. The Keepers are hiring mercenaries for protection, and if they are actually able to come, then the Court will have to go along with this charade. Keepers, as a rule, are less in tune with the darker side of The Dawn. The Sons of Bälech trust them very little, and because of this, they know much less of the corruption. The mercenaries, while not of much use in serious warfare, should be enough to fight off the size of any Orc crew whose loyalty can truly be counted on. The Dawn will have to let your little project play out, and the headmaster will almost certainly be disposed of. Baran, if you play along as though you're none the wiser, you will probably no longer be in any danger. I believe you were a 'casualty of war' in this scheme and also a victim to further remove suspicion that this was anything other than a 'tragic event.' As for you," the Warden said, turning to Arun, "you need to abandon your quest for pre-Dawn history. You and the Keepers may survive this one excursion, but if you keep it up, you will attract eventually the eye of the Son of Bälech himself."

Arun rubbed his right temple with his good hand; all the questions and implications… it was enough to make his mind explode. Finally he spoke. "So we're just to pretend we don't know any of this? Go about our merry way, like two graduates excited for their Task?"

"That's what you were when you left," Athaz answered. "And what you must continue to be. It would have been easier if you could just trust me, and I didn't have to reveal any of this, but you were correct. You had a right to know, and I couldn't keep hoping you would trust me blindly. But though we will appear as though nothing happened, we will act with all of the knowledge we have gained and the suspicions of our minds. We have horses now, which will allow us to take a much more winding path to Mizcur than we had planned while still arriving on time. Though we cannot ask for help, we will help ourselves. We will set a watch for tonight. I fear the headmaster will try to use assassins while we are in town. If he can have us killed, he may have hope of avoiding his unpleasant end that is coming. This is also why we must not arrive in Mizcur too early. On the Mossy Plain, we will see any encounter long before it happens. In town, danger lurks behind every dark corner or false smile."

By now the room was completely dark. Athaz lit his candle and handed it to Arun, who could see a thin smile on the Warden's face. "Well, I suppose neither of you will be able to sleep for a few minutes. As for me, my mind is freer than it has been for many nights. I will let you work out the details of who gets first watch, I will take second, and the other will take third. You can talk freely in front of me now, if you feel the need. But as soon as you can, put your minds at ease and try to get some sleep. You need to take advantage of these accommodations and get the best quality of rest you can, for it will be the last chance you get in some time, possibly for several weeks. Now, goodnight!"

With that, he grabbed the sheets and threw them over himself. It was only a minute before the two friends saw his breathing even and felt sure he was asleep so they could talk more comfortably. There may be no reason to fear him overhearing them now, but they still wished for some privacy.

"Well, that was unexpected," Baran whispered.

"You think?" Arun responded sarcastically. "I am having more trouble believing him than I did earlier tonight when I said I didn't think he would put us in danger unnecessarily."

"And I'm having less," Baran said. "My dad, when I was younger, would always tell us of how things had gone in the Court, any news he could think of. But as I grew up, he became more secretive about it. I just thought he was stressed and tired of talking about it. Even my mother feels distant from him at times. This would explain a lot. Don't get me wrong," he said, interrupting himself, "I'm still have trouble believing *everything* he's saying, but we still have to answer this question: Now what?"

"Now what?" was not easily answered, but after several minutes of thought, Arun tried. "I think we have to trust him, or at least go along with him for a while," he said. "If he's telling the truth, then obviously going back would mean our deaths. Let's assume he is lying or is wrong and we return ... then what? We have abandoned our Graduate Field Task for no good reason. We will fail and be forced into the Yeomanry. We can't prove he is lying, and we can't prove what he just said now. What if we aren't believed as to why we turned back? What if we were held liable for falsely accusing a Warden? I'm afraid we have to trust him. At least for now."

Baran wasn't happy with essentially stalling until they could find more information, but he didn't like any of the other courses lying before him either. He felt sure they could come up with a better one. "You go to sleep," he told Arun. "I want some more time to think." Arun nodded and blew out his candle.

But when it was time for Athaz's watch, Baran still hadn't thought of anything. He sighed as he went to wake the Warden before turning in himself. Athaz could see the young man had been wrestling with his thoughts. "Try to forget it for a while and get some sleep. You'll need it no matter what you decide."

CHAPTER V

Down River

The next morning, the friends made their way out of Desip's southern gate. For the first day, they decided to travel the route originally planned, in case any eyes were watching them leave the city. The horses they hoped wouldn't raise the suspicions of any Watchers - they were running behind after all, and one would be traveling slower than usual with a broken arm. At dawn on the second day, they would turn west and meander through the Mossy Plain for about a week before entering Mizcur from the northwest.

Arun had never ridden a horse before, and having his arm strapped against his torso was not making it any easier to learn. Baran had to help him get in the saddle, and Arun could barely direct the horse by the reins. Fortunately, Athaz and Baran were both in front of him, and Arun's horse was content to simply follow its leaders most of the time ... for the first day. After one episode where Arun could not turn the horse when he had decided to strike his own path, Athaz put on its halter and tied it to Baran's saddle.

"My pride is taking a serious hit." Arun laughed. "I feel like a spoiled child at a carnival."

"As soon as your arm heals," Athaz said with a grin, "I'll gladly work you overtime to rebuild your opinion of yourself."

"No, no thank you. That's quite alright," Arun said with only slightly feigned alarm. "I've been told humility is very becoming of a Keeper."

"Maybe when you're at The Tower." Athaz laughed. "But in the field I would rather you be able hold your head high as well as your own weight." Arun sighed. He did want his arm to heal quickly, but he couldn't help entertaining the thought of falling off his horse that came to him at that moment.

They stopped to make camp shortly before sunset. Or, more

precisely, Baran and Athaz made camp. Arun sat and watched, and in frustration asked how long he would have to wear the cast.

"You've still got several weeks before we can even begin contemplating taking it off," Athaz said. "Do you not remember what your arm looked like at the end of the fight?"

"I try not to," Arun admitted. "I was hoping my arm would be usable in that amount of time."

Arun suddenly found himself feeling like a complete fool. Why was he even out here? Why didn't he just pursue a typical Field Task, go and study some remote province to the north? To join a dig in progress with Keepers? Why had he pushed the envelope? He had put himself in danger and worse ... his best friend. And then there was Athaz. By his own story, he was already in trouble, but he had increased that danger by making Athaz reveal more than he should. Wardens who died in service, as Arun suspected was the goal now, knew their families would be taken care of for their entire lives. But disgraced Wardens? Arun now realized he couldn't think of a single family that he knew after they had fallen out of favor.

Arun looked at the Warden, who was surveying the land to the south. His eyes were far off, and he wore a concerned expression. In one sense Athaz was looking inward at dangers Arun could not see, but his gaze was also firm, focusing on the task at hand.

Arun realized Athaz was doing the only thing that could be done. No matter what happened, they had to survive this Graduate Task, and that would be challenge enough for the time being. Turning back was not an option, and wishing you could change the circumstances would only decrease the likelihood of surviving them. He walked over to the Warden. "I have a favor to ask," he said.

Arun had Athaz refit his throwing knife vest so that he could wear it on one shoulder, the knives exposed on the outside now. By the time the Warden had finished, darkness had made Arun's goal of practicing with his good hand impossible that night. With some of the discarded part of the vest, Athaz created sheathes for two of the knives from the discarded half. "Keep these at your ankles," his instructor advised him. "And during the day, while you are riding, accustom yourself to their weight by keeping a blade in your hand. Even if it seems pointless, it will help your throwing. And don't forget, always keep one knife on you as a dagger in case someone gets through."

As they continued journeying southwest, making their way toward the eastern bank of the Argom River, Arun would toy with the throwing knife in his hand, familiarizing himself with the weapons more fully than he ever had back in Hilae. Finding a shrub, Baran and Athaz cut and bound several of the thicker branches together and created a target for Arun to practice whenever they gave the horses a break.

After a week of meandering, they finally arrived at the Argom River. Baran and Arun gasped at the sight. It was wide, at least one quarter of a mile. To the northwest, they could see the Falls of Makrin, with a fine mist creating an everlasting rainbow. The travelers themselves were a good two hundred feet above the river, the path worn deep over the ages. The water below swirled in dark blue-gray patterns, mesmerizing if stared at long enough.

"By The Dawn of Bälech," Baran said under his breath. "It's more beautiful than anything I've seen in my dreams." Athaz rode up beside them. "Yes. Would you like to see the falls up close?"

They rode for about three hours to see the majesty of the Falls of Makrin. A large pool prevented them from walking directly up to where the water finished its decent, but it was still magnificent. Dozens of precipices of smooth limestone and moss jutted out, places of wondrous beauty that left men envious of the winged creatures that could reach the lofty havens with their unrivaled view. As the sunlight hit the spray from every stone that withstood the torrent day after day, year after year, rainbows were formed.

"The Falls of Makrin. One of the Five Wonders of Lugon," Athaz said, smiling. "Many times have I been blessed to witness its glory, and every time I am still left in awe.

They ate dinner, and no one spoke. It seemed sacrilege to interrupt the never-ending song of the Falls. Then they mounted their horses and rode most of the way back to where they had first looked over the Argom River.

They felt refreshed and clearheaded. They had not forgotten their problems, but in the face of such majesty, their problems felt small. Their existence felt small. Their own successes and failures were just one of many stories in a book of tales so massive that to think theirs were any greater or worse felt vain and ignorant. But far from being depressing, it was comforting. The world had seen such problems before, and it would see them again in various retellings. And through it all, there was Good that weathered all the characters and conflicts. Just to be a part of it was humbling and uplifting, and you couldn't help but Hope that, in the end, your part in the tale would be part of the Good that was still standing at the end.

* * * * * * * * * *

Ten days after leaving Desip, and three weeks to the day after leaving Hilae, the three friends found themselves looking on the city of Mizcur, the trading mecca of The Dawn. If Arun found Desip more beautiful than Hilae for its humble atmosphere, Mizcur's ugliness was greater for its opulent waste. Rare gems were thrust into the walls and crowded together, gaudy tapestries hung from every balcony as everyone tried to showcase their most recent economic success, and gardens with beautiful flowers still managed to make themselves repulsive with overcrowding and lack of thought in their arrangement.

"Found you at last," said a voice from the shadow of a doorway behind them. In an instant the Warden had his zweihänder out and readied, Baran had his sword out of its sheath, and Arun had a knife in his hand. "Whoa, what's this all about? And what happened to your arm?!" cried Descia. Athaz cursed himself for his jumpiness. The dig party would obviously be looking for them.

Baran, separated enough from his poor first impression to forget its lesson but still remembering the stinging mockery of his goal of being Warden, quickly said, "Orcs, that's what happened." Arun gaped at his roommate. "Nine, to be exact, but we handled them alright for a first battle, I'd say."

"Yes, this one has quite a bright future in the military," Athaz said, slapping Baran on the back so hard it knocked the breath out of him and nearly caused him to fall to the ground. "Even your budding scholar could make a decent fighter. But we'll talk about that later. Where are the others?"

"At the Tranquil Bank Inn," Descia answered. "But what on earth were Orcs doing in the lands you traveled?" Arun glared at Baran. Did the fool want to endanger more people?

"We never found out," Athaz said. "I sent a letter to the Wardens stationed in Hilae. They will investigate the matter more thoroughly."

Descia seemed satisfied. "Follow me," she said.

On the way there, Arun noticed she was no longer dressed as a Keeper. She wore common traveling clothes. She had a hood over her head, but when they entered the inn and she removed it, he saw her hair simply hanging past her shoulders instead of being kept in a Keeper's braid. Caught staring, he asked her about the style change.

"We don't announce ourselves when we travel," she explained to his question. "We are not Watchers who report everything to Hilae, and so when we are discovered, we are still tolerated pretty well. But we find our job easier if people do not know we are agents of The Dawn. Our goal is to study people, after all, and people act differently when those associated with authority are near."

The Tranquil Bank seemed anything but. The furniture was broken, repaired, and broken again. A cheap tavern near the banks where trading ships docked attracted unruly workers looking for cheap drinks and lots of them. "Sorry for the accommodations," Descia said sheepishly. "Since The Dawn provides for us most of the time, our actual compensation is pretty low. This is all we could afford.

Still, the Tranquil Bank did have a feast hall, and this was where Descia led them. A round of cheers greeted them when they entered the room." "Like I said earlier," Descia explained, "some of us have been waiting for decades to explore The Ruins of Lacris. Like Geown over there."

Geown was an elderly man who had hair covering more of his face than his head now, and all of it was white. He had a visible limp but was too proud to use a cane. He stood up and made his way over to Arun. "I understand I have you to thank for this opportunity at last," he said, eyeing Arun critically. "Why they gave it to you instead of me after all these years, I'll never understand, but I suppose thanks are in order. I have no family of my own, so I will leave what little I possess in this world to you, including my journal concerning pre-Dawn history. Better than the Watchers disposing of most of it. You and Descia here are the only two who would appreciate what I've spent most of my life researching."

Arun bowed awkwardly. "Thank you, sir. That means a lot."

Geown waved him off. "Merely an old man growing sentimental," he said as he limped back to his chair.

Descia leaned in close to Arun. "Don't let him fool you, he's always been sentimental."

"You've only known me since I was old!" Geown yelled without turning around.

"His hearing is also still in pretty good shape." Descia laughed, blushing.

Soon they were all eating. Their company measured about twenty from The Tower, plus mercenaries, who were not present. They were out on the town, enjoying their advance. If not for his arm, Arun could have forgotten his troubles for a while and simply enjoyed the excitement of what they were doing. And why shouldn't he? They had reached the point Athaz had hoped for. But one of the Keepers was making him uncomfortable. "Who is that one over there? Black hair and beard with a surly disposition?" Arun asked Descia.

"That is Nihl, and why he came … I don't know. He's never been one for pre-Dawn research. Still, he's favored by the Loremaster, and his rank is too high for me to stop him from coming." Arun had a strong suspicion why Nihl had come, and it made him sick. Would he ever be able to stop looking over his shoulder after what he learned from Athaz?

They had secured passage on three ships heading to Simpat in the morning, and the rest of the meal was spent planning how to divide the passengers. The cargo was already on board.

"Safer on the ships than here," Descia explained.

At the end of the meal, Athaz, Baran, and Arun said their goodbyes and headed to their room. Athaz breathed heavily with relief. "Well, I for one will sleep as soundly as I do in Hilae now that we have made our rendezvous with the Keepers."

Arun and Baran weren't sure how sound his thinking was, but it was certainly better than if Watchers had been waiting for them when they entered Mizcur.

* * * * * * * * * *

For the first time since the Orc attack, Arun and Baran woke up excited for their adventure. They had made it past the threat of the headmaster, so why couldn't they enjoy their Task now? Even if their knowledge kept their zeal from being what it had been before, they were refocused. Athaz had left a small note on his bed saying he had already left to make sure everything was ready. He would be waiting on the docks at a boat called "The River Daughter."

They arrived at the docks a couple of hours after sunrise. Athaz shook his head. "Should have known you two would sleep in. We should be gone by now."

"Don't worry, Warden. One of the lads will get to help make up the time, and I dare say I can find some work for his friend," an old gentleman said with a smile.

His perfect posture, keen gray eyes, and impeccable dress gave away his leadership role at once. This was Brasan, Captain of The River Daughter. When he was younger, he had sailed the Tempar Seas to the South on much more lucrative trade routes than what any river could offer. But as he had grown older, he grew weary of battling the ever-changing sea. He had plenty of coin to retire, but sitting and wasting his final years away was not his idea of living. He was a firm believer that the dullness plaguing so many of his fellow aging peers was a direct result of the lack of use of one's mental prowess. River trade may not be as lucrative, but it came with its own set of challenges, new puzzles for his mind to solve.

The River Daughter was large for a river vessel. It was a trading barge, sixty feet long and thirty feet wide. It had oars at five-foot intervals along both sides, each manned by two men, for when it sailed against the current. She was painted green with silver trim. Since Brasan had taken over her operations, her profitability had increased exponentially, and he had taken some of the extra funds to make her the finest river trading ship in The Dawn. He had only been joking, of course, about having Baran work on the oars. There wouldn't be a need for anyone to row today anyway. They were sailing with the current.

Descia was walking along the front of the ship, near the prow. Her hood and hair were down, the gentle wind causing her hair to slowly dance to the unheard melody of the wind. Baran was enjoying watching her graceful movements and, for the first time, relaxed facial features. Her dark green eyes were soft, possibly even happy. Baran thought her lovelier than ever, now that he saw a side he felt was more human. This was what she must look like when she no longer demanded the respect of those around her, and the effect it stirred in Baran was rather ironic. He felt foolish for his behavior earlier. How could he ever had hoped to impress her with such shallow attempts?

Arun noticed his friend staring and hoped what he knew was going to happen wouldn't happen. But it did. Or, it sort of did. Baran did approach Descia, but it was much meeker than anything Arun had seen in his friend before. He couldn't hear the conversation, but judging by their body language, it was going well.

"Good morning, Keeper Descia," Baran began simply enough.

"Good morning, Baran," Descia replied cordially in response.

"I was wondering ..." Baran tried to find the words he was looking for. "I was wondering," he repeated, "if you would be willing to enlighten me a little on the pre-Dawn knowledge we have. I confess I didn't prepare as well as I should. But seeing as how we don't have anywhere to go for the next four days or so, I thought … of course, if you don't want to repeat yourself, I—"

Descia held up her hand. "I would gladly go over it again with you," she said. "Provided you will be listening this time. And I will teach you many things. Athaz has taught you how to use your sword in defense of The Dawn. Let me teach you why The Dawn is worth defending."

She began a much more casual lecture than she had in The Tower, and Baran, to his credit, was listening intently this time. Every now and then he caught himself simply staring at her, but he did his best to focus on the words instead of the mouth that was forming them.

Descia knew very well he was attracted to her. She wasn't sure she returned those feelings, but was delighted he had taken the time to sincerely listen to what she knew. She thought Baran quite handsome, that was true. However, their first meeting when he was full of arrogance and pretense was fresh in her memory. Still, she knew she had been overly harsh with him. And if brash, proud behavior was to rule men out, she would be hard pressed to find anyone in the Court she could bear. And Baran meant well. That put him well above most of the Court Sons she had met in her life.

Arun was chuckling to himself when he realized there someone standing next to him. He looked up to see Captain Brasan observing him with a curious look on his face.

"I take it you're used to enjoying the spectacle of seeing him making a fool of himself?" he asked with a smile.

"Arun nodded. "I don't think he can help himself."

"Probably can't," Brasan replied. "But you shouldn't laugh at him."

"No, I guess I should help him." Arun sighed.

"Help him? You mean tame him?"

Arun nodded again, but now it was the captain who was laughing. "No, lad, that's not what I meant. I meant maybe you should learn from him. I saw you staring at her too, you know." Brasan gave him a small wink. "But I also saw it never even crossed your mind to go up to her. Why not? You plan on becoming a

Keeper yourself from what I understand. You have much more in common with her than your friend, but the thought never even occurred to you, did it?"

Arun was taken aback. The old man was rather forward and blunt. "I don't know," Arun stammered. "I guess I'm just used to not trying with people of the Court. I'm just a Gifted Yeoman after all."

"Doesn't that mean you are a member of the Court now?" Brasan asked knowingly.

Arun sighed. "You don't understand. In name, yes, I'm a member of the Court. But no one in the Court really acknowledges that."

Brasan snorted. "You're the one who doesn't understand. You have let your doubts stop you from ever trying to find out if there is something better out there. I'm not saying you should copy your friend's reckless style — it would be even more awkward on you. But I make it my business to know about any passengers I carry, and I know your friend doesn't have much more reputation than you. Your friend's route may be a little rough at times, but at least he has a destination. You are drifting in the doldrums. They may seem peaceful, but they are almost impossible to get out of, and many don't survive it. Think about what I'm saying." With that, he walked back down to check on his crew.

Arun looked back at his friend and Descia. Suddenly, she threw her head back in a full belly laugh. Judging by Baran's animated face, he was telling her some story from The Academy. Maybe Brasan was right. Maybe he was just shutting himself away out of habit.

"Next time," he promised himself.

CHAPTER VI

The Dig

The next few days passed quickly for Baran, who spent the majority of each day with Descia. Arun spent most of his time with Athaz, and the two were developing an unlikely friendship. Arun had the time now to realize he would be dead if not for the Warden's insistence he learn to defend himself. It didn't make up for the pillory incident, but now they reached an understanding. He had Athaz show him forms, blocks, and counters with the fauchard, and he practiced the footwork along with the Warden.

"Surprised to see you taking such an interest in combat," his mentor said on the third evening.

"So am I," Arun said. "But now I know I could never forgive myself if you or Baran were hurt or killed trying to defend me when I knowingly went into danger."

Early in the afternoon on the fourth day of their journey from Mizcur, the boat anchored near the bank at Simpat. It was a small town, similar to Desip but without the economic benefits of being nestled between Hilae and the economic center of Mizcur. The people were proud of their resourcefulness. Buildings had been patched and roofs re-thatched time and time again. Some were no more than mud huts. It was a place no one in the Court would be caught dead staying, but that suited its citizens just fine. Here, finery was simply a waste of resources.

Athaz pulled his two charges aside. "I will stay behind on the ship for now and meet you on the eastern side of town as you all head out the day after tomorrow," he said. "This town is known to sympathize with The Bewildered, though we are still many days up river from their southern strongholds. Wardens come here more often than not to quell rebellious mobs, and I would only cause you more trouble. Though I believe the significant danger has passed, you still need to be on your guard."

Arun and Baran promised they would be, said their farewell to Brasan, and made their way into town with the Keepers. The Keepers, though tolerated far more than the military, still desired secrecy as well. The explanation for the large company and dig equipment was that they were sent by the master of a mining guild in Mizcur, seeking the possibility of a copper mine in the Tikus Foothills, south of the Briar Patch Mountains. None of them could have really kept the guise up for long if the people had any serious concerns, but with farmers' crops in high demand and craftsmen calling for supplies that couldn't be brought down from Hilae, and all the local inns filled to capacity, nobody cared one bit if their story was true or not. The economic activity would ensure most of the people of Simpat lived comfortable year-round, at least until the snows came.

Descia, Arun, Baran, and Geown were all staying at the same inn, a small place aptly named River's Edge. Arun hoped that Descia's favor of Baran was more than friendly sentiment. For the first time Arun could remember since they had been kids, Baran was not drinking himself to death. He was having a rather detailed conversation about, of all things, The Rebellion of 737.

"It was Helite Katina that helped the people of Flur re-assimilate into The Dawn, correct?" Baran asked.

"Hey, I'm impressed you know that name," Descia said, raising her eyes with sincere but over-played, surprise and enthusiasm.

"Well," Baran laughed, "someone at this table hammered that one into my head," Baran said, elbowing Arun in the ribs. "Right?"

Arun smiled, grateful his friend hadn't completely forgot about him. Arun and Baran spent some time telling Descia about their planned presentation had the Field Task not been approved. They finished the evening discussing the plans for the dig and deciding to go to bed early for the hard hiking that would begin tomorrow.

Arun was almost asleep when a short series of flashes from the direction of the mountains came through the window. Almost unconscious, the sight merged with a dream of him riding a lightning bolt in terror as it struck a mountaintop. He was thrown down from the mountain and fell deep underground in darkness. Next, two opposing armies were rushing at each other, oblivious to his begging for them to stop before they crushed him in the middle. He awoke right as the two armies collided, but though he was sweating and startled, he couldn't remember the dream. Looking out the window, there was now only darkness. Laying his head back on the pillow, he tried to remember the vision, but eventually sleep overtook him. The quieter dreams that followed removed even the desire to recall the violence of the first.

Baran and Arun were reluctant to get out of bed the morning of their departure. Their horses, no longer needed, had been left behind in Mizcur. It had been weeks since they had traveled on foot, and the soft mattresses were preferable to the marching that would be demanded of them for the next two weeks at least. It was only about 120 miles to The Ruins of Lacris, but the mules would be pulling wagons of equipment and the Keepers that rode with them. Arun, Baran, Athaz, and the mercenaries would be walking. The trip would traverse the Tikus Foothills, making the going even slower.

After eventually dragging themselves into a standing position, the boys were forced to rush so the company wouldn't be waiting on them. It was still gray, before dawn, when they found Descia and Geown up at the head of the company.

"Glad to see we didn't have to wait on you this time," Descia said with a smile.

They found the Warden about two hours outside of town, leaning against a stone while he waited for them. He spotted his two charges and motioned for them to come beside him.

"Keep your eyes open," he said. "Though still a ways form the northernmost stronghold of The Bewildered, The Ruins of Lacris are sacred to them. They believe when Bälech conquered their forefathers, they were an advanced people, not leaderless, savage tribes. The Ruins mark the beginning of The Dawn. Or the beginning of the Long Night as they like to mock. To them, these grounds are hallowed: a reminder of the last time the peoples of

Lugon were free."

The company kept to the high ground as much as possible. The valleys were still soft from spring rains and melted snow from the Briar Patch Mountains, but they were forced to go down into some of them, which meant the occasional wheel getting stuck in the mud.

Baran and Arun kept their eyes peeled but saw nothing that alarmed them. Eventually, Baran stopped watching all together and focused all of his attention on Descia again. Arun noticed she indeed seemed to be truly reciprocating Baran's romantic sentiment. She smiled whenever he laughed, and she no longer even attempted to assume an attitude of superiority around him. One time, Arun even overheard her telling Baran stories of when she was a young girl and the trouble her older sisters were always getting her into. It was the first time she'd ever opened up about her personal history.

The next morning, clouds kept the sky an eerie pre-sunrise gray that the ground began to mirror as they traveled. It was as if the earth itself was still grieving here. When they entered the ruins, they saw why. Though the battle had been over 2700 years ago, the devastation wrought was so immense that nature had never reclaimed it. Grass refused to grow, rocks were charred black, and nothing stood higher than three inches off the ground. Death lingered here—not just of men but of a reality.

"I never dreamed it would look like this," Descia said as they stopped just twenty yards shy of the first pieces of broken stonework. "There may be nothing intact enough for us to study. History itself seems to have been silenced."

Arun found himself wondering if Athaz's hope that The Dawn was ever a beacon of light was true. This was not the work of a being who had united the tribes of leaderless men who was forced to squash a wild, unruly resistance. This place reeked of hatred and sadistic pleasure.

Athaz joined them from behind. "We came here for a reason." Baran, Arun, and even Descia turned to give him a dark look. Something felt wrong. This was no place to study. This was the grave to an era. To disturb the place of rest felt like digging up a corpse just to see the burial clothes.

"What will you say if we return without ever having lifted one thing from the earth here?" Athaz asked. "You all chose this errand, not me. You must now see it through."

Reluctantly, they set up the tents where they were. They had four weeks to survey the ruins and give themselves enough time to travel back to Hilae with a two-week cushion. But Arun wished it was less time. He shivered every time he looked out over the land, hearing cries of anguish, which he was sure were the last sounds carried by the air in this place. He was glad now that the apprentices were going to be doing most of the digging.

The first few days they found pieces of bone, but rarely one that was intact and never a whole skeleton. The victims were obviously never buried, but whether scavengers had scattered the remains or it was the destruction from the Divine used by Bälech, it was impossible to know.

They realized that if they were to find anything, they would have to dig much deeper to a layer from before the battle. There was nothing left of Lacris as it stood in its final days.

Three weeks into it, they finally had gotten past the layer of devastation and into one with artifacts that were still intact. What amazed them was their beauty, their precision, and their quality. Complex, geometric designs were just the beginning. The remains from the stonework architecture were beautiful, carved with skill like they had never seen. And forges. Forges were everywhere: plain forges for common use; ornate, decorative forges; tiny forge figurines. Whoever these people were, they were fascinated with the craft.

Excited chatter came from the apprentices. Soon after, two of them brought forward a humungous tablet.

"Writing!" cried Geown. "A written account of something before The Dawn! What a treasure!" It was true. Even if it was nothing more than an account of a mundane task, the tablet would enlighten pre-Dawn knowledge more than anything else ever recovered from that era. One of the apprentices carrying it said,

"Sir, do you not see the similarities?"

"Blazes of The Dawn's Sun!" cried Geown. "It's so similar to Bewildered writing!"

"And what of that?" Nihl asked with a sneer. "It's not unknown that the first Bewildered were the descendants of those who fled The Dawn's Light."

"It may be close enough to decipher," Descia said, her eyes tracing the fine lines.

Arun, Baran, Descia, and Geown excitedly talked with each new translated word. This was beyond their wildest dreams! But Athaz grew more and more grave with each artifact that passed before them. With three days left before the dig was to end, he called his charges over to him.

"You must never return to Hilae," he told them.

Arun looked up at him, waiting to hear an explanation. Baran outright laughed. "Not return? Where are we to go? And we have done nothing."

"You *have* done something," Athaz corrected. "You have witnessed something. It has long been suspected by some that Bälech was not a benevolent leader uniting warring tribes with his Divine abilities. You have now seen proof that some of what The Bewildered say is true. You will be silenced if you return to Hilae. Death may be one of the least evil ways your knowledge could be sealed away."

The three stood in silence for a while. "What about the others?" Baran finally asked. "They will be in as much danger as us, and we can't all just disappear."

Suddenly, a cry of alarm rose from the apprentices still digging. All three turned in the direction of the cry. The apprentices were running back to the tent screaming, "Orcs! Orcs are here!"

When Athaz looked, it was all he could do to not show the same despair that was in the eyes of the apprentices. It was an army, at least five hundred strong. The mercenaries totaled fifty. Even if the mercenaries had been professional infantry, this could only end in defeat. But Athaz was not one to accept death quietly, nor to let others fear it.

The Tales of Lugon

"To the hills!" he cried. "Gain the high ground! Guards, form a perimeter around The Tower scholars! Baran, grab your weapons and follow me."

As they were running, Athaz yelled to Arun, "Stay with the scholars."

"I can still throw," Arun began protesting.

"Then slay the Orcs that get through," said Athaz grimly.

The Warden's tone indicated this would be the end, and where they were wouldn't matter much at all. They kept following the Warden numbly. They should be terrified. They should be running for the mountains where they could hide. But the Warden's lack of hope stunned and slowed their minds. As Athaz continued directing those around him, his courage reawakened the two friends.

"Stay behind me," Baran said to Descia.

"Sorry I got you all into this," Arun said to all of them.

Athaz shook his head. "Don't let those be your thoughts now," he said, placing his hand on his young friend's shoulder. "We are all here for reasons other than you."

By now the perimeter had been set, and the friends turned to face their enemies, who were dismantling and destroying everything with unbridled mirth.

Baran put his shield over his back and notched an arrow in his bow. Firing would begin their demise, but there wasn't much point in waiting. "Mind if I have the honor of evening the odds this time?" he asked the Warden with a dark grin.

Athaz smiled and nodded. "Wait until after I begin a Divine command." He turned his focus onto the Orcs, who, confident in their numbers, weren't bothering to encircle their foes to gain equal footing in the hills. Narrowing his eyes, Athaz began his Divine command. "*Zol ete Bälech, a ver—*" Baran released the arrow, and his target fell with scream as the arrow penetrated the Orc's neck. "*—yn fa Anp …*" The Orcs nearby laughed at the pitiful beginning of the battle as they turned to grant the wish of their victims to begin the slaughter. "*—et falun cree.*" The Warden's eyes widened, and he raised his hands, fingers spread out and pointing toward his targets, palms out. "*Shrik!*" he cried, and out of each hand shot a dagger of ice that penetrated the Orcs with such velocity that each one hit three back. Six Orcs fell, never to rise again.

The Orcs cried out in anger at the unfair attack and began their charge in earnest. Arun threw his first dagger, and Baran loosed another arrow before dropping his bow for his sword and shield. Lacris was hosting a hopeless battle for survival once more.

But a sound from up high and behind came unexpectedly to their ears: a horn being sounded, echoing many times as it bounced through the foothills. "Death to Bälech and his legions!" cried clear, strong voices as the horn echoes faded. It was an army of Bewildered, two hundred strong. The Bewildered were charging toward them as fast as their mounts could gallop. Their eyes were fell, with long swords raised high.

"Bloody Bewildered!" Baran cursed. "They've come to ensure their filthy Orcs finish the job."

When they were fifty yards away, they suddenly split around the dig team. As they engaged the Orcs, a score from each side charged toward the middle about fifteen yards in front of the mercenaries and began establishing their own perimeter. The rest kept rushing by them. About twenty of The Bewildered force were archers, and they dismounted directly behind the scholars, firing volley after volley into the heart of the Orc army, as the majority of the force raced down the sides of the Orcs, containing them for their bowmen.

"The Bewildered are helping us!" Arun shouted.

Already, the Orcs between them and the front guard were dead, slain by the mounted Bewildered forming the inside barrier as some of the Orcs attempted to charge their foes. The remaining Orcs were in a state of confusion, not knowing where to turn. And the longer they waited, the fewer of them there were. The archers needn't worry about accuracy; the Orcs had bunched themselves so close together that missing was impossible.

Finally, after about half of their force fell, the Orcs turned and fled. Apparently this had been expected, for the archers quickly remounted, and The Bewildered that had posted themselves in front of the mercenaries now formed a protective shell around the archers as they moved in pursuit. Those between the archers and the Orcs occasionally dispersed to allow more shots to be fired before closing again to prevent any of the vile filth from even considering charging the bowmen.

Three of The Bewildered soldiers had stayed behind near Arun, Baran, and Athaz. Once he was satisfied that the threat was over, one began speaking to them as the others finished their bloody work. "We do not wish to kill you," said one, taller than the rest, who moved with a grace no human could match. "But do not force our hand. And, you, Warden..." he practically spat the words "... if you so much as twitch your lips without being told, I will stop your mouth with my steel. " He and the other two soldiers drew their blades and brought them to his neck, the one in front just under his chin.

Athaz gave a slow nod to show he understood. The rest of The Bewildered had finished their business and were now retuning. Not a single Orc would return to their filthy camp that night. The victors returning, however, looked grave. A youth, one of the archers, rode up to the tall one that spoke to Athaz. Arun thought him too young to be in an army; he could not yet be sixteen years old, though his face wore the worry of one twice that age. He had short, blond hair and green eyes. His frame was a little on the small side, but he was obviously athletic. In spite of the cares, which in Arun's mind did not belong on someone younger than he himself was, there was a freshness, vigor, and eagerness that older men do not face such worries with.

"Commander," the youth began. "The Orcs are slain, but we lost several men, many of them in my company. Unless you foresee more danger, we would like to return the bodies home so their families may mourn them properly."

"Yes, we will take them home," the newly identified leader said. He removed his helmet. His hair was white, but he still looked young.

"An Elf!" Arun instinctively cried in a hoarse whisper, though how he knew it, he was unsure. He could bring no memory of a drawing to mind. The commander turned. "You have seen one of my kind before, young man?"

Arun shook his head. The commander looked hard at him. "I don't know how I know, to be honest," Arun finally said. "It is like a long-forgotten dream that is suddenly brought to mind when it is unexpectedly mirrored in the waking world."

Therran's eyes lit up briefly, but he quickly smothered the flame. He turned to the dig team. "People of The Dawn, for the time being you are prisoners of the Savanir, or 'The Bewildered' as you call us. So long as you comply, you will not be harmed. However, we will be following secret paths, so you will be blindfolded."

"Are we supposed to walk blindfolded?!" cried Nihl incredulously. Knowing death was at least not imminent had loosened some of the braver, or perhaps more foolish, tongues.

"No," Therran said, trying to be patient. "Though your mules have been slain or driven off, most of your wagons remain intact, and we have horses. One wagon will carry our dead back to their families. The rest of you will ride in the others. I'm afraid you must leave your equipment behind as we have no room or horses to spare. Your Warden will be bound first so that you may know what is coming. He, however, will have one additional binding, because of his curse."

Athaz immediately understood and opened his mouth to receive the gag when it was presented. They then placed a hood over his head. A wagon was brought up to him. He was helped into it. Then his hands were bound behind him, then his ankles.

"Now, drop your weapons and let my men assist you."

Slowly, they all did as they were told. Baran, stood next to Descia and was the last to do so. He never would have if she had not placed her hand on his arm. "I'll be fine," she said. Then she walked up to one of the Savanir and let them place the hood over her head and bind her. Baran sighed as he put down his weapons. Captured. Somehow, it felt more terrifying than when he had thought they were going to die. He looked at Arun, still next to him. The young Savanir that spoke with Therran earlier approached them and waited.

Arun shrugged. "Guess this is one way to get out of going back to Hilae," he said as he nodded to a soldier presenting a hood to him. Baran wasn't the least bit amused by the jest.

CHAPTER VII

What Was Found Underground

The ride seemed to take forever in the darkness. Though hooded, Arun could tell they were heading north. They were obviously going through the foothills, north towards the mountains. "They must have a stronghold closer than even Athaz knew about," he thought.

As they bounced along, Arun soon learned having his head covered combined with the constant, unpredictable movements gave him a sort of sea-sickness. What made it worse was the fact that it was even harder for him to keep his balance. With his broken arm still in the cast, they had to bind his right arm straight against his side, much like his cast was doing for his left arm.

The young soldier had climbed in the wagon with them and placed a hand on his shoulder to help his captive keep upright after watching Arun nearly slam his head into the side of the cart twice. For the entire trip, he was both their guard and source for any information.

"I assume your stronghold is in the Briar Patch Mountains," Baran said at last. "Isn't that quite a distance to have us blindfolded?"

"I'm afraid so," the young soldier replied. His voice was stiff but polite. "But as I'm sure you know, the southern end of the mountains spans quite a bit of land east to west. We must keep as much hidden from you as we can. We wish this precaution was not necessary, but we are at war with each other, after all."

Arun had a different question in mind. "What is your name? How old are you?"

"Inoch, and I'm fifteen," the youth replied.

"Fifteen!" Arun said in amazement. "But you are already a leader in this army!"

Arun heard the young man laugh. "Not of the regular army,"

Inoch corrected. "I'm not at liberty to say much at the moment, but I'll risk this. The Savanir, though larger than we have ever been since the Long Night began, are still precious few in number. We have always been hunted and driven from the lands your emperor controls. For over two thousand years, our neighbors were the Savage Races: Orcs, Goblins, and Giants. Waiting to fight until the age your people consider adulthood is a luxury we do not have. Though we have some cities of our own, precious few are safe from the hordes of filth like those we saved you from today. Even for those like myself who grew up with them, we still must learn to fight, and we cut our teeth on the Savage Races. The regular army is normally reserved for battling your human military and Wardens, who are much more capable, intelligent fighters than the Savage Races."

Arun fell silent. Baran now spoke again. "I guess now you all regret aligning yourselves with them when The Dawn began."

"You speak as you have been taught," Inoch answered. "Has it ever occurred to you that if ever such an alliance existed, our hopes of escaping Bälech's clutches would be more likely if we still worked with them? Never has there been an alliance between the Savanir and the Savage Races. And there never will be, even if it means our destruction. You have much to learn about our ways, but soon it'll be clear."

Arun stiffened. "Are you going to torture us until we join you?"

"Xiarch, grant me patience!" Inoch cried in exasperation. "No, you were promised you would not be harmed. And you, Arun, will be unscathed if every single one of us must die to ensure your safety and well-being."

Arun grew concerned about how many of these Savanir knew his name. "How in Lugon do you know my name? And that I belong to it? I have never met any of you in my entire life."

Though they couldn't see it, Inoch was smiling. "Some of it we know from our spies within Hilae. Yes, we have spies even within your precious Court. Our eyes and ears are everywhere, and very good at staying unnoticed. But you have been watched for some time. It's not every day a young man from Hilae is interested in pre-Dawn history."

Feeling very uncomfortable of the implications of this conversation, Arun tried to change the subject. "Why do you say 'Bälech?' Surely you must know Bälech died ages ago."

Inoch rubbed his eyebrows with his hands as he let out a slow breath, frustrated by trying to remember all differences in how they saw the world. "Sorry. I forgot you call him 'Son of Bälech.' Really, it might just be easier to wait. I'm just going to confuse you. The Lady Lyr will be much better at answering your questions."

When they stopped for the night, they were all very relieved to discover they could take off their hoods when they were inside the tents. A guard was posted outside each one. Arun saw he, Baran, Descia, and Geown had been kept together. Athaz was nowhere to be seen. Their guard also served as their host, serving them food. The bindings on their feet remained; their hands, though still tied, were brought to the front to let them eat. The three younger friends were suspicious of the food, but Geown was eating heartily and seemed to be without a care in the world.

"We're alive, which is more than we'd thought we'd be before they showed up," he pointed out. "Even if this little ride ends in our deaths, I have a feeling we're going to see and learn things that we never would know no matter how many years we lived in Hilae. Some of us Keepers do actually venture out of our Tower, and I've risked my life for less before."

When it was time to sleep, the rope binding their wrists was tied to another rope attached to a stake in the ground, keeping their hands away from their ankles that were also held in place by another stake. They weren't immobile; the purpose of the stakes was to make escape impossible but not be cruel.

For two weeks, they traveled in darkness. Inoch, was always courteous, and eventually the friends relaxed. Not that they forgot their situation, but as the days dragged into weeks, a tentative acceptance settled upon them and with it the desire to enjoy themselves as much as they could. Early on, the conversations were short, just small talk to ease their nerves, but soon they became longer and more natural. In this way, Inoch learned much about them: their names, their pasts, and sometimes even asked questions. At first they were hesitant to answer him, but then they realized it wasn't like it could make things worse; except Baran finally pointed out to them that if the commander allowed his men to socialize with the prisoners, it was probably to get them to reveal something.

"Or because your status as prisoner is temporary," Inoch responded. "Most of you know less of your own empire than we do, or at least know less of what lies below its gilded surface."

Baran shuffled in his restraints. Athaz had warned them of something similar.

At the end of the day, Inoch made an announcement to Arun, Baran, Descia, and Geown in their tent. "Tomorrow, we will be splitting up. All groups will be going in different directions, lest we make our path so obvious even the most dimwitted Goblin could find us. Do not worry, it will only be for a few days. Still, don't try to escape. There are enough of us for multiple guards in each group."

Arun laughed quietly to himself. Where would he go? The last thing Athaz had told him and Baran, before the Orcs appeared, was death — or worse — awaited them in Hilae. It very well may be he was safer as a prisoner with his enemies than in his unwelcome home.

When they awoke the next morning, the three friends realized that they had been allowed to sleep in. "It's an easy way to make it more difficult for you to know where you and your friends are going, and you needed the rest," Inoch explained.

Hoods were again placed over their heads. The stench of stale sweat had grown worse each morning as the hoods daily soaked up the moisture from their hair. At least the material was lightweight; it breathed well enough to provide adequate ventilation to let in fresh air. When there was a breeze, they could smell the pines that covered the foothills, and, while one could not make out shapes, it was easy to know when something passed before them or when the sun was obstructed. Arun wasn't sure what they were made of, but it was something wholly foreign to him.

"What material is this?" he asked his captor as they traveled that day. "As unpleasant as the smell is becoming, they breathe well. But I still can't make out anything beyond light and darkness."

"Cloud silk," said Inoch. "A material we invented not long ago. In fact, you are heading to the place where it was first woven. It was a team effort, the brainchild of a human textile engineer and a Dwarven tailor. It is light, even in its densest weave, but it's almost as strong as a rope of horse hair."

"Dwarves? I thought they were extinct," Descia said.

"Not quite," Inoch answered.

"Fascinating." Descia said.

Geown chuckled. "Fancy a study of Bewil— Begging your pardon, Master Inoch ... Savanir races and technology, Descia?"

"Well, we were the first Keepers to study a pre-Dawn site. Might as well keep up the pace," Descia said with light sarcasm.

After the first day, their climbing and descending became much steeper. They must have made it to the Briar Patch Mountains. After three days of journeying alone with Inoch and his small band of guards, they heard other voices on the fourth day. "We are drawing near," Inoch explained. "You will all be together again soon."

And they were. But one voice Arun desperately wanted to hear more than any of the others was still missing. "Inoch, where is Athaz?"

"Who?" Inoch asked.

"Athaz ... the Warden," Arun explained.

"I'm sorry, Arun, I can't answer that," he said.

"Is he dead?" Arun's voice shook as he tried to control his anger and trepidation.

"No. He is alive, but I cannot say more than that for now. I am sorry. His path is very different from the rest of you. He is a war criminal. You probably are ignorant of most of what Wardens do, and I can tell you hold him in high regard. I don't want to ruin your opinion of him."

Baran spoke up. "Athaz would never act dishonorably, no matter what other Wardens you may have encountered have done. And they all look the same. How can you tell what Athaz has done?"

"I told you, I am not free to discuss it!" Inoch said, raising his voice. It was also a little harsher than he intended. "You will learn, eventually, what is to befall him. Some of it is not even decided."

"Such as whether or not he'll live," Arun said under his breath.

Inoch heard it, but let the matter be. It was an accurate guess.

It was nearing noon when everything suddenly went dark and the wheels and horse hooves began to echo around them.

"A cave?" Descia asked.

"You could call it that," Inoch answered.

Soon they realized it was a huge underground passageway; no natural cave would have been easily traveled by horses and carts. It was a full two hours before the wagon came to a stop.

"You must walk from here," Inoch explained. "I'm afraid your eyes must remain covered for now. But you will each have one of my men as your personal guide. Rest assured, you will be led with care."

They walked for another two hours, full of twists, turns, climbs, and descents. There were many passages, all to confuse any enemies that should happen to find the entrance to the underground stronghold.

"This place is massive," Baran said. "How have you managed to keep this secret for all this time, being so near to Hilae?"

"With extreme measures," said the solider leading him. It wasn't Inoch's voice. Baran had forgotten they had their own personal guides now. "In addition to keeping visitors, such as yourselves, hooded and disoriented, even our soldiers have their memories wiped of the passages and exact location, save for the commander. And the commander will kill himself before he allows himself to be captured, lest the Watchers are able to read his mind for the information."

Baran whistled. That was a bit extreme. "But then how did you split us up here?"

"Very observant. You don't have to know where something lies if someone is looking for when you arrive. They were given long, meandering directions that would eventually take all of them by a lookout near here that would guide them back, but the directions kept going for days after that. And we don't risk that much until we have no doubt that we are beyond the grasp of the enemy."

Meanwhile, Inoch was leading Arun. After three hours of walking, Inoch and his men brought the blind companions to a halt.

"We passed through our military stronghold three hours ago when you dismounted. Now we are before the gates of Menigar, one of the few cities we have been fortunate enough to keep secret from the Dark One for centuries. I'm going to remove the hood so you may see the wonder for yourself."

It took Arun several minutes for his eyes to adjust after traveling in darkness for weeks, with only candlelight at night in a tent. When his eyes finally adjusted, he saw before him a sight that left him breathless. It was an ornate gate of carved, jet obsidian. Carved on the left base corner was a solemn, angular face with closed eyes. The lines were filled thinly cut strands of sapphire. On the forehead of the face was script, beautiful and fine, also made of sapphire. The face reminded him of Therran, and he knew this must be the seal of the Elves.

On the right base was another seal: a hammer striking a chisel, carved from a single piece of pearl and set in a carved-out space that fit to perfection. Below the chisel where smaller pearls, pieces of the unseen item being shaped. When Arun looked closely, he saw a pattern emerge from the small pearls. What appeared to be discarded dust falling to the earth formed musical annotation. He wondered what song was prestigious and beautiful enough to be annotated with the pearl ink, but his attention was soon drawn elsewhere.

A great forge constructed of small orange topazes was at the top center of the gate. The slightest movement changed the hue of the gems as they caught the light, giving the impression fire actively burning. And for reasons he was unsure, Arun felt his heart leap within him more at the site of the forge than at any of the others, in spite of knowing nothing of smelting nor smithing.

Arun had not realized he was gaping when Inoch cleared his throat to get his attention. "If you are this amazed at the gate, maybe your eyes aren't ready to see the city yet," he said with a small laugh.

The gates opened, and Arun realized his captor's jest was not an empty boast. Under the mountain, the walls reached hundreds of feet above the ground they walked on. Glass bowls filled with some pale yellow liquid substance hung from an unseen ceiling. Arun realized they were giant candles with numerous large wicks. Their flames ever so slightly flickering in a small breeze; ventilation that had somehow been worked throughout the mountain.

The roads were paved in black and gray stone with large, rough cut rubies and orange sapphires placed here and there to give the appearance of embers flaring up as the light struck them. The buildings were made of the mountain stone, polished smooth as glass. Most of the buildings were carved into mountain itself, though some were made with stone brought in from elsewhere to accommodate the growing city population.

"By the D—" Descia caught herself. "I never knew men were capable of such beauty," she finished.

Inoch gave a smile. "This was designed by men, but not built by them. Menigar is an old Dwarven city, founded shortly before the Long Night fully eclipsed Lugon and one of the few places Bälech never discovered. The remaining Men and Elves that escaped the surrounding lands made their way here. The three races, while meant to be united in brotherhood, are not identical. Living too closely together increased conflict, and so the city was divided into districts. You are now in the District of Men."

A new voice none of the friends had heard before spoke up. "Enjoying your first look at Dwarven craftsmanship, Night Dwellers?"

They all turned and saw what they assumed must be a Dwarf. He was obviously past middle-age with graying hair, but some parts were still shimmering black, similar in hue to the obsidian on the gate. His frosty blue eyes countered his fiery, penetrating gaze. Though the term "Night Dwellers" was obviously derogatory, his countenance showed no hostility. It still made the friends feel a little annoyed after avoiding the term "Bewildered" for their captors' sakes.

"The only thing Kruthos takes more pride in than his own work is that of his ancestors'," Inoch said with a smile. "He'll be your guide for the next few days, Arun, though I'm sure we will meet again soon. I have duties I must attend to ... first and foremost to deliver your friends to their hosts."

The friends looked at each other with concern. "Don't worry, you will see each other again soon. In fact, tomorrow you can be in each other's company as much as you like, but four guests is hard to accommodate for most. We thought this preferable to the military holding cells."

The friends quickly agreed to that. Their minds were filled with some trepidation, but so far they had no reason to doubt Inoch's word. After his friends left, Arun turned to look at Kruthos, who had been speaking to him, though he hadn't been paying attention.

"Lady Lyr will meet with all of you soon and answer most of your questions," Kruthos continued. "But long speeches and new realities are not for weary travelers. Tonight, we will eat, rest, and tour this area of Menigar before we return to my home in the Dwarven District, and then ... Is something bothering you?" he asked a lost-looking Arun.

"Just not how I was expecting a prisoner to be treated," he finally said, not wanting to discuss it further.

"Bad word choice," Kruthos said. "Think of yourself more as a restricted guest who does not have a say in the matter." Arun dropped his head and stared at his host. "Okay, so I pretty much just defined a prisoner. Still, you are not looked on as such. You have been separated from your friends but will unite with them soon. Your weapons may be longer, but here you will find no ill will toward you ... unless you do something deserving of it."

"What about Athaz?" Arun asked.

"Who?"

"The Warden."

Kruthos let out a long, low breath through his nose. "Friend of yours? 'Prisoner' does best describe his status, and he will probably find little love anywhere among the Savanir. But don't give up hope!" he said, upon seeing Arun's gaze fall to the ground. "From what I understand, his behavior at Lacris was much to his credit. You may see him again yet."

Things were indeed much worse for the Warden than his charges, but still not as bad as they might have been. He was being escorted by Therran and nine other guards. They were not overly cruel, but rather taking no chances. He remained gagged the entire trip; it was only removed to allow him to eat, which he had to do with blades only a couple of inches from his throat. His hands were never brought to his front like his charges, and his hood was only removed with the gag during meal times.

Still, Athaz did not complain when he was able to speak during meal times or by unwarranted groaning when his mouth was gagged. After a week, this began to get Therran's attention. He desired to speak with the Warden. Their intelligence had told them that Athaz was in disfavor with the Son of Bälech, but they had not been able to discover any reason for it. He had never failed in any task given, which most likely meant Athaz was guilty of the crimes suspected of all Wardens. This strengthened Therran's resolve and he would not speak to his captive until they were safe in The Sanctuary in Menigar, where the Divine Tongue held no power. Though he was meek without being cowardly, the Warden still held his head high. His eyes, when they were visible, were neither afraid nor defiant. He didn't necessarily look content. It was more of a look of resignation and acceptance, but it didn't carry even a hint of self-pity.

One evening, while Therran was on rotation to guard the Warden, he pondered his question aloud. "Who are you, Warden Athaz?" It was a question he never thought he would have asked of any Warden. It didn't matter who they were. They had surrendered their identity to become the monsters they were. That they were all of the same appearance was fitting as they were all of one mind and heart.

Or so Therran wanted to believe. But this Warden's actions at Lacris, and even now, made him ask questions he did not want to think about. Had this one managed to keep his conscience intact, in spite of all that had been demanded of him? If he had, he would be the first. Or was he?

Therran shook himself. "Stoic actions can have roots other than a pure heart," and with that he shut down his mind for the evening and simply watched his captive until his shift was over.

Therran had long decided the Warden must be brought in for questioning and to face trial before the rest of the expedition arrived at Menigar.

Athaz arrived at the beautiful city two full days before his charges. He was as ignorant of this information as his covered eyes were ignorant of the beauty of the city streets his feet now walked, for his hood was still covering his face. His ears heard the curses and cries of hatred thrown his way. Though most seemed to have as little effect as they would have on a deaf man, there were a few specific ones that caused his head to drop in painful memories. This went unnoticed by his accusers, not that they would have cared anyway. Every one of them had suffered loss at the hands of The Dawn's most powerful and unnatural fighting force.

He was brought to The Sanctuary in the middle of the city. It was where meetings between the three races were held, as well as the courthouse and meeting hall for all official business conducted by the three Noble Races of Menigar. It was here that the Lady Lyr waited for the Warden to arrive and stand trial. She was the current seer and leader of Menigar. She was old, even for an Elf. More than four of her five hundred years before she Faded back into the Sea were spent. She was the mother of Verran, who in turn was the father of Therran and Vera. Like all Elves, occasionally her mind was called back into the Sea, granting her insight into those before her as well as hints toward potential futures. She was more gifted than most in interpreting these visions as well as seeing the paths that led to them. The same gift could be found in her granddaughter, Vera, who many believed would take her place in leading one of only three major cities still standing from before the Long Night.

It was in this middle section of the city Athaz was brought. Nothing of the Divine worked here. When the city was dug from the mountain, they began to notice their Divine commands over the stone lost effectiveness and eventually ceased to work at all. At the center of the wide area was a smooth, curious, white stone. Not daring to touch it, the Dwarves carefully enclosed it in a small case, barely moving it from its original location and instead built around it. The perimeter of where the Divine ceased to work was named The Sanctuary.

It was not the only place of its kind, but it was the only one known that was underground. The city was in its infancy when Bälech began his conquest, and the Dwarves realized this might be one of their last bastions of defense. Fortunately, it was never tested as Bälech never discovered it. Though he long believed there was a stronghold in the mountains near Mizcur, he thought it was on the west side of the Argom River, not in the Briar Patch Mountains.

While The Sanctuary could protect them from the Warden's Divine abilities, it would also cut Lyr off from her connection to the Sea. And now she desired that connection more than ever. Ever since they had learned of this expedition and the Warden to lead it, Athaz had been a curious subject of discussion. Some even wondered if his heart was still tender, even after years of serving as a Warden of the Dawn. No blemish could be found on his record, yet here he was leading a couple of young students as a chaperone. What had he done to fall into disfavor?

Athaz blinked as the hood was yanked off his head. Therran removed the gag but left the bindings on his wrists. "Your Divine abilities will have no power here," Therran informed him. "Now you will face trial for your crimes. Lady Lyr will be here to preside and render judgment in a few moments."

Athaz only bowed. Finally, he asked in a hoarse voice, "If I am to speak, may I have a drink of water?" Therran ordered a guard to fetch his captive a drink. When he had received it, Athaz thanked them. Thoughts plagued Therran again. Who was this Warden? A bell rang, announcing the approach of Lady Lyr.

"I have not much time," he thought to himself. He sprinted up the steps to the balcony Lyr was approaching, praying he was making the right decision. He found his grandmother just as she was getting ready to present herself to the prisoner.

"Therran, what are you doing here, you should —"

"I know, my lady," he answered. "But I must speak with you. I pray I am not falling victim to a ploy, but he has asked nothing. I ask you put this matter in Xiarch's hands. Grant the Warden an opportunity to face The Sundering."

Lady Lyr stared at him. Therran thought she would dismiss him curtly, but she did not. She had been dreading making this decision while out of touch with her kin in the Sea, but maybe her kin in Menigar were providing her the insight she needed.

"We will see," she said at last.

It was all Therran would get, and he knew it. He bowed and returned to guard the prisoner.

"The trial will now begin," Lady Lyr announced, making herself visible to Athaz from her balcony well above him.

"I am Lyr, Seer of Menigar, where you are now prisoner. What is your name, Warden?"

"Athaz," he replied evenly.

"Already, I see some of what the Commander sees in you. You are fearless, but not insolent. You carry yourself with a dignity, which is uncommon for those of your … kind."

Athaz stood resolutely. This farce of a trial was unnecessary and the sentence of death should be carried out swiftly. He never understood why rulers always insisted on a show of seeking justice when they already knew the outcome. Besides, it wouldn't change the accuracy of the charges or the eminent consequences, whether the trial was a sham or true.

"You are charged with the murder of all the Savanir you have slaughtered. Should we doubt our assumption of your guilt? All of you look the same in our eyes. What is your plea?"

The Tales of Lugon

"Doubt?" Athaz began. "No. As for my plea that I have killed many of your allegiance in battle ... I do not deny it, but neither do I feel responsible for their deaths. It was your ancestors that began this war, and you continue it to this day, so I could argue their deaths were on your hands." Curses erupted as they demanded the trial be brought to a close and the Warden executed.

"*However*," Athaz said, regaining their attention by using the word of exception. "I have been ordered, and obeyed, to kill those who surrendered or never raised a hand against us at all, which went against my own conscience, even if they were ultimately at fault. I have done this more times than I can remember even if I so desired. Therefore, I must still plead guilty."

Now it was the Lady Lyr's turn to think. "Your honesty is appreciated," she began. "Though your guilt has not been lessened by it. Now I ask you another question. As by your own admission you are guilty, is there a reason we should even entertain the notion of sparing you?"

Athaz believed he was being toyed with. "Your Commander, I believe, would do me the service of a quick death instead of asking me such pointless questions, but I will answer. Yes, I can think of reasons for pardon: for my family, for the people under my care, such as my charges you also captured. But such pleas reached my ears and I ignored them. Therefore, the only mercy I ask for is that you treat my charges better than I treated yours: that you show them mercy. The only mercy I ask for myself is assurance of this."

"Understood," the Lady Lyr responded. "But I would have you ask for mercy for yourself."

"I will not grovel like a whipped dog!" Athaz growled.

"Ask, or you will die not knowing the fate of those you claim to care for!" the Lady thundered.

Athaz stared silently, his jaw clinching and his nostrils flaring in rage.

"Very well," she said. "Commander Therran, execute this murderer."

"Wait!" Athaz said. "Mercy," he mumbled.

"Louder, Warden," she said.

"I ask for mercy," he said, choking back tears of pride.

"So you will humble yourself," said the Lady in a gentler tone. Athaz was about to lose his mind with indignation, but Lady Lyr raised her hand. "I did not have you ask for mercy for my amusement but so that you might receive it!" she said. "The fate of your companions you shall now know, but your mercy does not end there." She made a motion with her arms, and others clothed in official robes stepped forward, bearing a plain, round stone encased in a glass box.

"Though your actions damn you, you have found favor in my eyes, largely based on the testimony of Commander Therran, who believes he sees Xiarch may have use for you."

Athaz couldn't resist a small laugh before he checked himself.

"Laugh if you wish, Xiarch will determine your fate, not me. You will have your unnatural burden removed from you, if you can survive it."

Athaz's eyes widened in understanding. "You are going to try to tear me from the Divine?"

"That will happen. The Silent Stone was found when this chamber was constructed over three thousand years ago. No Divine abilities work here. The Silent Stone was discovered in its heart. Here, the rocks absorb the Divine around us. But this stone will draw it out from those who touch it. It is a horrible fate for Dwarves and Elves, but since Bälech destroyed Man's ability to wield the Divine, and in your case poured some of his own taint, it may prove to be your salvation. However, Bälech's command over the Divine is strong. Only six times has this been attempted and only once survived. Still, if you are favored by Xiarch, as Commander Therran suspects, then we will leave it to him whether you are to live or die."

Athaz looked at the stone with fear, but not for the reasons those around him suspected. For decades now, his only defense against the horrible things he had committed was that there was nothing more powerful than the spirit of Bälech that enabled his heirs' absolute control of the Divine. If something else existed that could render that power mute... Athaz felt sick at the thought of it. He almost hoped nothing would happen when he grabbed the stone that was now being presented to him. Then he realized what a selfish thought that was. If there was a greater power than Bälech, it was cause for the world to rejoice.

"Maybe if it does exist, it will kill me," he thought. He knew from the moment it popped in his mind that it was a cowardly thought. But he was so ready to rest. He feared for his family, but he didn't know how he could save them now. He feared his guilt if he lived.

"Still, I would die knowing," he suddenly said aloud. The glass lid was raised as he looked down at the stone. Slowly, he reached in with both hands, still bound, and grabbed it.

At first, nothing happened, and he cursed himself for being foolish enough to think something greater than his wicked emperor existed. But right when he was about to drop the stone, a searing pain shook his entire body. He fell to the ground, writhing, unaware of all that was going on around him. He would have dropped the Silent Stone to escape the pain, but his mind was locked in a battle. He felt the strands of the Tainted Divine powers fused with his soul evaporating. The agony was beyond anything he had ever felt, but there was also a sweetness to it, like a man dying of thirst suddenly drowning in a vast lake. He knew to drink might kill him, but drink he must. He felt the final aspect of the Taint leave his soul. Darkness enveloped him as the robed figures raised his body and carried it out of The Sanctuary.

CHAPTER VIII

Revelations

When Arun awoke the next morning, he found his legs still asleep. Their circulation had been cut off by the rail they were hanging over at the knees in Kruthos' guest room bed. Still, it was worlds better than waking up with ropes digging into his ankles and his right arm.

He heard a knock on his door. "You up yet?" came Kruthos' gruff, friendly voice.

"Awake, not up," Arun replied.

"Well, you might want to get up. Your breakfast is already cold and soon won't be fit to eat!"

Arun swung his feet over the bed and waited for the pain to subside as the blood rushed back through his legs. When he made his way into the Dwarf's kitchen, he found flapjacks and some type of syrup waiting for him — and more than he could eat, though he put a good dent in it. It was the first time he had eaten unsalted food in weeks.

"So, my host-captor, what is the plan for today? Enlightenment, I suppose?" Arun asked.

Kruthos grunted, knowing Arun was trying his best to make light of a situation he had every right to be suspicious of. "Not much to learn today. We'll meet up with your friends and get that arm looked at. When did you break it?"

"Third day after we set out. We ran into some Orcs that were supposed to be tracking us, but they overestimated our progress. This was the lesser half of a steep price I paid for being a reluctant student of combat training," Arun said.

"That puts it at what? A couple of months or so, right? Have you not had it looked at since?"

"Athaz was going to inspect it during the dig, but obviously there was a change in plans," Arun responded dryly.

"Fair enough. Still, let's get to a human medic after we meet up with your friends."

That was the first bit of good news since the Orc attack that made Arun genuinely excited. It also made him hopeful; it would be odd for his captors to be concerned about his arm healing properly if their long-term plans were cruel. He hoped the medic would find out that Athaz had been wrong, and he could keep the cast off.

They passed through the Dwarven District and into the Elven District. Kruthos was leading the way to an underground pool Therran was fond of visiting. Sure enough, they found him there, staring into the water, his mind lost in a world his body could not enter.

"Elves are tied closely to the water," Kruthos explained. "That's another long story, but one that can easily wait for another time. We can approach. He is still aware of his surroundings, though most of his thought is in the Sea at the moment."

They walked up to Therran, who slightly bowed his head without facing them in acknowledgment. A few seconds later, he looked up at them.

"Good morning, Kruthos. And you, Arun. It is nice to be able to see you a little more comfortable, though I'm sure you are far from feeling at home here."

Arun bowed awkwardly. "Thank you, Commander."

Therran waved off the formality. "Unless you plan on joining my company, Therran will do. Now, what can I help you with? Or did you actually seek me out?" he asked.

"We just need information," Kruthos said. "We were wondering if you could tell us where Inoch dropped off his companions last night. Then we're going to get his arm examined by a medic."

"I can have them brought here," Therran said. "I do not know all of their hosts, but Inoch will probably be glad to help, even with it being his first day off in months. He'll probably join you, if you let him."

Arun was caught off guard by the request. Sure, Inoch seemed decent enough, at least compared to how he had expected The

Bewildered treat them, but he was hardly ready to socialize with someone who had kept him tied up for more than two weeks.

"Maybe tomorrow," Arun said finally. "My friends and I would like to be able to talk freely among ourselves. Inoch has been our constant ... companion for a while."

Therran laughed. "Delicately put, Master Arun, though I hope you don't judge Inoch too harshly for carrying out his duty."

Arun assured him that wasn't the case, that he thought highly of him. "But we still felt ... and feel rather trapped."

Therran nodded. "Of course. No one can blame you for wanting some privacy. This will take a couple of hours. Why not go ahead and get that arm looked at while we fetch them?"

So they made their way to the District of Men. Arun was still in awe over the craftsmanship of the ember road that reflected light from the overhanging candles, when he heard singing in the distance. As they drew closer, he could make out the words, and he felt his heart soaring within him.

> *To Breathe in Life things yet to be*
> *And Bring to Light what minds can see*
> *To Melt and Smelt*
> *To Bend and Blend*
> *We Forge a place for all to stand*
> *A land we Build by hand...*
> *Of Man!!*

Arun hadn't even realized his feet had come to a stop. His heart was filled with the desire to create things never seen and to find new uses for the mundane, to see visions take material form.

Arun was brought out of his reveries by Kruthos repeatedly clearing his throat. When Arun turned to him, Kruthos gave a small laugh. "So, even Night Dwellers still feel the call to their Task."

"I'm sorry?" Arun asked confused. "What Task are you referring to?"

As they continued walking toward the clinic, Kruthos began to explain Savanir lore to him. "Though you have heard of Xiarch from your life in Hilae, the teachings you heard are much different than ours. And I don't exactly have to try and convince you that a good deal of it was filled with deception. But it has been passed down to us that each of the Three Noble Races were given a Divine Task. The Dwarves had the Task of Craftsmanship, to shape Xiarch's world of Lugon into the most beautiful place in the heavens. We are born with an innate and unquenchable thirst to mold raw materials into things of beauty and use. The Elves were given the Task of Knowledge and Wisdom, to understand and share Xiarch's wisdom he imbedded in the order of his universe. Men were given the Task of Forging, to continue Xiarch's work of creation by bringing new things into existence by combining that which already exists. The three are constantly feeding off each other. For you need tools and knowledge of what exists and to continue to Forge, and when you Forge, Elves have a new branch of lore to study and Dwarves a new element to shape. If I were to guess, you just felt the Task to Forge as you heard Men singing at their work."

Arun wasn't sure about all of that. He felt more interested in the Elven task, but by now they had arrived at the clinic. The medic cut open the cast and looked at his arm. Arun was shocked to see numerous scars. "It's mending well. Whoever did this certainly took care in setting it, but it appears their tools were crude," the medic said. Arun again found himself wishing to see Athaz. The medic continued. "Hmm, looks like we could remove the cast and just keep you in a sling for a few weeks. After that, you should be able to begin strengthening exercises, but you'll have to go slow, especially at first."

Arun thanked him for his time and left with Kruthos to return to the pool and meet up with his companions.

They were the last to arrive at the pool. Baran had his arm protectively around Descia, but it may have provided more comfort for himself than security for her. Geown was excitedly talking with his host. He was an Elf of some standing, it seemed. His dark blue tunic was filled with a golden, fluid script. But unlike those discovered at

The Ruins, this writing obviously was laid out in a horizontal path. And while known Bewildered writing had always been graceful, Arun realized the Elven script didn't have a single corner, dead end, or retrace; it flowed like one long, continuous narrow stream.

Baran spotted him first and waved him over. "Glad you're alright as well," he said.

"I don't think we have much to complain about as prisoners other than the status," Arun replied.

Baran had to admit that was true. The hosts, their tasks complete until the evening, went on their own business. Inoch informed them they were free to explore the city for the next several hours. The friends wandered aimlessly, taking in the sites, but mostly just enjoying the limited freedom they now had after weeks of being blind, bound, and guarded. Kruthos chose to stay with them, as much to be of service as to watch them, but he hung back far enough he would only hear them if they called for him.

For the first hour, they simply fellowshipped together. At times, they talked about the wonders of the city. Other times they just enjoyed quiet companionship. Eventually the conversation turned to what was weighing on all their minds.

"So, what are we going to do now?" Baran asked.

"Patience, my young friend," Geown said. "We don't have a lot of choices at the moment. We don't know what they have planned for us, and even if we needed to flee, we can't right now. We don't know the way out. What we do know is that there is a military stronghold between the city and our escape to the surface."

"But what are we to do if given the choice?" Descia asked. "Should we return to Hilae? It is doubtful we will be allowed that option, given that we are in an undiscovered stronghold of The Bewildered. Even if we can, should we?"

"I will not," Arun said. "Athaz was warning me and Baran against returning when the Orcs appeared."

"Why would he do that?" Descia asked.

"Because we are wanted dead," Baran answered.

"What? That's impossible."

It was at this point the friends revealed what Athaz had learned from the Orc's mind during their first attack and what they suspected it meant.

"I'm sorry we had to keep that secret," Arun said. "Athaz believed ignorance was your best defense."

"I'm going to kill that fool Warden myself if The Bewildered don't!" she said angrily. "Ignorance is never a good defense! Nor am I convinced that was his only reason. Did it ever occur to you if he had sent word to me and the others from The Tower we could have simply pretended to have not been able to raise the necessary funds?"

Baran's eyes widened. Again it was Arun that came to the Warden's defense. "Descia, you were as eager as we were to go. How could he convince you of the danger in a message without saying it plainly? And had you canceled the trip after receiving any message, no matter what you claimed, it would have brought suspicion on all of you, not to mention how devastating it would have been for his wife and son. Family of a Warden traitor? I don't want to know the fate that would await them."

Descia fell mute. Geown spoke again. "Like I said, patience. You have gotten yourselves all worked up, and we are no closer to a solution or plan than when we started."

At this point, Kruthos came trotting up. "I have just received word that Arun and Baran's presence is requested elsewhere. We need to make our way back to the pool, where Inoch will be waiting to assist the rest of you as I bring Baran and Arun to The Sanctuary."

After Inoch arrived, Kruthos began leading Arun and Baran toward the center of the Menigar. "The fate of your Warden has been decided. Don't bother asking me ... I was not told. Before it was announced, Commander Therran asked that you two be told first because of your friendship with him."

The two friends weren't sure they wanted to rush to learn the news or wait until the following day and learn with everyone else. Kruthos brought them into a small room under the balcony where the Warden had received his sentence. At a desk sat an older middle-aged man clad in the robes of a priest of Menigar. Though hooded, they could see he had a gray beard with some yellow flecks throughout, suggesting it had been blond long ago. He was writing furiously, though he had no candle to light the room, just a small window into the outside of The Sanctuary.

"The priest was here when the Warden stood trial and knows his fate. I pray the news is good," Kruthos said. Then he turned and left, shutting the door behind him.

"Well met," the man said. "Forgive the dimness, but my eyes are quite sensitive to light, at least for the moment."

"Sir," Baran began. "We were told you could tell us the fate of the Warden that was brought here as a prisoner."

"The Warden is no more," the figure said coldly. Arun's head fell and Baran, in a rage, instinctively reached for his sword before he remembered it wasn't there.

The man laughed. "You couldn't touch me, even if you had your weapon." Suddenly the man threw back his hood, stood erect, and grabbed a long sword unseen from the other side of the desk. "For Athaz is still quite formidable, even as an aging man."

It took the two friends a second to realize what the man was implying. When they did, doubt clouded their features.

"And stop calling me 'sir.' I told you I would tire of hearing it."

Doubt was suddenly replaced by a hope they feared to let in. "How in The Dawn's—" Arun began, but Athaz cut him off.

"Never speak in awe of land ruled by that accursed traitor in front of me!" Athaz said vehemently. Then he softened. "But if you doubt that I am who I claim, feel free to test me," he said, pointing to the wall. There lay Baran's sword and shield. Arun wished his arm was healed. Then he realized his mentor had the fauchard in his hand, apparently lying behind the desk as well. He handed it to Arun. "Hold this while I train with Baran for a while. Then we'll pick up our lessons where we left off at Lacris."

Arun took the fauchard with his good hand. "I'm already convinced," he said. "Maybe it's because I wanted it to be true so badly, but I feel if it weren't for my eyes, I would have no trouble believing it at all."

Athaz shook his head with a smile. "You shouldn't be so easily swayed, but I would be lying if I said I'm disappointed. I have a feeling I will have enough trouble convincing others."

By that point, Baran had girded himself with his sword and secured his shield. Athaz first put him through his paces before the real sparring began. When it did, it didn't last very long. Athaz came over top, and when Baran raised his shield, Athaz bashed him in the gut with his own shield, just as he had the first day they trained in combat. But this time Baran was up in a flash, even if he could barely breathe.

Athaz laughed. "Well, at least you learned that lesson, but we really have to work on you exposing your body when you block high. Are you convinced?"

"Definitely … feels … the same," Baran wheezed.

The friends had a great reunion with their mentor. Athaz discussed what he had learned: the limits of Bälech's power, his crimes from the past that he now knew were in service not only to an evil ruler, but one whose power was not as absolute as he had thought. Arun and Baran described Menigar for him, as he had not been able to see it, too busy revealing what he knew of The Dawn: her military, tactics, strengths, weaknesses … any intelligence that could help in the future. Though he seemed healthy, they still were unsure if his body would last long after The Sundering. Eventually, though, Baran asked what they had been dying to know.

"How did they return you to your pre-Warden form?"

Athaz laughed. "This is hardly how I looked before I was a Warden, though I recognize my features: brown eyes, a hawk nose—though now longer than I remember. Sadly it appears not only did my hair not keep its color, it seems to be disappearing. Still, this is how I should look at my age, as near as I can tell. I am fifty-three years old after all. But as for how this happened," he continued. "In this room we are now in, 'The Sanctuary,' as the Savanir call it, the Divine Tongue has no power here. When they shaped this room, they found in the very center a peculiar stone that actually draws out the Divine from those that touch it."

"Wait … the Elves can use the Divine?" Arun asked.

Truth Unearthed

"Yes," Athaz replied. "And so can Dwarves. And at one point apparently so could all Men. But each race was only given a very limited ability in the Divine to pursue their Task. Elves have power over memory to search others for knowledge. It turns out it's very similar to what I did to the Orc, but they do not have to invoke the power of Bälech, like Wardens. It is simply a natural ability for them. Dwarves can move and shape objects, as their Task is craftsmanship. And Men, to help with their Task of Forging, can create fire, melting down elements to rebuild them again as they see fit. However, when Bälech established his empire, he used his own Divine abilities to remove their natural powers. The few men that escaped him have mostly mingled with those who cannot, and very few have any ability left in the Divine. I knew of this already from my time as a … dog of that foul creature. For Bälech hunts these men fervently, forcing them to become Watchers, Wardens, or Healers. You may have heard of them in legend. In The Dawn, and sometimes in the Savanir, they are now referred to as wizards. Elves simply call them Pure Men, for their abilities have not been tainted by Bälech. Still, with no masters left, few wizards are able to control their abilities or use them for anything constructive. Most with the gift live and die without ever knowing it. And, from what I understand, you all will be tested to see if any of you possess Divine abilities."

"How will they do that?" Arun asked.

"You will be given a simple command to see if the Divine still listens to your call. The words will prove powerless from the lips of Elves, Dwarves, or Men that have lost their gift. Anyway, back to my Sundering; I was forced to touch the Silent Stone, both a penalty and mercy for my crimes."

Baran, and Arun especially, shifted uneasily as Athaz shared that news. Had he really been guilty of the horrific crimes the Savanir hinted at?

Athaz picked up on their discomfort. "Yes, I am guilty of terrible crimes, which I beg you not to ask me about. I did those things for many reasons, but chief among them was for the sake of my family, and I fear I would do many again for them. But I am deeply

The Tales of Lugon

ashamed for another reason. I followed him in despair. Despair that no hope outside of Bälech could be found. Never have I been more wrong."

"But how do you come to believe these Savanir so easily?" Arun asked. "How do you know you are not trading one evil for another?"

"I am not truly a member of the Savanir. I have been granted time, as you will, to decide what I will do with my newfound freedom. Truth be told, my number one concern is for my family trapped in Hilae ... if indeed they are still fortunate enough to have been left in peace. They must be freed. I may not ever completely trust the Savanir, but we now have a common enemy. Afterwards, I may join them, or I may take my family and hide in the most remote place I can find. But I won't find better allies in my mission against Bälech."

Another man, in similar dress as Athaz, knocked on one of the columns to make his presence known. "Begging your pardon," he said. "But Lady Lyr requests the presence of all three of you in her chambers."

Athaz bowed. "We will come immediately," he said. "Lady Lyr is the leader of Menigar and to whom I owe my life and what little of the dark history of The Dawn I did not know," Athaz explained as they headed out of the small building into the wider area of The Sanctuary.

Lady Lyr sat on a high-backed chair, dressed in a simple, beautiful dark blue robe with her hair fanned all around her. She wore a golden ring with the same Elven seal as the door on the gate to Menigar, and like the seal, her eyes were closed in deep thought when they first saw her but opened as they approached. On her left was Commander Therran and on her right was Vera. Though Lady Lyr was beautiful and did not show her age in wrinkles or graying hair as human women did, their age was the only way to tell Lyr and Vera apart. Vera was filled with fire, and her eyes eagerly searched for new answers and knowledge to pressing problems, whereas Lady Lyr's eyes were focused inward in reflection, seeking understanding and wisdom from things already seen.

Lady Lyr rose from her seat. "I am pleased to see you again, Athaz. And to finally meet your charges you speak so highly of. Baran, your courage and valiant nature is already known to us, and we hope you will find it pleasing to join us as we seek to protect those cut off from The Dawn because their knowledge of its true nature. Arun, we will discuss you in detail in a moment. You already know my grandson, Commander Therran, who saved your expedition from the Orcs." She reached her hand back to Vera, who accepted to be presented. "This is my granddaughter, and likely successor. She is called—"

"Vera," Arun finished, amazed that he already knew the name.

All eyes turned on him and he blushed. "I do not know how I know. But when I look into her eyes, I feel like I should."

Vera smiled and bowed her head. Therran, in great distress, walked over to his sister. "He also knew I was an Elf before I introduced myself. How does he know you?"

"Alas, the path I chose can no longer be hidden, and the clumsiness of my abilities in my youth repays me. Arun and I met many years ago, the night before he was taken to Hilae from his hut in the Yeomanry and a year before I came of age during a visit to our friends in the Makrin Mountains."

"Why did he not speak of this meeting before?" Lady Lyr asked, though she feared she knew the answer.

"Because he does not remember it," Vera said simply. "When he fell asleep, I removed the memory from his mind, though apparently not well enough, and placed him back in his own bed, for both my protection and his own and, as it happened, for the sake of the Savanir. And now, Arun, it is time you learned what the Sea showed me in the water of the lake near your house as I searched your mind."

Vera closed her eyes, reliving the moment that had transpired fifteen years ago. "I saw you, Arun, in The Tower of Hilae, showing Elves the histories of The Dawn as they kept them. I saw Dwarves building houses for themselves outside of the caves they now hide in. And I saw men formerly of the Yeomanry working for the benefit of their families and themselves. I knew the Sea must be showing me that you would be at long last the one to deliver us from the Long Night.

Vera gave a weak smile, "Finally, the Sea spoke a warning to me:"

> *Should this future you seek to see*
> *Forsaken by your own will you be*
> *A life in exile 'till you Fade into eternity;*
> *A drop of rain longing to return to the Sea.*

Suddenly Lady Lyr rose from her chair, stepped forward, and grabbed Vera's arm. "Enough!" Turning to the three guests, she said, "I must beg you to leave us. I will call you again at another time."

After the three Men had left the room, Lyr turned to her granddaughter, grabbing her by the hand and leading her into her private bedroom. Vera was not spared even that short walk before the rebuke began. "You altered his memory?! Without consent or even informing him? Do you know what you have done?!"

"What I had to do in order to save our people," Vera replied evenly. "I knew the price I would pay. I heard the Sea's warning. I chose it willingly."

"What about the price our people will pay?" Lyr said with the chill of ice in her tone. "Being willing to touch the Silent Stone for abusing your Elven power would be disastrous enough, but the implications that will come of this should the boy succeed ..."

Doubt crept into Vera's mind, and Lyr felt it immediately. "That is the same doubt I felt in you the night you met Arun, only now it is magnified many times over. You no longer believe the vision you saw?"

"Oh, no I do ... at least part of it, the delivery of our people." She paused. "But I haven't seen Arun happily walking with our people for nigh two years now. Perhaps it's best if you see my memories of that night. Maybe you'll see something I didn't."

Lyr's movements showed no hesitation, but Vera could feel the fear building in her grandmother as she reached up to her head and began the Divine command.

Vera's mind rushed back to that night as she relived it with her grandmother, now seeing that night from Vera's eyes and mind: the singing by the pool, Arun staring her. Lyr listened to their conversation and then Vera's songs. It was at this point she experienced the visions. She saw Vera's hope of seeing the peoples of the Savanir walking freely with Arun, still several years older than he was now but conversing happily with them. And then, she saw the battle. Eagerly, she waited for Arun's face to appear, but the view was always obstructed. By the end of the vision, she still had learned nothing, but instead saw Vera diving into Arun's mind, trying to remove the memory of their encounter.

Lyr wanted to withdraw, and she could feel Vera trying to pull out, but she must know. After reliving their conversation, she finally released Vera. Rage and sorrow gripped her vocal chords as she coarsely whispered. "You lied to me."

"No, I didn't—"

"You *lied* to me and to yourself! I should have pressed you that night when I felt your doubt. And when I asked you for assurance, you fully committed to it, believing it yourself, knowing full well that I would sense any hesitation a second time. Never in my worst nightmares would I have imagined you deliberately deceiving me, much less risking our people for it."

Lady Lyr raised her voice. "You never saw Arun delivering our people, merely that he would be alive during its occurrence. I was right, the Sea was beginning to move to you, preparing you to lead our people. The Sea was giving you the Hope I longed to see for nigh five hundred years! But in your eagerness you have risked everything! And don't think I didn't see your doubt about even the battle taking place now. That vision is weakening too. But it certainly seems that Arun won't be around regardless!"

She paused in her anger. Vera now felt sorrow overtaking it. "And that verse was not a warning of the price to pay for a noble action. It was a threat for a crime. The Sea was preparing you to lead our people, but when it sensed your intent, it tried to frighten you away from this folly. Rather than our leader, you would be exiled, hated. That is the path you have chosen."

Lyr felt the shock through Vera's mind. That interpretation of the Sea's words had not occurred to her before. "The only question now..." Lyr forced herself to continue "...is how many reasons they'll have to hate you. I only hope that you haven't cost us the vision of hope that you were given."

Vera tried to process what her grandmother was telling her, but she couldn't. "I thought I was doing the right thing," she whispered.

"No," Lyr corrected her again. "You convinced yourself you were. There is a difference. And you will pay dearly for it."

Vera stared through the floor, beyond the room, flitting on the edge of conscious thought. "What must we do?" she asked at last.

"*Do*?" Lyr asked. "We will *do* nothing. We will pretend to the rest of the world that we have never had this conversation. You are still trying to manipulate events. There is a time for action. You raced ahead, before waiting for all the information you needed. Now, we will do what you should have been doing for the past twelve years. We will wait and hope we haven't run too far down on this path to turn back."

* * * * * * * * * *

Arun needed to sit as soon as they were back in the Elven District. His mind was racing. Confusion. Anger. Even guilt. Now he realized he was the reason everyone was not only at the dig but why they are now forced to pick sides in a war where they had all been bystanders previously. The biggest question was "why?" Why him? How in the world did she expect him to save them? And why should he? Who were they to him? Sure, they had saved his life from the Orcs, but apparently that was no act of simple kindness. He had no love for the Savanir, and his feelings were quickly turning from cautious gratitude to revulsion.

Baran sat next to him in silence, equally stunned and confused. Athaz stood next to him, placing his hand on Arun's shoulder. "Do not act hastily," he said, knowing his young charge's emotions were in turmoil.

"Why shouldn't I tell these people they have it all wrong?" Arun asked angrily. "That they have set us all up for some vision I was not privy to, that they never bothered asking me before they put their plans into motion?"

"For starters," Athaz began, with an even, matter-of-fact tone, "while I do not discourage your refusal, how you refuse may greatly affect the rest of your life here. For here you will spend it, regardless of if you help them or not. Doubtless Bälech was ignorant of the Savanir's designs for you or you would never been allowed to leave Hilae. But if he doesn't know yet, he soon will. That a Savanir army was ready to ruin his plans to destroy us has undoubtedly reached his ears, and I can guarantee you he has not been idle in the weeks since then. Yes, the Orcs were under his command. I have wondered before if he had commanded some of the filth, but it was not confirmed until our battle. He may not know the location of Menigar, but, as I informed Lady Lyr and Commander Therran already, he knows of its existence. The Savanir are not the only ones with spies that have infiltrated enemy ranks. And now that the Savanir believe that their time of victory is at hand, that prophecy and who the Savanir believes it refers to will be known to him. You will be hunted by Bälech for the rest of your life."

Arun slammed the flat of his good fist into the wall behind him. "So, not only is my past life gone forever, but thanks to their misguided belief in my identity, I am now an enemy to the most powerful empire Lugon has ever known. And my refusal to aid the Savanir in their hopeless rebellion against him may cause my neighbors that I now cannot escape to hate me. This Graduate Task keeps getting better all the time!" Arun raked his hair with his free hand before getting up.

"Where are you going?" Baran asked.

"I don't know, but my feet won't be still. Go tell everyone what you learned just now. I'm sure I'll be able to find someone to take me back to the rest of you or to Kruthos' tonight. Who would refuse such a simple request from their prophesied savior?" Arun asked bitterly.

Baran started to go after him, but Athaz stopped him. "He needs time, and he's got a good head on his shoulders. The sooner he walks out the emotions, the sooner he'll come to the right decision."

Arun meandered aimlessly throughout the Elvish District. Eventually he noticed many of the Elves were looking at him with knowledge in their eyes. Containing his anger to a low growl, he made it a point to walk in a straight line toward the District of Men. Hopefully, he wouldn't stand out there.

When he made it to his new destination, a few eyes still glanced his way, but they were directed at his sling. At least they weren't staring at some foretold hero.

However, it was not merely self-pity that haunted Arun. Even if it had been another in his company, Baran or Athaz—either of whom would have made more sense—he still would have been trying to dissuade them of this fool's hope. Arun knew The Dawn was unbeatable. Athaz's military experience was proof that though The Dawn may have lied about its history, its present state had been no idle boast. The Savanir themselves acknowledged that they lived in hiding, mostly in small camps or even among the towns of The Dawn. Menigar was one of very few places that held any strength, and it would not be able to resist a determined siege from a global empire.

Of course, hopelessness of success doesn't mean they shouldn't resist, he thought. But it wasn't just the hopelessness. *Do they honestly believe that they'll just be liberating Lugon? Leading us all into a paradise?* As an aspiring Keeper, Arun knew better from countless examples. Even in a single town, if Power was suddenly no more, a vacuum appeared. Infighting for leadership, attackers from the outside … it brought chaos, even on a small scale. But worldwide? Arun shuddered at the thought. The Savanir did not have the forces needed to rule most of Lugon. There would be mass starvation as bandits attacked trade lines. Cutthroats would rise to power. No, it was not for himself that Arun hated what the Savanir were trying to accomplish; he feared for all of Lugon should they actually succeed.

But what do I do for now? Where do I fit in all of this? Eventually his mind began to organize its thoughts to the rhythm of his walking feet. *This isn't my problem. They are the ones clinging to a miraculous prophecy — because a miracle is exactly what it would take to overthrow The Dawn. Athaz and Baran will help me carve out a life for myself here, even if all the Savanir turn their backs on me for refusing the play along. After all, what are they going to do? Force me, a scholar, to lead their armies? Threaten to kill their 'savior' if I don't play along?*

He started to raise his hands in a mixture of frustration and relief, when he was reminded of another reason he could not possibly be their hero. "Yeah, I'm going to deliver these people from Bälech with one hand nearly tied behind my back and the skill to barely kill a single Orc." He laughed. Separating himself from the expectations, the whole situation was actually very ridiculous.

It was at this time he realized the great overhanging fires were dimming. Apparently it had taken him longer than he realized to reach this obvious conclusion. He made his way back to the Dwarven District and asked one of the stout fellows for directions to Kruthos', which, as expected, were gladly given.

When he arrived, he found his friends all gathered around, even Athaz, at Kruthos' dinner table. Arun could not relax, for also in the room, sitting on chairs in the far corner, were the Lady Lyr and Vera, both with their eyes fixed on him. Arun gave them a cold bow as he took a seat near Baran. "If you are here to tell me more about my future as your savior, I'm afraid you're wasting your time. It's not me."

Lady Lyr nodded. "You are perfectly within your rights to refuse this role, nor would we force it on you. I apologize for not explaining that before I rudely dismissed you, but my granddaughter's meeting you and the forgetfulness she caused you were revelations I was not expecting. In my shock, I acted hastily and foolishly. Forgive me."

Arun blinked stupidly. He was expecting a fight and instead was issued an apology. "You are not going to try to force me, or at least convince me, to participate in your war?"

Lady Lyr shook her head. "No. Visions and foretellings are dangerous to force." Arun wasn't sure, but it seemed the seer was looking at Vera. "That was part of my concern, that Vera had influenced you into taking this path. Also, as I pointed out to my granddaughter, the vision never exactly says what your role is, only that you will be present." Vera shifted in her seat, her eyes showing she wished to speak, but wisely she remained mute.

Arun stood and bowed more sincerely this time. "I shouldn't have doubted you would respect my choice. You have done nothing but act with hospitality toward me and all of us that you saved."

Lady Lyr gave a slight nod in acknowledgment of his gratitude. "We came for two other reasons. One is to test you for Divine ability; we have already seen something that surprised us …" She turned to Baran, who smiled awkwardly.

"You're joking …" Arun said in disbelief.

Baran's voice was sheepish. "I was the most surprised. Well, more surprised than any except the Elves at any rate. Does wonders for helping me trust them. And I know it was me … I felt the warmth of the fire leaving my heart, flow through my arms, and depart through my hands. It was … well, I don't quite know how to describe it, really."

"What did you do?" Arun asked.

Baran nodded over to the fire in the stove.

"Which we now need to put out. You not only need a target, but something to contain your fire command if you are off target," the Lady said.

Kruthos smothered the fire in the stove, closing off the lid and sealing it for several seconds before releasing it. When the smoke cleared, the seer motioned Arun to the stove.

"Hold out your right hand and repeat EXACTLY what I say," she said.

Remembering what Athaz said about the Divine, Arun didn't need an explanation as to why he couldn't err. The Elf seer did not close her eyes. As this was not her Task, the words were nothing more than an ordinary foreign language to her.

"*Fureigh san bor, ilum de pro.*"

Arun waited for a full five seconds before he repeated the phrase. When he finished, he held his breath. Nothing. He looked at the Elven women. They nodded. "You can relax now. Your blood is too weak."

Arun was actually relieved. He looked over at Baran and then back to the Lady Lyr. Vera gave a small laugh.

"Normally he would need to train before even attempting this again, but these are unusual circumstances," the seer replied to his unasked question. Baran, somewhat embarrassed by his own eagerness, went back to the stove. He remembered the words but decided to wait for her to say them one more time, lest he do something catastrophic.

The Lady Lyr repeated the command, and Baran echoed, "*Fureigh san bor, ilum de pro.*" Immediately a small line of flame left his outstretched hand. When it reached the dry wood, a full-strength fire immediately erupted and began burning its fuel.

"By—" Arun cut himself off, realizing the exclamation was not appropriate here.

Descia laughed. "At least he didn't yelp this time." Baran gave her a slight scowl.

After a few moments, the Lady Lyr spoke again. "There is one other more somber reason we have come to speak with you. My granddaughter's actions demand punishment. She will be forced to touch the Silent Stone."

Arun, and especially Athaz, began to protest, but Vera was actually the one who stopped them. "This must be so," she said. "For even though it was for my safety, Arun's, and the fate of my people, if we were to cast aside the punishment for altering minds whenever we felt the circumstances justified it, we would do so far too often. No, the only way to ensure that mind-altering is done either against the will or unbeknownst to the target only at great need is to make it a conscious sacrifice of those who do so. But," she said with a smile, genuinely touched by their concern for her, "I have been granted time. The seer believes that my … decision …

may have unintended consequences in the near future, especially if those consequences harm any of you. So, I am to be spared until such things come to pass or the natural years of your life are spent, for such time does not seem long to the Elves."

The two Elven women rose and, with the grace of a slow moving stream, made their way to Kruthos' door. As they left, Lady Lyr turned to Arun to bid him farewell. "Xiarch guide you and protect you."

The mood was considerably more somber, but it was Arun that actually seemed to be the least fazed. "I for one will not join their war. I do not believe in prophecy, nor would I believe I'm their hero even if I did." Turning to Kruthos, Arun softened his tone. "I am sorry," he said. "You all have treated me well and risked much to save me and my friends, but I'm afraid you made a mistake."

Athaz stood up. "My path, at least, is clear," he said. "I must save my family. If word gets out I survived, they will likely be tortured and killed in my stead."

"Then my path is also clear, at least for a limited time," Baran said. Athaz tried to stop him, but Baran refuted him. "You no longer wield the Divine. You will need fighting companions, and I know Hilae better than any soldier of the Savanir."

Descia put her hand on Baran's arm. "My father," she began, "is in the town of Abscos, on the northern bank of the Argom River near the Meros Wood. If Athaz is reluctant to take you, fearing for your safety, you could assist me. He, too, is in danger."

Baran was miserable. He felt he was more desperately needed by Athaz, but he and Descia had grown close since that day on the ship when he humbled himself to her.

Athaz came up to him. "Help her, my friend. I value your sword, but you should use it to protect those who cannot defend themselves, and my mission will depend on secrecy, not force. And I do not know for sure that they are still in Hilae at all."

Baran nodded and sat next to Descia.

"I also will go with Baran," Arun announced. Kruthos and Athaz began to protest, but Arun said, "I have made it clear I am

Truth Unearthed

not the hero that is sought, and I will not be shepherded like some sheep waiting to be sacrificed for others," he said darkly.

"But your arm ..." Kruthos began.

"If we can get some aid shouldn't be an issue."

Kruthos knew Arun needed to stay within the bounds of Menigar at least until his arm was mended. He also believed Arun deep down knew this was foolishness, but he also knew forcing the young man to stay against his will would only make him more likely to try something desperate. "At least wait until I see if I can get Therran to let Inoch accompany you," he said finally. "I know he would be more than willing and is very capable in combat. And maybe I can reach Brasan again."

Arun and Baran's questions about Inoch were temporarily held in check as they looked at him, surprised that he knew the ship captain. "You know of Captain Brasan? Did you all arrange for him to be our guide? He's part of the Savanir too?"

"Yes, yes, and no, not exactly. While we keep our strongholds a secret, we provide goods that are restricted or rationed by The Dawn. The profit traders get on the black market from these wares is incentive for them to help us out from time to time if the risk for them is not too great. Of course, Brasan has never met me, doesn't know my real name, and certainly doesn't know I'm a Dwarf, and I would ask you to keep it that way."

That made everyone feel better about the quest. Water would be safer than land. They began to discuss lighter things when suddenly Geown cried out impatiently, "Anyone remember me? Well, I'm going to tell you something whether you want to hear it or not. The Savanir have been gracious enough to furnish me with a house and valet and are allowing me to live in retirement. So it appears my troubles are over, and I expect to hear regular reports from all of you to give me something to think about. Somebody has to start chronicling this adventure!"

CHAPTER IX

Journeys Begin Anew

Arun, Baran, Athaz, and Descia spent a week together, all but the last getting ready for their respective journeys. Descia fought long and hard to go with them, but the others pointed out she knew nothing of combat and had never traveled on land without horses and carts. Speed was necessary for all involved. They needed to get their loved ones and then get out as quickly as possible.

As the week progressed, a small sense of control and normalcy returned; they were finally deciding for themselves, to an extent, what their next course would be. However, Arun and Baran were unable to stop worrying for their former mentor, but then Arun received some unexpected news one night when he returned to Kruthos' home. "I'll be accompanying Athaz," he said. "My Divine abilities in shaping material can greatly aid his stealth, and I have skill with combat axes if needed. Lady Lyr has already blessed the endeavor."

Arun couldn't help but hug the Dwarf. "Thank you, friend. You have proven yourself over and over, and now you risk everything for the sake of one of us, and now I know you do so without expecting anything in return." Kruthos patted his shoulder when released from his young guest's grip—and he truly was only a guest now, no longer a prisoner.

The week soon passed, but the friends did not say goodbye yet. They would be together for the blindfolded trip back to the Tikus Foothills. Even Descia would join them for this; an extra gate guard for Menigar was accompanying them to guide her back. This time they accepted the hoods without any trepidation, and the journey passed much more quickly with conversation, both with each other and their guide, Inoch. As they made the sightless journey, they began to discuss what they would do when they returned to

Menigar.

Athaz spoke first. "I plan to settle with my family inside of Menigar, at least for a time until it is safe for us to travel without being hunted. After that, we shall see."

Baran was whispering—as everyone rightly guessed—with Descia. Apparently there had been much discussion on this matter. "I still don't know where I fall in this war, but I think we can all agree in defending peoples from the Savage Races. I plan on joining the patrols, hopefully under the leadership of Inoch."

"I would be honored," Inoch responded. "We can put in a request with Commander Therran when you return."

"I hope to see if the Elves have use for a human researcher," said Descia. "There is so much to learn, so much many peoples and even races I never dreamed of. In some ways, this is a scholar's paradise, even if the means of arrival hadn't been ideal."

The three-hour walk was followed by another two hours of riding, every horse tied to the pommel of the one in front of it. Each one of the departing friends had a horse to call their own, a gift from the Lady Lyr. They felt the wind brush their faces, and the hairs on their skin seemed to reach for the sun at the sensation that had been kept from them for almost two weeks.

"I hope you don't find it rude," Arun began to Inoch, "but I think I would go without ever seeing the wonders of Menigar again than spend another two weeks without the sun and fresh air."

"While some would be hurt at the insensitivity of such a comment, most of the Savanir would still agree with you," Inoch responded. "All of them, perhaps, except for some of the Dwarves."

"But even we long to be out in the free world again, to craft with wood and earth, and not stone alone," Kruthos informed them. "We just can't bear the thought of our work and our ancestors being forgotten,"

They rode in silence now, the weight of the parting paths weighing heavily on them. After about four hours of riding at a trot, they knew the sun had sunk below the horizon. They rode for another two hours before Inoch brought them to a halt and had them remove their blindfolds.

"We trust none of you to deliberately betray us to our enemy, and therefore it has been agreed you should have your sight restored much closer than when you came. Also, there is this ..." Inoch dropped from his horse and moved toward the trunk of a tree whose branches they found themselves under. Moving the brush aside, they saw the tree had been marked with a small triangle, each side made of thin strokes of sapphire, topaz, and pearl.

"You will find trees like this one throughout the Tikus Foothills. If you ever desire or need to return to Menigar and one of our people is not with you, camp in one of these locations. You may not see us, but we will see you, and within a week's time guides will arrive to escort you back to our stronghold."

Baran and Descia walked a ways off to share a more intimate farewell before she rode back with the gate guard. They saw her hand him an envelope before turning their backs to respect their privacy. Some moments are not meant to be shared.

The company did not set a fire. At the request of Lady Lyr, they would not do so until they reached the eastern bank of the Argom River. But they ate well. The Dwarves craftsmanship apparently extended even into the culinary arts, and friends of Kruthos had ensured they would be well provisioned with an assortment of cheeses and flavored breads that Bälech's own chefs would have envied. The group would travel together due west, striking the Argom River and following its banks north, back into the town of Simpat. From there they would split up. Arun and Baran would seek out Captain Brasan, hoping the messengers had found him in time and he had taken the commission. If not, they would ride their horses on the northeastern bank of the Argom River to meet Descia's father, Paleon, and purchase a wagon and hitch team with funds provided by the Lady Lyr to make the journey as comfortable as possible for the aging, retired scholar.

Athaz and Kruthos would be journeying north on the mountain side of the Grigor River, even though Athaz wouldn't be easily recognized. Bälech had surely informed some of his agents to be on the lookout for him. The Sundering had not removed one telling mark; the plow tattoo still identified him, as the ink that formed the stain was not of Divine origin. But for most eyes, he could walk completely unknown among the general populace. Kruthos, however, would stand out a little more. Even hooded, he was still no taller than a youth of twelve, but his beard hung below his belt, and he had muscles that belonged to a laborer in his prime and skin that was worn and leathered by years of work wrought by his skilled hands. They might still run into other travelers in the mountains but none that were on friendly enough terms with The Dawn to alert them to unusual sightings.

On the twelfth evening since setting out, they could see lights in the distance they knew belonged to the town of Simpat. Baran and Arun looked at each other, each thinking the same thing. The town had not changed at all in the few weeks since they had last seen it, but their eyes certainly saw it differently. Never would any town in what had once been their home be a place of rest or refuge. Rather, they must have disguised features and use guarded words and looks. Once friendly places and faces must now be kept at a distance, sometimes completely avoided.

Athaz grimaced. His long, hard life lessened the strangeness of the sensation his charges felt, but not the depression. He had looked upon the settlements where he would now only find enemies before. His love for The Dawn had died long ago. Seeing it now as an enemy seemed the obvious end of a miserable journey that he had hoped for so long, against all odds, would redeem itself in the end. It hadn't.

Kruthos broke the silence. "Well, I guess it's time to get ready. Arun, it's been a couple of weeks, and this will be easier without the sling. Go ahead and take it off." Arun didn't have to be told twice and quickly took his arm out of the sling as Kruthos began rummaging through his pack. "Ah, here they are!" The Dwarf produced two razors, two wigs of long, black, tangled hair, three bowls of liquid tightly sealed, and a pouch filled with animal hair. "Tomorrow our ways part. Athaz has shed the disguise he wore so long that he can walk with little care of being spotted. But your image is doubtless known to all of Bälech's agents by now." Here he turned to Baran. "And you would stand out in any crowd." Baran shrugged, and Arun couldn't help a small smile. His friend had always been easy to spot.

"Of course, you will be wearing hoods, but it would be best to change some features. If you show a couple of traits known to be contrary to your true self, it will keep curious minds from wondering what else is concealed."

Inoch, too, began changing his appearance, though not the color of his skin or hair. His Savanir clothing was replaced with drab, muddied travel garments. He burned the Savanir clothing in the campfire.

Kruthos tossed a wig to each of them and handed one of the bowls to Athaz, motioning for the two friends to come to them. "Might as well get used to wearing these things now, and it would be good to ensure they are secure while we can fix any problems easily. Can't have these wigs falling off at an inopportune time!"

Arun sat in front of Kruthos, Baran in front of Athaz. The two elder adventurers began shaving their young friends' heads.

"What's in the third bowl?" Baran asked.

"Your new skin," Kruthos answered. "Black hair on your fair skin will arouse suspicions, not quell them. That is a skin dye."

"Won't it come out when I sweat?"

"Ha! If it does you let me know and I'll drive Rostein's business into the ground," Kruthos said, laughing. "You fret for nothing, Master Baran. The Savanir have perfected this technique for our survival over the centuries, and this blend is especially meant for human skin. You won't even be able to wash it off in water unless you mix it with some of this soap I'm sending with you. Your skin will stay this color until it falls off with the dead skin in the coming weeks, and I'm sending enough with both of you to last you several months. Your pale skin will be darkened enough your own mother wouldn't recognize you, even if your hair were still red."

"Fitting to get a new face with a new life," Arun said lightly.

"Do not say such things!" Athaz said quickly. You are concealing your identity, not altering it."

Truth Unearthed

Arun regretted his joke immediately. "Sorry," he apologized.

Athaz smiled. "None needed. You did not offend me. Rather, it pains me to see you think you are losing yourself in your present situation."

Arun grunted his agreement as the Dwarf began placing the wig on his newly shaved head. Inside, he wasn't so sure. His face may be restored with much less effort, but what about his place in this world? What he had been was lost forever. His newfound allies had designs for him to which he would never yield. Arun closed his eyes, forcing himself to simply focus on the wet adhesive, the wig that tickled, and the tug of the Dwarf's firm hands. No need to get himself frustrated again with those thoughts!

"Alright, all done!" Kruthos said proudly.

Arun went over and looked at his reflection in the river. Since he couldn't recognize the face staring back at him, he knew no one else would. The Savanir had concealed his identity perfectly. At least until he grew a new skin.

The next morning was a solemn one. The time for parting had come. Arun felt the need to say something. There was a real chance he would never see Athaz or Kruthos again. Athaz knew his young friend's struggle. "Don't trouble yourself with words, Arun. Sometimes a simple farewell is best." With that he mounted his horse and Kruthos mounted his. They raised their hands with smiles and sped off.

Arun knew at least one thing he wanted to say. "Thank you!" he cried, cupping his hands around his mouth to yell louder. It was for both, though most certainly the feeling was stronger for Athaz. His mentor was already a good ways off, but he pulled up his horse, half turned his steed so he could see Arun, and gave a small bow. Then he turned again and was gone.

Baran and Arun girded their weapons for the first time in weeks. Though Arun couldn't dream of using his yet, simply carrying it gave him some comfort and would give unfriendly eyes more pause. They mounted their own steeds with Inoch and began walking them toward Simpat. They were in no hurry. The longer they took to get there, the higher the chance Brasan would be there; the quicker they got there, the sooner their guards would have to be up.

"Wonder what is being said of us back home. Err ..." Baran stumbled. "Well, what used to be home anyway."

Arun wondered as well. He probably wasn't being missed that much. Unlike Baran, he had no family, not even many connections. It was true that Baran was not overly close to his family, but they were still family. Suddenly, he realized how selfish he had been to not think about his best friend's personal loss up until this point.

"I am sorry I dragged you along in this," Arun said to his friend. "You had a promising life ahead of you and a family."

Baran, riding on his left side, raised his fist before lowering it. "You're lucky that arm still needs time to heal. Stop being so arrogant! You always blame yourself too much. I wanted to come, and my motivations weren't nearly as genuine as yours. Besides..." Baran paused for a minute, looking at Inoch "...I have met those I would have gladly struck down without pause before. No matter who is right in this war, I am glad I will not be killing any of the Savanir now."

"Who says you would have been able to?" Inoch asked with a playful, cocky grin.

"Is that an invitation to be a sparring partner?" Baran asked, also smiling.

"When time and situation permit, certainly. Though our number one concern is getting Descia's father to safety. Perhaps while we are on Brasan's ship, we can test each other while still making progress."

They could have made it to Simpat that day, but it was too late to find Brasan. They instead chose to camp about five miles out in the shelter of a cluster of trees to avoid an unnecessary night of unfriendly eyes. The river, maybe a half mile to the west, flowed peacefully, barely audible. Inoch took Baran and Arun over to the river's edge and told them in detail of the lands beyond its western banks, including the Forest of Ours and the Makrin Mountains and what settlements they would find help if they ever needed it. "Not many support the Savanir, but there are plenty that have no love for The Dawn; if you keep your head down and ears open, you would likely be able to find some help, maybe even meet someone in our network."

After a while, the talking ceased and they were simply enjoying the pleasant summer evening. Baran approached the river; its reflective water was dark, like the obsidian gates of Menigar. The moonlight reflected off the caps of the waves like glinting diamonds. They could just make out ripples in the water. "It is beautiful," he said at last. "With its rolling and rippling currents, it almost feels alive too."

Arun approached the slow moving river. He could just make out his silhouette in the darkened mirror. A dream, though he now knew was the fragment of an erased memory, came to mind. A beautiful voice singing. A young, comforting voice, and he knew it to be Vera's, though he had no face left from the broken memory. Still, he pictured her as she had appeared in Menigar, and it fit perfectly. The fate she was trying to force on both of them came fresh to his mind. He was glad to have escaped Menigar, at least for a time. Though still angry, ever since he learned she would be forced to touch the Silent Stone, he knew she must not have made the decision lightly. She probably felt justified. *That's why I'm so angry,* he realized. *She believes she had the right to choose!* A drop of rain hit the back of Arun's head, and he looked up. Clouds had gathered above while their vision had been cast toward that which was below them. Already, he could hear a solid rain in the west, even with his vision limited by the surrounding night. The three of them quickly made their way back to camp, seeking the shelter of the trees and tents, wishing they had chosen to enter the city.

CHAPTER X

Paying the Price

The next morning Arun, Inoch, and Baran quickly packed, though Arun's process was a bit slower with his weakened arm. They soon made their way to Simpat's gates, hopeful that Brasan was already there. Perhaps they could be out before dusk and not spend a night worrying about unfriendly eyes while they slept.

As they walked under the gates, Arun and Baran raised their hoods, pulling some of the wig down so that the black hair was easily visible. They quickly made their way toward the docks, eagerly searching for The River Daughter, but her distinctive form was nowhere in sight. Discouraged, they made their way to the inn that the messenger had been instructed to direct Brasan toward, a seedy tavern known as The Siren's Sleep. They quickly took up a table in the corner and ordered three pints of ale, keeping an eye on the entrance for Brasan and hoping no one would take notice of them.

Arun and Baran would have balked at the accommodations not very long ago. Now they understood this was merely a meeting place where they could go unseen; the eyes of those around them were too busy keeping an eye out for their own safety. Everyone in this room was much more eager in avoiding being seen than paying attention to unconcerned parties. Inoch actually was the most uncomfortable. He was much more accustomed to meeting his enemies in combat with his sword drawn. Here he might brush up against them and feel a knife being slipped into his back before he ever saw the hand that wielded it.

They hadn't been there five minutes when a voice came up from behind them, "Took your sweet time."

The friends turned in unison, Baran and Inoch unsheathing swords and Arun drawing a knife. The man raised his hands to show his unarmed state. It was true the man was no threat, but now they had the attention of the entire crowd. "You'll need to control yourselves better if you want to live," the man said quietly.

Looking into his eyes, Arun suddenly knew him. Brasan saw the recognition in his friend's face and raised two fingers to his lips.

"Sit down," the captain whispered. "We will have to wait until some of the attention you attracted dies. And guard your tongue until we are out of this wretched rat hole!"

The four of them sat together. Brasan ordered a glass of wine — or what passed for wine in this outhouse of a tavern — and brought out a deck of cards, absently dealing them. Any observer paying close attention would have realized they were just tossing cards at random, taking tricks at their fancy. It only took ten minutes until most of the guests were completely refocused on their own affairs, but it felt like ten hours to the younger men before Brasan said, "Follow me."

They kept close behind the altered captain. He had let his beard, formerly short and neatly trimmed, grow long and wild. His head was now shaven, and his attire was that of an old sea dog whose work was not worth his board, much less his pay. They hurried down alleys, staying off the main streets, always cutting back north. Finally, they approached the wall that circumnavigated the town. It was only ten feet high but perfectly smooth, making climbing impossible. The captain let out three low whistles followed by a shrill one. Instantly, two ropes were thrown over. Arun was wondering how many weeks this would set him back in his recovery when Brasan went straight for a pile of garbage, tossed some pieces of trash sitting on the top to the side, and pulled out a large plank still in good shape that had a thick metal ring on each side. As Brasan fastened one end, Baran came up and did the same with the other.

"You first," he said, motioning for Arun to sit with his feet facing the wall so he could help those on the other side by walking.

Reaching the top, Arun saw a cart with straw had been placed below. He jumped and recognized the three men as Brasan's crew on The River Daughter. Two of them quickly untied the ropes from the plank and threw them back over for Inoch and Baran, who soon made their appearance on the wall. Brasan was last.

"Quickly now, we don't want to miss your horses," he said as he began trotting away from the town.

They had not walked far when a youth came running up, bringing Arun and Baran's horses with him.

"Took some doing, but I got them. You swear these are their true masters? I don't want to hang for horse thieving. Especially when I'm not keeping the horses."

Arun nodded. "We are, kid, and you have my thanks."

"I would prefer his coin," the boy said, looking at Brasan. The captain tossed him a small bag. The boy took a quick look, closed it back up, and put in his vest's breast pocket. "You have my services any time you need them!" he said before sprinting off.

"Now we can talk freely," Brasan said.

"Good," Arun said. "Because that seemed a little extreme."

"Not if you knew the stakes. Even disguised, you were fortunate to not have been spotted passing through the gates this morning. Waren was keeping an eye out for you, hoping to lead you around the city before you ever entered it and you could have kept the horses. But his lack of activity made the guards question what he was up to. By the time he had put them at ease, you were already approaching the gate, and he couldn't do anything without raising suspicion. He came straight back and informed me you had gone into the town. I rushed to the inn, but I was beginning to fear for you when you took so long."

"We were hoping to find your ship or see you pulling in," Baran said. "We didn't want to stay the night if we could help it. But things must be even worse than we realized."

"They are. As you no doubt guessed he would, the Son of Bälech now knows the Orc party was slaughtered by the Savanir and that you live. And as you also must have known, you will be killed if found. But something else has him restless. He has put out descriptions of everyone that was involved in your expedition, including myself and my men. We were supposed to report to the

Watchers so we could help 'locate the lost students and Keepers.'"

"My men and I had no idea of the Orc attack, but we also knew the Savanir were looking for you. At the time, I simply thought they had sneaked a message to you and you left voluntarily, but either way, we knew better than to answer the summons. But we did not expect to be hunted. One of my men disappeared while we were in dock at Flurn. We searched all over for him the following day; never have I had a man not send word, even in an emergency. We never found him.

"But when I returned to the inn that evening, the master hailed me before I went to my room. 'Thought you were gone,' he'd said in his usual friendly manner. 'Friends of yours from your sailing days on The Sea Hearth came by looking for you. Told 'em they had just missed you. They seemed pretty disappointed. They left but came back about twenty minutes later. Told me to give this to you if you came back.'" Brasan paused. "I should have been suspicious immediately. I had not heard from any of my crewmates from my first command in over thirty years. But my mind was still on my missing sailor ... at least until I opened the box." The captain stopped, his eyes seeing horrors as fresh in memory as they had that evening. "One of his hands was in the box, holding a letter. It detailed everything the Watchers had learned from him, including all of our dealings with the Savanir. There also was a warning to submit ourselves to questioning easier than he had. The final words read, 'You cannot hide. We are the Watchers, Eyes of the Son of Bälech. We see everything The Dawn's Light touches. Your man felt the urgency of our message should be delivered by his own hand. It has been done.'"

Brasan continued. "I sprinted to every tavern where my men were staying. I got to most of them in time, but not all." The captain's face contorted with the miserable thoughts that flashed through his mind, knowing what those he did not find had faced. "I quickly sold The River Daughter for a tenth of her worth, told my crew to leave, especially those who had a family, which fortunately was few. The three you see here—Arnost, Damon, and Waren— are the ones who refused to leave my side. Since then, we have done some digging. We learned of the Orc attack and the battle. We knew you had been rescued by the Savanir, which would not please the Son of Bälech. I fear I have only found more questions, not answers. You are not the first citizens of The Dawn to have turned to the Savanir, but never has this been the reaction from Hilae. Our friendship demanded I aid you, but I will not deny my search for answers might have driven me to you had my fondness for you lessened."

Arun hung his head. How many more would suffer for the Savanir's prophecy?

Inoch decided to spare Arun the tale. "Brasan, we should have been transparent with you from the beginning about who we believed you were transporting, but we did not know they were in danger, and therefore put you in danger, until shortly before they boarded your ship. In short, an Elf of ruling lineage has long been keeping an eye on Arun, hoping to bring him to the Savanir to aid us in our fight against Bälech, or who you know simply as the Son of Bälech. None on your ship knew our designs; we alone are to blame. Both for keeping you in the dark and also for not securing better intelligence." Inoch paused, debating whether or not to share anything else. Finally he did. "Our future seer had a vision from the Sea that echoed an ancient prophecy."

"What role did you think they would play?" Brasan asked in frustration and confusion.

Inoch hesitated. "That Arun would one day defeat Bälech in battle."

Brasan could barely control the rage boiling within him. No wonder the Watchers were hunting him and his men. They were now enemy combatants. But Arun spoke up before he could launch his tirade.

"Many have suffered because of their desperation," Arun said hotly, and Inoch looked at him in alarm. "But Inoch played no role in the decisions that have robbed you of your men, me and Baran our future, and Athaz of his family. In fact, it is for fear of Descia's father's safety that we have ventured out of hiding, knowing we are dead if caught, hoping to convince him to join her there. It seems her fear is justified, and I wished we had moved faster. If you would like a chance to face those responsible as well as protection from The Dawn, the Savanir, I believe, will take you and any you bring with you into safety." Arun paused and Inoch nodded his agreement. "Perhaps you can talk some sense into their leaders, urging them not to pursue a 2500-year-old rhyme passed down from their ancestors." That phrase stung Inoch, but he said nothing. "If you no longer want to aid us in our task of reaching Paleon, no one would blame you. Baran and I are simply trying to minimize the damage already done, and Inoch was kind enough to assist." Arun decided to leave off the fact Inoch was probably just as motivated to keep him alive; Brasan's fire didn't need any more fuel.

Brasan walked in silence for a while. Finally, he said, "I will aid you, and I hope the Savanir will aid me in helping my men, all of whose lives are now in peril for their folly. Still, I would not leave you in your quest to save a life."

Baran, grateful for all the assistance he could get to save Descia's father, thanked him profusely. "But how are we going to get there in time? You have no ship, only three men, and The Dawn has obviously heard rumors of the Savanir's designs for us, and as misguided as they are, he seems to be taking no chances."

"Paleon may not be in as grave of danger as you think," Brasan said. "Mind you that he just as easily could be. But the official word on the expedition is that most of you were slain in the Orc attack, including the Warden, but that some of you survived by fleeing. The Watchers were using the guise of saving the survivors for a long time, though it has certainly worn out its usefulness by now. Still, it was a large expedition, and they can't have everyone related to those on it disappearing. I am sure he is being watched, but there is still a good chance he is free, possibly even unaware of the eyes upon him."

Everyone sat quietly. Arun and Baran were giving their friend a chance to sort out his thoughts. Inoch was trying to wrap his head around the unintended casualties his people were causing. As a patrol leader, he was used to being revered, even by Night

Dwellers, since he normally only came into contact with them after saving them from an imminent attack from one or more of the Savage Races.

"The Son of Bälech is a paranoid fool!" Brasan finally cried in frustration. "Your stories would answer all questions if it actually made sense for him to fear this prophecy. But the Savanir are hopelessly outnumbered, out-resourced, and, with thousands of Wardens now in his service, hopelessly overpowered. Is he really frightened by old prophecies that gave hope to life-weary exiles over two thousand years ago?!"

They walked in silence. It was Baran who broke it. "Unless there's more to the prophecy than false hope," he reasoned. Arun looked at his friend in alarm. "No, Arun," Baran said quickly. "I don't think you are the hero. But the Savanir have something strong enough to perform The Sundering, and the Elves and Dwarves, and even myself, certainly seem to have powers you and I don't fully understand. Maybe the prophecy is real, even if their timing is off."

"I never thought you the religious type," Arun scoffed at his friend.

"I'm not. But you have to admit, in the past month we have learned and seen things we would have laughed at before we set out from Hilae. As Descia says, we don't have to know they are right to know that we were fed lies our entire lives concerning many things. We grew up believing only Bälech, his descendants, and his Augmented servants could wield the Divine. Not only can Elves and Dwarves wield it, but even I can a little … and none of us received that power from Bälech. We have always assumed Bälech was the source of the Divine. Obviously he is not. And if he is not the source, than the source — if there is one — would presumably be more powerful than he."

Arun looked at his friend, not sure if he was more astonished he had not realized it before or that Baran had thought that through on his own. "You've always chewed on things longer than you let on, but I believe Descia is certainly adding to the quality of your thinking."

Baran grinned. "Didn't have a choice. She was getting bored with me before."

Even Captain Brasan smiled at that. "That you two are doing well is the first good news I have heard since the day we parted."

They reached a Yeoman's barn that Brasan had made arrangements with before nightfall. The farmer himself came out with his wife and brought them dinner.

"We don't have much, but food is plentiful," the lady of the house said.

"It's wonderful," Arun said with a sincere smile. If only he had stayed a Yeoman's son! So many would be spared the misery they were now going through.

When their hosts had left for the evening, Brasan gathered them together to discuss plans. He pulled out a map of the region. The light was fading fast and this was no place to light a candle, but Arun could just make out "Hilae" in its northeastern-most corner, the Green Peaks in the southwest and Mizcur was dead in the center.

"Here is Simpat," Brasan said, pointing to a dot in the eastern shore of the Argom River, just north of the Tikus Foothills. "The first part of the journey is simple enough. We journey north along the river until the Grigor joins it at Mizcur, where we set out together before the dig. The Argom River flows into Mizcur from the northwest." Brasan then pointed to another dot in the northwest, along the banks of the Argom River. "Here, right before the river turns mostly south toward Mizcur, is Abscos, where Paleon lives. On the eastern and southern sides of the river are the Makrin Mountains. We must decide now our route. The fastest is obviously to stay on the eastern and northern banks of the Argom, the side where both Mizcur and Abscos are located."

"But you fear being spotted, even outside the cities?" Baran asked.

Brasan nodded. "Mizcur is the economic hub of this region of The Dawn. Not only are the waterways used, but traveling along the banks is common, especially for non-merchant travelers."

"So the Watchers keep their eye on them," muttered Arun.

"Aye." Brasan sighed.

"So the question becomes," Inoch began, "do we want to turn into the Makrin Mountains via The Grass Blade," he said, pointing to a narrow, long gap between the Makrin Mountains' western slopes and the Forest of Orus, "where we are the least likely to run into agents of The Dawn and passersby who could give information to any who ask ... or do we risk the banks all the way to Abscos, or journey on the bank until Mizcur before going around it north to the Mossy Plains and cut east?"

"The Mossy Plains are easily traveled. We could probably get to Abscos almost as quickly as the banks," Arun reasoned.

Baran's military training made him speak up. "True," he answered. "But as we learned when we set out from Hilae, we will have no cover if unfriendly eyes spot us."

"Exactly," Brasan said. "And we are actively being sought out."

The company sat silent for a while. Arun looked over to the three crew members still throwing their lots in with their captain. "Any thoughts?"

They shook their heads. Arun tossed his hands into the air, placing his hands behind his back as he fell into the straw behind him. "If only we knew Paleon's situation! We could know the urgency of our mission and decide on the proper path."

"But we don't, so we will have to make our decision as best we can," Inoch said.

Arun turned to Baran. "This is chiefly your quest. What do you say?"

Baran stood up to pace. Five minutes passed, and still he muttered to himself, eyes running back and forth, envisioning unseen scenarios. Finally he said, "The western shores of the Argom River. The mountains will be close by if we need to take cover, but speed is of the utmost importance. We can't take the time to cross over the mountains twice to use The Grass Blade."

"But how do we cross the river?" Arun asked.

"Most Yeomen have small craft to get back and forth," Brasan said. "I'm sure our friends here will lend us a hand or be able to point to someone who can."

With the agreement of the entire company, the matter was settled. The friends finished the cold remnants of their supper. They set three watches. Arun, Baran, and Inoch were on first watch, then Brasan and Arnost, and finally Damon and Waren. "Do not extend your watch," Brasan said. "We must all rest well tonight, for this will be the last of our friendly accommodations for some time." With that, he turned over and seemed to immediately fall into a deep slumber.

Arun, Inoch, and Baran sat in the doorway side by side so they could talk without disturbing their companions' rest. It was a cloudy night; no moonlight or cheerful twinkling would ease the dark thoughts of what they had learned today. When their watch was over, the dreams that came over them were as haunting and murky as the night around them.

Morning came and Damon and Waren roused their companions to a breakfast brought by the Yeoman farmer, already about his work before the sun's light woke the other companions. Mornings were cool now, but while summer's heat had been left behind, the trees still had plenty of green leaves side by side with the more colorful ones on their branches; the clime would be moderate for a while yet.

They ate quickly. It turned out the farmer did have a small raft, but it could only get one horse across at a time, meaning crossing alone would take up the better part of the day. But there was nothing for it. The farmer couldn't help them much. He had his work to tend to, but of course they would have to get him for the final trip so he could bring the raft back.

Brasan and Waren went first with Brasan's horse. Each horse came alone with its rider, with Brasan bringing over Waren's horse last. When Brasan came back to the eastern shore on the final time and had placed the luggage on the raft, he retrieved the farmer. Before leaving, they all thanked him profusely for his kindness. Brasan slipped some gold into the man's hand as he shook it. The man was about to refuse, but Brasan insisted. "If you don't consider letting us sleep in the barn to be worth something, at least don't insult your wife's cooking. That was better than anything we would have had in any inn. And I'm sure the next time a trader passes through, there's something you can get her in our stead to show our thanks."

The farmer bowed deeply and departed with no more argument, and the company quickly mounted their horses. With the course laid out, speed was now their number one concern, and they only had a few hours of daylight left in this first day. As tempting as galloping at full speed would be, they couldn't overwork the horses; most of the horses they would encounter would be thick-bodied horses more accustomed to methodically pulling plows than keeping a useful journeying pace. Still, they did keep the horses moving at a good clip, and there was little talk as they followed Brasan, who knew the shores along the Argom River better than any of them.

That night, they kept the same watch teams as they had in the barn. The next morning, Brasan woke them up in the gray light of the false dawn. He was eager they should reach where the Grigor joined the Argom within the next seven days. The Argom south of Mizcur was one of the most traveled places in The Dawn, but once they were east of Mizcur, their journeying would be a lot safer. The eastern region of the Argom, for many leagues, was made up of small villages of the Yeomanry that mostly gathered lumber from the Meros Wood, whose materials were gathered quarterly by the Watchers. The summer shipments should have already arrived, and the autumn shipments wouldn't start making their way for another two months at least.

The weather held and during the evenings Baran and Inoch sparred while Arun and Brasan held council. Waren, Damon, and Arnost spent the evenings fishing to see if they could get some fresh meat to go with the breads and cheeses for dinner, and most nights they were successful. On the last evening before they were come to the joining of the two rivers, as they watched their two friends sparring about fifteen yards away in the fading light, Arun quietly asked the captain, "I know I'm not their prophesied savior.

Truth Unearthed

Personally, I think their war is hopeless, but is it worth fighting? I mean, should I hope they can win? Is justice delayed and freedom for a few worth what they will put everyone else through? The Dawn may not be perfect, but at least it is stable. Peace has got to count for something."

Brasan didn't respond at first. He himself opened his mouth and closed it five times before finally answering, "The Dawn is stable off the backs of slaves. The Yeomen are forced to work for the betterment of those who are currently in Bälech's Sons' ever fickle favor while they themselves see nothing for their work. The emperors are constantly building up new glories, but they share very little of that glory with anyone else, and what little is shared is never truly given. Most families fall out of favor in the same generation they rose to power, and none have seen it for more than five generations. It's a show with the same characters but an ever-changing cast, the only constant being the imperial family. And most of his subjects never even see the show; they work until their bodies give out to provide the props necessary for the Son of Bälech's amusement. Oh, there are a few merchants and craftsmen who manage to scrape out a living in the cities, but mostly its peons and dupes playing their parts for the amusement of a line that thinks they are gods among men. Is such a "stable" empire really worth protecting? Is The Dawn peaceful or are the people cowed? I would think the latter, and you would as well if you had ever seen the treatment of the majority of the people of The Dawn."

Arun remembered the whipping post incident. For a long time, none of the Yeomen had looked him in the eye. When some did, it was only for a dreadful instant that conveyed more fear than long words could have ever expressed. Was it the same everywhere? He knew the majority of The Dawn's populace were Yeomen.

Brasan paused for a while before speaking. "No, as much as I have suffered because of the Savanir's actions concerning you, I cannot say they should lie down and submit to the Sons of Bälech. In the end, I believe they will have to. I believe the events set in motion at The Ruins have numbered their days. But when I see the people of this land, I cannot help but believe we were meant for so much more than this. As long as The Dawn is in power, the only hope most people have is landing in the Son of Bälech's favor and dying before they or their children fall out of it."

Arun's memory again flashed back to the whipping post and the image of the young boy whose cries he would never forget. If that was going on under his very nose the whole time, who knows what life was out in the more remote areas? And there were the Orcs that had attacked them at Lacris. Could Bälech, or the Son of Bälech, whichever he was, truly be leading such armies? If that was true, then every city that had been attacked by the Savage Races might have been the doing of the very ruler that was supposed to be protecting them.

The more he thought about it, the more he didn't like it. To his knowledge, no major city had ever been attacked by the Savage Races. And what better way to keep the majority of your people submitting to you willingly than saving them from disasters you create?

But the land is stable, and that must account for something," Arun thought. *If The Dawn were defeated, most of the land would fall into chaos.* That much at least was guaranteed, but at that moment Arun had another, much more terrifying thought: one born from the possibility that the Emperor commanded the Savage Races. *What if we get overwhelmed by other foes if he's gone?*

"Oof!" Arun was snapped out of his thoughts as Baran fell with a thud only a yard from him. Arun looked at Baran's upside down face contorted in pain, which made it look like a disturbing grin instead of a grimace. Arun shook his head. "I've never seen you bested by someone younger than you," he teased.

Baran was up in an instant. "Normally, people younger than me haven't seen combat," Baran gritted, but in pain not bitterness. "Still, I'm seeing openings. He's not as good as Athaz." With that, Baran went back into the fray. Arun realized he had never actually seen Inoch in melee combat before; he had been on horseback in the rescue at Lacris. Inoch was using a sword and shield, but very different from those used by Baran. Where Baran's sword was short and broad, Inoch's was at least another third longer, and in place of a large, rectangular shield, he wore a small, round buckler over his wrist, in which hand he also held a long knife.

Emboldened by his success so far, Inoch was getting a bit reckless, thinking he overmatched The Dawn's soldier in training. Instead of waiting for an opening in the flow of the fight, he went low to try and force one with a move that had worked earlier, expecting Baran to bring down his shield or at least sidestep. Instead, Baran stepped on his wrist, brining Inoch to his knees while coming over the top of him with his sword as he closed the distance. With no choice, Inoch raised his buckler to deflect the blow, but it never came. Baran swung his shield in toward Inoch's exposed face, bringing it to a stop inches short, then let out a laugh.

"Finally!" he said. "I was beginning to doubt myself." He released Inoch's hand so that he could clasp it. "Your skill is amazing! No one with military training at The Academy would stand against you."

Inoch smiled but also reproached himself. "I got cocky. Commander Therran warned me that the hardest part of transitioning from patrolling against the Savage Races and fighting The Dawn's regular army would be the ever-increasing awareness and tactical changes in my opponent. Previous victories will do little to comfort me if I get myself killed with such immature thinking."

Waren came up. "Dinner will be ready soon. Plenty of fish to be had tonight, and we thought you wouldn't mind the delay if we didn't have to ration the meat."

Everyone agreed with that. Dinner would have been perfect if not for the conversation of how they should keep out of site near Mizcur? Should they go up into the mountains for a couple of days or try to make it across by cover of night?

"I should think the mountains would be best," Inoch suggested. "While time is critical to our mission and bank travel aids us in that aspect, I think here it would be worth the delay for a couple of days to ensure we are not spotted."

"But we are on the far bank," Baran pointed out. "It's not like the Watchers would be able to spot us from the city walls."

"Possibly not, but you shouldn't underestimate them. They may be near the river itself, and even if they aren't, we would be very likely to be noticed by any boats pulling in, whose passengers would no doubt mention the odd sight of travelers at night when there is fire and food to be had if they weren't so obviously avoiding it. We would appear unfriendly even to eyes not looking for us," Brasan pointed out.

It didn't take much talking after that to persuade Baran to take to the mountains for a few days. "Our destination isn't far. Once we reach it, it will be a straight shot on the fastest path to Descia's father. Mizcur is the last town we'll encounter with a strong presence of The Dawn's higher ups," Brasan assured Baran. "Speaking of our next destination, Lamphine is a small outpost town for those living near the Forest of Orus, which brings lumber for trading. It's a few days march east on the northern slopes of the Makrin Mountains."

Baran straightened up at that name. "Lamphine?"

"Yes. You are familiar with it?"

"Not really, but it's the town I was born in," Baran said. "It was where my father lived and warned a company of soldiers that there was a Bew— Savanir ambush ahead; that's the reason we were given a place in the Court at Hilae. I don't really remember it at all. I was two when we moved away."

Inoch's eyes lit up at that news. He whistled. "You might want to keep that news to yourself back at Menigar," he said. "Obviously that was before I was even born, but we lost a great many men when we found ourselves turned from hunter to hunted in that counter-ambush. You've met some of the families that lost loved ones that night, though most were from a different stronghold. I'm sure the Lady Lyr and Vera know, but I'm not sure Commander Therran knew. He lost many friends in that battle. He never would have disobeyed orders, but he would never have aided you beyond them had he been aware of that bit of information."

"More pressing than that now, though," Brasan interrupted, "...would anyone recognize you? Did you ever visit after your family became a part of the Court? I had planned on restocking our foodstuffs there, but that may not be an option."

"We never visited," Baran said. "I think we'll be good. My hair might trigger some memories, but not in its current state. And this skin dye removes any family resemblance."

"Good enough for me," Brasan said. "Tomorrow we make our way into the mountains. I'm afraid the horses must be left behind, as there are no paths and the climbing will be steep. But for now let's get some sleep. It goes without saying the watch needs to be sharp tonight with Mizcur so close."

The next morning Brasan woke up even before the gray light, uneasy. Something was amiss. No boat had traveled by them now for two days. He woke up the others up, eager to be gone, though he only told them it was to make up for the delay the mountains would cause. He sent the others on ahead as soon as they were ready, promising to catch up. He wanted to make sure nothing remained of their camp. Perhaps he was becoming paranoid. Still, it wouldn't hurt to make sure.

Unbeknownst to him, unseen eyes were watching his every move. Skodus laughed at the old man's feeble attempt to throw him off. Those military fools had let the youths and Brasan escape from under their noses in Simpat. Watchers were never so careless. Still, the soldiers had their uses — their willingness to ignorantly die for his master if nothing else. It should hardly come as a surprise that anyone that weak-minded should never be left to handle any task that requires creative thought. He had taken command of this squadron in Mizcur personally to ensure no more failures would delay the Son of Bälech from his prize. Closing his Divine scope that allowed him to hear the sounds of the place being viewed, he motioned for the colonel, whose men he had commandeered, to follow him. "One of our target's companions has graciously informed me where we may take our prisoners."

"Take five of your men to the south bank. Ride until you are a day and a half's footmarch from Lamphine. Send the horses back and take hiding positions in the mountains where you can see the bank, where they will be passing. When they have passed out of sight, you will follow them west while staying in the mountains for two more hours before tailing them the rest of the day along the bank. Be sure they never see you. Keep marching into the night until you see their campfire in the distance. Hide yourselves again in the mountains. In the morning, give them an hour head start and then pursue them. Do not engage, but make as much of a disturbance as you can without being obvious about it. They will not want to confront you; they are unaware that we know of their plans. Act as a sergeant training some new recruits. They will surely speed up in their attempt to avoid you. Chase them. Me and my men and I will be waiting."

The colonel didn't miss the insult of not recognizing him as the commander of the troops but saluted his understanding. Skodus handed him two stacks of parchment to disperse to the men. "These two are to be taken alive. You are not to kill them."

"What if they were to escape?" the colonel asked.

Skodus smiled darkly. "If they escape, you and your men will be executed for aiding in a traitor's flight. If you kill them, you will wish for death long before it comes."

The colonel swallowed back the lump forming in his throat. "Understood," he said when he felt he could do so without his voice cracking.

"Doubtful," Skodus mocked. "You are dismissed."

The colonel saluted and quickly about-faced, eager to be out of the room. "Watchers!" he spat when he believed he was out of earshot. "Cowards. Nothing without their tricks and threats. There's teeth behind them to be sure, but always the teeth of other tools held in check in the same fashion!"

The Watcher of course heard him, but it only amused him. Skodus knew his own ability in combat was quite formidable. But one should never let skill stop you from fixing the game. "Military fools," he laughed again.

CHAPTER XI

Bad Tidings

Kruthos set to work preparing the food while Athaz set up the tent, of which they only had one; someone would always be keeping watch. Taking only one tent allowed for more supplies. Tonight it was Athaz's turn for first watch. The person who got the first watch also got to set up the tent while the other cooked their meal. It had been Kruthos' idea, based on a Dwarven festival custom. During community festivals, everyone's meals were prepared by someone else, fostering appreciation for their neighbors' skills and effort in preparing the dish. Kruthos had modified it a bit: first watch would prepare the resting place for his comrade, and first rest would cook what the watchman requested (granted, the menu was limited; it was first rest that was the true gift).

But Kruthos had made little progress with the former Warden. It had been almost two weeks since they left their young friends a day's journey outside of Simpat, and Athaz had not shared many thoughts with the Dwarf. He had told him the names and descriptions of his family, which would be necessary for their mission, but Athaz had shared precious little about them—and even less about what kind of relationship he had with them.

Kruthos had always known that some Men kept to themselves; indeed, it seemed some of his human friends had only really begun to open their hearts when their span of years was nearly spent. But Athaz was proving to be incredibly hard, even for a human, to reach. But Kruthos also knew that Athaz was no ordinary Man.

Chuckling, Kruthos thought of the frustration some of his Elven friends would experience. Dwarves may be communal, but it was nothing compared to the Elves. A Dwarf recognized the interconnectedness of all things; Elves almost didn't see where one thing ended and another began. That was to be expected. Their connection with the Sea, their ability to see into each others' minds, and even their own individual fading and rebirth blurred not only the lines of individuality and community, but even past, present, and future.

Kruthos was unaware that he was smiling, amusing himself with such imaginings until he saw Athaz staring across the campfire at him. He jumped, nearly spilling their dinner.

"Good thing I have first watch tonight," Athaz said, a small, rare smile of his own making an appearance in front of the Dwarf. "What happy thoughts pass through your mind tonight?"

"Just some thoughts about a friend of mine back home, an Elf." Kruthos passed the sausage over to his companion.

"You will have to enlighten me," Athaz said. "What little I have seen of them ... laughter is not something I associate with them."

"You haven't been around them long, and you have mostly seen their leaders in a time filled with weighty decisions," Kruthos reminded him.

Athaz conceded the point. He envied his companion. Thoughts of those that would normally bring a smile to his face only brought worry now. Lilleth, his wife whom he loved more than she knew, was most likely in a dungeon or on the streets as a beggar, if she was lucky. And his son, Caedin, would be publicly shamed and beaten before being dragged to the dungeons. Even old Palit might not even be spared. Bälech had eyes everywhere. It was likely they were aware of the unapproved favors the two friends had done for each other over the years. He never imagined how dearly his friend might one day pay for it.

And now, against his better judgment, he had allowed himself to grow fond of the two young men who were meant to unknowingly lead him into his deathtrap, as surely as he was supposed to do the same for them. Baran he felt would be fine. He was skilled with a sword, and while he could not be certain the youth would not one day face similar nightmares as he did now, the odds had certainly shifted in his favor. And at least they would not be in service to the cruel deity that had stolen all Athaz once held dear: his life, his honor, and now his family. No, for whatever comfort it was,

Baran was in little more danger than he would be if none of this had transpired. But Arun he feared for still. While he wished his scholar friend had stayed behind, Menigar may have posed as much of a threat to the sensitive young man's sanity as The Dawn did to his body. Earlier, he had thought Arun might have made a fine soldier because of his natural fighting skill and his ability to use it when pressed, but now he realized that was not so. Arun was too easily influenced by others—a fault in anyone and a fatal one for a soldier and very likely for a young man mistaken for a hero.

Athaz looked down and discovered his plate was empty. He hadn't even tasted the food as it passed over his lips and into his stomach, his mind once again filled with fear for the few who he could not reach.

"Your thoughts seem a bit heavier," Kruthos pressed.

"They are," was all Athaz said in reply. It was terse, but not harsh. Kruthos sighed. "Alright, well neither of us gets enough rest to squander the time meant for it. Wake me up in four." With that he put out the fire and turned into the tent.

Athaz stared up at the Briar Patch Mountains, every now and then a flash of silver starlight striking off some stream or river. He knew Kruthos wanted to help, wanted to ease his troubles with companionship. It was not misunderstanding or lack of trust in the Dwarf, nor even a lack of desire for his friendship that kept him guarded, it was necessity. Odds were they would both fail and be killed or worse … captured. It would be impossible for everyone to make it out of Hilae alive, and Athaz could not risk Kruthos staying behind with him when he secured their escape. His duty to The Dawn had always kept his son at a distance from him. Never had he received the love of his child. Caedin respected him. He had even been grateful to him, grateful for the life he had provided, and grateful for the protection Athaz afforded him and every other citizen of The Dawn; Lilleth had raised him well, after all, but Athaz had rarely been there … and it seemed he was never there when he was needed most. And since Caedin knew him chiefly by title, both as father and Warden, the change of fortunes had most likely destroyed any positive emotions associated with the man whom he cognitively knew as father. Over the years, even Lilleth's affections had eventually grown cold. She would always love him, he never doubted that, but the years of solitude had made him more like a cherished memory, one whom she knew somewhere still lived and loved her, but that knowledge only caused more pain. He hadn't been home for their anniversary since the year Caedin had been born. How old was he now? Fifteen? Could it have really been so long?

Athaz cursed himself, but even more he cursed Bälech. In one sense, he had willingly given up a life of hearth and home. At the time he had not realized who he was serving. There had been so many opportunities to turn back, though they did not seem possible at the time. Yet his own failures and blindness did not excuse the illusionist who had entrapped him.

Suddenly Athaz saw a campfire being lit near the base of a mountain, about half a mile away. He could also hear voices shouting and immediately knew these were no fellow travelers; they were not even human. Quickly, he slid into the tent and roused the Dwarf.

"Enemies near," he said before slipping back out into the night. Athaz quietly left the campground, carrying his zweihänder — not the Divine weapon he used to carry, but a beautiful steel blade crafted by a Dwarven master smith.

Being near the river bank, Athaz was below the campfire, which would aid him as he got close enough to hear. He bent over and silently crept, taking cover behind boulders and bushes when possible. About twenty yards away, he found himself not only below the reach of the fire light but also behind a large rock, where he was able to rest with his back to it and lean his head just past the side so he could hear their conversation as well as see the savage faces holding council. There sat three Goblins, two Orcs, and a Giant. That was alarming; the Orcs and Giants only partnered in desperate need. But at the same time he was fortunate; they would be forced to use the Communal Tongue. Suddenly, he felt the Dwarf's presence next to him. He looked at him and while tugging his own ear. The Dwarf nodded.

"Well, take your rock-face back to your cave, Grot, if you are so miserable. We can get the job done without you."

"And your stench ain't exactly a thrill for us to be around either," said the other Orc. "And take your worthless Goblins with you. They couldn't track your fat sister and her ogre feet if she had been stomping through a field of mud. And they ruin the trails for those who can track!"

"Shut your mouths, or I'll shut 'em for ya!" Grot responded. "The master will have my head and worse if I return empty-handed and with no news. But not before I make both of you feel the pain that awaits me if we fail this mission! We wouldn't even be here if your filth could gut more than whimpering captives pleading for their miserable lives."

"You say that one more time, and Dun and I'll show your plump gut just how effective we are;" growled the first Orc. "We were about to slaughter that miserable Warden and his brats when that Elf and his friends arrived on their wretched horses. Not only was most of my command killed, but I had my eye on a nice lass next to one of the boys. She looked a lively one that would have been … feisty." He smiled at the thought.

The Giant smiled at his fellow filth's fantasy. "Yes, female humans can be quite lively! Have you ever …" Athaz's knuckles turned white on the hilt of his sword at the thought of what would have befallen Descia at the hands of these brutes. The Orcs were roaring in laughter, and even the Goblins were jumping up and down, enthralled with their superiors' stories and barbarism.

The conversation became much friendlier after that, the vile creatures hatred for each other momentarily forgotten in the tales of torture inflicted upon the innocents they both hated.

Suddenly, Athaz and Kruthos quickly turned behind them, drawing their weapons silently. Someone approached from behind. It was another Goblin. Apparently unaware of their presence, he sprinted on by, but his nose caught something. He sniffed, panicked, and bolted toward the fire.

"Damn him!" Athaz cursed. Kruthos rose quickly and let a throwing axe fly. His aim was deadly, even in the dark. The Goblin shrieked his last breath.

"Damn him!" Kruthos echoed.

"Enemies!" Grot cried. Quickly, Athaz and Kruthos sprinted around the bottom of the hill. If they could get on the other side, they would still have some element of surprise.

Dun was the first to reach the fallen Goblin, yanking the axe free. "Master's whip!" he swore. "A Dwarf axe?!"

Kruthos cursed himself for a fool; if any of these creatures survived, it would be known that the Dwarves were on the surface, aiding Arun, which would only intensify the hunt.

"That's our expected messenger, grab his bag," Grot yelled.

Messenger! Both Athaz and Kruthos' minds began racing at the word.

"Hand me that bag," Grot demanded. Dun threw it to him.

By now Athaz and Kruthos were on the right side of the fire where they had come from.

Grot quickly read the contents. "You…" he pointed to a Goblin, who came slinking up to him, the stupid creature not sure what to expect "…burn this bag and everything in it."

Athaz questioningly made a throwing motion at Kruthos. He nodded back and reached behind his back and pulled his final throwing axe.

The Goblin was approaching the fire now. With a yell Athaz charged. The Goblin turned to flee with the bag but had an axe in his back before he had taken two steps toward his company.

"The Giant is mine!" Kruthos cried, a hate-filled fire burning in his eyes as he sped past Athaz and pulled up his two combat axes. Dun grabbed his whip and lashed out at the Goblins. "Attack cowards!" he yelled. It was an accurate description, as only their greater fear of Dun spurred them toward the Man and his sword.

But Goblins are only a threat in numbers. In one swing, Athaz had gutted both of their stomachs and they fell, screaming.

Kruthos leapt toward the Giant's face, cross swinging his axes in an attempt to decapitate his foe. Grot countered by planting the end of his club in Kruthos' gut. Adding to the Dwarf's momentum, he catapulted the Dwarf through the air. Kruthos landed on his back with a thud, and the Giant lunged, intent on smashing his club into Kruthos' skull, only to see Kruthos roll away at the last second. The two began circling each other, both of their attempts at a quick kill avoided.

Athaz was trying his best to keep both Orcs in front of him, but the Orcs knew their advantage and weren't going to let it go. "Give it up, old man," Dun cackled. "At your age you couldn't take either of us alone."

A thought came into Athaz's mind. "Kruk zilg nacht ot vungh!" For a fatal second, Dun dropped his guard and jaw with widened his eyes upon hearing the old man's retort and challenge in the Orc-tongue. His face was left with that permanent expression as Athaz's blade ran through his gaping mouth, coming out the base of his skull, before quickly kicking the body away and withdrawing the sword to deflect an oncoming overhead attack from the remaining Orc.

Grot yelled in frustration as the nimble Dwarf dodged each and every attack, always nicking his much larger foe with a small gash before Grot was able to recover from his swing and move his leg out of the way. Grot's only hope was that Kruthos would tire; if he could land one clean hit on the runt, it would be the end of him. And Kruthos was slowly tiring. Fortunately, Grot's patience ran out first. Instead of trying to avoid Kruthos' axe after another miss, the Giant instead attempted grab his tiny foe, intent on squeezing the life out of him. Kruthos lunged under the massive hand and quickly sliced the Giant's left achilles. Grot roared as he fell in pain. Kruthos was on him in an instant, axes flying furiously toward the Giant's face. Hopelessly, the Giant raised his club and attempted to block and move his head out of the way. He called for aid, but none would be coming. Finally, the Dwarf broke through the Giant's crumbling defense, planting an axe deep into his foe's forehead.

When the final Orc realized he was alone, he swore. Diving past Athaz's next swing, he sprinted toward the campfire, picking up the bundle beside the Goblin that had been the second to fall as he passed.

"Runner!" Athaz cried, and Kruthos was quickly behind him as they chased the Orc toward the fire, but the Orc was already putting distance between them. Seeing the messenger Goblin still with the other axe in his back, Athaz yanked it free as he ran run and tossed it up before moving aside. Kruthos understood immediately, caught his axe, and with every fiber in his brawny arms hurled the axe at the escaping Orc, catching him in the leg behind the knee. The Orc fell but was up again instantly. Losing his speed advantage, the two companions ran at a much more manageable pace, catching up to him quickly. The Orc wildly swung his blade, only to have Athaz sever his arm from his torso. The Orc finally fell, knowing he would never rise again, and looked with intense hatred at those that would soon end his existence. He spat at them, and Kruthos would have ended it there, but Athaz waved him off. Even in his miserable state, the Orc laughed. "Well, Warden, so you do live, even after the rabble tore the Gift from you. Yes, I suspected it was you from the beginning; a gray-haired human daring to take on a hunting party of the Clans, out in the middle of nowhere. That fool Dun apparently never had the thought cross his mind until he heard you use our language … always slow, that one. And only a Warden would try to glean information from a Clan Race. Well, unlucky you, I probably know less than you. My orders came from Chief and Grot, and I don't think your bulgy companion left Grot with much to say.   My dying comfort is knowing what awaits you, the young humans, and the Rebels. Oh, and there is one thing I know," he said as he was fading from the loss of blood. "Your woman's and brat's location." Athaz grabbed him by the throat. The Orc laughed. "I'd be dead before you could make me talk, but I'll tell you anyway. The Tennebrom. Go ahead, save them … if you can and … if they'll still have you!" He was trying to laugh some more but no longer had the strength. His chest sank, never to rise again.

Athaz grimaced. The Tennebrom housed prisoners for which Bälech held a special hatred. Older than The Dawn itself, its history was long and terrible. Located on the northeastern edge of the Briarthorn Mountains, prisoners would be marched out of Hilae for a week before they took the ferry that never moored on the southern bank.

"Well," Kruthos said, "at least we got the location of your family. That's all we needed. Good riddance!"

Athaz didn't say anything but scooped up the messenger bag and headed back to the light to read the letter.

"Fire take them all!" he cursed after finishing its contents. Kruthos turned. "They have found Arun and Baran," he sighed.

Fear filled Kruthos' eyes. "Captured?"

"No, or at least not when this letter was written. Apparently they were spotted in Simpat, but someone, Brasan most likely, got them out of the city using neither the gates nor docks."

"Well that's a relief," Kruthos said.

"They are still in grave danger, I fear." Athaz said. "Watchers found their trail headed into The Grass Blade, through the Makrin Mountains, and they are tracking them. An ambush is lying in wait for them closer to town. We have no way to reach them before they are trapped."

Kruthos paced back and forth. "If only that filth had been able to tell us more before he expired!"

Athaz looked gloomily into the Dwarf's eyes. "He did, my friend, and the news is grave."

Kruthos impatiently waited for Athaz to finish. "The missive pays special attention to Arun; it has considerably more on the importance of his capture than Baran's. Arun is to be taken alive at all costs. And our wretch said a fate not only awaited me and my charges, but the Rebels ... the Savanir.

Kruthos now understood. "He knows our plans for Arun."

Athaz nodded. "Long has he been content to wage a slow war with the Savanir, fighting them from afar, letting the Savage Races do the dirty work to keep your numbers small. But no more. Soon The Dawn's army will throw its full might into the Savanir, including the Wardens."

Athaz looked at the bodies. Normally, they would dispose of them, but there was no time. "We need to contact the Savanir. All strongholds need to be ready for not only battle, but siege. And if your people have a way of quickly communicating, it is the only

The Tales of Lugon

hope we have of aiding Arun and Baran."

Athaz turned to Kruthos. "I know you would go with me, but my duty is to my family. Yours is to your people. For that, and our shared friendship with Baran and Arun, we must part."

Kruthos shook his head. "No. The quickest way I know to reach the Savanir would be to find one of our agents in Mizcur, and we only passed east of Argom and Grigor two days ago. If we ride hard, we can reach it in a day and pick up fresh horses. It's dangerous for both of us, but surely your hope of rescuing your family is much stronger with two, even if we are delayed a couple of days. And I will most likely need your help to make it through Mizcur undiscovered."

Athaz's eyes turned north. How his heart ached at the thought of even a small delay! But the Dwarf was right. "To the horses," he said, his thoughts still trying to find a better solution as they ran toward their campsite. When they reached their destination and quickly packed, no other plan had come to his mind. He took one last look in the direction of Hilae. "No rest until our message is delivered. We ride!" And with that, he spurred his horse to a full gallop.

CHAPTER XII

Where a Candle Shines Brightest

Though they did take occasional short breaks in an attempt to keep the horses going, Athaz's horse collapsed from exhaustion an hour before sunset the following day and still five miles from Mizcur. Perhaps it was for the best; they would now have the aid of darkness in trying to hide Kruthos' nature from the local populace when they reached the gate. Athaz pulled out a cloak from his bag, and the Dwarf tucked his beard into his shirt, pulling the much too large cloak over him. Especially next to the towering Athaz, still over six feet tall even without being a Warden, Kruthos easily passed for his grandson at night with the clothes hiding his beard and brawn. Still, they had to be quick. An aging man with a young child wandering the streets at night would attract attention, possibly from the Watchers directly, but more likely from a ruffian they would be forced to fight if he got too close to Kruthos. The latter would raise the whole city in alarm.

Kruthos knew the location of the agent, an innkeeper in a small tavern at the northwest end of town. It didn't get much business, but that made it ideal. "The Gilded Coffer," Kruthos whispered to Athaz. Hearing the name, Athaz took them a meandering route toward the place, always taking the roads he thought they would be least likely to encounter anyone on — or for people to find a body of a thief that got too close.

"Goes by Krimly," Kruthos said as they approached the door. "But his real name is Aster. When Krimly introduces himself, tell him you seek lodging for two, and then add that you found his inn by the light on in the upper room, a comforting sight tonight. Follow that by noting how *the candle always shines brightest in the dark.*"

Athaz nodded as they approached the door and went in. There

were a few patrons, drinking while Courting the Deck, but it was mostly empty.

The portly innkeeper stopped wiping down a table on the far end of the room that had recently been vacated by guests that had retired for the evening. Kruthos kept his head down and pulled the cloak closer to him like he was cold, hoping it didn't look terribly suspicious to the other patrons given how warm the inn was kept by the roaring fire in the fireplace.

"Good evening, friends. I'm Krimly, the innkeeper here at the Gilded Coffer. And what can I get for you this fine evening?"

"Just lodging for two, thank you. I am tired. Not as young as I used to be. I like to be in bed early, and my young grandson here has no business in the events of an inn at night."

"Quite right!" laughed the innkeeper. "Anything else?"

"Well, maybe it's just the thought of an aging man remembering better days, but I was hoping you might help us with our luggage to our room. Your inn looked so welcoming to weary travelers with the light on in the upper room, and I guess I just began thinking that maybe in this place old courtesies continued."

"Certainly," the innkeeper said, still being friendly but now paying more attention with the first half of the code spoken.

"Much obliged," Athaz said. As they approached the final stair and were out of earshot of the other patrons, Athaz finished the phrase. "Your manners in this generation stand out like your upper room light. The candle always shines brightest in the dark."

"I suppose it does," Aster nodded, not looking back. He opened the door and led them in. When Kruthos closed the door behind them, they turned to see Aster with a dagger he had hidden in his waistcoat drawn. His voice lost its kind demeanor. It was now harsh and suspicious.

"Who are you? The last message I received just three days ago said not to expect any contact for at least another month. You will find there is plenty of strength and not just fat on this body if you are not true friends of the Savanir."

Athaz and Kruthos raised their hands. "If you let my companion take off his cloak," Athaz began, "you will find all the assurance you could wish for that we are friends." Aster nodded, and Kruthos shed his cloak and untucked his beard. Aster's dagger dropped to his side as he relaxed. "Well, I've never heard of a traitor of the Stout People, that's for sure, though I can't say I've ever met one personally. This *is* an honor."

"No time for pleasantries, brave friend," Kruthos said.

"Agreed, but I'm asking the questions first," Aster said, his voice lowering to a whisper. "It's not just my neck but many lives that will be in danger if I don't act properly. So let's start with just who you are and what you're doing?"

"I'm Kruthos, a Dwarf living in the original Savanir stronghold of Menigar. This is Athaz, a former Warden that survived The Sundering and has been of great aid to us with his intelligence concerning The Dawn's military tactics. As for what we are doing, we were on our way to attempt to free his family, but we intercepted an enemy communication and are in desperate need of help in order to save two youths of extreme importance. I assume you heard of the new hope that came to us a few weeks ago?"

"I've heard rumors, but being within the Shadow, it is a rule that I know as little as possible, lest sensitive knowledge be torn from me in Bälech's dungeons," Aster replied.

"Well, the enemy already knows, so you might as well too. A young Man, Arun by name, who Vera believed to be the hope prophesied of old, has been recovered."

Kruthos continued to explain everything up to that point, how they had been forced to essentially kidnap Arun due to the Orc attack at Lacris, Athaz's former Warden state (at which point Aster began stealing looks at Athaz whenever Kruthos' eyes turned aside), and, finally, the knowledge of the enemy concerning Arun's location and the impending siege of the strongholds.

"We must get word out to the nearest group patrol or other agents as soon as possible to save Arun ... or rescue him if he is already captured," Kruthos finished.

Aster nodded. "Yes, but the Watchers are suspicious of me. They don't know anything yet, and I've been able to keep the books so that the aid I receive for the inn's continuing function stays hidden, but the lack of patrons and the continued operation, instead of moving toward the docks or at least along one of the river banks, has aroused suspicion. I will indeed be forced to move soon or no book doctoring will be able to satisfy their questions. And for that reason, I certainly can't leave, nor can either of you — at least not as you came in. I have a young lad that runs errands for me from time to time. It would look odd this late, but even disguising you might not be enough. Having a patron leave that never entered might make them take even a closer look."

"Is he trustworthy?" Athaz asked.

Aster nodded. "In the best way, Aphen is ignorant. But I fear for him. He's a good kid, and I don't want him mixed up in this."

"We must hope for the best," Kruthos said. "Many lives depend on this message."

Aster nodded and quickly scribbled a note on some parchment. "In code of course, and addressed to my cousin, a clothmaker, asking for blankets for two new customers, apparently my previous patrons stole some last night. The boy will bring these back. I'm hoping that eases suspicion. Of course, I'll have to file a claim if they confront the boy, which will mean my inn will have to go dark for months. They will use the investigation as excuse to investigate me."

Opening the door, he lumbered down the stairs to wake the boy with his message. Soon they heard the boy complaining on being roused from his dreams as he stumbled out the exit and slammed the front door behind him. Aster returned with a piece of paper in his hands.

"One more thing," Athaz said, now that the needs of others had been met. "We need horses and to trade the one we have left. We leave at daybreak."

Aster nodded. "A little closer to the river just south of here there is a man who trades in horses; many people need to be rid of or gain a horse when they arrive or leave here. You will overpay, but I take it that's the least of your concerns." They confirmed it was. "Alright, I'm going to wait for my boy. I will not be at ease until he returns without trouble. Goodnight!" In a whisper he added, "And

Truth Unearthea

Xiarch aid us!"

* * * * * * * * * *

Aster began pacing the floor. His boy should have been back an hour ago.

"That's it! I've got to go look for him," he finally said. "At least I can be honest about my mission this time if confronted."

Grabbing a lantern and lighting it, the innkeeper made his way down the route he felt Aphen would most likely have taken. About halfway there, his heart stopped. There lay the boy, face down in the road, the blankets underneath his arms, still carrying them, where he had fallen. Aster in shame found himself hoping it was only a ruffian as he lifted the boy's face. Alas, it was not. His eyes bore the look of one who had died with his mind being searched by the Watchers. Aster cursed Bälech and his minions as he began sprinting as fast his legs could carry his large body back to the inn. The hidden cell the boy had visited would already be on alert, if still occupied, after receiving the message. He burst through the door and sprinted up to Athaz and Kruthos' room.

Kruthos had his axe drawn, and even Athaz had enough time to roll out of bed and have his zweihänder at the ready after hearing the door thrown open. Seeing Aster, they lowered their weapons. Aster was already busy grabbing things hidden in floorboards and behind furniture. "We must flee!" he said hoarsely. "Watchers killed Aphen, searching his mind as they did. They would have learned nothing of your identity, but they will definitely know the location of the cell and suspect my two visitors are at minimum sympathizers with the Savanir. Take the horses for my wagon that are stalled in my barn. They are not terribly fast, but they are better than nothing. At least they will outrun any pursuit on foot."

"And you?" Kruthos asked.

"After I start a fire in here, I will rouse my patrons to flee. Hopefully in the chaos, I will be able to at least make it to the cell and burn it before being captured. Only Xiarch can get me out of the city tonight."

The Tales of Lugon

Kruthos looked at Athaz, who nodded. "We are coming with you. The Watchers undoubtedly now have that house on lockdown. You are going to need help."

Aster nodded. "The fire will start here. This room is kept specifically for friends of the Savanir, but wait until the other patrons begin fleeing before making your way to the barn."

They nodded and went down to the common room and into the kitchen. In less than two minutes, they could hear the fire burning down their room and Aster raising the alarm. Kruthos re-donned Athaz's cloak and hid his beard. After three patrons had made their way out of the door, they too sprinted out, feigning fear for their lives.

"This way, child!" Athaz yelled panic stricken as he pulled Kruthos toward the barn, as if he were a child lost in shock. Not far behind them was Aster. Kruthos had already removed the cloak, having made it to the barn safely. Nothing would hide their intention now that they were riding with the innkeeper.

"Take those two!" Aster cried. "They are the faster members of the team." Taking a third out of the barn, he sent it screaming with a hard slap to the backside, Aster mounted the last and led the way out at a gallop.

Already, a crowd was gathering. "Isn't that the innkeeper?" some asked as he flew past them. "Why is he leaving? Shouldn't he …" But already they were out of earshot. They would hear plenty of charges, true and false, in the morning.

They rode the horses hard toward the cell. The streets were mostly empty, but a few night travelers had to jump out of the way of being trampled. Soon, they were approaching the cell location.

"Lap around the block. Search for an ambush before we stop!" Athaz called ahead.

Aster waved to show he heard. They did circle, but they found nothing. Slowly approaching the cell house from an alley, all was quiet … and too dark for a place that should be on high alert.

"Watchers waiting in ambush, most likely," Athaz whispered. Aster nodded.

"We can burn them alive, then," Kruthos said.

Truth Unearthed

"Not likely," Athaz said. "Watchers have more ability in the Divine than Wardens, though subtler. And we can't risk killing any Savanir inside."

Kruthos' eyes burned with violent intent. "Well, fortunately, Aphen never laid eyes on me. They do not know about me, though they are about to learn! Athaz, Aster, go up on the rooftops. If any Watchers are in there, they will soon be joining you. I will raise the earth to the ceiling, stopping just short not to crush any friends inside."

They both knew what he meant and that indeed he could, as shaping earth was within a Dwarf's Divine abilities. Still, it was a shock to prepare for.

"Go on," he told them. "No need to wait for me. This will take some time."

All three dismounted. Aster and Athaz quickly found a ladder, and, as silently as possible and keeping their shadows cast by the moon hidden from the streets, they made their way to the buildings next to the cell, one of them on each side. Aster prepared a fire accelerant in a small glass globe and lit a small piece of firewood he had brought with him from the inn. As soon as he could see there were no bystanders, which he did not suspect there to be, the battle would begin, surrounded by fire.

Well, this will alert the entire Dawn far more than my axe ever could have, Kruthos laughed grimly to himself as he finished the Divine command. Aster and Athaz steadied themselves at the sudden shake and prepared to leap. Two seconds after the minor earthquake, a curse from inside was heard, and the thatched roof was somehow tossed aside. Seeing no allies, Aster threw the globe of accelerant first, followed shortly by the lit wood. Athaz steeled himself, for indeed it was a Watcher with three soldiers.

"Soldiers first!" he cried, leaping in. Neither would have survived their charge, but the soldiers were stunned by the sudden earth upheaval and unexpected fight, and the Watcher was busy avoiding the flames surrounding them. Armor stopped Athaz's zweihänder as he swung at the head of the first soldier, but the force broke the man's neck. Aster's dagger found the heart of the second through his target's back. Before Athaz's first victim's body fell to the ground, he finished the third soldier with a thrust through the gut, easily piercing the softer, supple armor that protected it. As the third soldier crumpled to the ground, the Watcher was now on the offensive, heading toward the former Warden, knowing his foe after seeing the weapon of choice and the skill of its wielder.

"Down!" cried Kruthos, who had been watching and saw the Watcher, now alone, on the offensive.

Immediately, Aster and Athaz leapt from the raised ground back onto the street, rolling to break their fall. While they were still in midair, and before the Watcher had time to jump, the ground suddenly gave way. With a yell, the Watcher fell; there was now a pit below the street, with the debris of the ruined house falling on top of their enemy.

"To me!" cried Kruthos.

Athaz and Aster ran full speed. They had not gone ten yards when suddenly they were knocked off their feet by a much more violent earthquake as Kruthos slid a massive wall of earth from the ground below them to crush the Watcher. They heard the Watcher shriek in terror before it was suddenly cut off by the slam of the moving earth hitting the opposite side of the pit.

"Quick! Before the whole street caves in!" Kruthos yelled.

The two were back on their feet, panting hard by the time they reached him. They didn't stop running when they reached Kruthos. His power over the earth was terrifying.

"That should stop him," Kruthos said. "I am sorry the evidence didn't get to burn completely, but it should take them a while to recover it at any rate."

The two men were still panting and just staring at him.

"Oh, right, you've never seen an Earth Mover at work before," he laughed. "Well, it was my first time using it in a real combat situation, but I am one of Menigar's last lines of defense. "I—"

Suddenly the ground on which Athaz and Aster had been standing on only moments before caved in completely, falling at least fifteen feet.

"Last line for a reason," Athaz said with a grim laugh. "Doesn't look like there will be much left of the home, even if the enemy was defeated."

"We do need to get away from here. The ground is unstable and agents of The Dawn will be here soon. Look, already people are coming out of their houses. Let's see Aster off in the direction of the aid sent to Arun and the others before we head out. I'll explain the rest on the way."

They rode their horses quickly, though not harshly; they needed them to last now.

"Menigar is much different," Kruthos explained as they rode. "We dug empty chambers and networks everywhere. We know exactly how much earth to move and exactly how far to move it, and each section has its own Movers assigned to it, so we can do it quickly. The first command took so long because I was trying to avoid any unnecessary destruction, which was difficult not knowing the area. Once we were in combat, I had to act much faster and keeping the earth around us stable was no longer feasible."

They were now near the gate, and they slowed up. As they feared, it was on alert, the strange events of the evening had the guard active, weapons drawn.

The three took a quick council. "Let me and Kruthos ride through, hard," Athaz said. "Someone is getting chased, and we don't want you to lead them to those aiding Baran and Arun, or all of this was for naught." Aster nodded. When they remounted, Kruthos grabbed Aster's arm.

"Your job is nearly thankless, and you never see the places or faces you risk your life for. With your post destroyed, I suggest you make your way to Menigar. After you retrieve Arun and Baran, use my home as your own until I arrive and we can get you settled. You know what to look for, I assume."

"The marked trees in the foothills?" he asked.

Kruthos nodded. "Farewell and may Xiarch guide you!" With that he spurred his horse into action with Athaz close behind. Just to make sure all followed them, Athaz sliced the neck of one of the guards as they rode past. When they exited, the two turned north.

"In the Name of The Dawn's Light halt!" cried the watchmen

as they began their hopeless chase on foot. Quickly, Aster made his way out of the gate and turned south, hoping to catch up to his allies that by now would already be miles ahead.

CHAPTER XIII

On the Trail

Still in the mountains, Arun, Baran, Brasan, and his men were now only about a day's march out from Lamphine and would be returning to the bank of the Argom River. All of them were eager to return to the river bank. Not only was speed vital to their mission and safety, but hiking through the mountains was incredibly exhausting. Brasan never complained and did his best to hide his exhaustion, but the captain had not traveled by foot in decades, and his knees were as weak as any old man's. Even the young legs of Arun and Baran ached; it was as though they could feel every fiber in their muscles. When it seemed Brasan might soon collapse, one of the two friends would suggest a small break, though whether it was purely out of concern for Brasan was hard to say.

The company was getting ready to take their afternoon break and lunch when they heard something that made their hairs stand on end.

"Double time, you lazy mutts! Don't you know we're at war! We will be on the move soon, and none of *my* men will slow down the army's progress. Move it!"

Creeping over the large hill they had just come down, the companions couldn't believe their eyes. "Soldiers out in the middle of nowhere?!" Arun exclaimed in a hoarse whisper.

They were still a good distance off and wouldn't have heard without all the yelling, but he still couldn't believe their bad luck.

"Conditioning training, by the looks of it," said Baran.

Yes, but is there more here than it seems? Brasan thought doubtfully.

"There's only six of them," Baran continued as they hid behind the top of the hill. "With the element of surprise—"

Brasan cut him off. "A victory would kill us as much as a defeat. No doubt those men are expected to report back to someone before long, and when they don't, a search party will be sent out. Even if we took time to hide the bodies, we couldn't get rid of all traces of their trail or the battle, much less ours that they would begin to follow."

"They're coming this way," Arnost informed them.

"Hide or run?" Arun asked.

Brasan grimaced. "I don't like this," he muttered under his breath, then aloud, "We have no choice but to run. Lamphine isn't far. We are just going to have to get there a little quicker today than expected. But let's get to the banks. It will be easier for us, and if it is conditioning training, we won't be followed."

Fortunately, they hadn't fully unpacked, but Arun's arm was slowing them down. When they finished gathering their things, Brasan announced their course. "Back to the bank!" Then, for the first time since voicing his suspicions, "Eyes in front! This may be more than coincidence."

The group was forced to keep the same speed as the soldiers behind them, which was a brutal pace. When they made it to the bank two hours later, they paused to catch their breath. But the sound of the sergeant and his men was still behind them.

"Maybe they're coming for a drink?" Baran hoped in vain.

"Run for it!" cried Brasan. "We cannot risk a fight."

"But if they see us running, won't that raise suspicions?" Arun asked.

"Damn it all!" Brasan swore. "Yes, you're right. Back into the mountains! If they follow us again, we will have no choice but to fight."

Already tired from a hurried, careful descent, they began the much more exhausting job of fleeing into the mountains. After they had gone some distance, they stationed Waren behind while they ran ahead for another half hour or so. If they pursued them into the mountains, Waren was supposed to blow Brasan's old whistle; he used it to give combat orders in sea battles when it became too loud to hear his shouting.

At last they stopped. Arun began to wonder if they had the

strength left to fight. He and Brasan were looking completely spent, and even Baran and Inoch looked like they were utilizing every effort just to stand erect. "We will rest here."

Brasan said. "The fact that Waren has yet to signal is a good sign at least. Maybe they really were replenishing their canteens."

They had been resting for about twenty minutes when a voice hailed them — a voice cold and unfeeling that seemed saturated with a cruel mirth.

"Greetings, Captain Brasan, formerly of The River Daughter," Skodus said in a voice that froze the blood in their veins.

The company turned and realized there would be no more running from a battle. Skodus had brought two dozen soldiers with him. Their lack of bows allowed a fleeting thought of possible escape. But it didn't last long. Skodus was tall and gangly, even in the armor he now wore. He looked sickly thin, and he still wore the robes and hood of the Watchers over his armor and helmet. His eyes, no longer human, could still be seen emitting their pale orange light. Perhaps it was the shape of the lights, but you could tell a smile was hidden in the shadows of that hood — the smile of a veteran hunter who had his game hopelessly cornered.

"My esteemed captain," the Watcher began in a tone that could have been either mockery or a poor attempt at friendliness. "You and your former shipmates need not fear me. I am not the Watcher assigned to your affairs, and it seems you have stopped smuggling with The Bewildered. Of course, you are traveling with one of their fighting whelps..." he paused to look at Inoch "...but I'm sure you were unaware of this. And the boys' crimes you might never have been aware of. If that is the case, you and your men may be on your way."

Brasan and his men didn't say anything, but neither did they flinch. Hatred shone from their eyes.

"Ah ... of course," Skodus said, shaking his head. "Honor demands you not abandon your companions in trouble, and I hear you are a very honorable man. Fortunately, the honor lies in upholding the law of the Son of Bälech. If you stand aside as a good citizen, it would only be fitting for me to put in a good word for you regarding that previous affair."

The restraints on Brasan's tongue fell, completely cloven by his disgust at the despicable bribe. "Those who do not possess honor should refrain from persuading others with it, even more so if they do not comprehend it! Abandoning my companions is at stake here, but more for the one's you tortured, breaking their bodies and minds until you squeezed every last sensible utterance from them before you killed them, only to make room for others. I will die defending these young men, but I would have gladly suffered the fate of my men a hundred times over just for the chance of wiping every one of you monsters off the face of this world!"

There was no false sweetness in tone when Skodus spoke again. The mixture of rage and mockery made the hairs stand on the necks of everyone present. "Old sentimental fool," he said. At that moment, Waren's whistle was heard. "Ah, your final companion arrives, and with him, the six-pronged whip that drove you here. We shall wait for them. Perhaps your men have more reasonable minds than the captain they have been burdened with."

Arun turned to yell for Waren to run in another direction but was suddenly buckled by an unseen blow that penetrated deep into his gut, knocking the wind out of him. "If you thought your Warden's abilities in the Divine commanded respect, you will find mine are to be feared even more," Skodus laughed. "It is true that Wardens' abilities are in combat and Watchers' abilities in interrogation, but you would be amazed how effective our techniques are in battle for disabling your foes." At that instant, Baran also crumpled. "I'm not so easily distracted. The next person who tests my patience will suffer far worse."

Soon enough, Waren came over the last hill. Baran was still on the ground. Arun had gotten back up, but his hands were on his knees, and he was sucking wind as he tried to refill his lungs. Seeing the trap, Waren slowly made his way to Brasan, Damon, and Arnost. He gave a shallow nod at Damon with Arnost returning it to show he, too, had seen before he casually made his way next to Brasan. By the time Waren placed himself on the far side of Arnost and the captain, the colonel and his five men were now looking over the hill at them. Baran slowly staggered to his feet while Arun was finally able to stand straight again.

"Well," Skodus began again. "Now that everyone's here, I will make you an offer that your senile captain refused. Never let it be said The Dawn is unmerciful. Will you — "

Before he could finish the question, Waren, Damon, and Arnost simultaneously catapulted themselves as though they had been released from fully wound crossbows. Damon flung a knife at the Watcher as he and Waren charged at him while Arnost grabbed his captain, yanking him toward the five guarding the passage back toward the river and yelling for Inoch, Arun, and Baran to charge with him.

Skodus screamed with fury and was about to use the Divine on Damon when a second dagger came flying from Waren, holding him off for a little longer; Damon already had his second and final dagger at the ready.

"Kill them!" Skodus shrieked at his men. "But take The Academy brats alive!"

By this point, Arnost, Brasan, Baran, Inoch, and Arun had already made it where the six, now five thanks to a dagger from Arun, had been standing. "Behind me!" cried Baran.

Knowing their goal was escape and not victory, he left his sword in its sheath and lowered himself behind his shield as his comrades lowered themselves behind him. Arnost and Inoch flanked Arun and Brasan, covering the sides of their retreat. As they passed the men that had chased them into the ambush, they heard the death cries of Waren and Damon.

Skodus and his men were now on their tail, with the Watcher only pausing for a brief second to permanently discharge the colonel for letting his prey escape through the back gate.

They scrambled as fast as they could back down the steep slopes of the mountains. But in their haste, their worst fear was realized as Arun lost his footing, and in an attempt to not re-break his arm let himself fall but got his ankle twisted underneath his full weight. He immediately knew it was hopelessly sprained.

The Tales of Lugon

They all stopped. It would be impossible for all to escape now, but Brasan knew someone must escape. It was clear they wanted Arun and Baran alive, or they would have never even known the Watcher had been there before darkness took them all.

"Baran and Inoch, you must continue alone," he said.

"You think I'm going to abandon you ... abandon *him*?" Baran asked in disbelief, looking at Arun. "As if I would let them kill my friends so that I could escape!"

"We do not have time to argue!" Brasan said. Their pursuers were peaking over the last hill they had just crossed. Brasan quickly explained. "Arun will be captured, not killed, and that will happen whether you are here or not. Only if you escape can you find help before he is brought to Hilae, and you two are the youngest and strongest left. Arnost and I will remain behind to slow them down, every second will be vital."

Baran was about to refuse when Arun looked at him and with a cold voice asked, "Don't you have someone who has a higher claim on you than I do now?"

Knowing any more delay would be the ruin of everything, Inoch yanked Baran to his feet and dragged him away, keeping Baran from speaking any words or even making eye contact with Arun. Cursing Inoch and himself, Baran yanked free from Inoch's grasp but kept running.

As he made his way, Arnost and Brasan readied their swords. "I am sorry," Brasan said to his final faithful follower.

"Don't be," Arnost said with a perfectly steady voice. "I drew the short straw. That was why I had to be the one to run."

Baran was sprinting, his heart wanting to explode with shame. He kept replaying Brasan's final words to himself over and over to keep his feet moving as he blindly followed Inoch. At last they leapt into the river and began to swim.

By now Skodus and his men had encircled Arun, Brasan, and Arnost. Knowing they would be dead before they finished raising their weapons for an attack, the captain and sailor stood firm, knowing the best delay tactic they had would be to amuse the Watcher for as long as possible. However, a quick death would be more pleasant.

"Half of you, continue chasing the other brat! Don't come back until you have captured him. You will be better off dead than to return alive empty-handed. Kill The Bewildered pup." Immediately, those closest to the bank turned to give chase.

Skodus spat in disgust at Brasan's face. "Convinced your men dying for you was glorious, did you?"

Brasan didn't even bother removing the vile fluid from his face. If anything the captain stood straighter. "I am proud to say I had no part in that and was as surprised as you were. The only part I played was surrounding myself with honorable men, which, as I told you earlier, you clearly cannot comprehend."

"So you love your men so much do you?" Brasan reached to stop him as Arnost braced himself right before he felt the blade plunge into his stomach and stuck out his back. Brasan futilely looked on, held in place by four men as Arnost sunk to his knees, coughing blood. His gasping and gurgling made Arun's stomach tumble, begging for release from his clenched teeth as he swallowed everything back down.

"Fortunately for you, my amusement must be shortened by my need for haste. He will only struggle for fifteen minutes before he drowns in his own blood. Of course, I can think of one way to make both of your exits from this world just a little more painful." He motioned the four men holding Brasan as well as one other toward Arnost. Brasan was forced down to his knees while Arnost was forced up to his.

"Knowing you would rather suffer than your men, your death will be swift, while your sailor's slow. But the last thing he will see is your head being removed from its shoulders before his eyes are put out. A fitting end for your *honor*."

As the sailor and his captain looked into each other's eyes for their last moments, Brasan, in a final show of defiance, and an attempt to comfort faithful Arnost, knew what to say. Waiting until the sword began its strike that it could not be stopped, he left Arnost one final word, "Godspeed," as the blade fell.

If there was any doubt the Watcher had missed the defiant

aspect of it, it was soon dismissed. Seething with anger, he yanked Arnost's head up and put out the eyes most cruelly. Even as Arnost yelled and gasped for breath, he managed to wheeze an appropriate farewell to his captain. "May fair winds bring us again to safe harbor."

When Arnost finally finished struggling, Arun finally released his stomach and his tears.

"Don't trouble yourself with their fate," Skodus mocked, his composure now fully restored after watching Arnost slowly lose the ability to cling to life. "If you must weep, weep for yourself. There is far worse ahead of you. Come along. It won't do to keep the Son of Bälech waiting."

Arun struggled to his shaky feet. As he was pushed forward to begin his limping march to Lamphine, he looked one last time at the face of the only stranger that had helped him with pure altruism since this insanity had begun. He had feared he might collapse from the sight, but instead he found his knees steadied themselves and, in place of fear, a light now shone his eyes. It was gone in a moment but simmering just under the consciousness of his mind that was scheming for an escape. A seedling for vengeance was shooting its first leaf from deep within, feeling the warmth of the wrath that could feed its growth. Without instruction from his mind, his eyes shifted to the soldier that now held his vest of knives before his thoughts and eyes returned to the ropes that bound his wrists.

For a moment, Arun's mind retreated back into panic as a familiar voice called out, *Don't be a fool! The Dawn is unassailable!* Only to be reminded of the aged face of Athaz, who at this moment was on his way to rescue his family. "Not quite," he growled to himself.

* * * * * * * * * *

Baran and Inoch struggled to swim as fast as they could until they had put some distance between them and the bank. Baran was struggling just to keep his head above water, though.

"Lose the shield!" Inoch yelled at him.

Truth Unearthed

Baran cursed both his stupidity and the loss of the shield as it sank to the bottom of the river and his struggle eased considerably.

"Swim with the current toward the bank," Inoch panted, now next to him.

Baran did as he was told, and his fear of drowning all but vanished between fighting less of the current and the work of his legs lightened, only having to carry his wet clothes and small sword. Hearing voices, they turned back to watch the men that had been chasing them sprinting further downstream back toward Mizcur.

"They are going to search for a narrower point to cut us off," Inoch said. "But we'll be across by that point."

After several minutes, the two found themselves lying down on the banks, panting from exhaustion.

"Can't … rest …" Inoch said. "They'll … be coming."

"Where to?" Baran finally got out.

Inoch just kept staring at the ground, breathing heavy. "I don't know."

"What do you mean you don't know?!" Baran yelled in frustration, finally catching his breath. "Are you telling me we abandoned our friends just to sit and wait for the soldiers to come round us up? You all seem to have hideouts everywhere!"

"In the forests and mountains, yes, but not in an open plain that acts as the doormat for Bälech's capital!" Inoch shot back. Calming himself, he added, "We need to think. Panicking won't help."

"I'm not panicking!" Baran yelled.

Inoch was barely able to hold in a retort but was glad he did when he saw Baran slam both fists into the ground, screaming in frustration. *Of course*, Inoch realized. *It's not our situation that is upsetting him.* Walking over to Baran, he held out his hand. "Come on. We need to think, but we can't sit around while we do it."

Baran finally took it and pulled himself up.

"We might as well keep going west," Inoch said, taking his sword out of its soaked sheath and drying it on the grass. Baran followed suit. "Keep it out. Your wet sheath won't protect it."

"I'm not an idiot. I was training for the military, you know." The words were empty, though. Baran knew he would have drowned like an idiot had Inoch not told him to drop his shield.

Inoch suddenly laughed.

"Well, there's no need to laugh. Even if I am an idiot..." Baran said, annoyed.

"Not you, me," Inoch said, shaking his head. "We still have to go to Lamphine."

Baran blinked at him. "Did you hit your head while we were escaping?"

"Look at us. The lack of sheath for our swords won't bother us at all because we have nothing else to carry. We have no food, no way to get food, and both Arun and Descia's father are to the west. Kind of obvious which way we have to go, and I actually had to think about it!"

"And the soldiers coming?" Baran asked.

"Will probably catch up to us and it will be a miracle if we aren't killed, but hey, at least we know what to do," Inoch said as he began walking up the bank.

He must have hit his head, Baran thought to himself following him.

They had been walking for about four hours and had stopped to rest, when they heard what they had been dreading ... yelling from the east. They could just make out the figures, but something was off. Inoch put his ear to the ground.

"Horses?"

"You definitely hit your head," Baran now said aloud.

"I'm telling you, those are riders heading this way. More than one, but certainly not as many as we had soldiers chasing us."

Sure enough, four horses finally appeared on the horizon.

Inoch and Baran readied their swords, Baran feeling almost helpless with his short blade without its accompanying shield. Inoch, too, had lost his buckler, but at least he could reach a little further. *Not that either of us would fare well against mounted enemies,* Baran thought grimly.

Their actions had apparently been noticed, for the lead rider began rummaging behind him and finding a horn let out a shrill call.

Inoch's mouth gaped. "Drop your sword!" He flung his aside and began sprinting toward the horsemen.

"Inoch, wait!" Baran shouted, following after him.

"Drop the sword! They'll think you're chasing me!"

Baran pulled up from his run. "What?"

"Allies!" Inoch yelled over his shoulder.

Baran let his sword fall from his hands, but it was from shock, not obedience. "He's gone mad with despair!" But when the horsemen were mere yards away, they suddenly pulled up and the lead horseman dismounted as Inoch ran up to him.

"Well met indeed!" Inoch said, grasping one of the men by the forearm with a single strong shake. "Who are you, though? You are no patrol. If our situation was not so hopeless, I would be a lot more suspicious, but as it is, you are our only hope."

"You must be Inoch, then?" said the leader. When Inoch nodded, the leader continued, "My name is Blake, and we are one of the cells hidden throughout The Dawn to aid fellow Savanir in our enemy's strongholds. Aster, here..." he nodded to their rotund companion "...keeps an inn for us and is our spy. Athaz and Kruthos sent word you were in danger, and it seems they were right. Where is the rest of your company?"

Baran at this point had caught up. "Arun's been captured," he said, trying to keep his voice level.

"The others were killed, sacrificed themselves to make our escape. Arun fell and injured his ankle in the chase. There were around two dozen led by a Watcher. Brasan ordered us to flee while he and his final companion delayed them. He seemed confident Arun would not be killed, at least not at that point. They could have killed us very easily in their ambush without a battle had that been their goal."

"We were chased, though not by all of them. By my count, there were around nine looking for a place to cross the river and catch us," Inoch continued. "You must have just missed our pursuers because of your horses and speed. They are on foot."

"I see," said Blake. "Aster!"

"Yes, Blake?"

The Tales of Lugon

"Stay with them. If anyone attacks, send Baran on your horse back toward us. They need rest, and while your work as a spy has shown courage—"

"I'm not used to moving speedily. I'm very aware of that Blake," finished Aster, who was indeed looking the most exhausted.

Blake nodded. "Glad we brought the bows now. Alright!" Blake turned to his two other companions. "Let's put an end to our friends' pursuers so that we can focus on helping Arun."

With that, all but Aster turned their horses and galloped back the way they had come.

In the meantime Baran, Inoch, and Aster exchanged news of how Athaz and Kruthos had known they were in danger and had sent for aid from the trap the Watcher had set to capture Arun.

Blake and his two companions to returned after a couple of hours. Between their horses and bows, it only took a few minutes to slay The Dawn's foot soldiers once they had been found, but they had to make sure the bodies slept on the bed of the Argom with no chance of finding their way to Mizcur, lest a larger and better equipped pursuit replace the previous one.

"The soldiers will not trouble us further," Blake said as he rode up to them. Inoch thanked them again for their timing and aid, but Baran simply looked down the river.

"What's wrong?" asked Aster.

"Nothing," lied Baran, shaking his head. He smiled and shook Blake's hand in a similar manner that Inoch had done when they had first met. "Thanks, Blake and ..."

"Aldo," said the first.

"Garren," said the second.

"Thanks," said Baran, now smiling. "The Savanir seem to have a knack for showing up when I'm about to get myself killed."

"Sorry we couldn't get here before," Blake said. "Arun might not have been captured."

"Unlikely," Inoch said. He then recounted for them the ambush and the number of soldiers. "They had been tracking us for days, obviously. You would have just gotten killed, possibly before

Truth Unearthea

you ever even made it to us, and our situation would have been hopeless. As it is, Baran remains free, and we have a chance to save Arun. If we act quickly, we might surprise them before they suspect their soldiers were unable to capture us. They will not expect a rescue attempt for Arun at least for a few days. After all, who would tell our forces of the ambush?"

"But we'll have to be swift to take advantage of that," Aster said. "They know that the Savanir will be keeping eyes on Arun and will quickly realize something is amiss."

Blake nodded. "Inoch, ride with me. Baran, you're with Aldo. We must make it to Lamphine before nightfall, and we must go back to where the soldiers first forded the river. The Watcher will be able to see anyone that is on the northern bank of the Argom. We must reach the place where the soldiers will cross the river. Once we are within sight of the city, we will have to take to the mountains. We will have a few hours to rest and plan our strategy. Arun must be freed by dawn tomorrow. Let's go!"

They took their time. With horses, they would easily reach Lamphine early that night, but they had no desire to see its borders until night cloaked their entry. They halted behind a bend in the river a mile or so from Lamphine, about an hour and a half before sunset. Blake and his companions dismounted and changed into the burlap clothing worn by the Yeomanry (except Aster, who had never needed to disguise himself before), applying a fresh layer of mud from the river bank for good measure.

"Are there any Savanir cells in Lamphine?" Baran asked.

"Possibly," Blake answered. "As a rule, I don't know who they are or where they are. If we had a day or two to search, it would be worth the effort, but we don't have that kind of time. The Watcher will already be on alert as the night passes with his men not returning. They may plan on transporting Arun first thing in the morning, regardless. We are going to have to do this on our own."

Blake and Garren set out. They were concerned about needing an excuse for their travel at the gate, when, much to their relief, they saw a group of Yeomen pulling in logs from freshly cut trees. They fell in line with a group dragging theirs. "Need a hand?"

Blake asked. The Yeoman in front nodded, not bothering to stop his work to answer. Bypassing the gatekeeper without a word, they carried the log to the ship bound for Mizcur and made their way back toward an inn they passed just inside the town's walls. Quickly changing back into standard traveling clothes in the ally, they asked for lodging for six. Though they doubted they would be resting tonight, paid innkeepers tended to be less inquisitive.

First came Baran, Inoch, and Aster, followed by Aldo, who had kept an eye on them as he blended in with the Yeomanry as his fellows had before him. When all six were in the inn, they met in one of their rooms.

"Garren, Aldo, and myself will do some quick scouting, as we are the most familiar with the habits of Watchers," Blake said to the others. "You all should rest while you can. Even if sleep does not come, gather your energy, for we do not know when we shall be able to rest again."

They were not gone long. They returned in just over an hour. The others were already sleeping. Worried as they were, they were all exhausted. So were Blake and his men. He sighed. It was now midnight, but even he and his men needed to rest. They hadn't slept since they set out last night.

"Give me two hours," he said wearily. "Keep an eye out in case they try to leave in the night. Once you rouse me, rest yourselves. When daylight breaks, we must tell them of our plan and move out."

CHAPTER XIV

A Foe to Friends

Arun looked from side to side as they approached the gates of Lamphine. Supposing he could by some miracle escape his captors on his bum ankle, unless he could find a way to distance himself quickly, he would only be recaptured. To his dismay, there were no horses. The people of Lamphine lived off of the forests and the Argom River. There was very little need even for draft horses; the Yeomen here were not farmers. Some simply cut down trees or gathered other resources from the forests. Others were carpenters that made whatever supplies The Dawn required of them. In all cases, most never left the town. Even the few that accompanied their goods to Mizcur rode on small, simple boats that would be recycled for materials before making the long walk upstream towards home.

Arun almost despaired upon realizing the hopelessness of his situation. This meant his only chance of escape would be to hide onboard a boat and pray that it left before the alarm was raised and Skodus searched the boat. His oppressive fear continued to rise when he heard Skodus order the gates closed behind them.

They walked along the road, heading toward the eastern edge of town, where a ferry would set them on the opposite shore upon the Mossy Plain. Once on horseback, there would be no hope of a rescue fast enough to catch them before he was returned to Hilae.

Turning off the main road, Arun saw they were stopping in front of a house. Something was off, though Arun could not put his finger on it at first. But when they entered and his eyes could only see darkness even in midday, he realized this building had no windows. A shiver he could not stop made its way down his spine as his mind began to think of why a Watcher would have built a windowless house.

The Tales of Lugon

"Fureigh san bor, ilum de pro ..." For a brief instant Arun's heart sparked with hope upon hearing the phrase Baran had used in Menigar, but it was extinguished even as the chimney logs erupted into flames. *"... Shrik!"*

"Guard the door," Skodus' unnaturally thin, cold voice ordered. Two soldiers quickly turned and went back outside.

"Restrain him," he said to those remaining. Arun was roughly forced into a plain wooden chair with his wrists tied to the armrests. Arun stifled a cry as they forced his injured ankle to one of the legs.

"And now, Arun, you and I are going to have a little talk," Skodus said as he advanced toward Arun, bending down and looking his prey in the eyes.

Arun gaped in horror. For now he realized that it was not a trick the hood's shadow hid the Watcher's face. The black, charred skin that was missing in several places had a sickening glow from the fire hidden within, its full brightness only visible in the empty sockets that no longer carried human eyes.

"What ... what are you?" Arun asked half to himself, not really expecting an answer. "Even Wardens don't—"

Arun was interrupted by a hot hand held over his mouth that muffled a cry. He screamed in pain at its touch. "Do not compare me to one of those wretches!" he said dangerously. Arun threw his head back and forth in an attempt to move his face away as his screaming continued to be silenced by the hand he desperately wanted to escape.

Skodus released him. Arun could already feel the blisters forming around his mouth. Arun felt his stomach lurch at the sound of the cold chuckle coming from his captor's hood. "Now even your screams will torment you further."

Arun's anger vanished. All hope for escape or rescue vanished. In their place was nothing but overwhelming dread.

* * * * * * * * *

The next morning Blake woke everyone up.

"Quickly! We cannot let them get on the open plain or Arun is

Truth Unearthed

lost forever."

Baran, Inoch, and even Aster followed the three scouts from the previous night to the windowless building. If there was any doubt that such a structure was likely where Arun was being held, the two guards dispelled all traces. They were visibly tense, an uneasiness born from a threat within the windowless house more so than any without. "Aster, I believe you can help us out the most here by creating a little disturbance that would entice them to open the door?"

"No plan?!" Baran shrieked.

Blake was more than a little annoyed at the reminder of how ludicrous this was. "Get Arun and make a run for it. I can't see through walls! Even we can't make intel appear out of thin air!"

Without further interruption, Aster stepped out into the street while the others followed Blake as he quickly went around the block to get near the building from the other side. Perfectly impersonating one of his former patrons on a morning after a night where they had downed a few too many, he sauntered over to the guards.

"Dawn's Light b—praised," he slurred.

"Get lost, you damned drunkard," the closest guard to him spat.

"But I'bn robb'd bline!" Aster wailed.

Both guards lowered their spears. "You come a step closer and it's more than your coin you'll lose this morning! Hey, what are you doing?!"

Aster grabbed a spear in each hand and yanked backwards with all his considerable weight, causing the guards to yell in dismay. The door opened with another guard about to scream at his comrades if their intention was to get Skodus to torment them when he tired of Arun. Instead, his eyes widened as Blake lowered his shoulder into the door and sent him sprawling.

Chaos erupted. Blake and his men quickly scanned for the Watcher lest they all find themselves stunned by his invisible blows, but almost immediately five more guards were on them. That would have been the end of all of them. But as Skodus hid in a corner of the wall shared with the door with a pale, unconscious

Arun at his feet, Baran and Inoch heard his unnatural voice forming Divine words. Baran turned, and when he saw the state of his friend, all of his fury and guilt of having abandoning Arun before surged through him as he leapt with his short sword held high in both hands to cleave the vile creature in two. Skodus easily dodged the attack, and the battle fully engaged.

Knowing giving his opponent a single breath would be his death, Baran lunged constantly at the Watcher, grabbing any item nearby when he missed to hurl it at his foe. It was hopeless. He moved too slowly. Skodus needed only to bide his time. Still, the Watcher was getting angry. Few Bewildered were stupid enough to attempt to take up a sword against a Watcher. *"But of course! The fool doesn't know!"* Skodus realized. As he continued to dodge Baran's attacks, he taunted Baran. "You dolt, don't you know the hand that strikes me down kills its own master?!" Baran paused only for a moment before he realized his error, but it was enough. *"Pron morte a —"* The command was cut off as a shriek of fear and anger escaped Skodus' hood, followed by Aster's own agony as Baran looked on in horror as the friendly innkeeper's blood gushing from every orifice of his body.

Baran and Inoch were both staring at Aster, who was still writhing and screaming. "Don't let his sacrifice be in vain! Quickly, get Arun and run!"

Baran shook himself back to reality upon hearing his friend's name and quickly threw his roommate over his shoulder, flanked by Arun and then by Aldo, and Garren, and lastly Blake, who was covered from head to toe in blood, much of it his own.

As they ran toward the southern gate they entered in last night, a horn rang out behind them. "Cut left. Make for the boats!" Blake shouted to those ahead of him.

Time seemed to stretch as they feared being waylaid at any moment, or worse, the pier held against them. But at last the boats came into view, including the one full of lumber they had helped load during their disguised entrance. They leapt on board as the Yeoman readying to shove off fled the armed mass of madness bent on boarding their craft. Aldo and Garren grabbed the poles and began pushing with all their might, and Inoch cut the ropes tying them to the pier with his sword. Unfortunately, some soldiers had indeed guessed their plan and were now coming to try and board while they were still among the piers. They would have to fend them off until they got to the river where the current would help them pick up speed.

"I'll watch Arun. Protect Aldo and Garren!" Blake's weakening voice commanded Baran and Inoch. Baran hesitated for a moment. "Go! If we don't get out of here, it won't matter that you stand guard over him!"

Baran quickly laid Arun in the midst of some of the cargo and went to protect the polemen.

They made it through the open waterway. Five soldiers had already ran ahead, and now one leapt up on the unguarded prow of the boat.

"Inoch, Baran, to me!" Blake called wearily. He had run up to meet them to slow their progress but was very quickly being forced to retreat. His arms were weakening from blood loss. As Inoch and Baran attempted to make their way across all the cargo, Blake stumbled backwards and fell. The foremost soldier leapt over him, making straight for Arun. "Not this time!" Baran yelled, leaping toward him and thrusting his sword into the soldier. Though Baran's aim was true, his charge was overzealous and both he and the soldier tumbled into the river. Kicking his sword free as the soldier sank to the river bottom, Baran came back up quickly, calling and searching for help. Garren saw him and ran over to the very back of the boat and tried to reach Baran with his pole, but it was too late. Inoch had heard his cry too and was running toward the back of the boat after having dispatched the other enemies at the front. His eyes widened as he looked over at his friend and behind him. Baran turned in the water to see more soldiers pursing them from the city.

Turning back, he saw Inoch preparing to disembark. "Don't!" Baran yelled. Inoch stopped and looked up at Baran treading water with fear but resolution in his eyes. Seeing that his warning had been heeded, Baran climbed out of the river onto the bank and made for the mountains.

* * * * * * * * *

As evening fell, Arun finally opened his eyes. The stars were twinkling in the dark purple sky of dusk. For a while, he did not move or say anything. Had his capture been a dream? No, his heart still ached as he remembered Captain Brasan's death. Had he died himself? Surely, Skodus would not have let him sleep so soundly and awaken to the beautiful evening sky. Then he noticed that his bed swayed, and the stars slowly moved by. Was he on a boat? He did not want to move. He didn't want to do anything lest the dream end and reality come crashing back on him. When at last he got the courage, he slowly sat up and looked around.

"Greetings, Arun." A man caked in blood-soaked bandages was sitting at his feet, leaning against a stack of timber. "I am Blake, leader of a Savanir spy-house in Mizcur. I'm sure you have a lot of questions, and when you're ready I'll answer them."

"No, Blake, I'm afraid that task should fall to me." Arun turned and almost leapt for joy to see Inoch, but something was terribly wrong. Inoch was avoiding his gaze. Confusion clouded Arun's face.

Arun quickly stood up. "Baran!" he cried, looking all around him. Not seeing him on the boat, he scanned the shore and was about to cry out again when Inoch put his hand on his shoulder.

"I'm sorry, Arun." Inoch said. "As we made our escape, a guard attempted to pull you off the boat. Baran leapt to your side and drove his sword into him but fell into the river with his foe. We were being chased, and he waved me off as I prepared to go after him. The only good news I have is we saw him make it into the mountains with no immediate pursuit."

Arun sat in stunned silence. He thought he had handled everything up to this point rather well. He had no close personal ties to Hilae itself; the only people he was close to had entered exile with him. Knowing that the most powerful person on Lugon wanted him dead was unnerving, but there were too many other things to occupy his mind: Athaz's family, Descia's father ... and the prophecy. The prophecy. A sense of fear filled his mind as he recalled his decisions in Menigar, more wholesome than the dread he experienced at the hands of the Watcher, but all the more terrifying for its purity that rose up within him. *I will not sit by ...* Stripped bare of his defenses, Arun realized the real reason he had come was not to help Baran but to prove to the Savanir he wouldn't play by their rules. How much would Baran suffer for his pride?

Turning away from Inoch, Arun sat looking back toward Lamphine. He was thinking of Baran, but he also didn't want any of the others to see the tears he now knew he wouldn't be able to stop. He felt childish. He had acted childish.

Arun couldn't stop his shoulders from shaking. Now that he realized they knew, it surprised him how little it bothered him. So long as they didn't try to come up to him, he didn't care. *Just don't put your hand on my shoulder*, was his only thought.

A touch came anyway. It was not a hand and not on his shoulder. Rather, a warmth behind him steadied him. Inoch was sitting back to back with him. After dreading a pointless gesture, Arun was shocked by how much this solidarity that still gave him privacy comforted him. He shoulders quickly stopped shaking and the flowing tears slowed.

When Arun felt he could speak without his voice breaking, he asked, "When are we going to look for him?"

He had meant the question for Inoch, but it was Blake that answered. "*We* are not. You are going back to Menigar where you should never have left until you were fit to travel. At daybreak, Aldo and Garren will disembark at the south side of the river and begin making for our hidden outpost that we keep in the Makrin Mountains. There will be other members of the Savanir there that can navigate these lands blindfolded. Baran will be seeking water and shelter, no doubt, and those men will be able to quickly find him. I will accompany you and Inoch to Menigar. With Aster dead and our faces known, my cell can no longer continue operation in Mizcur, and Menigar is where my orders will come from. They will want a detailed report of everything that has occurred. And do not argue about searching for your friend; the Lady Lyr may have had patience for your foolhardiness, but I will not. As you have already seen, it costs me lives, lives I hold much dearer to me than yours. From what I know of you, and have seen thus far, a mistake must have been made. You cannot be the savior prophesied to us."

Inoch felt Arun tense, but his words were not the angry outburst he had been expecting. "I understand. I see now that the closer I am to anyone, the more danger that person is in." His tears had finally stopped.

Now Arun's mind and heart were occupied by an inner battle. He wanted leave and save Baran, but now he realized he would have to rely on the Savanir — as much it repulsed him. He didn't want to owe these people anything. Ever since he had met them, they had bent over backwards in a vain hope that the desperate ravings of a fallen society thousands of years ago would come to fruition. *Not entirely true*, something whispered inside of him. *They could have just saved you, or you and your friends, but even Nihl was saved and treated well.* Begrudgingly, Arun admitted to himself this was true. *Blake doesn't believe you are the savior they seek, but he's still going to seek out Baran.* Also true. *You are a vain, proud, fearful creature.* And now the two sides of his mind were united. Ever since he could remember, he had felt superior to the world in which he belonged. He had been taken from his family by an empire that cared nothing for him. Since that time, he had successfully navigated the system so it had to give him what he sought, even manipulating The Dawn to send him to a site it had never allowed anyone to venture to … which was why it had sought to end his life. Even among his peers, he had earned Baran's friendship and protection through his intellect. For the first time in his life, Arun had no sway, much less control over those surrounding him. But they certainly held such things over him.

"You alright?"

Lost in his own thoughts, Arun hadn't even felt Inoch get up.

"I will be, assuming they can find Baran before he gets himself killed because of my stupidity."

Inoch look bemused for a second before he smiled. "You'll let us help you?"

Arun looked around to where Blake and his men were at the front of the boat. He nodded toward the back, and the two walked to the very edge of the vessel.

"I don't have much of a choice. Haven't since the day we met. But I'll stop sulking about it. I still have no plans of overthrowing The Dawn for you, but I said that much back in Menigar and every last one of you promised aid with no strings attached. I will now accept it on those terms. And I'll attempt to be grateful for it."

CHAPTER XV

Worrying About the Future, Wandering in the Past

Athaz and Kruthos circled around the north of Mizcur and headed due east, back toward the Grigor River. They didn't push the horses hard, knowing that the pursuers would never catch them on foot and that they would lose not only the initial time on their fruitless foot chase but they would have to return to get mounts before the pursuit could begin in earnest. They praised their good fortune that the land had apparently not seen much rain lately, which meant the soldiers would also have to dismount regularly to track them. Still, The Dawn's military horses would indeed be faster than Aster's wagon team, so while the pace was manageable, they kept their rests to a minimum. They would be setting the horses free once they reached the river, for there was no way to get them across. If they covered their footprints decently and were lucky, their pursuers would follow the horses and leave them as they journeyed into the mountains.

Athaz looked longingly to the northeast as they continued to ride through the night. He could be at The Tennebron in just over a week's time with horses on this open plain! But the plain would be watched and secrecy was the only thing more necessary than speed. Indeed, even taking a route through the mountains, new measures would have to be taken. Ever since they had happened upon the party of united Savage Races, the likelihood of success had significantly decreased from their already dismal chances. Bälech knew, or at least thought it possible, he had survived the battle at Lacris and might be aiding the Savanir. He also knew the Savanir's faith in Arun and the prophecy. The entire Dawn would soon be mobilized for war, and he and a lone Dwarf were hoping to rob Bälech in one of the strongest prisons just outside his own capital.

Truth Unearthea

As the gray light of morning began to soften the stars still illuminating overhead, they pulled up for a rest. But they did not set up camp. They did not need the delay of preparing or taking down their tent or packing up their supplies.

"Your turn to sleep my friend," Athaz said to Kruthos. "I need to think, and even Dwarves must tire eventually."

"They do," admitted Kruthos. Pulling a single blanket to throw down over the dew-laden grass, the Dwarf threw himself to the ground and was soon snoring heavily.

And so they alternated for the next two full days, pausing only every eight hours to alternate the member that would rest for four. When it was Athaz's turn to stand guard, his mind would race with thoughts of their goal, but it only served to frustrate him, which in turn caused him to scold himself. He had been on many campaigns and fretting over circumstances you could not control only made it more likely you would be overwhelmed by them. He had been in tight situations before, and a combination of levelheadedness and (he had to admit) occasionally luck had kept him alive. But this was different. He had lost his fear of death early in his youth. Indeed, there had been times he had selfishly desired for it to come. But he also knew this was different. If he failed, it wasn't his life or even the lives of his men that he was worried about. It was the only two people left in the world whose cries could still tear at his soul. He wished that Kruthos would return home to Menigar if asked, but he knew asking would only anger the Dwarf.

If Kruthos was to be believed, most Dwarves felt he yielded too easily. "Clayish," they called him; it was because of this Kruthos had often mediated between Dwarves in disputes between his people and the Elves or Men in Menigar. If Kruthos was clayish, Athaz wondered how the Lady Lyr, even with her wisdom, persuaded them when they didn't agree with her council.

At the end of the second full day since the two had fled Mizcur after alerting the Savanir to the plight of Arun and Baran, Athaz and Kruthos had finally reached the western bank of the Grigor River. Their captors still had not caught up to them. Moving up stream about a mile, they found a wide area where the current weakened.

Quickly chopping down a couple of shurbs nearby, they tied their luggage to the broken bushes to help keep their baggage dry and not weigh them down as they swam around.

"Guess this is where we part with our four-legged friends," Kruthos said.

Athaz nodded. "Yah!" cried Athaz as he slapped them both on the backside, sending them running south along the bank. "Eventually they will return to Mizcur, where they still believe home is, but hopefully they will at least keep the soldiers from following us immediately."

Kruthos nodded. "I'll go on ahead first. I'm sure your experience in trailing is much better than mine." Tying his axes on top of his baggage, he pushed out half of the sparse goods they had with them and waded out into the bank, swimming toward the far shore.

Athaz did his best to hide their footprints. Ideally, he would have dug up the stumps from the bushes, but with no time to do that, he would have to pray they didn't think too deeply on the issue. Placing his Dwarven zweihänder on top of his baggage as Kruthos had done with his axes, Athaz swam out into the river.

Once they had reached the other side, they quickly made their way up and out of sight and into the mountains' knees. Finding a spot they could look over and see the river, they cast off their clothes to dry as much as they could in the cool night. At least they could dry their bodies with blankets; hiking the mountains would be a challenging enough task without the pain of raw skin with every step.

It was Kruthos' turn to watch, though they would both rest before setting off again. Now hidden in the mountains, there was no need to constantly travel exhausted, to the point of collapse. He was to wake Athaz in six hours.

Five hours into his watch, as Kruthos sat huddled under a blanket to keep warm as his clothes were stretched out over a nearby rock, he heard voices across the river. Peeking over, he saw as their pursuers had caught up to where they had crossed the river. Only one was carrying a torch, making it impossible to get a rough count. But then more lights shone out as several of the men lit their own torches. Kruthos counted at least a dozen soldiers. Xiarch save them if they did not follow the horses!

For the next ten minutes, every passing second felt like an eternity. The soldiers were all scanning the ground. They were obviously puzzled. No doubt they had seen the horses' prints heading back down south. It begged the question of why they had been heading north to begin with. Eventually Kruthos watched as every soldier he could see remounted their horses, following the river south at walking pace.

With his watch nearly over, he decided to wake Athaz.

"It's a little early," he said apologetically, "but our pursuers seem to have taken the bait. They were obviously puzzled, though, so I thought it might be good for us both to stand ready for the next half hour or so."

Athaz grunted and sat up, wrapping the blanket around him as he stumbled out of the tent. They did not say anything, lest a soldier had crossed and could overhear them. It seemed Athaz's skill and the aid of night had been enough. Confident they were safe and ready for his six hours, Kruthos went in the tent and immediately fell asleep.

Athaz began humming a tune to himself. Looking at the stars above had brought back a bittersweet memory. Or rather, the memory was sweet, but it pained him to think of it now. It took him a few tries before he got the notes right; it had been several years since he had let himself remember happy thoughts with his family. It was an old folk song of a warrior who pledged his undying vow to the maiden he loved before he marched to war to protect their lands. It had been nothing more than a foolish attempt at romance the first time he sang it to Lilleth, after they had moved to Hilae when he had become a Warden. It had caused his first unpleasant encounter with the Watchers, and he had not permitted himself to sing it often since then. Though the notes may have taken some time to come back to him, the lyrics were imprinted on his heart as they were on the day he had naively sang them to his young wife - the words of a warrior promising to return home. He had been a fool in those days, but at least he had been sincere.

Long after he reached the end of the song and was silent, Athaz still continued staring northward, remembering on that night how he had comforted her, somehow assured her he would be there. But the warrior in the song had charged headlong into battle to protect their home. Now home was the very place that sought to destroy Lilleth, and he had not been there. He had never been there, it seemed. What had they told her? Would they still tell his family he had died in disgrace for failure? Or had they condemned him as a traitor? There would be no end to the lies and deception they might tell her to justify their actions against her and their son. If he had been beside her all these years, she would know he had never ceased loving her, would never have done anything to put her in jeopardy. But he hadn't. What he would not give for one more tender embrace from her! To see his son as a proud young man, not a disgraced prisoner for the life and failures of his father.

"Perhaps," he began to hope but shook the silly thought free before it could take form. But whether there was hope or not, he knew one thing for sure: Bälech would not have them! Looking at the sky, he knew he still had maybe four hours left before it was time to wake Kruthos. When they finally set off, he would be putting the fabled stamina of Dwarves to the test.

* * * * * * * * *

Athaz roused the sleeping Dwarf. "Think you can keep up with me today?" Athaz grinned when he said it, but there was a fire burning in his eyes that did not escape the Dwarf. "I'll certainly try, but you look ready to outrun the wind." The smile disappeared as the fire in Athaz's eyes roared into an inferno. "Only wings could add to my speed."

They set off at once. Athaz turned just deep enough into the mountains to keep the river, and thus themselves, out of sight. At one point the Briarthorn Mountains had been the center of a Dwarven kingdom. Though Athaz's pace was tireless, there was no way to quickly crawl and scramble over the stones that barred their path. Stones of any significant height where there was nothing

Truth Unearthea

near at hand to climb forced the pair to search for a way around; the stones' smooth surface offered no place to grip, not even for the clever hands of a Dwarf.

On the third day since abandoning the horses at the river's edge, the sun was obscured by dark clouds. By noon it was raining. At first, this was a blessing. The water rushed down into tiny streams that allowed Athaz and Kruthos to refill their water skins. But soon the rain had become a downpour, and the tiny streams that had restocked their water now formed treacherous rivers. They had to stop and find high ground as the water pooled in the ravines and rushed in faster than it could leave on its westward course to the Grigor River.

The next few days, their progress was even slower. Some of the water had collected in basins, forming pools that forced them on an even more meandering route as they traveled north as best they could. A week passed. Already they would have passed Hilae easily if they had not needed to stay hidden in the mountains. Even so, Athaz knew they must be nearing the northern edge of the Briarthorn Mountains. The water pools were becoming fewer and fewer as the water found drains to escape through or evaporated. As good of news as this might seem, it actually presented a problem. Their water was running low again, and they would need to refill their skins soon. Doing so this close to Hilae risked exposure. Watchers always kept a lookout on the land surrounding Hectare's capital.

On the eighth night, they discussed it over dinner. The question was when and where they could refill their skins one final time as far from Hilae as possible without having to go back down to the Grigor until they were a safe distance passed Hilae. Of course, they didn't know their location perfectly. Athaz reckoned they were less than two days away from the capital. Kruthos pointed out it would be better to go too far and then backtrack a bit before drawing water than to go too soon. But they were already dangerously low on water. They finally decided to go one more day before turning down the western slopes.

The day was nearing its end, and they saw no sign of the capital.

The Tales of Lugon

The mountains' western end seemed to be constantly getting closer, hinting that they were indeed nearing their northern edge. Suddenly, they came to a clearing of sorts. Kruthos stopped walking, a look of awe on his face. He thought all of his peoples' ancient history had been beaten down and washed away long ago. But there was no doubt about it. There was still evidence of a road here, pieces of broken stone surrounding larger ones in their center, evidence he knew to be of the ancient Dwarven kingdom that once called this land home. Kruthos' stop caused Athaz to pause and turn to his companion. He was getting impatient, but he immediately stopped his rebuke as he saw the look of love and anguish in the Dwarf's eyes.

"Go on ahead, Athaz," the Dwarf said as tears began to well up unbidden. "I shall not tarry long. No Dwarf could forgive himself if he did not take a moment to remember his ancestors and the greatest achievement of his people."

Athaz looked up at the sky, which had begun darkening some time ago; there was perhaps only half an hour of daylight left. Any more and he would have pressed on as Kruthos had told him, but as it was they would have to stop to make camp soon.

"I will go the western edge of the circle," he answered. "But we shall make camp here, and you will tell me of this place. For I see in your eyes a love that I have not seen since Menigar, only now it is far stronger, but there is also a deep sorrow." With that he turned to let his friend take in the wonder that he himself was blind to.

Kruthos did not come until the darkness had settled for a full hour. "We should both sleep tonight … and long. We will need it for the days ahead. My ancestors' spirits are deep in the rocks here, and the preservation of this place is proof of it. I have heard you Men say that a piece of your soul went into your work; it is a nice sentiment, as far as it goes for your kind. But it is an actual fact for Dwarves when they work. And this was the most significant piece of work for countless Dwarves for several generations. It is a testament to their power that, so close to Bälech's dwelling, the place has been preserved at all. No evil thing will disturb this hallowed ground unless the Evil One himself accompanies them.

Truth Unearthea

We are surrounded by the ruins of Kelbragh. And I now know where we are. We are in its capital city of the same name, only a few hours' march from the northern edge, back when there were roads. We will be within sight of Hilae long before sundown tomorrow."

Kruthos knew the history as well as the sad story of its downfall. He told Athaz some of it that night. The entire record of that great civilization was in the tomes in the Library of Menigar (for those that take the time to decipher the ancient Dwarves tongue), but recorded here is only a short recount of what Kruthos told Athaz:

Millennia ago, before Lugon knew of Bälech, the Cruach Dwarves came to the Grigorian Plateu, a huge stone mesa that forced the Grigor River coming from the north to the east as it continued its southward journey to the Meridonian Sea. There was little soil above the rock, and it presented a unique opportunity: to create an above ground Dwarven kingdom. The Cruachs had always been fascinated by the beauty of the woods, and here they saw a chance carve out trees from the bedrock of the earth itself. Carving the treetops first, the Dwarves burrowed to find their forest floor, fashioning branches, some of which became bridges between the trunks of the trees, on the way down. The Kingdom of Kelbragh, The Stone Forest, over the centuries flourished in beauty, trees inlaid with blossoms of pearls and emerald leaves in the spring and rubies and yellow amethysts to create fall colors. Bark comprised of streams of silver ran up and down the trunks and branches. Kelbragh, the only open-air Dwarven kingdom, became their crowning jewel.

Its fall preceded even the coming of Bälech. For Bälech had not assaulted a world united but a fractured one, where not only the three Noble Races no longer stood together, but nations within each race distrusted and fought one another. A great war between the Dwarves had left the nation desolate. The majestic trees, toppled and broken, became a mere collection of crisscrossed thorns. The silver and gems were looted over the course of centuries thousands of years ago, and even their veins had been smoothed by countless rains and many centuries of wind.

"It is a pity our ancestors warred with one another," Athaz

noted. "Bälech might have been defeated before he ever rose to power."

"That," Kruthos agreed, "is certain. If ever he does fall, it will be of great importance to remember it. Bälech is merely the instrument, but we wrought our own ruin. I only hope we have become wiser after our long time of suffering." His face clouded. "But I doubt it."

It was more than a sobering thought. Dwelling on it, Athaz almost for a moment felt the despair that naturally accompanied it. But there was too much at hand to worry about the fate of the world and its future. The force that was driving him now was the force that has driven all peoples to continually push on toward their uncertain futures — the pressing needs of those they cared about in the present. The future would have to wait. His family called him onward for now.

The next morning, Athaz woke to find Kruthos already up, breakfast cooked, and gear being packed. "Too overwhelmed to sleep?" he asked his friend.

"Far from it," Kruthos responded. "I slept more soundly than ever in my life; I could literally feel my ancestors surrounding me, as I will one day surround those that come after me. I feel more rested than I would after a week in my own bed. It only made sense to let you rest while I got things ready."

Athaz ate his breakfast while Kruthos stowed away the blankets and made final preparations. But as he bent over, Athaz saw something barely sticking out past the Dwarf's beard. He didn't get a good look at its design, but he recognized the material. It was *lucarum*. In appearance, it had the beauty of pure gold, only richer, with a stronger red-amber appearance. But whereas gold was soft and malleable, *lucarum* was hard and brittle like iron. It was rare, and only the greatest jewel crafters were even able to lay their hands on the precious metal. Fewer could do anything with it. "Where did you find *that*?"

A fierce jealousy leapt into the Dwarf's eyes, but it only appeared for a moment. "You recognize it?"

"I have only seen anything like it once before, inlaid in Bälech's signet ring."

Kruthos spat in disgust. "The ring belonged to the Elven lord, fashioned here in these very mountains. Only Dwarves have ever shown the skill to shape *lucarum*. Needless to say, we never fashioned anything for him. He took possession of that ring in the Fall of Lacris. This piece..." Kruthos gestured to necklace "... was likely nothing more than a favored necklace by a noble lady of Kelbragh. But," he said as he heaved his pack on his back and extended a hand to help Athaz to his feet, "the fact that such a treasure has lain buried for so long until we should pass this way, I will take as a token that better days are dawning for my people."

After a brief moment where he seemed indecisive, he lifted the chain from his neck and presented to Athaz. Whether it was the spirit of its crafter or some art long lost, the thread that held the pieces of *lucarem* together was still in tact. The shapes were that of leaves and berries, fitting for the kingdom Kruthos spoke of the night before. The detail captivated Athaz. Strokes finer than he had believed possible were cut into the necklace for veins.

"A simple design for its time, which is why I believe it to have no greater lineage. Even for a master craftsman, shaping *lucarem* is no easy feat. A member of the chieftain's family commissioning the piece might be willing to pay for multiple attempts, but for a jeweler working on his own, it was best to remember the main value was in the metal itself."

Athaz gave the necklace back to the Dwarf. "I hope you are right about this omen, my friend. But for now we must make haste. We have stayed too long. And we still have the water to fetch."

Kruthos smiled. "That won't take as long as you think."

Kruthos took Athaz about half a mile back toward the center of city ruins of Kelbragh. There was some broken stone in what used to be a circle, but was half caved in. "This is the Kopahain, the ancient well of the Cruach Dwarves. The well reaches deep into a river that runs underneath the mountains. To drink from it is to partake of the strength of the mountains themselves. I have already drunk from it, and we shall now fill our skins and take the ancient strength of my people with us."

The Tales of Lugon

If Athaz had wondered about Kruthos' tale of the Dwarves ancestors pouring their spirits into their work before, they were removed. First the necklace and now this. The well should have been unusable eons ago. But the stone crank and bucket were still attached to the rope. What Kruthos had said about Dwarves pouring themselves into their work, was most clearly demonstrated in the rope, and Athaz gazed in wonder at it. The braided fibers were not plant matter but hair, Dwarven hair. Whether the spirit of the Dwarves that had made the rope or some other magic imbued it, Athaz did not know, but there was a great Power that kept the rope as strong as the day it was attached to the well.

Athaz waited patiently as Kruthos filled their skins. There was no need to tell him it was no place for Man to claim the water from the well. When Kruthos was finished, he pulled the bucket back to the top of the crank and placed a rock at its handle to keep it from falling.

After a brief silence, he said, "When I bring back word of the Kopahain with this necklace, the Dwarves will come back to the surface to attempt to reclaim this land, even if it means the end of our people."

"Will you tell them and risk that?" Athaz asked.

"If I survive this venture," Kruthos answered, "I will have no choice. To keep such a secret would be a greater treason than to take up arms against them." Kruthos looked over the ruins in silence one more time. "Alright, let's get your family," he said as he turned eastward.

For the next week, their trek through the mountains continued as it had before they found the ruined capitol of Kelbragh. However, now there was the added fear of accidentally straying too far north. Exposing themselves to the eyes on the walls of Hilae would doom them, but turning too far to the south in these mountains could add a day or more to their travels. Already, Athaz feared they had taken too long. It had been several weeks since they set out from Menigar, and there was no way of knowing how long his family had been imprisoned before that. Also, they were already deep into autumn, and the nights were beginning to get cold. And then there was the issue of water. They were already rationing it to keep from needing to return to the banks of the Grigor until Hilae was safely behind them.

At night, they would discuss their plans for getting into The Tennebron and locating Athaz's family. They did not discuss escape. "I'll get us out," was all Kruthos would say. And Athaz was content to leave it at that. Chances were they wouldn't reach the escape phase. If they did…well, after the display at Mizcur, Athaz had no doubts the Dwarf could cut off their pursuers. The only question would be if only their pursuers would be dead when he was finished.

On the eighth day, they turned northward. By nightfall, they were able to look out to the west. All was clear. They probably could have turned back toward this river a day earlier at least. They could just make out where the river bending to the south as it sloped away from them. The Tennebron would be reached in less than two days' time if they walked along the banks of the Grigor. But at last the debate they had carried on for the past week must be concluded. Did they want to come down on The Tennebron directly from the west by going through the mountains and try to scale down the mountain, or would they march around in the foothills and try to find a way past the wall?

"It's like choosing which axe your executioner will swing," Kruthos said in a mirthless chuckle.

"Not quite," Athaz responded. "We'll get a chance to run if, by some miracle, he misses. Nothing forcing us to stay behind and wait for him to try again."

Kruthos thought for a moment. "My Divine abilities could get you either in or out, but not both. If we climb down the mountain, I can move the stone and earth to gain entry, killing a lot of them in the process. But immediately the entire guard will be mobilized. They probably know your new face by now, and they'll know where to trap us, and we won't be able to get out. We'll have enemies on all sides. But if we choose to try to sneak in —"

"We might be able to reach my family before anyone knows

what's going on," Athaz interrupted. "And if we manage to reach them, they'll be forced to chase us because there is no obvious place we'd make for to try to escape."

"Exactly," Kruthos said. "And I can cut them off from one direction, just not every direction at once."

And so it was settled. They would try to sneak around the foothills to gain entry. Neither one spoke of the tremendous amount of luck it would take to find his family quickly enough. There was nothing that could change that.

The two companions trudged up and down the foothills, following the curve of the Briarthorn Mountains. On the first day, no one would have guessed they both knew it was likely their final full day in this world. They spoke casually, not in hushed whispers, of good memories and future plans. Indeed, when the conversation occasionally turned toward what lay ahead of them, the change in tone mirrored the intense anticipation in their eyes. Athaz, of course, was eager to search for his family. But Kruthos' fire came from another source: revenge.

For millennia, the Dwarves had been hiding for the survival of their race. But never in all that time had they forgotten what drove them underground. Bälech, of course, had been the mastermind, but it was the Savage Races that had laughed even as they climbed over the corpses of their own kind to continue the slaughter of the Dwarves during their final stands. The Giants were most abominable to Dwarves, meant to mock their very identity. But the Orcs were almost equally hated, for it was their cruelly imaginative weapons that killed them thousands at a time, or slowly tortured those who were captured. Kruthos had not told Athaz about the uproar his departure had caused. For no Dwarf had been above ground for more than a day or two, and never far, until he accompanied Athaz.

Now that the enemy knew of the prophecy and of Arun, there was no longer a need to be secret. Instead, he planned to make sure his presence was felt. If they knew he acted alone, all the better. Let them fear what one Dwarf would do, so that when Bälech drove them into Menigar, or any other stronghold that housed his people, the terror of what awaited them would make them weaker.

When it was time to make camp for the night, they retreated into the foothills. They lit no fire, but set no watch. They both would need to be at full strength. Prudence could no longer help them. They placed their trust in Luck now. As they prepared their supper and beds, their casual manner at last faded. Eating in silence, they both were mentally preparing themselves for what awaited them tomorrow. Sleep found Kruthos first; Athaz stared passed the stars in thought. *Too late*, the whispers in his mind tormented him. *Even alive ... too late!* Tossing and turning, he finally found an uneasy sleep.

CHAPTER XVI

The Tennebron

Kruthos also was up first, shortly after the sun had risen. He prepared a small breakfast for himself and Athaz, who woke just as the Dwarf was finishing up. After they had both eaten and packed everything away, they began the final stretch toward The Tennebron. It was near noon when they stopped for what would likely be their last rest. They only drank some water before refilling their canteens. Knowing the price of rounding the final corner in view of an ancient Orc stronghold, they turned into the foothills. It was only an hour later when they began hearing the sounds they had been anticipating for so long: The Tennebron's din comprised of commanders' harsh orders, the agonizing cries of slaves under their burdens or the whips of their tormentors, and a dozen other sounds creating a symphony of suffering that never ceased.

Suddenly another sound, clearer and nearer, but by no means less ugly rose above the unending, miserable sounds of the prison. It was that of Goblins speaking ... or trying to at least. It was only a few, no more than four Athaz reckoned. The hills made it difficult to tell the exact direction, but they were both sure it was to their right, in the direction of the mountains — and The Tennebron.

There was nothing to do but engage them. Trying to sneak around the hills would just likely end up causing them to be spotted. Plus, four Goblins were a small threat in combat, provided you were looking at them. Anyone, even Goblins, can stab a foe in the back. Athaz unshouldered his zweihänder as Kruthos readied his combat axes. Slowly making their way toward the voices, as best they could while avoiding the hilltops, they eventually spotted the Goblins on top of one of the hills.

"Leave one alive," Athaz whispered. "I have a plan."

Kruthos nodded. Seeing the Goblins facing northward, they

crept their way to the southern side. With a final nod to each other, they silently climbed the slope. The massive strength of the Dwarf was enough that even his one-handed axe managed to unseat a Goblin's head from its shoulders at the same time Athaz's sword impaled the nearest Goblin in the back. The first two Goblins fell without knowing what hit them, but the dying bark of Athaz's target alerted his companions to their danger. Not even taking the time to remove his sword from the felled Goblin, Athaz leapt and tackled another as he tried to flee, while Kruthos had never stopped his initial run over the hill and easily overtook his target before he could get up to full speed.

Athaz had his hands full, dodging the Goblin's teeth and keeping its hands away from his weapons while trying to avoid killing him. He yelled to his companion, "Finish yours off. This will be our captive." The Goblin's shriek was cut short as Kruthos' axe came across its throat.

"Take his arms for me," Athaz told Kruthos. The Goblin snapped his jaws at his new captor, but Athaz's hands were now free and he gave the Goblin a punch to the ribs. "*Okh!*" he commanded, using the Orcish word for "no." Goblins had no speech of their own, but they have a rudimentary understanding of basic commands of their Orc or Giant masters. The Goblin stopped and stared at Athaz, a look of dumb confusion plastered on his face.

Athaz had Kruthos stand the Goblin up. After binding his wrists and arms behind his back, Athaz gagged the Goblin to ensure he remained quiet. "Alright, let's go," he said to Kruthos. "And release our prisoner, push him in front of you, and he'll walk between us."

Kruthos was perplexed but did as he was told. Athaz headed back toward the river. They hadn't taken ten paces when the Goblin bolted back toward the mountains, slowed by the odd balance caused by his bindings. It was at this point Kruthos understood and laughed.

"I'm not sure if I should be more amazed at your cleverness or his idiocy," the Dwarf said as they turned to feign chase.

Athaz shrugged. "They are little more than beasts. The truth is, I have always pitied them. They are violent creatures by nature, but their cowardice and stupidity would make them rarely a threat to anyone but themselves if it weren't for the other races that control them."

"A twisted nature ..." Kruthos was about to begin another sermon against Bälech and his breeding of the Savage Races, but Athaz stopped him. It probably wouldn't have taken the Goblin twenty minutes at full speed to reach his destination, but with his current situation, it was much slower going. This was only hampered by his fear and panic as he would occasionally stumble. Even Kruthos began to feel that maybe Athaz was right for pitying the creature. Not only had he been foolish enough to try to escape, but he hadn't been able to figure out that they were not trying to catch him, even with all of his stumblings, which sometimes took a while to recover from when he landed in a valley and could not use his hands to get up. Even in his panic, the Goblin would occasionally slow from exhaustion. But finally, over an hour later, Athaz and Kruthos knew they were getting close. A large mountain was looming in the distance, and the sounds of The Tennebron were growing ever clearer, but the most conclusive sign was that the wretched creature was now attempting to call for help through his gag. They closed the distance between them and their guide; the gag wouldn't stop him from alerting others once they were close enough. If seen, it wouldn't help at all.

Coming over the last hill, they saw what the Goblin was heading for: the opening of a tunnel in the base of the mountain. Athaz finally put the creature out of his misery. They had found what they dared not hope for until now. The Tennebron had a back door.

Athaz and Kruthos charged for the tunnel. There were sure to be guards, and they would have no way of knowing if any ran to raise the alarm before they tried sneaking in. "Let me go in first and follow a few seconds later," Kruthos said over his shoulder as he kicked his run into a higher gear. Athaz acknowledged he understood and began making for the side of the mountain next to the tunnel as Kruthos charged into the darkness.

Athaz immediately heard Orc voices crying in shock and alarm and soon heard steel clanging against steel and instantly knew that Kruthos' axes had found their mark by the duller thud of the axe against bone under flesh. He soon followed in.

Two feet into the cave the tunnel took a left turn, and his eyes saw only three torches floating in a sea of black. But judging by the sounds of the fighting, and only hearing one voice other than his friend's, Athaz had an idea. Loudly unsheathing his sword, he cried, "Death comes from behind!"

The Orc tried to roll away from his current opponent and take up a new position to cover his flank, but Kruthos was too quick for him. Diving toward the Orc, one axe found the Orc's back and the other came on top of his helmet, splitting it and cracking the skull, leaving the Orc senseless. By this point, Athaz's eyes had adjusted enough to the darkness to administer the coup de grâce.

"Well fought, my friend!" Scouring the Orcs' bundles didn't yield much, just some old bread as well as some meat they didn't dare take with them. As guards for The Tennebron, there was a high chance it was the flesh of Men. Eventually, though, Kruthos did find something that might be of use: a scroll. He unfurled it, hoping for a map.

"Find something?" Athaz asked.

"Nothing of use, it appears. I was hoping it was a map, but it's just script," Kruthos responded.

Athaz came over and looked as he could read some of the Orc language. "I see nothing, but that is unsurprising for me in this light. Let me take it to the entrance." Athaz returned very shortly. "It's a guard rotation schedule. The good news is that a shift had just started an hour ago, so we aren't likely to run into many moving companies. And, at least for now, we don't need a map. Only one path to follow. Twice your Dwarven eyes have proven their superiority underground. Lead on, friend!"

They made their way slowly to keep their noise to a minimum. The tunnel ascended steeply into the dark. There were small patches where Athaz couldn't see the floor underneath him between the great gaps between the torches that provided the sparse lighting. It was only just big enough for Giants to walk through single file without constantly ducking, yet when they came this way they often had a knot or two on their heads by the end of it. Though it was only just big enough to serve its purpose, the only thing the companions had to watch was their footing because of the crude, hastily cut floor. For fifteen minutes, they heard and saw nothing. Kruthos nervously ran his fingers up and down his axes. Athaz, though less fidgety, strained his ears for any threat. It was a prison; guard duty certainly centered on keeping people *in* rather than out, but this was uncanny.

In truth, the Orcs had become lax, neglecting their duties that they did not enjoy. The guards at the back door were primarily there for show. The only thing they really kept an eye out for were the Watchers or occasionally even the Emperor himself. *He* usually came to the front gate with pomp. It was the Watchers who particularly enjoyed the opportunity to catch the Orcs in their laziness. The Orcs that were caught soon learned there were others experts in different forms of torture than their own kind. When a visitor was seen to be on his way, one of the guards would rush back to "sound the alarm" and everyone made a great show of being industrious. The illusion would be kept up for about a week afterward. The work itself ceased the moment their guests left. But one mustn't think the Orcs of The Tennebron were lazier than the raiding parties that tormented the Savanir. In fact, the Orcs of the Tennebron invented more tools for the use of torture used by their kin than any other Orc population. Indeed, they were the envy of all their brethren, though not for their creativity. As the jailers for the most notorious prison in The Dawn, they were incredibly well-provided for and didn't need to fight and plunder to sate their hunger — in addition to more base desires.

It was thanks to this idleness that in just under an hour of climbing up the tunnel that Athaz and Kruthos found themselves looking at a stone blocking their path. On the other side of the stone, they at last heard the sound of guards talking. Athaz and Kruthos spoke softly.

"Well, do you want me to move the stone before the guards can react but create a crash loud enough to wake the dead? Or would you prefer me to try a longer command that will cause the stone to crumble and risk the guards overhearing it and running off before we can enter the room?" Kruthos asked. Athaz paced back and forth as he mulled over which was less likely to end their mission before it had really begun in earnest. The biggest problem was that they still did not know where his family was being kept or how to get there.

"Quickly, we'll have to risk the noise," Athaz finally responded. "Those inside may shrug off an unexpected noise they only hear once. But there is no way they'll ignore a warning from a fleeing guard."

Kruthos nodded. "Anything else you need to prepare before I start? We're in this to the end once I start the Divine command."

"No," Athaz answered. "It's time."

Athaz couldn't hear the command Kruthos uttered; he had said it quietly to hide their presence up until the very last instant. The stone door leapt backwards, smacking the opposite wall before falling to the ground. Before the stone ever landed, Athaz's zweihänder had found its way through the neck of the guard he could see from the aft side of the doorway, leaving him unable to scream. Immediately releasing his sword, he stepped past the doorway and turned to tackle the other guard before it realized the situation. Quickly, Athaz's hands found the Orc's throat, throttling and stifling any cries for help. The Orc was flailing wildly, trying to grab Athaz's face, poke his eyes … anything to escape his demise. But by now Kruthos had entered the prison and planted his axe deep in the creature's skull, ending its struggle.

Looking around, they didn't see any sign that their entrance had caught the attention of anyone else in the prison. They quickly pulled the bodies back deep into the tunnel in the direction they had come. Then they took in their surroundings.

They were in the main part of the prison now, but apparently this way was seldom used. They could turn to the left or right, but could not go straight ahead. Though still crude stonework, these were true halls, wide and with sure, if plain, footing. There were even signs hanging overhead. Signs! And script! Reading the script of the one to the right as they had come in, he slowly translated the scribbling. "Prison Barracks, Yard, and Quarry: Dissenters, Doubters, Disappointments."

"Not that way," Athaz muttered under his breath. Going to other sign, he read. "Officers' Quarters, His Excellency's Quarters, The Breaking Rooms." At the final words, Athaz's vision flew back to the Orc whose mind he had read months ago, when he, Arun, and Baran had just set out from Hilae. Memories of the Orc came flooding back. He had been stationed here, and the Breaking Rooms were the place where all those horrors that had caused him to lose control that night had taken place. In a panic, Athaz ran as fast as he could while keeping his noise to a minimum, and Kruthos quickly followed. That would be the place the family of a traitor was taken. Try as he might, he couldn't stave off the thoughts of his family suffering as those he had seen in the Orc's mind. Without realizing it, he had broken into a full sprint.

"Athaz. ATHAZ!" Kruthos yelled hoarsely, grabbing his companion by the arm. "The terrors in your mind will continue if you get yourself caught!"

Athaz's eyes returned the world in front of him, and he breathed heavily. "Thank you," he said without looking back and continued at a brisk but quiet pace.

Their progress was severely slowed when they approached the Officers' Quarters. They passed the first two, hardly daring to breathe, even though the doors were shut and they heard nothing. The third door was not shut. An Orc had taken a captive to his own chambers for his depraved fantasies. Kruthos felt sick leaving the poor woman to her torments. The knowledge that saving all the prisoners was impossible did little to ease his conscience. Worse yet, from that point on, they were forced to stop at each door and listen. Each room presented new auditory horrors with the Orcs' limitless depravity and imagination. Cries and howls that no living creature naturally knew how to form comprised the language of this living hell. But Athaz never heard the voices of those he was looking for.

A sign pointing around the corner read "Breaking Rooms." Rounding the corner, Athaz stopped so quickly that Kruthos jerked to the side to pass him instead of running into him. It was like staring into a mirror that showed both past and present: a young man with long blond hair but the gray eyes of his mother, whose motionless body he was now carrying, stood before them. "Caedin!" Athaz gasped. The boy took a quick hard look at the man he knew must be his father before sprinting right past him, revealing the five Orcs that were escorting them back to their cell.

A raw, primal hatred that blinded Athaz to all things past and future engulfed him. All he saw were the cruel eyes of his family's tormentors, their faces still frozen in their hideous laughter that had paused in slight confusion when the young man took off.

"DAMNATION AND DARKNESS TAKE YOU ALL!" Athaz roared.

With a strength he had never possessed even as a Warden, Athaz lunged forward, split the first Orc in twain from head to navel. Before the corpse could fall, he kicked it off his sword and spilled the guts of the second that did not back away in time, leaving him mortally wounded before his comrade's body had even hit the ground. Kruthos, axe in hand, suddenly pulled back. Nobody in this Man's path was going to survive the onslaught. Turning, he saw that Caedin hadn't stopped running. "Caedin!" he called as he started to follow him. Athaz needed no help in this fight.

The Orcs, though they possessed weapons, were not well-armored nor prepared for any sort of confrontation. For years they had been feeding their violent natures on helpless victims whose attempts at fighting back on occasion only broke up the monotony and added a bit of fun. But now they had a Man, whose age was more than offset by his experience, condition, and rage. Not even realizing they should turn and call for help, the remaining three formed a line across the passage and snarled as they ran toward their attacker and their doom. With another yell, Athaz drove his sword through the belly of the middle with enough force to send the Orc flying back several feet. Letting his sword fall with its victim, he pinned the Orc's arm to his right before its sword could make contact. Swinging the helpless Orc between himself and the last combatant, the final jailor unwittingly stabbed his comrade in the back. Easily removing the sword from the dying grip of the Orc that had served as his shield, Athaz threw the body out of his way and decapitated his final foe in a single swing.

Athaz retrieved his own sword from the belly of the Orc he felled earlier before turning back the way the way they had come. There, he saw Caedin still holding his mother's motionless body. Kruthos stood next to them. "We must be quick," Kruthos urged. "I can stop the pursuit if we can get back to the tunnel leading to the back door, but there'll be no sneaking around now."

Athaz looked at his wife as his son held her. He couldn't tell if her slight movements were her own breaths or just the movements caused by Caedin's trembling muscles and labored breathing. "Is she …"

"She lives, for a little longer anyway," was the cold, curt reply. "If you get her outside to see the open sky one more time it will be more than either of us thought you'd do to ease our pain." The words cut, but there was no time to respond.

Kruthos led the way, hacking at any Orcs that peeked out of their rooms to see what all the commotion was about. Some were able to see it coming ahead of time and tried to lie in wait to attack Caedin and Lilleth. Those that did found Athaz ready for them as he brought up the rear. About halfway back up the passage, they heard horns blowing.

"There goes the last hope of the back passage not being held against us…" Kruthos muttered under his breath. As they turned the last corner, they found what they expected but had hoped would not be there. Ten Orcs already stood between them and the back passage, but fortunately some had been busy trying to get the stone back into place and had only just begun to lift it.

"Kruthos! Turn into the passage. Kill any you find and begin your command. Caedin, guard him from any that make it past me. Don't stop your command once you start. If I am left behind, so be it."

With that, Athaz sprinted forward to get in front and plow a way through for those behind him. Kruthos turned into the tunnel, followed by Caedin hunched over to protect his mother from any that tried to get past Athaz. There were no Orcs in the tunnel. They were too focused on trying to cut them off before they reached that point. Kruthos turned to face the door and put his hands on the ground, but he wasn't speaking.

"I don't know what he told you to do," Caedin growled, "but I can tell you're not doing it!"

Kruthos looked at the young man with eyes that could have cut through granite. "I'm not leaving him behind, no matter what he told me to do." With that he reached behind him and pulled out his combat axes. "If you want me to work on ensuring our escape, you go help bring him back. The two of you together should be able to work your way back here ... unless you wait for the rest of the guard to show up."

Caedin's snarl could have cowed a wolf, but he gently set his mother down before snatching the axes and sprinting up beside his father. "Fall back, you old fool!" he called as he came up to Athaz's right shoulder. "The Dwarf won't start unless you do!"

Swearing under his breath, Athaz began to step backwards as he continued to fight. Caedin's use of the axes was clumsy enough, but the few Orcs that got close were off-balance from dodging the great sword and made an easy target.

When they had taken only five steps into the cave, a sudden shaking knocked all parties off their feet. The ground directly in front of the passage's opening shot up, hitting the roof of the main passage with a thunderous clap that cut off the terrified screams of the Orcs. One Orc had managed to get inside the passage. Realizing his doom was upon him, he made a lunge at what he hoped would be the easiest kill ... the unconscious woman lying on the floor. Simultaneously, father and son fell upon him with a yell of savage fury, the Orc's severed arm falling well short of its target but much closer than the rest of him that Athaz had stabbed against the floor, dead.

"That should hold them for a bit," Kruthos said. Looking over at Lilleth, though, any mirth he had faded. "Come, let's get out of this place."

Athaz tenderly picked up his wife. Caedin burned at the sight, but he said nothing as he walked beside them, and Kruthos led the way. It wasn't much faster than their entrance, between the unsure footing, dim lighting, and Athaz's precious burden, but at long last they made it out. It was the middle of the night, most likely another three hours before dawn.

"We must tend to her now," Athaz said as he set Lilleth down gently on the grass. Only now was he able to see the horrors that had been wrought on her body. Broken bones that had mended amiss, only to be broken again. Burns everywhere. The rags offering little cover through the torn fabric. Tears of rage welled in his eyes as he uncorked his water skin and held it to her lips while cradling her head. Rage at the Orcs, yes. Even more rage at Bälech. But none of it could compare at the rage he felt toward himself.

Lilleth choked on the water, but it roused her. She began to eagerly drink, eyes still closed. Her breathing was ragged and thin. Kruthos turned and walked some distance away. Not even with the finest physician's in Menigar would this woman survive for much longer, and he did not want to distract from what little time the broken family had left.

At last, Lilleth did open her eyes. She saw her son's face first and smiled. When she looked into Athaz's face, she stared for a long time without saying anything. With a faint groan, she reached for his shirt, trying to grasp it. Athaz immediately stripped to his torso, revealing the tattoo she had chosen long ago. She looked back into his face.

"I told you I would always remember," Athaz said softly as his voice broke. "Forgive me."

Lilleth was trying to speak, but was too weak to form the words. Bending down, Athaz heard her whisper. "Our son … is who … you owe … such words …" She took a few more breaths before continuing. "But you … have freed him. For that alone … all malice … is gone … for my part." "One more thing … I ask …" Athaz's eyes responded *anything*. "You … are not … blameless. But we …

Truth Unearthea

both ... have suffered ... much ... Mine ... ends ... soon." Athaz knew where this was going, but did not interrupt. "End ... *him*."

Pushing Athaz gently away, she grabbed her son's wrist and knelt down beside her. "Don't ... believe ... their lies. Try ... to forgive him ... in time."

"I'll try," Caedin said as he pressed his forehead against hers. After a few seconds, she reached for the water skin, and Athaz held her while she drank again. Suddenly, she laughed. It was weak, but there was wry smile on her face. "Athaz ..." she said quietly. He bent down beside her. "There was a night ... long ago ... when you held me ... and I looked up at the stars. Do you ... remember what I said?" Athaz couldn't stop his crying now. All he could do was nod. "I was right. I could. And it ... looks like I will." Athaz wept as he kissed her tenderly. When he pulled up, she turned to her son. "And ... with our son ... It is more than I had dared hoped for. Since that day ... *he* ... came into ... our lives."

She pulled her son close to them. She stopped talking and closed her eyes. For a few moments, she lay there, smiling. Suddenly, Athaz and Caedin realized her breathing had stopped. They wept.

Hearing the tears, Kruthos came back. "We must move. The blocked passageway will only buy us as long as it takes them to come around the mountains. Half a day at most."

"We will not leave her," Athaz said, holding a hand to silence Caedin's protest.

"Of course not," Kruthos said. "We make for Kelbragh, and my ancestors will guard her for countless more generations."

"Your people will allow it?" Athaz asked, caught between gratitude and skepticism.

"Not only will they allow it, when reclaimed, all will know her story. For without her, and you, Kelbragh might have been lost for another thousand years."

Athaz carefully covered Lilleth's body in one of his spare cloaks. Though it had been almost twenty-four hours, they did not stop to rest before beginning their journey. Athaz walked on, numb to all physical pain. When Caedin offered to carry her, Athaz shook his head. "As you carried her in life in my stead, I must at least carry her in death. But," he said as he looked at his son, "the honor of laying her to rest will be yours."

At about noon, they rested. Athaz and Caedin first while Kruthos kept watch. Five hours later, Kruthos roused Athaz. During his watch, Athaz did what little he could do to preserve Lilleth's body until they reached her burial site. Well into the night, he roused the others and they began their march again.

They made it back into the Briarthorn Mountains early into their second march. Without worrying about straying into unfriendly territory, Kruthos cut a path as straight as the terrain would allow for the ruined capital city of Kelbragh. After three days with short rest (which kept them moving during the day and resting at night), they were fairly certain that the pursuers had either given up or gone the wrong way; they most likely never suspected the party to travel so deep into the Briarthorn Mountains, which would be the longest and most difficult path to any known settlement. By the end of their fifth march, they had reached ruined city.

Kruthos led them to the structure where he had found the necklace. Stopping a few yards short of the entrance, he said, "Here, among my people, Lilleth shall sleep deeply and soundly, until the time where Men's souls shall leave Lugon."

Athaz laid his wife's body where Kruthos directed.

"We have no tools to bury her," Caedin said quietly.

"Follow me," Kruthos said.

They followed him north of the old home and soon were out of the ruins. Finding one of the "thorns" that Athaz now knew to be a fallen stone tree, Kruthos climbed on top. About fifteen feet from the tip, he stopped and placed his hands on the stone. From where they were, neither Athaz nor Caedin could hear him, but they knew he was speaking the Divine. A loud crack signaled he had finished. All the stone in front of him crumbled into broken pieces. Athaz went to pick up the first piece, but Caedin stopped him. Remembering his promise, Athaz nodded and walked back to his wife's body.

For most of the night, Caedin carried stone back and forth. His hands were bleeding and raw by the time he finished. When he was bringing the last stone, Kruthos came with him. "It's going to take all three of us to bring back her marker," he said.

They followed him back to where he had caused the stone to crumble. Athaz realized he cut some more stone from the source. Below, he found the headstone. It was three feet high, the surface slanting toward the viewer with its base. Its back was straight, forming a right angle to give it balance. Kruthos, in the manner of the Dwarves, had carved out the scene of the passing that the marker would honor: there was Lilleth, with Athaz and Caedin on either side of her, heads bowed. Lilleth's face was turned up towards the stars, which had not been forgotten. Athaz couldn't bring himself to say anything. All he could do was put his hand on Kruthos' shoulder for a moment before walking over help lift it.

It was not easily moved, and by the time they reached the grave, the sun was peeking between the peaks of the mountains. In the daylight, the level of detail Kruthos had put into the piece could finally be appreciated. All of their features had been captured with such precision that anyone who knew them would have recognized their likeness. Athaz also realized the stars formed musical notation, similar to the gates of Menigar.

When Athaz inquired about them, Kruthos replied, "It's the melody I heard you hum all throughout these mountains." Exhausted and needing shelter from the bright sun, the three of them went inside the ancient house and found a place to lay their blankets.

When they awoke, Caedin surprised both of them by announcing he planned to go his own way. "Mother told me to try to forgive you in time. For her sake, I acted as though I could. For her memory, I have kept my peace as we traveled to bury her. But a beautiful carving doesn't make its image any more representative of the truth. You don't even have any idea what she did to keep you in Bälech's good graces. And you still managed to screw it up. The family of a traitor—"

"It was *we* who were betrayed, son," Athaz interrupted. He couldn't fault Caedin for his anger, but he would not take the charge of traitor. "I gave my life for The Dawn. Though I didn't realize I was doing it until it was too late, I gave yours and your mother's as well. All with the thought that you and she would be protected from the fear and hunger we both knew before you were born.

"I'll own that I should have taken you and your mother and fled when you were still very young. Your mother pleaded with me to do so, once. I didn't listen. And by the light I have paid for it! By the time I realized my error, we could not flee. If hating me eases your own pain, I will bear that, but you will know the true traitor in all of this. And I promised your mother I would end him. And I mean to ensure it happens. I had hoped to keep you both safe, but now I see that cannot happen."

Caedin's rage had been building, and he was about to retort when Kruthos cut in, "Caedin, surely even you must realize that your life is in danger anywhere in The Dawn. Why not at least come to Menigar and think about your course of action?"

At the name "Menigar," Caedin quickly turned his gaze to the Dwarf, giving him a curious expression. It only lasted for an instant. So quickly did it disappear that Kruthos couldn't place it beyond shocked, but he felt uneasy.

Caedin walked up to his mother's grave, thinking about the offer. When he came back, he said, "I accept. But..." he looked at his father "...I will not travel with this man. Let me follow some distance behind you." It was an odd request, but there wasn't much they could do to persuade him, and Kruthos knew Athaz would rather have the odd arrangement than let his son return to Bälech's grasp.

"Stubborn, ungrateful, arrogant youth ..." Kruthos muttered under his breath, but all anyone heard was a curt, "Fine!"

Silently, they began their southward march, the mission ended.

CHAPTER XVII

A Long Journey with Few Steps

Baran quickly made his way up into the Makrin Mountains. He had to put as much distance between himself and Lamphine as quickly as possible. For two hours he climbed and ran, using the roots of trees to hide his footprints as often as he could. He thought of nothing except hiding from any pursuers that might be following him, pursuers he daren't take the time to find out if they even existed. If they caught up to him ... He thanked his luck that he hadn't dropped his sword in a panic. It was a miracle he had even freed it from the soldier's body.

At that thought, he suddenly stopped. Had he just killed a Man. Not a mindless Goblin or a vile Orc. A Man. Remembering how easily he had done it was unsettling, but easily explained. Arun was in danger. He had acted on instinct. He had always wanted to be a soldier to defend others. But that was back in Hilae, back when all he knew that existed outside of Dawn were the mad Bewildered or traitors that deserved the sword. But he had known many soldiers growing up in Hilae. Most had been good men with families. Baran was overcome with a desire to know the man's name. Was he married? A father? Who had he just killed?

He didn't have time to think about these things. He had to move. He managed to make his hands and feet focus on the task at hand, but not his mind. He banged his head repeatedly against unseen branches. Finally, he realized he needed to stop or he would have no idea where he was. Leaning against a tree, Baran composed his thoughts.

"Why do I feel so guilty when I was just trying to save my friend?" he asked himself. *"Was it because he probably was just someone serving his nation, someone that did not deserve to die?"*

Certainly that was part of it. He remembered how grateful he was he had learned of the Savanir before he had ever taken arms against them. *"I wanted to join the Savanir's army to help defend them. Even if I mainly fought Orcs, Goblins, and Giants, fighting The Dawn's soldiers would eventually be inevitable.* The thought stumped him for a while. Had he deceived himself? Had the dream of being a soldier simply been a boy's fantasy that wouldn't stand up in reality?

When the answer came it hurt much worse. *You didn't hesitate. And you won't hesitate next time. If someone tracking you came over this hill, you would run your sword through them on instinct again. You didn't think about the meaning of the life you ended until hours after the fact, even though the man lived the life you envisioned yourself leading. You killed a man that you, more than anyone, should have known was likely a good man. And it was easy.*

Baran felt sick, both at what he had done and how close he had been living a life of slaughtering the Savanir without even having a moment of remorse like the one he was having now.

But I do feel remorse, he realized.

This debate with himself wasn't over, but it was over for now. Water. Shelter. Food. Those were the things he needed most. Putting the alarming questions and rationalizations aside, Baran began thinking about the task at hand: survival. The Savanir would likely come looking for him eventually, and Arun wouldn't rest until they did. Looking around, Baran searched for the highest point nearby and began climbing. It was slow going; he had no climbing gear, and he didn't dare risk a fall of any considerable distance lest he break his leg, which would almost assuredly seal his fate.

After a couple more hours, he realized he wasn't reaching any higher than his current point. He turned around to look below. Baran faced the Argom River. "Not going down there again if I can help it." He attempted to circle the mountain near his present height to see the other side. It took a while. Even as high as he was, he wasn't anywhere near the peak, so it was a long way around. He had to be careful to avoid a steep fall. Some ledges he daren't risk and many he did were still narrow enough to warrant plenty of caution.

Truth Unearthea

At last a young but fairly large tree created an impasse so he could go no further around. At least he had made it to a point where he had a good view to the south. It was by now evening and the air was cold with a late autumn breeze, amplified by his damp clothes. His legs were raw now too. But most of all, he was exhausted. Scanning the valleys below, he noticed a little to the southeast that the vegetation was thicker than most of the other valleys. He sighed. It was a long way down, and he wasn't quite ready to get back to his feet again.

"Wait a minute!" he said aloud to himself. With nervous, excited laughter, he looked at the tree above next to him. Using his sword as a crude axe, Baran hacked off several branches. When he had a decent pile, he backed away a few feet and laid them down on the other side of him. It wouldn't do to set the whole tree on fire. Remembering every exact syllable he learned from the Lady Lyr, he placed his hands out in front of him, toward the bundle of limbs. "Fureigh san bor, ilum de pro!" A bolt of flame hit the branches. Yellow and brown leaves immediately curled up, and Baran laughed with wonder at this new power. This would make survival much easier! Quickly, he took off his clothes and encircled them around the fire to dry, sitting as close to it as he could stand.

After a few minutes of self-contentedly looking into the fire, Baran looked out over the Makrin Mountains again. Even as tired and distressed as he was, he couldn't help but notice the majesty before him. Even the power to summon fire at will seemed like nothing compared to the glory before him. With the sun setting in the west, each of the taller mountains displayed their glorious cliffs and trees laden with beautiful autumn foliage on one side while the other already slept in a peaceful night with their shorter brethren. Baran's thoughts turned to Descia. What was she doing right now? Probably throwing herself fully into studying the history of the Savanir since the inception of The Dawn. He wondered how often she stopped and thought of him? Knowing it was unlikely, he entertained the fantasy of taking her up here one day if they were ever able to walk freely in the open air again. He remembered from discussions in Menigar there was an outpost of Elves deep in the Forest of Orus. Perhaps they could start at Lamphine and leisurely make their way down so she could interview them about what it was like living as a hidden outpost of the Savanir out in the open air, as opposed to ancient Dwarven cities where most of the Savanir populace was hidden. Panicked, he reached inside the breast pocket of his inner shirt. Taking out the envelope, he knew the letter was almost certainly ruined, but he could still feel the jewel inside. He sighed in relief. Relaxed once again, his mind returned to their farewell.

"If you don't come back with that and my father," she'd said, "don't bother coming back."

There had been tears in her eyes when she said it. She hadn't said anything about him staying safe, but he had been grateful to her for keeping those worries unvoiced. It kept him from having to try to come up with something to say. He answered her with a kiss. She understood him and didn't expect him to say anything. While still in his embrace, she put the envelope in his breast pocket, where it had stayed since. After she had placed it there, she broke away from him and left without looking back.

The fire had begun dying during his musings when a sudden gust of wind from behind extinguished it and woke Baran out of his reverie; already he would be traveling mostly by moon and starlight by the time he reached the valley. His muscles were cramped from sitting still for so long, and he knew he should have waited until he set up a permanent camp before allowing his mind to drift like that, but he couldn't be too upset with himself. Even if it had been an idle fantasy, his spirit felt refreshed from the beauty his eyes had seen, as well as the one his heart remembered.

Baran stood up and carefully made his way down the mountain, making as straight a line as he could. It didn't take him nearly as long as he thought it would. This was primarily because he only stumbled occasionally and rolling downhill proved to be a much faster, even if more painful, means of travel. The sun had only been down for about thirty minutes with the last bit of light just beginning to fade when he arrived in the valley he had seen from above. Exhausted, hungry, and now badly bruised, he could only hope this valley may have a water source, as he had guessed because of the dense vegetation he observed before.

A downside of this valley having so much vegetation was becoming ever more obvious: very little of the moon and starlight made it past the canopy of leaves overhead. Many times the only warning he received of a tree in his path was the feeling of the roots sticking up near the trunk. He continued pressing on in what he hoped was a relatively straight line. It might have been better to wait until morning, but by this point, Baran's desperation for water overpowered any other thought. After an hour of wandering blindly, he stopped. Was his mind playing tricks on him? A faint sound of rushing water sounded like it was coming from his right—he had no idea what direction he was facing by this point. Slowly, he made his way toward the sound as best he could, trying to ignore the echoes bouncing off the tree trunks. Eventually, there was no doubt about it. It was water moving very rapidly with loud splashes as it beat against objects in its path. Maneuvering as fast as the darkness would allow, Baran made his way until he found its source. A narrow river was flowing down a steep mountainside. Thousands of years of flowing water had carved out a deep track for its bed, but there was no way down the cliff to the water below. Here the trees coverage was not nearly as thick, and he was finally able to see a fair bit into the distance. Just over two hundred yards ahead was where the land flattened and the water spread out. Excitement provided new energy to his weary and bruised muscles, and he made his way down the last part of his journey.

The crashing water had carved a deep pool into the ground. Rushing into the shallows, Baran began scooping water into his mouth to quench his overpowering thirst. So intense was the need and the relief, for full minute he didn't even notice the cold. Cursing himself for not at least taking off his clothes before venturing into the water, he retreated out of the water and back onto land, quickly drying his sword and disrobing before the cold fingers of the night air could aid the wet clothes on his skin in freezing him to death. He quickly gathered firewood from the nearby trees and rocks from the pool's edge. Stacking the wood, he raised his hands at the pile and repeated the only Divine command he knew.

"Thank you, Lady Lyr!" he said aloud. He only knew one command, but he couldn't think of a better one to know for a man needing to survive in the wild. Fire would not only keep him warm and dry, but also keep any hungry predators at bay. Baran briefly considered the danger of unfriendly eyes finding him because of the fire but quickly dismissed it. He was in a valley, surrounded by trees. "And it's a moot point anyway," he realized. With no blankets or tents, the need for warmth would have outweighed the need for secrecy.

Baran warmed himself by the fire for a time. The desire to sleep was becoming overpowering, but there were still a few things that he needed to do before he could finally rest. He ventured back among the trees. Eventually, he found what he was looking for: several fallen limbs of about the same size. Carrying them back near his fire, he set them down before walking back to the water's edge, carefully keeping himself dry this time. Quickly scanning the rocks in the shallows, he found a triangular one that suited his needs perfectly. Taking it in his hands, he went back to the fire and began digging holes in a circle around it. After each hole, he placed one of the small limbs he had found and packed dirt around it. When he was finished, he draped his clothes over the limbs. "Perfect!" he said aloud to himself.

Baran waited for his clothes to dry, forcing himself to sit up so when his head would droop, it would wake him up every time he began to doze off. He'd check and rotate his clothes each time. When they were finally dry, he put them back on, forced himself to go back into the woods one final time, and brought back as much wood as he could carry. Putting all the limbs in this final load, along with everything he had left from his earlier trips, he flung himself next to the fire and fell into a deep slumber.

The fire died late in the night, the air around Baran cold enough that had he been awake, he would have felt miserable, but sleep numbed him. The sun rose the next morning, warming Baran's still unconscious body, and still Baran slept. It wasn't until nearly noon when the sun reached its peak that finally the young man's eyes blinked open. And still he did not get up. It wasn't until his stomach's protest became an incessant symphony of growling and rumbling that he finally forced himself into a sitting position, groaning from the increased protest of his bruised muscles that hadn't received much benefit from his rest—thanks to the dirt bed on which he had slept.

Stiffly walking to the pool, Baran knelt by the water's edge again to refresh himself and drink the cool water. In the daytime, he could see the pool was about twenty-five or thirty yards wide and continued for maybe fifty yards before the waterway narrowed back into a fast flowing river again. "Now, if I can just find some food, I'll be the happiest fugitive ever," he said with a grin.

He tried setting snares for rabbits and other small creatures first. Though he had indeed taken survivalist classes in The Academy to prepare for his life as a soldier, he had never had to make them out of materials he could find lying around, much less actually used them. The biggest issue was the lack of any type of string. The grass here wasn't long enough. The few vines he found were too thick. After a frustrating hour without even having finished a single snare, he gave up.

"If only I had my bow and a few good arrows!" he moaned out loud. But there was no use in whining. How long would it take the Savanir to find him he wondered? *Long enough to get really hungry,* was the obvious answer that floated into his mind. He looked at his sword, trying to think of any use his only piece of gear could be. All that came to his mind was the soldier he had killed yesterday. "Nope, can't think about that yet," he said aloud again, trying to force it away from his mind.

He looked down to the end of the pond. "Of course!" he realized. The water in the pool didn't seem like it was flowing, but that was only because the width and depth of the pool made the water flow more slowly. *But I bet it picks up where it narrows again, and it might be easier to find fish there.*

It didn't take long to reach the eastern end of the pool. The water's current became more and more obvious as its path narrowed back into becoming a fast flowing stream. He even saw one fish swimming near the bank. Without thinking, Baran's hunger took over his arms, and he quickly made a stab at it with his sword, but the only thing he did was kick up mud when he missed, obscuring his vision and making a second attempt impossible before the fish swam away.

He continued on until the pool began to narrow toward the upcoming river. Fish began to appear in greater numbers. He made more stabbing attempts, but it was never fast enough. He was now nearing the end of the lake when he saw a tree that had been dead for quite some time washed up near the bank. Peering into the water, he saw fish hiding among the branches and limbs that were in the water. Suddenly, an idea occurred to him. He climbed on the trunk of the tree, which disturbed the water, and most of the fish fled. "They'll be back," he thought to himself. Finding a branch that had fewer twigs to obscure his vision, he placed his sword a few inches into the water and waited. After a few minutes, some of the fish began returning. "Come on," he silently pleaded.

At last, one fish began making its way, ever closer, to being directly under his sword, but it stopped just inches away. His stomach protested his refusal to stab, but Baran held firm. After what felt like an eternity, the fish at last swam under the tip of his blade. Releasing all his pent up energy and desperation, Baran pushed his sword through the creature and into the lakebed below. Not chancing losing his prey, he held the sword in place until the struggling fish stopped moving. Carefully switching into a better position, he reached into the water with his empty hand and grabbed the fish's tale, pulling up his prize.

It wasn't much, but it was something. He cooked it at his camp. "Next priority is setting up camp closer to the food," he thought to himself. When the fish seemed fully cooked, he removed it from the fire. No one would call him a chef, looking at the state of his meal, but being so hungry Baran savored every bite.

Over the next three days, Baran's success continued, but it was slow business catching enough fish to keep his belly full. While he waited, his mind had plenty of time to contemplate his personal crisis.

With the thoughts he had wrestled with earlier, he realized no scenario existed where he would not defend those he cared for. The question that now bothered him was if his sword was ultimately a tool for "Good", or merely what was convenient for him. The Dawn had proved it was merely a sham led by a crazed emperor and lapdog nobility. But its people? Well, they were people. Evil people, good people ... they covered the whole spectrum. The Savanir? On the surface they seemed better. Baran knew that if he spent more time with them, there would be plenty of individuals that would prove every bit as evil as well. "And," he thought aloud, remembering Arun's words. "They are too worried about survival to backstab each other." But that can hardly be used to credit them. Speaking of Arun, the Savanir fought to keep him safe only because of their self-serving interest in his well-being.

Should he fight with them? The soldier's face he had killed floated back to his mind. *How many like him would I kill?* he wondered to himself. A realization struck him. The threat of extinction might make the Savanir willing to fight, but it was their confidence in fighting for Xiarch's vision that had them believe their pursuit to be noble.

Baran, more than any of the others was aware the Savanir knew things that The Dawn had kept secret from him. But was Xiarch truly there? And if he was, was the person the Savanir spoke of an accurate portrayal? If not, then all of their nobility was self-aggrandizing nonsense.

But what if they're right? The uncomfortable thought took shape in his brain in spite of his mind's attempt to stop it. What would that mean for those in The Dawn that were the same as Arun and him? Just people wanting to live the best they knew how. Many of the same soldiers that were killing the Savanir felt they were fighting the same fight as the Savanir — in the defense of Truth and their people — only they were winning for the most part.

A paper on The Bewildered he and Arun had written (well, mostly Arun) came back to his mind. The dangerous nature of faith. It was faith that strengthened the resolve of The Bewildered, and as such, they had concluded that faith was dangerous. But now he could see that the people of The Dawn were just as much in the throes of faith as everyone else. Athaz was walking proof of it. Faith was a main component of a conscious psyche.

But could it be so bad, then? Baran refused to believe that Men, or even Dwarves and Elves, were doomed to fight vain struggles. *Misplaced faith is the cause of countless wars. But how do we know if our faith was misplaced when its very nature is that of trust?*

Baran pondered this for several days, but never came up with a satisfactory answer. He probably wouldn't have come up with any answer anyway, but on the sixth morning after becoming separated from his company, the debate ended when he woke up to find Aldo and Garren sitting some distance away. Two other men he did not recognize sat behind Blake's men, one of which was looking over his sword. *I slept a little too soundly,* Baran thought to himself.

"Well, this one at least seems capable of handling himself," Garren said looking at Aldo, but obviously meant as a compliment for Baran to hear. "I believe he could have gotten himself home and saved us the trouble."

Baran laughed as he looked around for his friend. "Arun didn't come with you?"

"Wasn't allowed. He's almost to Menigar by now," Aldo answered. "And for once he seems to finally be listening to sense. Good thing too, because I'm pretty sure Blake would have broken his legs to stop him."

Baran grimaced. He knew it had been said in jest, but with where his thoughts had been the past couple of days, the joke fell flat on his ears. Baran also knew that if Arun had become compliant, it was most likely out of guilt, and he feared for his friend. He knew the Savanir leadership would never hurt him directly — that would hurt their designs for him, but if Arun started to go along with them and their prophecy …

Baran had a crucial decision to make. Should he go back and help keep Arun from being manipulated? Baran shook his head. He

Truth Unearthed

couldn't. Descia was counting on him when she was unable to act as she wished to save her father, Paleon. And the old man himself was in danger he did not realize and grieving for a daughter while she still lived. *I'm sorry, Arun. I can't protect you this time. You'll have to find your own strength.*

"I'm glad Arun is safe for the time being," Baran said. "But my mission still stands. I do not ask you all to come with me. I know you have lost many men already, so I will follow you back to the nearest city or hideout you have. From there, I'll make my own way."

Garren shook his head. "You will not go alone. Did you think we came all this way out here just to bring you some food? Or that we have not lost men before? Blake does not believe Arun could even deliver a meal to a patron at an inn, and from what I have seen thus far I agree with him. But Lady Vera's actions for the past fourteen years have set things in motion, whether for good or ill. Nothing can stop that now. This mission was blessed by them knowing what the cost might be. And quite frankly," Garren said with a shrug, "our mission just became a lot easier. The Dawn may be keeping their eyes open for you, Baran, but they are actively hunting Arun."

Aldo fetched their bags and an additional one from the other Savanir scouts that had helped them find Baran. One of them also unbelted his sword and handed to Aldo. They saluted each other before the scouts took off. Baran was shocked at how quickly he lost all track of them once they reached the trees.

"Time is still of the essence though," Aldo said to Baran, "and we have spent too much time in talk." He threw the additional bag and sword at Baran's feet. "Are you ready?"

CHAPTER XVIII

Finding a Path

Baran followed behind Garren and Aldo. They were still traveling due north, as much as the Makrin Mountains would allow.

"The good news," Aldo said as they trudged uphill, "is that you camped a bit to the east, and Lamphine will not be in sight when we reach the Argom River, so we'll only have to worry about patrols. Once we get a local to ferry us over, we'll take an arching route through the Mossy Plain to reach Abscos to avoid any unwanted contact along the river."

"The better news," Garren continued as they now began their descent, "is that we will be able to use the river most of the way back. It will be faster, and as long as you don't stand up to greet the patrols, they won't think anything of Yeomen shipping their goods all the way to Mizcur. Of course, we won't quite go all the way before we have to disembark, but it will save us a lot of time and effort."

The Makrin Mountains along their northern peaks, thankfully, had very little depth north to south, and the trio was out of them just as the horizon began to partially cover the sun. Clouds were rolling in, though, and they were dark with rain. They reached the river just as the cold precipitation began to fall and night fully enveloped them. It wasn't a hard rain, but it was enough of an annoyance that Baran was frustrated by what he saw.

"Of course we would manage to find a downpour in the middle of a field without a farmhouse in sight," Baran muttered as they scanned the areas to the west and east of them.

"Well, it's not that bad. We'll just have to head eastward until we reach one. Shouldn't take long; they build next to the river for obvious reasons," Aldo explained.

"But why to the east?" Baran asked. "Abscos is northwest of

here."

"Because," answered Aldo, "we appeared to have turned a little to the west in the mountains, and I don't want to risk getting any closer to Lamphine."

"Alright," Baran said. "I just hope you're right about it not taking long. This appears to just be a field of grass, though, not grain, so I'm not sure why they would have a shelter out here."

Aldo just smiled. Thirty minutes later, Aldo's guess turned out to be right. There was a low-roofed building of some sort, but it obviously wasn't a house. For one thing, there were no walls, but the biggest giveaway was its occupants. Sheep. Hundreds of them. All in crowded pens with narrow paths between them.

Aldo laughed. "This couldn't be any better!" Baran gave him a confused look. "Where there are sheep, there is a shepherd. Watching sheep is normally the responsibility given to a young Yeoman; he'll almost certainly be open to ferrying us for a chance at a little coin."

It took them a while to find the shepherd, who turned out to be a youth around twelve years of age. He had fallen asleep on the job and was a little startled to see three strangers, mistaking them for bandits. Garren, who was the smallest and least intimidating, finally managed to calm him down. "We just need a little help getting across the river. You've got a small boat around here, I'm sure. Think you could give us a hand?"

"I can't leave my sheep," the boy said, suddenly becoming conscious of his duty. "And why should I help you?"

Garren laughed. "You make some good points. Tell you what, my friend here," he said, pointing to Baran—and whom the youth was obviously most terrified of, "will stay here and watch your sheep. And I'll give you two silver pieces for your help."

That proved to be more than enough motivation for the boy. He led them down to his parents little dingy, which Aldo and Garren carried back up to the shelter. Aldo and Baran went across first. This allowed the boy to ferry Garren across. The moment Garren alighted on the shore, the boy shoved back off and turned downstream to take the boat back to where it belonged.

Baran laughed. "Apparently two silver pieces does a lot to ease a shepherd's conscience."

"Don't judge him too harshly. It's probably more money than he's ever seen in his life."

They marched north for two hours, during which time the rain finally stopped, before they finally made camp. They built a fire and placed their wet clothes around it, changing into some dryer ones they had in their packs. After dinner, Garren volunteered to take the first watch while Baran and Aldo quickly found sleep.

The journey for the next several days had Baran in high spirits, in spite of occasionally worrying about Arun. They traveled unhindered. The weather was kind, they slept undisturbed at night, and they had plenty of food, even if it did become a bit repetitive. He had become so accustomed to facing danger at every turn, he had forgotten that it wasn't a mandatory component of traveling. In fact, when thinking of Arun, he realized this was how the trip to Lacris should have been like. That memory brought back others of all his ambitions and plans. Funny that it now seemed like the life of someone else; it had been his only a few months ago. But he actually wasn't upset. He was living a life of adventure, which he had always wanted. He never would have met Descia, and just being with her would have been worth trading all those hopes and dreams. And he realized he and Arun might continue a friendship that probably would have faded quickly after their graduation. *If Arun can find himself,* came the reminder. *He will,* he forced his mind to answer the doubtful voice.

They traveled quickly on the Mossy Plain. The ground was flat, the mossy turf soft and springy, and there were was no need to take pains to hide themselves from unfriendly eyes. By the end of the fourth day, they could just see the silhouettes of Abscos' tallest buildings casting long shadows as the last bits of sunlight began to fade behind the western horizon. On the fifth day, they traveled due north, just making their way into the southern tip of the Meros Wood. From there, they marched westward along its southern edge, hiding from unfriendly eyes that might be watching from

Abscos. They ran into some Yeoman foresters, but they were too busy with their labors to mind or question the travelers in their midst.

Though they could have turned south and reached Abscos early in the night, all three agreed it would be better to rest in the woods; once they reached the town, there was no telling if Baran would be noticed. He still wore the disguse (the tools to remove it left behind when he tumbled in the river), but after the episode at Lamphine, it might be as well known as his true face. And that was only one of a number scenarios they may face. If there were problems, it would be better to encounter them at the start of the day, well rested.

They rose as soon as the sun came up. Meandering a bit so as to not look like three adventurers with a definitive purpose, they made their way slowly to the outer buildings. Abscos had no wall; it was far from any Savanir strongpoint, and the Savage Races had been driven from the Meros Wood long ago and never returned. In fact, outside of Hilae and trade hubs like Mizcur, Abscos was one of the more peaceful settlements in the entire empire, and it had none of the former's political intrigue. It was that quiet nature that had led Paleon to choose to spend his retirement there.

They asked a woman making her way through the streets where they might find an inn. It wasn't far, and following her directions, they indeed found The Oak and Stag Inn shortly after leaving her.

"Greetings, friends," the innkeeper shouted as they entered his establishment. "Not often I receive new patrons in my establishment," he said, looking them up and down. All three felt a bit uneasy as he did so. "We are looking for Paleon," Baran finally said.

"Ah," said the innkeeper, and his face fell. "Friends of his daughter, were you? Well, I'm glad you came then. Perhaps you can help the old fellow out. He hasn't ventured out of his house in weeks. I take him some vittles on occasion, especially if business has been slow. No need to let them spoil and all. But he's been mighty depressed since he got word of his daughter's slaughter at the hands of the Orcs in that raid." Here the innkeeper shook his head. "No one in their right mind would have ever ventured down that far near The Bewildered and Savage Races, but that's of course no comfort to a man that lost his little girl."

Upon finding an open source of information, Garren had an idea. "Tell you what, why don't you tell us what we can do to help after fetching us some breakfast."

It took a good deal longer than they had anticipated; assuming the innkeeper actually had hired help to serve his customers, he certainly seemed to have found his calling. Eventually, after more than an hour of winding conversations and tangents in which the innkeeper thrice solved every problem The Dawn faced, they got directions to Paleon's house. It was just outside of the town's southwestern edge.

"Good," said Aldo when they were finally on their way. "We'll be near the river."

It was about ten in the morning when they were passing the last houses in town and laid eyes on the house that matched the innkeeper's description: a low, one-story white house made of stone with a green wooden door and green trim around the windows and a roof that sloped toward the river. It wasn't overly large, but most of the houses in the area were built of wood with thatched roofs. Baran remembered that Keepers made little money compared to most of the officials in Hilae, but it was apparent they still made a good deal more than most of The Dawn could ever hope to earn.

When they made their way up to the door, Baran stepped forward and knocked. "Leave me," came a voice from within, barely loud enough to be heard outside the door. Baran hesitated for a moment, trying to think of something to say to bring the man to the door. "I come bearing tidings concerning Descia."

There was a pause before the door barely opened, revealing a sliver of the man's face. "What could you possibly have to tell me that I have not already heard before?" he asked.

In response, Baran took the envelope out of his pocket. Some of the letter tore with it, but that didn't matter. The jewel alone would get them in the door at least. The emerald was simple in design, just a square cut, but nicely done, and it caught the light beautifully.

What marked it as unique was what enclosed it. A silver setting with a two rolled scrolls crossing each other underneath a tower. Under the image was the inscription, "Knowledge is the most sure foundation."

When the man held it in his hands, a dry sob came raggedly from his chest as he opened the door enough to reveal his small, recently thinned frame. "Where did you get this?" he asked.

Baran looked him in the eyes. "I was with her that day, and I have news to share, if you'll hear it."

The man opened the door fully, motioning for them to follow him. Sitting down at a plain but well-made table in the kitchen, they silently waited while he looked at the jewel. "You were with her?" he asked.

"Yes."

After this, Paleon sat in thought. "So, I guess they lied about there being no survivors?" Baran sat up. There was no incredulity in his tone.

"Yes. I have to say, I'm shocked at your easiness in accepting it," Baran added.

Paleon looked at him hard. "Only the young are shocked when authority is shown to be susceptible to falsehoods." He fell silent again. Baran knew he was afraid to ask, but he also knew the man wanted no help in asking. At long last, he asked, "Does my daughter live?"

Baran smiled. "Yes."

"How did you survive the Orc raid? I assume that at least was true; they brought back some of the bodies. Certainly more of the Orcs than our loved ones."

Here, Baran motioned to Aldo and Garren. "Comrades of my two friends you see here. We were rescued by The Bewildered."

"The Savanir?" the man said, for the first time, genuinely surprised.

Aldo answered, "We are pleased to see you know our proper name."

Paleon waved him off. "Most Keepers do, though my daughter was young and hadn't been on many ventures yet. Most of your spies that are caught have brushed shoulders with my order. We rarely reveal you intentionally. That would give us away and make our research more difficult, but the Watchers know that we're most likely to talk with sympathizers since we actively avoid revealing our connection with Hilae."

Paleon tried to pull out the letter, but it had bonded with the envelope. The ink had also run. "I guess she wasn't using her own supplies. Oh how I would love to hear from her personally after all this time!" he sighed. Then, finally, he smiled. "Well, I am sure you must be on your way, but you are certainly free to rest here as long as you like. I'll be grateful to you till the day I die."

Baran shook his head. "We weren't sent to just deliver a message. You are in danger—"

"Indeed he is, as are all traitors," the voice had come from the window, and in less than a second the intruder had gone to the door and kicked it open—unnecessarily, for it hadn't been locked.

The brief moment had given Baran, Garren, and Aldo enough time to stand and ready their weapons, but Baran's heart sank when he saw their opponent. It was a form he was very familiar with: six-six muscular frame, black hair, and beard. A Warden had them cornered.

"Looks like one of those ship rats was right. There was a young man that was sweet on Descia. They told a lot of tales to try to stop the torture, but after hearing of this one and the other student traveling this way, we thought that particular tale might have actually been true." The Warden paused to unsheathe his weapons, twin scimitars. They were well made, and his ease with them made it clear he knew how to use them. *But they aren't Divine weapons*, Baran realized. At least they wouldn't have to worry about changing weapons.

The Warden continued his self-contented speech. "I believe I just heard you offer known enemies of The Dawn quarter, and the sentence for that is death."

Paleon was by far the calmest of them, but at this he actually laughed. "And you were shocked that I so easily accepted that my great Emperor lied to me," turning to the Warden he said, "I suggest you leave the spin and propaganda to those with more wit than you, cur."

Baran looked at the old man in surprise and admiration. *It's like deja vu of the day I met Descia,* he thought to himself.

"Shut up, old man," the Warden said, annoyed.

But Paleon only laughed harder. "No Divine disguise can hide your age, young one."

With an angry shout, the Warden charged at them. Baran stepped between their enemy and Paleon, raising his sword to intercept the strike. The Warden would have liked to use one of the other scimitars to strike at Baran, but Garren and Aldo were attempting to take advantage of his eager charge. With a wide seep, he forced them to defend against his attack as he landed and rolled out of the way. He may have been a hothead, but he was a Warden; he would not be easily defeated.

The small house made for an odd arena. On one hand it limited the Warden's wingspan with his dual blades, but it also made it much easier for him to keep them from encircling him. With his enemies forced to come at him from the front, and his superior skills, it would be difficult to best him.

Baran charged first, but Garren and Aldo quickly followed up on either side of him. Baran's momentum carried him to the wall as the Warden dodged his straight stab to the right before raising his scimitars to block Garren's overhead swing, kicking him back. Aldo tried to quickly change direction with his sword going toward the Warden's exposed underarm. But quick as lighting, the Warden had ducked underneath and sliced at the back of his opponent's leg as he ran by. With a cry, Aldo felt his hamstring cut like a taut rope and crashed into a shelf of tomes and scrolls.

"One down, two to go," the Warden laughed. In fury, Garren grabbed his sword with both hands and was swinging and stabbing at the Warden, closely followed by Baran. Though he had no breath to mock them, the Warden's years of training were showing, as neither of them were unable to land a blow. They were exhausting themselves in their efforts, but the Warden was efficiently deflecting their blows. Fatigued, Baran reacted too slowly and felt the scimitar meet bone on the top of his forearm, causing him to drop his sword. The Warden went to shout in triumph, but instead a gurgling grasp came from his lips. Paleon appeared from behind the Warden with bloody hands. "You had three left to deal with, young fool. No amount of skill can make up for the stupidity of ignoring foes, however weak they may seem."

The Warden's scimitars clanged against the stone floor as he fell to his knees, the look of pure disbelief on still on his face. "Looks like you were right," Paleon said, turning to Baran. "Let me grab just a couple of things and I'll be ready to go." He went to the back room and came back with a small, wooden box, some old shirts, and a satchel filled with parchments. He and Baran then put each of Aldo's arms over their shoulders and walked him out of the house. Garren came out a few seconds later. He cleaned his sword on the grass as well as Aldo's that Paleon had used to strike the deciding blow. Paleon had already borrowed Baran's sword and cut up the shirts for bandages.

"Any message you want to leave for anyone?" Baran asked.

Paleon shook his head. "Any true message would only endanger whomever I gave it to. "Besides," he said, looking at Baran. "I'm going to be with my family again, and that is all I can ask for. The Dawn will say whatever it finds most convenient. It's what they always do." Then, more quietly, he added, "And what we've all been forced to do."

With Baran and Garren carrying Aldo, Paleon led them down to the river where they washed and changed out of their bloody clothing. Then they followed the river toward town. Spotting a Yeoman loading timber, Paleon hailed him. "You have the papers this delivery is for?"

"Yes, Keeper, always."

"Easy, friend," Paleon said with a smile. "My cohort has injured his leg and is in need of a skilled surgeon at Mizcur. Your boat will be crowded with your load and even just four, so I thought I'd take the delivery for you."

The man smiled. "I've heard rumors you've done some mighty big favors for Yeomen before, but I only half believed them. Looks like I'll have to start convincing some of my fellow doubters." He gave Paleon the papers as Baran and Garren carefully laid Aldo among the timber. Once that was done, the Yeoman tipped his cap to them. "My old lady thanks you as well. She hates it when I'm away."

Paleon bowed. "Don't mention it. You're the one doing me the favor." With that, he turned and boarded the vessel, and Baran and Garren took the oars and shoved off.

As they floated along the water, Baran looked south and east toward where he knew Meingar lay. Descia would be overjoyed to see her father again, and that thought made him smile. *I just hope Arun's sorted his thoughts out. Sometimes he thinks too much for his own good.*

CHAPTER XIX

Doom

"Good news, Arun," Inoch said. "Lady Lyr has said you don't need to wear the hood, you can walk freely and just have your mind wiped."

Arun shook his head. "Give me the hood. I'll be here for some time, but I certainly hope not permanently, and..." Arun shivered involuntarily "...I now know that *they* would be able to squeeze any information they wanted out of me if anything was left behind. Remember, I knew Therran was an Elf and even had a shred of memory of Vera from my childhood." Arun rubbed his mouth where the blisters had been without thinking about it. In truth, it had been one of the least painful parts of that day that seemed to last forever. His body had at one point felt like it was on fire from head to toe. He had learned that night that Elves sometimes put mental blocks around memories, but apparently those could be shattered if the person wanted to access them enough. But it was the moment that he realized his helplessness and terror overwhelmed him, as the scorching hand covered his screams, that stuck out the most. It wasn't because of the pain, but rather the empty eyes and thin voice that made him realize his torment would never end.

"Not permanently?" Blake asked. "And here I thought you had learned some sense." His tone was rough, but not cruel. He was riding a horse that had been brought for him once the lookouts had seen his condition. When they first dropped off Aldo and Garren, he had been covered nearly head to toe in bandages his wounds were so numerous. Most were healed now, though he still wore a few bandages in places where the cuts had reopened because he moved too vigorously.

Arun didn't respond. He had learned to not be stupid in his resistance to the Savanir, but he still had no plans to attempt to fulfill Vera's vision.

"Come, Inoch, give me the hood. At least I know you won't stab me while I wear it this time!"

Inoch gave him a look and threw the hood in his face. "You are a real smartass, you know that?"

Arun genuinely laughed as he caught the hood and put it on himself. "Now you sound like Baran."

"Well," answered Inoch, "I'm beginning to think he is smarter than you."

Arun's face was hidden as he shrugged. "Perhaps."

They made their way, Inoch once again guiding Arun through the underground twists and turns. The combination of the *clip-clop* of the shoed hooves of Blake's horse and his eyes seeing nothing but blackness caused flashbacks in Arun's mind. Though his limbs were free this time around, he now knew with more certainty his old life was gone forever.

When they reached the gate, Arun took off his hood. Even knowing what awaited him, he couldn't help but be in awe of the gate's craftsmanship. Yet, he still couldn't fully enjoy it. *Vera must have been a very young Elf, living a sheltered existence within these walls,* he thought, *to have placed so much faith in any vision that had a Yeoman defeating Bälech.* As they walked along the streets, a woman quickly and deliberately made her way toward them.

"Descia!" Arun said in amazement when she got close enough for him to recognize her. She looked very different. Her hair was now cut short, too short for a Keeper's braid. She was dressed in the manner of Savanir women, wearing a light-weaved tunic with short sleeves and full-length pants. Her shirt was fiery red, while the pants were black with red flames running up them. *A fire leaping from the coals. Very fitting for her,* thought Arun.

She strode right up to him. It was easy to forget how short she was, even when looking directly down on her. "You're lucky we just got word from the other Savanir stronghold in the Forest of Orus," she said. "Or you'd wake up with amnesia from the day after you let them convince you not to stay with Baran."

"Easy!" said Arun, taking a step back. Descia instantly closed the distance again. "You have more recent news than I do. What do you know of Baran? I have not heard anything since Garren and Aldo went to search for him."

"They found him, and Garren and Aldo went with him to find your father. That's the last I heard."

She took a few steps back. "They told me why you agreed to let him go alone. I'm not happy about it, but I understand." So did Arun. She had wanted someone she trusted with Baran, and she wasn't yet comfortable with the Savanir.

"He really is safer without me," Arun said. "I wouldn't have left any other way."

Descia backed off a bit. "I know you wouldn't have. And I really am glad to see you back safe."

"Excuse me," Inoch said. "I assume you can help Arun find his way? Blake and I need to report to Lady Lyr."

Descia responded just by waving them off. Turning, she then motioned for Arun to follow her. "Really, I'm happy they're gone. I need someone with a Keeper's eye to look over some things anyway."

This intrigued Arun.

"I have been studying their histories," Descia explained. "And I stumbled across something very interesting." She looked at Arun. "A myth concerning the origin of Bälech." Descia would have just taken him to the libraries right then and there, but Arun reminded her that he had just spent weeks without a proper meal or bed. "Or bath," said Descia, her nose scrunched up.

They went to Kruthos' house, where Descia had been living since they had all left on their various quests. "The human women were too smothering," she explained. "All so eager to 'help,' when all I wanted was some quiet and a chance to observe and research. The Dwarves are kind enough, but for the most part ignore me unless I ask them something directly."

"My kind of neighbors!" said Arun with a laugh. "They might not be quite as distant with you," she reminded him.

Arun exhaled slowly in resignation. That was a reasonable guess. Once inside, Arun, remembering his way around easily, went into the toiletry room and began pumping the water into the bath. He didn't have time to warm it, but just getting all the grime off felt wondrous. While he was washing, Descia went to a nearby tavern and brought back some freshly roasted lamb, a huge slice of cheese, bread, and spiced wine. After Arun had dried and dressed himself in some of the garments he had left behind, and eaten the best meal he had tasted in weeks, Descia led him to the greatest Elven treasure that yet survived in Lugon: The Library of Menigar.

Arun was accustomed to huge libraries; he had studied in The Tower many times after all. But comparing the two was impossible. The Tower had perhaps six or seven stories, sparsely lit by candles. Their tomes were stored on sturdy, simple shelves. The first difference Arun noticed, though, had nothing to do with the quality. The levels in this library, though still circular, went down, not up. When Arun thought about it, it made sense. But the effect it had was completely different. Instead of seeing information you could climb to reach, if you spent too long looking down at all this knowledge (the floors continued for so long that Arun's eyes cease to be able to tell them apart), one could become overwhelmed by vertigo, and you feared falling into a deep sea that was as dangerous as it was glorious and beautiful. In the middle were countless lifts leading on from each section to the one below it and above it. Most levels had a few. The floors were all lit in different shades. Arun was sure there was a meaning for this, but he was clueless as to what it might be. So many different hues, he couldn't possibly think of a purpose for all of them.

"How were you able to find anything in this ocean?" Arun whispered in awe.

Descia gave a small laugh. "Now I know how I must have looked to the Mosytes ... That's their equivalent to a Keeper. Here, let me show you." She took him to a desk where an Elf sat, his eyes seeming both distant and near. She then explained he kept a massive tome, an index containing every possible area of study. Once you picked your subject matter, other tomes would be brought over, showing all works pertaining to your subject.

"See those strings?" Descia asked, pointing them out to Arun.

"Once you select your book, he'll pull on one in some sort of code. Depending on how far down the library it is, it takes a different amount of time to come up here, but I've never had to wait any longer than ten minutes. And we don't have to wait at all; they've allowed me the use of a storage box where I can keep materials for up to three days. I discovered the scroll I want you to read shortly after you left, but when I heard you were coming back, I recalled it, along with another."

Arun followed her over to a cabinet (there was no lock), and she pulled out several scrolls, shuffling through them until she found two of what she was looking for. "One of these is a scroll of my own creation, a translation into the script of The Dawn," she said, handing him the first. "And this," she said pulling out another, much more ornately written with several beautiful drawings, "is the original. It took me a week to translate it, looking at a translation guide. Some of the words either had no equivalent or referenced a word so archaic I decided to do a little modernization. But what I found was distressing for the future of all of us, but especially you, should they try to coax you into their design."

It was then that the Nochanes rebelled against Xiarch. Bälech, once of great influence among his brethren, found himself forbidden from joining in the assault of Xiarch's gates. He alone doubted they had yet the strength to overcome The One from whose speech had uttered them into existence. Though but echoes, they had hoped to amplify their own Divinity and drown out Xiarch and all his Kingdom. But when his designs to place himself at their head were revealed, his warnings were believed to be nothing more than a ploy to sow doubt among his brethren. As the Final Rebellion of the Nochanes led to their demise, Bälech found his binds loosed. But, sensing Xiarch's reach extending into their own lands, he forsook all that he knew in terror; creating a rift in the planes, he sent his Divine Nature hurtling into the vulgar Lugonian world. Capturing the body of a mortal through deceit, Bälech stalled the Wrath of Xiarch, for he remembered the Vow Xiarch had made with the Noble Races, who would be free to act as they saw fit until the End of Days.

Arun re-rolled the scroll, his face hard. He had read what Descia wanted him to see. After a minute, Descia said, "I took that to mean that it is not merely the soul of a creature that inhabits The Dawn's Emperor. Bälech himself is a being, without a body ... or at least not a body as we understand it. His power in the Divine must be nigh limitless that he and his brethren would even think they could oppose the Creator using his own power against him. Certainly beyond anything we could hope to challenge."

Arun nodded. "I take it to mean that as well."

Descia shook her head. "If they could not withstand him at the pinnacle of their civilization, what makes the Savanir think you or anyone else could possibly overthrow him now?" she asked.

"I don't know," Arun admitted. "The Elves see things we do not, Vera and her family especially. But Vera was young when she chose this course. Perhaps even Elves, in their youth, are as susceptible to wishful thinking as our kind."

Arun handed the scroll back to Descia. "Thanks for showing me," he said wearily. He began walking back to Kruthos' house. "Of course, it is just a myth," he reasoned to himself. *Elves and Dwarves were myths too*, his mind retorted. Once he entered Kruthos' home, he dropped himself into a chair and stared at the unlit fireplace. It all felt so pointless. He wasn't angry anymore; he had become too tired. He was a little frightened still, but there was no need to panic yet. Perhaps it would all blow over in a few years, and the Savanir and the Dawn would return to their grudging acceptance of the status quo. Of course, Arun didn't really believe that. But that small hope was his chief source of comfort as he dozed into vague, uneasy dreams.

* * * * * * * *

For the next couple of weeks, Arun continued going to the Library. He spent most of his time reading on the history of the Savanir since the beginning of The Dawn's empire. They had settlements all over Lugon, but most were small and all were isolated. From what Arun could gather, there were two other major strongholds. Far to the North, there was one primarily consisting of Dwarves. With the help of a few Elves and Men, they had managed to create subterranean farms in the warm places deep under the surface. The other was far to the west, several months journey westward from the Forest of Orus into the Agna Desert. It was named Marviss. Comprised mostly of humans, it was the only stronghold above ground. But it was a city of tents, mobile out of necessity, letting the unforgiving desert crush any forces Bälech sent to them. Reading records of their history and customs, they seemed almost barbaric. But they were staunch allies of Menigar — or at least equally opposed to Bälech. The rest of settlements were small, or sometimes just pockets of resistance, hidden within The Dawn itself, much like what Arun had seen in Mizcur.

At the end of the second week, shortly after eating lunch, Descia came running back into the house and threw herself into Arun's arms in a hug that threatened to squeeze the life out of him. "They're on their way back! Baran and my father! And they'll be here any day now!"

Arun tried to say something, but she had knocked most of the air out of him, and her arms were so tightly enclosed around his ribs he couldn't breathe, leaving him only capable of making puffs of air come out with sound that died on his lips.

"Whoops, sorry," she said, laughing.

Arun smiled awkwardly. "I'm just glad my arm was healed before you did that. Try not to squeeze the life out of my friend when he gets back, if you can help it."

Sure enough, three days later Baran and Garren rode in on horses while Paleon and Aldo were riding in a cart, all escorted by Inoch. Paleon had spent the final bit of his money he had brought with him to ease their trip by land. Garren and Aldo quickly said their hellos before heading toward the medics, and Descia jumped into her father's cart, throwing her arms around his neck. The old man started crying. "Oh stop it!" she said, but the command might have been to herself as she felt her own tears assault her.

Baran dismounted and came back to the cart. She went in to kiss him, but suddenly stopped. "What did you do to your hair?!" cried Descia, just now noticing.

"Hid it from agents looking for it," Baran said with a grin.

Truth Unearthed

"And everyone else!" she scolded before giving him the kiss she had stopped short of before. After an uncomfortable length, Paleon coughed vigorously. Descia rolled her eyes, but Baran couldn't help but feel embarrassed. "Here, my child," Paleon said as he presented the box he had brought with him to his daughter. "Mother's jewelry box," she said.

"You got my letter, then?"

"Well, so to speak. Your beau over here couldn't keep it dry," he said with a chuckle. "But I would have brought this to you regardless. As far as the man himself, I would say I've gotten to learn him better in these past few weeks than most fathers ever do with their future son-in-laws." he said, grinning at Baran. "Once this whole mess settles down, you both have my blessing, not that it comes with much tangible reward anymore."

"Good to see you back," Arun said to Baran.

Baran looked his friend over with an eye that Arun wasn't accustomed to. Was he ... looking for something? But Baran's normal grin quickly replaced the searching gaze. "Well, it went pretty well. Only had to fight to escape his house."

"Speaking of houses," Arun said. "Inoch, can Baran and I stay with you ... if you have the room? It's going to be a little crowded with four of us in Kruthos' house."

"Of course!" Inoch replied. "You'll have the house to yourself most days. As you noticed, I'm kept pretty busy."

It was still a few hours until dinner, so they all split up with the promise to meet at the tavern near Kruthos' house. Inoch led his friends to his own house. It looked small on the outside. Upon entering, it looked even smaller.

"I'm afraid it's not much compared to Kruthos'," he said somewhat apologetically. "I only have one guest room, but I'll sleep in the common area so you can each have a room." Arun and Baran simultaneously shook their heads. "No, you won't," they said.

"But—" Inoch was getting ready to protest, but Arun gave him a look that left it clear he wasn't budging while Baran brought himself up to his full, considerable height. "If you think you can keep me in there, feel free to try it."

Inoch sighed. "Fine, but the lighter sleeper should take the guest room. I come and go as Therran dictates." He quickly gathered some extra bedding and placed it on a couch.

Arun was looking over the place and noticed a lot of sword hilts and dagger grips without blades. "What are all of these?" he asked.

"Oh, just a pet project of mine. I've been trying to design new guards out of different materials to better defend our hands against various weapons. I'll tell you more about it later, but I must be going. I need to return to my watch at the gate." And with that, he was gone.

"So, what do we need to discuss?" Baran asked as he picked up one of Inoch's hilts.

Arun took the hilt from his friend and placed it back down on the table. "Descia found a myth concerning the origin of Bälech. He's not merely an old soul inhabiting new bodies. If true, he's a Divine, immortal creature; his very existence is composed of the Divine as we are of matter. His command over it is almost limitless. He might as well be a god for all it matters to us."

Baran's mouth grew tight. "That Elf may have visions, but she's a damned fool to think any of us could deliver her people from such a creature. So," he said, turning to Arun, "have you come up with a plan?"

Arun shrugged. "Hope Athaz gets back without being followed and that in a few years this all blows over?"

Baran looked at him again in a way Arun wasn't used to. "You remember what we pulled you out of. More than anyone else, you know that's not going to happen."

Arun looked at his old friend. They hadn't been separated long, but the change was obvious. "You've changed."

Now it was Baran's turn to shrug. "Perhaps. You definitely need to."

"What's that supposed to mean?" Arun asked.

"It means you can't try to hide any more. Growing up, we protected each other from those that tried to knock us down and keep us there. But I can't help you against the designs they have for you, other than try to make sure you don't get lost in your own head while fighting against them."

Arun sighed as he sank onto the couch. "I know. My recklessness nearly got you killed. It did kill Brasan and his men. But I won't make that mistake again. I just don't know what course of action I should take. But, this time, I won't be rash."

Arun had his arm covering his eyes as he looked toward the ceiling, so he hadn't seen Baran fetch a mug of beer from a barrel in the kitchen he had found. Slamming it down on the small table next to Arun's ears, he made his friend jump much in the way he had done for years at The Academy.

"At least I've always been good at snapping you back into reality," he said with a grin. There was the friend of his youth!

With a smile, Arun responded, "That you have."

* * * * * * * * * *

Athaz followed his son, who in turn was following Kruthos, as they walked on the eastern side of the Argom River. Fearing their faces were too well known, rather than going into town for horses or a boat, they had instead slowed their travel by venturing back into the mountains as soon as cities and towns became visible. They returned to the river once they were well beyond them. Athaz spent as much time in the rear guard as he could; he had probably seen more of Caedin in the past three weeks than he had in the previous ten years. However, Caedin still refused to speak him beyond what their travel mandated. "Hand me the flint," had been the longest sentence his son had spoken to him. Of course, he hadn't spoken much more to Kruthos, though occasionally he asked something about the Dwarves of Menigar. Athaz knew that a normal relationship with his son after all these years was likely impossible; he really didn't even know what one would look like, but he had hoped the frigid ice would at least begin to thaw over the weeks they had spent together.

They were nearing the Tikus Foothills and would soon be turning in to where the Savanir scouts would be looking for them. A sudden, icy breeze came rushing up from behind them, reminding them early winter was in full swing and that the snows would be coming soon. Shaking off the cold, Athaz was glad they had finished in time, if barely.

The following day, Kruthos turned them due east, away from the river. For another four days, they tramped up hills and down valleys. The trees, spread out great distances apart and relatively short, had traded in their final bits of green foliage for reds, browns, and yellows three or four weeks ago. Though some leaves still stubbornly clung to their branches, they were beginning to fall in earnest. Athaz reckoned in two more weeks the trees would be fully bare. He was glad he would be underground by that point.

In the middle of the fourth night after they had left the river, they made camp but only for a short sleep; Kruthos had told them a scout would be sent to fetch them under cover of darkness. Caedin stirred occasionally; it seemed he was searching for something in his pack, but he eventually settled and lay still. Shortly before midnight, Kruthos' ears detected the sound he had been waiting for. He stood in front of their fire and gave a brief hand signal to let the still unseen scout know they were not under duress and remained unfollowed. An Elf appeared before them

"Well met, Therran," Athaz said with a grin.

"Well met, indeed," Therran replied. "Where have you been? Our spies haven't heard head nor tails of you since you left. We knew you had at least made it into The Tennebron. The uproar was great enough that Bälech himself went down there. But we haven't heard of or seen you since. We feared you had been captured."

"No, and if you couldn't find any trace of us, hopefully neither could the enemy. I have to admit," Athaz said after a brief pause, "I'm somewhat shocked to see you here. You seem a little … overqualified for this task."

Therran shrugged. "I wanted to see your family for myself, among other reasons." Therran paused for a moment as he surveyed the camp. "I know you would never have stopped before you found your wife. I am sorry you were not able to do so in time." Therran stepped up to introduce himself to the young man.

"Caedin, is it? I am Commander Therran, it is a pleasure to meet you." Caedin glanced up for a brief second to halfheartedly shake the Elf's hand, but Therran did not release him. "Let me see your face, young Man."

Caedin tried to get his hand free, but Therran's grip was as strong as death. "Unhand me, fiend!" Caedin cried.

"Let my son go, Therran!" Athaz demanded.

"If you wish to turn his face toward me yourself, then do so!" Therran responded. "I saw a faint glow. If these are the eyes of one who has drank the Divine Draught, Bälech will not have needed to track you."

Kruthos was up in an instant and grabbed Caedin's head and turned it toward Therran.

"Hold Caedin still," Therran told Kruthos.

Athaz's hand went to his sword. "Release him, or death shall take one of us soon!"

"Hold your sword, Athaz! I mean to free your son, not harm him. Bälech has seen much and heard much from your son's perspective. I will wall off the tainted part of his mind, but first I need to know how much."

Caedin struggled furiously, but held in Kruthos' arms he might as well have been a young child trying to escape from bitter medicine. "Release me! Your pain will be multiplied tenfold for every injury I endure! The Son of Bälech will kill you all! And this wretched world will know his name alone!"

Therran grimaced. "Brainwashed as well." Looking into Caedin's eyes, he grabbed the young Man's head to steady it. *"Appertodos!"*

Caedin stopped struggling, unable to flinch or blink from the Elf's all-seeing stare. For five full minutes, no one hardly dared to breathe. At last, Therran, still commanding Caedin's attention, spoke. "All is well, he has yet to learn anything he did not know before or wouldn't have learned after your raid on the prison. Well, nothing other than my name and face. Now, to seal his mind. *Sempri isalligo* —" But suddenly with a cry Therran fell back, and Kruthos released Caedin. "No!" the Elf was screaming in terror. "Kill me! Kill me quickly! My mind is open to him! I cannot keep him out … Kill me!"

Kruthos was unarmed, and so reluctantly Athaz half-raised his sword. Suddenly, he gasped in pain as one of the Dwarf's axes came down across his spine and continued into his left lung. Kruthos turned to see Athaz slowly fall in spite of his attempt to remain standing, revealing Caedin's blood-spattered face filled with a mad glee. "The traitor now knows what it means to be stabbed in the back!"

As Kruthos made a move to grab Caedin, he became distracted as Therran's cries went into another plane of terror. "HE KNOWS!! He has seen Menigar!"

"And with that knowledge, Elf, you die first among your remaining ilk!" Caedin cried as he leapt toward the Elf.

Kruthos' tackle came too late, and Caedin planted the axe deep into Therran's chest, just below the throat.

* * * * * * * * * *

"Damned wretched fool!" Bälech screamed as his vision was cut off. The screams of the soldiers who had survived Arun's escape still echoed throughout the torture chamber. Their fallen comrades had been the lucky ones. "Quiet, traitors!" he screamed at them. With a Divine command, he clenched their jaws and sealed their lips, muffling their screams so he could think. Bälech stalked around, wroth that Menigar had so long hidden under his very nose. Needing a release for his anger, he grabbed a nearby hammer and began bludgeoning the soldiers to death to quieten them even more. He could have been more creative with the Divine, but ever since he had taken on flesh to keep Xiarch at bay, he found physically relieving his stress to be very effective. When the final soldier stopped whimpering even after repeated blows, Bälech stalked out of the torture chambers. He had an army to muster.

CHAPTER XX

Of Elves and Men

At last, Kruthos managed to catch Caedin. He would have strangled the man then and there, but Athaz weakly called out to him, "Spare him, I beg!"

"Sentimental old fool!" Caedin shouted. "I am your son no longer! Spare me indeed! Spare me of his groveling and pleading. I'd rather be dead than endure it any longer. Where has this devotion come from? Did the Elves alter your mind too?"

With that, Kruthos lifted up his fist, hammering the back of Caedin's head and knocking him out cold.

Kruthos quickly bound Caedin from head to toe before going over to tend Athaz. The cut was deep, and Athaz had not moved since he had fallen. His wheezing was indicative of his lungs filling with blood.

"Spine's been cut," Athaz said in a whisper.

"Kruthos nodded silently in agreement, holding's his friend's head up. "Promise me, something. When your people retake Kelbragh, you or your descendants will lay me on the other side of Lilleth's marker."

"It will be done," Kruthos vowed. Athaz was choking so much it made talking nearly impossible. "Ask … Vera … Caedin …"

Kruthos understood. "I will."

Now unable to speak at all, Athaz simply mouthed, "Baran" followed by "Arun."

Before Kruthos could respond, Athaz's features relaxed, and his eyes stared at the stars overhead without seeing them.

"You needn't have asked. I am only sorry I failed to bring you back to them."

Two hours later, a tangent of soldiers came out when Therran did not return, Inoch among them. Kruthos had wrapped both the commander and Athaz in cloaks. "Kruthos ... what foul deed took place here?"

Kruthos recounted the grim evening. Inoch walked over and uncovered his Commander's face, his hand covering his own when he saw it. For a few moments, he stood there, forcing himself to accept what was in front him. At last, he inhaled deeply before clearing his throat.

"So," he said grimly. "Open war is upon us. At last."

It was a dark night for Menigar. Baran, Arun, and Descia had all gathered to welcome Athaz. They only heard of the horror that happened merely minutes before the bodies passed before them. Baran wept openly. Arun was too dazed to react. The cart that bore Athaz passed by him before he was even fully aware of what was in front of him. So lost was his mind in thought that it was a good twenty yards behind him before he turned so his eyes could follow after it. When he did, he saw Vera and the Lady Lyr running to the cart carrying Therran. When they saw his face, Lyr clutched him to her bosom weeping, and Vera's wails echoed throughout the city. For a brief second, Arun forgot about his own pain. Never since meeting the Elves had he felt any connection to them. They seemed to accept news, joyful or terrible, that would send others into emotional extremes as if they had been informed of the weather.

Arun was ashamed of himself, but he could not stop his mind from thinking that maybe Vera would begin to realize the foolishness of her actions. He reproached himself immediately and hung his head in shame of what he had thought. Sorrow filled his mind as he remembered Athaz's fate. At that moment, Kruthos walked passed them, and he laid a hand on Arun.

Baran was behind him, eyes red from weeping, though he had steadied himself for the moment. "I am sorry," he said.

Caedin was bound and at that moment being pushed by guards by them. Bälech must have tormented him with that face, for as he passed, he called out to Arun, "Now you have lost what should never have been yours!"

The pommel of a guard's sword hilt silenced him as he was driven down the path. Kruthos turned to face all of them. "Meet me in my house this evening. I must give a report to the Lady Lyr and city council on what has transpired and make the best of what little hope we have left."

As they waited in Kruthos' house, they realized Menigar's great fires were not being lit, even as the hours continued into the morning. By the command of Lady Lyr, the fires were extinguished for a day of mourning, both for Therran and also for the dark days ahead. Small candles alone provided light.

When Kruthos at last returned, he was weary. But he steeled himself for what he knew would be the worst part of these wretched hours. He first revealed what had happened once Therran revealed himself. "We've never seen such a Divine command before, not even the Elves. It was a counter command. When Therran attempted to wall off the part of Caedin's mind linked with Bälech, he must have spoken a trigger. Elves are deeply linked with the mind, and Therran was trying to delay the search for me or Athaz to kill him. But, according to Lady Lyr, the very act of trying to erect barriers most likely made it easier for Bälech to find what he sought. When Athaz thought about intervening, Caedin attacked him. Therran he killed once he warned us that Bälech found what he sought. I was a fool. I let my guard down before we were safely within Menigar. I was unarmed and didn't even see Caedin grab one of my axes."

Kruthos pulled out two pieces of paper from his pockets. "These were addressed and sealed to you. They were found on him during preparation of the body for tomorrow's funeral. There was another for his son as well, but I will keep that for now."

Baran and Arun looked over the letters addressed to them, sealed in plain wax with no insignia. "I assure you, no eyes have seen their contents," Kruthos said quietly. "Also, you and your friend's presence is requested at the council immediately, Arun. And with that, I must attempt to get what sleep I can. Once we lay our friends to rest, preparations must be made. The doom of the Savanir, one way or another, is at hand, and we must be prepared to face it."

When the Dwarf left them and entered his room, Baran tore open his letter. Descia made her way to his side and read it with him, bearing more of his weight as he continued reading. Arun didn't dare read his now. He would wait until he was alone and could react honestly with himself.

Once Baran had composed himself, he and Arun went to the council, guided by Descia. They were meeting in the same room where Athaz's identity of a Warden had been ripped from him. A council of eight members — three Men, three Dwarves, and two Elves stood on the balcony, with Lady Lyr at their center. Arun briefly wondered why there were only two Elves before he realized the obvious answer. Of course their military leader would have been on the council. *Bälech couldn't have found a better target if he had tried*, Arun thought bitterly to himself.

"Bring them chairs," Lady Lyr commanded. "Sorrow is a wearisome burden, and heavy decisions will make it more so."

"We are fine, Great Lady." Baran and Descia turned, somewhat surprised, to see it was Arun who had spoken. "I see no chairs for you or your people and heavier burdens lie on your shoulders than mine."

A brief, faint smile appeared on the Elf seer's lips. "I thank you for your thoughtfulness, but while these will be the worst times since the Great Night began, we are more accustomed to weightier matters than you. Indeed, the first of many decisions has been made, and that is why you have been summoned." She paused and looked to the right of the three friends. They were shocked to see Vera staring straight up at the council, jaw clenched.

"My granddaughter's vision that she placed faith in becomes ever murkier. It began to cloud the day the vision was made known to you. Arun, though you are generally kind and intelligent, it was clear from the time of your arrival that you lacked strength, foresight, and steadiness required to be what was hoped. Part of why you were allowed to leave as early as you were was because there was no need for mind-vision to see you must mature before you could accomplish what we hoped. So deficient in this virtue were you that I feared keeping you here against your will, even for a brief time for your own safety. It would ruin any hope that you might one day trust us enough to bring down the creature whose existence has threatened ours for millennia, under whose rule you and all others who sought Truth and Growth would be killed for their desires rather than encouraged. But I chose ill. Though my granddaughter's vision fades, it is I who am to blame, not her. And now, at last, it is obvious that it will never come to pass. You are not a warrior, and any hope in stealth is now ended. The Dawn's full might will march on Menigar. But, as you have made clear, you owe us nothing. You are here through no choice of your own and have suffered much. Though we cannot atone for our errors, we would see no more harm or pain inflicted on you for our account. Therefore, gather yourselves. Once Athaz is laid to rest and you pay your respects, flee. The world is wide, and though a civilization may not hide, a small number of its people may. You, as well as a select few of our own people, must attempt to survive in the open. You may also take what companions from the city are willing to go; Inoch, I am sure at least, will travel with you. Kruthos has already told me he shall as well. He vowed to watch over you before Athaz's life left him. May fortune in future days be kinder to you. Farewell."

The council turned and left. Vera came up to them and bowed before Arun. "Forgive me," she said before turning to leave.

Arun reached out and touched her shoulder to stop her. "One day, I will, but I won't ever be able to repay you for saving our lives ... or for revealing a new world to me. So, you must settle for my gratitude instead."

When Vera looked into his eyes, she saw he was sincere. In his eyes burned a fire of great anger, but deeper in his mind she saw great depths of Gratitude and Sorrow that would put out the fire - one day. Bowing again, deeper than before, she turned and hurried out. Arun, Baran, and Descia returned to Kruthos' house, the events of the past several hours, and its possible ramifications, repeatedly playing through their minds.

Therran's funeral was held first, less than twenty-four hours after his death. Arun was shocked that those in his command did not carry their weapons, but rather were dressed in tunics covered in script. It brought to mind the time Arun had seen him by the pool, lost in memories. When he said so out loud, Kruthos responded, "Therran's spirit, and all the memories contained therein, are returning to the Sea. Whether those memories be of war or peace, joy or sorrow, they tell the story of this world, and in such knowledge is their chief delight — that their memories will live on in the Sea, to be remembered by those that care to look for them."

"But aren't Elves' spirits immortal and won't he be reincarnated?" Arun asked. "I get that it's sad, and it will be some time before those who loved him will see him again, but this is simply a long yet finite separation."

"His spirit will reenter this world at some point," Kruthos confirmed. "But the memories and his identity will stay in the Sea. Therran is no more. When that spirit returns, those he knew may be in the Sea still. Even if his contemporaries of this life were his again, they may never meet, and neither would know the other. Such memories and knowledge greatly affect how the spirit interacts with the world around them. Certain traits may transcend individual lives, but even those might have their expressions altered by circumstance. The spirit's life will continue, but 'Therran' will not."

Arun then understood their great sorrow. Never would Vera know her brother again. Lyr would never see her grandson again. The Elves may have eternal lives, but not eternal identities. They melded and shaped themselves to their environment much like the water they loved. Arun found the idea of a never-ending life, but transient identity unsettling. But, then again, he was a Man, not an Elf.

Four Elves picked up the cot on which his body lay. Vera, along with another Elf maiden, carried the front end, where his head lay. At his feet, Arun saw Inoch and another, much older soldier. In front of all of them was the Lady Lyr, carrying a torch. They followed her as she began her journey through the Elven District of Menigar. She made her way to the outer wall, where she paused and two Dwarves stepped forward. Speaking a Divine command, the outline of a great archway appeared in the rock. It glowed faintly before emitting a bright light, after which the wall began to slowly lower into a previously hidden recess in the ground, revealing a great tunnel. The tunnel was smooth with ornate script and images along the walls, telling the stories of countless Elves who returned to the Sea since the beginning of the Long Night. Into this tunnel, the procession entered, followed by all the mourners in attendance, including Kruthos, Arun, Baran, and Descia.

They began to descend deeper in the mountain, down a smooth, gentle slope. Arun could not tell how long they had been walking, but it must have been at least an hour when, at last, the Lady Lyr stepped up to a simple circular stone platform, polished smooth as glass. Beside the platform ran a small river. The pallbearers walked right up to the edge of the water before laying the burden down with the utmost gentleness. Here, Inoch and the other soldier turned to face Lady Lyr, bowing their heads. She returned the bow before the two men joined the other mourners in the crowd. Next, another Elf came up to the platform to hold the torch for the Lady Lyr, and she, along with Vera and another Elf Arun did not know, knelt beside the body. Vera held one of her brother's hands while Lady Lyr held the other. The Elf woman that Arun did not recognize caressed his face, and her cries were louder than the others.

She's his wife Arun realized.

The Lady Lyr and Vera stood first but waited patiently until Therran's wife also stood. Lady Lyr picked up both corners of the cot where the commander's feet lay, while the other two grabbed a corner each at his head. Walking into the water, they laid the cot down again and held his body in place as the current washed over it. After a few seconds, Therran's body began to fade, like mist in the morning the sun. It only took a moment, and soon the three women were only holding his garments.

The crowd began to turn around of its own accord; those closest to Therran would remain behind for a while longer, mourning together in private.

Descia began the somber walk back, holding Baran's hand. Arun and Kruthos soon began walking behind them. "I don't think I'm going to be able to hold it together for Athaz's funeral for anywhere

The Tales of Lugon

near as long," Arun thought aloud after they had exited the tunnel.

Baran nodded his head in agreement.

"There is no shame in sorrow, but if you wish to keep your mourning a private matter, Athaz's funeral will be much shorter," said Kruthos. "Though his aid given after The Sundering is appreciated, his actions as a Warden would make it … painful for the Men of Menigar to accept him to rest with their dead." Kruthos waved down their indignant protest. "Whether this is right or wrong is moot because of Athaz's own wishes. If the Savanir survive, somehow, I have vowed to exhume his body and place it beside his wife's. And though I will have to tell the story at another time, his place in Dwarven history will silence any complaints. But until his wishes can be fulfilled, he will rest in my family's tomb."

At Kruthos' house, the party silently bided their time. Arun suddenly remembered the letter Athaz left him. Pulling it out, he read:

Arun,

I am sorry that, if you're reading this letter, we never got to know each other in happier times. I would not leave this world without expressing how much I have come to admire both of my two young charges. You and Baran have grown and matured much over the course of a few short months. In you, Arun, I have seen your resolve blossoming as your timidity fades. You have made mistakes and will continue to make them. But you can at least now learn from them instead of looking down on others from the Keeper's tower. I know you still don't know your place in this new world yet, but I commend you for now beginning to look for it.

I have a final request I would ask of you. I hear my son in his sleep, and I fear the enemy has used my absence to poison his mind, especially during his time in The Tennebron. I ask you to do what I did not. Stay with him. I know from your file that you and Baran formed a brotherhood out of necessity, covering for each other's weakness. Caedin will hate you at first. Stay with him anyway. I, too, come from a Yeoman background. I thought that joining the military would keep my family together, unlike so many that, like your own, were split apart. That all changed on the day I became a Warden.

Long ago, I had a chance to stop it, if I had the intelligence to simply throw a piece of paper away. I know you would have had the foresight to do so (just as you see the unrealistic expectations the Savanir have placed on a world without Bälech). Instead, I still clung to a hope I always knew, deep down, was false. I hope that you, as his brother, will be more faithful than I was as his father. Set my son free from the lies of the evil I served for so long.

Though your bravery in battle only shines when all is lost, your courage to seek the Truth is what led you down this path. Do not worry about the visions or designs the Savanir have for you. I do not claim to know much about fate, but I can tell you from my own experience that trying too hard to shape the future, in any direction, often leads to the very thing you tried to avoid.

Farewell, Arun. If the Savanir are right, may Xiarch have mercy on me and may we meet again when the world is made anew. If not, I die blessed in the days we spent together.

- Athaz

Arun stared at the paper for a long time, in shock. It didn't seem fair that death had allowed Athaz to express himself freely while simultaneously denying the opportunity for Arun to do so in return. A feeling unknown to Arun welled up inside of him. The only man Arun had ever looked up to had left him with a task. It didn't seem fair or even possible. Caedin was still raving mad, now in the prison of the Savanir. But Arun was determined to try. This was not a prophecy to meet but a command to be obeyed.

"Arun ..." Kruthos knocked on the other side of the door. "It is time."

Athaz's body had been brought to Kruthos' house, lying on a cot similar to the one that bore Therran earlier. No one else would be accompanying them. However, made aware of the discovery of Kelbragh that Athaz shared with Kruthos, the Dwarves of Menigar quickly crafted grave clothes in his honor. A white hammer and chisel crest identical to the one on the gate had been embroidered on the black silk wrappings. Baran and Descia carried the front corners while Arun carried both in the back as they followed Kruthos through the Dwarven District.

Similar to the Elves, they stopped at an outer wall. Here, Kruthos gave a Divine command, and another archway opened. But there was no tunnel. Instead, they immediately entered a huge cavern. The roof was over a hundred feet above them, and the four walls of the room were many times that apart. Inside this enormous room were many long, low buildings, none more than ten feet high, though some were stacked on top of each other.

They walked along the narrow corridors. Arun noticed at the front of all of the crypts was a barrier, and each barrier had different emblems and scripts. Kruthos stopped in front of one that displayed a landscape Athaz would have recognized had he been able to see it. It was a forest of stone, with emeralds, rubies, and amethysts for the trees' leaves.

When Kruthos removed the barrier, they entered. It was a long hallway, with stone beds two high, lining both the left and right sides. Underneath each bed was a small family tree. When they had gone perhaps thirty yards or so, they came to an empty bed on the left, where they placed Athaz's litter.

"Look," Descia whispered, pointing to the stone underneath. Athaz's name and Lilleth's name had been inscribed, a line linking them, with a line leading to Caedin's name underneath. But on the other side of Athaz's name, another line linked an image of a zweihänder. Underneath that line were two lines inscribed: "Baran" and "Arun".

Kruthos spent a moment kneeling beside the body before motioning the others to do the same. When the others stood behind Kruthos again, he bowed one last time. "Farewell, son of Man," he said. "May you find Xiarch's favor and your eyes, when next they open, see those you love once again, never more to part." Then they turned and left Athaz to his rest.

CHAPTER XXI

The Best Laid Plans...

The next morning, Inoch guided Arun to the Lady Lyr, who had summoned him once more. After they had bowed to council, she spoke, "The time has come for you to depart. Already Bälech's main army has issued forth from Hilae. Other armies under his banner are amassing as well. Intelligence believes Bälech means to have them muster at Simpat, where some of his scouts have already arrived to ensure he is aware of any movements we may try to make. Even the most conservative estimates put his numbers in the tens of thousands. You must leave now or you risk being pursued, as your face is well known to any in Bälech's service."

Arun bowed. "I have decided to stay here. I will honor Athaz's final request of me, and I will not leave his son. Besides..." Arun shrugged "...it's not like he'll give up searching for me. As unlikely as victory seems, my best chance is for the Savanir's defenses to hold. As such, I will contribute in any way I can. I'm no soldier, but perhaps fresh eyes in your library can find something hidden by familiarity."

This unexpected turn caused an uproar among the council, and Arun noticed with some contempt that, though they may not believe in him defeating Bälech now, apparently even this offer was in the hopes that he would live long enough to do so one day. When he felt they had bickered enough, he raised his voice, "What kind of gift is the recipient not allowed to do with it as he pleases? I told you before I will not be herded into your designs."

There was silence for a moment before Lady Lyr spoke again. "Very well, Arun, but no more will my people attempt to aid you." *About time*, Arun thought to himself. "Conduct yourself as you see fit, but, like all residents of Menigar, you will be expected to do as you're told and aid in the defense of the city when the time comes.

For now, that means you will be quartered with Inoch. He and Kruthos seem to be the only people in Menigar who can get you to act with any sense, and Kruthos' abilities will be vital in preparation of our defense. Now," she ended with obvious frustration and disdain, "you are dismissed. Trouble us no more."

Arun bowed, though he felt like laughing. Had she forgotten he was only there through their own plots? He hurried away before they could think of something else to say, a stunned Inoch following behind him. "You certainly know how to fluster the council."

Arun shrugged. "If you all didn't trust them so blindly, my friends and I would be dead and your city would still be safe." Inoch's face became bitter after that remark, and Arun softened his tone. "Don't get me wrong, I am grateful, but they can't feign altruism was their motivation. There is no need for me to act as if I am forever in their debt."

On their way back, Arun noticed something different about Inoch's sword. "Did you get a new blade?"

"No, but I did put on a different hilt," Inoch replied. Suddenly blushing like an artist whose work was unexpectedly noticed and unable to decide if he was happy or worried about the attention, he continued, "We have time now, if you want to look over the others you saw earlier?"

Arun nodded. "Of course!"

Arriving at the house, Inoch let Arun inside his personal room. There were dozens of hilts mounted all over the wall. Some seemed purely defensive, designed to either deflect blows away from the hand or catch incoming blades. But others, Arun noticed, were very offensive in design. One had stone knuckles over where the wielder's knuckles would grab the handle, with sharp spike protruding from each one.

"You've used all of these?" Arun asked.

"Not all. Many of the earlier ones never, but this one…" Inoch unbelted his sword and scabbard and tossed it to Arun "…is my newest one to be equipped." The guard extended in four directions, with small, dull blades extending parallel with the main blade. Each one turned inward and back toward the hilt at the end. "I use this one to catch my opponent's blades and pull it out of their hands. Sometimes, when others particularly like the design, the Dwarves start to make them for the other soldiers. Not only do I not have the time, but their craftsmanship is superior to mine. But," Inoch finished, taking the sword back, "I still like to use my own crafted by my hands. Foolish, I know, but I like trusting my own work in battle."

The next few days saw Baran and Inoch training with the Savanir army while Arun and Descia spent their time in the library. They would spend the majority of each day translating ancient legends surrounding Bälech and the Divine, ending each day with reading and reviewing what the other had found. Though they searched incessantly from morn till night, they found nothing that could help them defeat their foe. Every night before returning to Inoch's place, Arun would take his fauchard and run through his paces as best he remembered them from Athaz's lessons. He wished he had a sparring partner, but Baran and Inoch were both preparing with the army. He also practiced throwing his knives, but he doubted they would be much use. Finally, he would stop by the prison to attempt to see Caedin, though the young man was still in the throes of madness.

Kruthos had asked Vera to cleanse his mind, but it was feared that Bälech may still have some link with him. They could not risk Bälech learning more than he already knew or what measures were being taken to prepare for the oncoming battle.

In the coming days, many preparations were made. The Savanir in the Forest of Orus sent their army to aid Menigar, but it was meager, as its location hid fewer to begin with. Much to the chagrin of the council, those in the Agna Desert refused to send anyone. They claimed that they could send no aid that would avail Menigar, which was probably true enough. But there was also the obvious fact that they believed the desert would continue to protect them.

"Fools!" a council member had exclaimed after hearing their response. "The desert will one day destroy them if they are unable to leave it, which is exactly what will come to pass if we fall here."

Twenty-four days after Arun had refused to leave, the alarms rang throughout Menigar. Bälech's army was less than two days' march away from the mountain. Inoch came rushing into the library and spotted Arun and Descia working feverishly. "Find anything?" he asked. They shook their heads, not even lifting their eyes from the work. "I'm afraid I have orders to bring you with me," Inoch said to Arun. "Every able-bodied person with any weapons' knowledge is commanded to gather. The army is greater even than we feared. More than forty thousand march on Menigar, including three hundred Wardens and thousands of Healers."

Arun nodded and closed his translation tome before pushing the scrolls he had been working on over to Descia. "This is beyond stupid!" she yelled at Inoch. "He may have some rudimentary knowledge of how to fight, but you are robbing me of a valuable partner, and if the army is indeed that large, it becomes even more clear that our hope lies in finding something hidden in the past!"

She would have continued, but Arun stopped her. "That might be," he said, "but we couldn't go through all of these documents if we had ten years to search. At this point, we need either a miracle or for Bälech to trip over his own feet. Besides," he said with a smile, "I have to make sure your fiancé doesn't do something to get himself killed if he tries something that pops into his head before he thinks about it."

Descia tried to bite her tongue, but she couldn't stop herself from swearing, "Men ..." under her breath.

Inoch led Arun to a place where he was suited with some very lightly padded armor, and then they went to retrieve his weapons. Baran was also in Inoch's camp, along with the other young soldiers. There was a lot of tension. Most of them had only fought against the Savage Races. The idea of fighting trained men, not to mention Wardens, with less than an eighth of their enemy's forces, left many feeling hopeless.

"The frontline is filled with many men that served under Therran," Inoch explained. "Most of us would simply get slaughtered if we tried to take them on directly. Baran will be joining the archers; they will be our primary means for keeping the Wardens in check. Though we aren't likely to kill many, if we can

keep them moving it will make wielding the Divine very difficult."
Baran nodded, remembering playing the same game with the
Watcher when rescuing Arun.

"Our biggest concern is going to be running out of arrows. We
are going to need to thin their numbers significantly before we
run out. That's where the Dwarves come in. They'll be stationed
with the archers, waiting for the enemy to wander near the traps
prepared throughout the mountain."

"That's right," said a gruff, familiar voice. Kruthos took off
his helmet and bowed. "I heard you had come to the front and
decided to come say hello. I'll be counting on you to keep any that
get through the frontlines away from me."

"Yes, that will be our role," Inoch said. "We will be the front
guard for the archers and Earth-Movers. Here…" Inoch went over
to a cart filled with gear and picked up small bronze shield "…
there will bronze pavises forming a wall, but use this to shield
yourself and the others from attacks that might get through. You'll
be stationed behind the shield wall, alongside Baran and Kruthos."
Inoch continued. "Our plan for now is to guide them into the
traps. When any Warden has lost enough men, special strike forces
will attempt to quickly take him out. The wildcard will be Bälech
himself. He marches with them, though it is believed he plans on
merely observing his final victory over the Savanir."

Before the day was done, the entrance had been sealed with
stone by the Dwarves, but it would not delay Bälech long. Its main
purpose was to allow them to hear when their enemy reached the
path to Menigar.

That night, everyone not on watch lay next to each other trying
to find rest. Arun and Baran were beside each other. Like the rest
of the camp (and most of Menigar), neither slept. No one would
be returning home until the battle reached its conclusion. They
whispered some meager attempts at conversation as they lay in
the dark, but it was pointless. There was nothing that could be
said to break the sense of dread and nothing that needed to be
said regarding their friendship. So, at last, they just looked up in
the darkness above them. Arun was intrigued by the seemingly

infiniteness of it. Though the roof of the cavern was only a few hundred feet above them, the black abyss his eyes perceived created a sense of looking further into a nothingness than the infinite sky dotted with stars immeasurable distances away. If one wasn't careful, it would be easy to forget the overwhelming darkness ended just beyond where they could see.

As Baran peered into the darkness, in his mind he could clearly see Descia, undoubtedly spending the night in the library, only sleeping in short bursts as exhaustion overtook her. He had tried to persuade her and Paleon to go with those who had been sent out shortly after the murder of Athaz and Therran, but she had refused, and her father swore he would sooner die than not know the fate of his daughter again. Like every other soldier that night, he knew there was nothing to save those he loved. He was placing his faith in the Dwarves to kill the footmen and the strike teams to kill the Wardens. The strike teams were placing their faith in the Dwarves for the same thing and archers to silence the Wardens. The Dwarves were placing their faith in their comrades as well. It was a circle of dependence that allowed them to bear a burden no mortal could possibly do alone.

There were no pre-tremors before it came. A deafening explosion sent the entire army jumping to their feet as one. Bälech had breached the mountain, and the first parts of his army would be there soon. Men, Elves, and Dwarves ran to their posts, checking supplies they had already gone over a hundred times. The Battle for Menigar was about to begin.

When the front of Bälech's army reached the barricade that the Savanir had erected about half a mile out, almost half of his army still stood out in the Tikus Foothills, waiting to come in. About two hundred feet out, the army had stopped and stood silently with grim, fell faces. Savanir leaders ran up and down their line, quietly telling their men to hold steady, but, upon battle being joined, "Make every mother's son believe every horror story they ever heard of The Bewildered!"

Arun smiled. Elves as witches, Dwarves with golem servants

Truth Unearthea

that did their bidding. Wild Men that served their devilish Dwarf and Elf lords. These were the stories Bälech had fed his own people. It may only help until they became more terrified of Bälech than the tales they heard as children, but the lies Bälech had sowed still might prove a valuable ally.

Out from the line stepped a man with an elaborate black robe with orange and green trim. He had rings on every finger, two on each index finger. The way he strode so boldly from the soldiers boasted of a man who was so used to being feared he had forgotten how to fear himself. He produced a long scroll and began reading a list of atrocities The Bewildered had committed against The Dawn. The reaction among the Savanir varied from amusement to disgust. Baran and Arun saw a Dwarven commander come up next to Kruthos and whisper something in his ear. Kruthos gave a slight chuckle and nodded as the man continued reading the crimes of the Savanir. After a full five minutes, he concluded, "For such crimes, The Bewildered are hereby commanded to lay down their arms and surrender—"

No sooner had the word "surrender" left his lips than the ground below him shot up into the darkness above them. If the man had made any sound of fright at the being raised to such a great height so unexpectedly, no one heard it. But they all heard his terrified scream as the ground dropped back into place twice as quickly as it had risen, with the man always just a few inches above it. The click of the ground reaching back to its original location also signaled the end of his screaming.

The stunt had the intended effect. The entire army of The Dawn shuffled backwards a few steps, and a murmur rose among them. But the Wardens were screaming at the men. "Fools! I'll do much worse to you if ever I see anything but your backs. Charge!"

The unexpected benefit of the Dwarven spectacle was the archers had now been able to mark the Wardens yelling at their troops, and they began firing at once. The Dawn's soldiers brought ladders to try and scale the barricade, but they were cut down by the veteran Savanir army that waited on the frontlines. One frustrated Warden joined his men in the charge. "Warden! Warden!" cried the archers.

No sooner had they said it than a group of Elves leapt over the frontlines and sprinted straight for him, cutting down any men that attempted to stand in their way. With blinding speed that neither Man nor Dwarf could match, they closed the distance quicker than Arun would have thought possible. When the first Elf reached the Warden, they found the he had just finished a Divine command. *"Shrik!"* Fire leapt from his hand and consumed the first Elf before he had time to scream. The Warden then deflected the spear of the second and put his own dagger into the Elf's throat. But as he raised his sword to engage the third, a fourth he had not seen came from below and thrust his spear under the shoulder of the Warden's raised arm and lifted him off the ground before planting him to it. They were on him in an instant. A small host from the frontlines had followed behind the strike team and now surrounded them as they finished off the Warden and protected them as they made their way back behind the barricade.

The Savanir army cheered. But though every large group may have a few fools, Bälech had not maintained his grip for over two thousand years with empty boasts. The Wardens lined their soldiers in front of them, creating a great wall of shields with gaps for them to send out their Divine commands. Some marched into traps prepared by the Dwarves and either were crushed or fell to their deaths. But their numbers simply couldn't be countered. As the corpses began to pile, the Dawn marched over their own dead or propped the crushing walls with the bodies of their fallen so they could continue to advance. The Savanir tried to fight them as they came, but whenever they tried, a swarm of Divine attacks met them, from several directions, ensuring at least one always found its mark.

As the day wore on, things only got worse for the Savanir. Once the Dwarven traps became congested, The Dawn's army began to lose fewer men. The Savanir still slew three for every one they lost, but it would not be enough. Baran had run out of arrows, his fingers covered with blood. Inoch had stopped him from going to the frontlines. "There'll be more on the way, and we have the gate to fall back to," he had said. That was two hours ago. But finally, a horn sounded and the slow retreat to the gate began. Three hours after that, Arun and Inoch sat around a table in a building that normally housed a tailoring business less than a tenth of a mile from the gate. Baran and some others were lying on the floor on pallets, trying to get some rest

"The gate they will find much more difficult to take," Inoch said.

"How many did we lose? How many did we kill?" Baran asked.

"We lost two thousand and estimate their casualties nigh seven thousand, probably fifty of their Wardens," he answered.

Arun slammed the staff of his fauchard on the ground. "Nowhere near enough, then," he said.

Inoch didn't answer. The situation was indeed looking more and more hopeless, especially since most of the soldiers the Savanir had lost were their most seasoned fighters.

"How long can we hold them at the gate?" Baran asked. Inoch was slow to answer. "Probably not more than two days," he said at last. Arun swore, "Damn! The Wardens are destroying us. We can't win against such power." Inoch reproached him. "We must not give up. If we do, the outcome is certain. But as long as we fight," he said, holding his sword up to each of their faces in turn, "then, however small, there is hope." Arun looked at the sword and the hilt their friend had made as he sighed. "I wish Athaz was here. He might be able to provide some tactic. Especially since Athaz was much more acquainted on Bälech's Divine Nature."

"What do you mean, 'Divine Nature?'" asked Inoch.

"Hmm? Oh, maybe I misunderstood. There is a scroll in your library that talks about how Bälech's existence is purely Divine; he has no body of his own as we know it, though obviously he can manipulate one. It's one reason why I know I could never beat him; I don't even have Divine abilities."

A fire lit in Inoch's eyes that perplexed Arun. He continued to watch as his friend's face contorted with ideas quickly coming together. "Of course … of course! But … wait, I'll never …" Suddenly he looked up at Arun. "We have to go. Now." Leaving Baran behind, Inoch ran as fast as he could to his house, Arun following in confusion.

The Tales of Lugon

About thirty minutes after the two friends disappeared into the house, Inoch dashed out, sprinting toward the Elven District. He had two missions, and he knew which to do first.

As he suspected, Inoch found Lady Lyr, Vera, and the rest of the council of Menigar going over battle plans as well as trying to figure out how they could evacuate more of the civilians who had stayed behind to aid in the battle. When Inoch crashed through the doors, they lifted their weary heads, too relieved for the momentary distraction to rebuke the young soldier.

"My Lady Lyr," Inoch began, "I have news that must be for your ears alone." The seer, for the first time Inoch had known her, looked as ancient as she was. With a resigned smile, she motioned him to follow her as she walked away from the table to leave the rest of the council to continue without her.

"You make bold use of my trust that I place in you," Lady Lyr began, just so Inoch wouldn't get too comfortable. "But I guess we don't have the time for you to run out of favors you have collected for all the times you assisted Therran before he fell."

If Inoch's mind were not on more important matters, he would have felt ashamed at even that mild rebuke, but there was no time. "Milady, Arun plans to duel Bälech."

Strong doubt stormed over Lady Lyr's face. "Vera, join us," she called out to the table. Vera's face showed more frustration than resignation, but she saw the same grim reality before them just as her grandmother had. "Have you received any vision from the Sea that would hint toward a possible victory should Arun face him in battle?"

Vera's face fell downcast. "No, I have not. But why this useless line of questioning?"

"Because Inoch has just informed me that Arun wants to duel Bälech."

"What?!" Vera's incredulous face looked into Inoch's eyes, but he returned her gaze with a determined calmness.

"Yes, Lady Vera, that is his plan," confirmed Inoch.

"Foolish boy!" she thundered.

"No more foolish than the one who put him in this situation,"

Truth Unearthed

272

Lady Lyr said evenly.

Vera regretted her outburst. She knew all of this was ultimately her fault, but she was still too young to acknowledge it to anyone but Lady Lyr, and only then in private.

"Rest assured," Inoch said to intervene, "Arun has no delusions about the odds of success. But, as he just pointed out to me, all plans likely lead to the same result. Though he himself has no experience with Xiarch, he acknowledges he has learned much since being in Menigar. He figures that trusting to Xiarch is as good a plan as any. If nothing else, the delay in setting up the duel will buy us more time to repair our defenses and see if we can help any more civilians escape."

"He said that?" Lady Lyr asked, searching Inoch's eyes. His eyes would give away a flimsy story without her needing to read his mind. "It is a generous gift if given, but it does not line up with what we have seen of him thus far."

"Yes, milady. Believe me, I've tried to dissuade him from this plan," Inoch said with earnestness that set them back. "I wanted to try something different, but he wouldn't even consider it. I admit it was worse. I just didn't want him to die like this."

Seeing Inoch's sincere grief put aside any doubts Vera and Lady Lyr had that Arun was truly volunteering to face Bälech.

"He only asks one thing: that we seek Xiarch's protection for him however we may. His exact words were, "I have never seen anything more powerful than the Emperor, but if one exists, and you have his ear, I'm going to need the help."" For a second, Inoch paused. He wanted some sense of permission for what he was about to do. "And that I assist him in any way I'm able."

The Lady Lyr nodded her head. "Of course. You may tell him he goes with our blessing and prayers. Now, leave us to use this new information and time as best we can."

Inoch saluted and quickly walked out of the room. *That should keep them occupied while I carry out the next step,* he thought to himself as he made a beeline to his next destination.

The Tales of Lugon

* * * * * * * * * *

Five minutes after Inoch left, Arun rose from his chair as he, too, prepared to leave. The plan was foolhardy. There was zero chance of defeating Bälech. That alone gave him the conviction he needed for his plan. But once Arun made this offer to the Emperor, there would be no going back. It wasn't what he wanted, but it was the only way to save Baran, Descia, Caedin, Kruthos, and Inoch. As he left Inoch's home and began the walk toward the prison barracks that held Caedin, Arun had to keep telling himself that this deception was necessary.

When Arun arrived, he saluted the guards and made his way down to where Caedin resided. Athaz's son was still laughing maniacally. "Oh! There you are," he said with a malicious grin. "I wondered how long you would be able to stay away until your relationship with my treacherous father mandated your conscience to come try and save me one last time. Fool! It's you who needs a savior! When Bälech destroys this thorn in his side, I will walk over your corpses as his new vessel!"

Arun grimaced. Turning to the guards, he said, "Leave us. He may be more willing to speak to just me, unarmed, than with you near. He's chained. You needn't fear for my safety." Dropping his voice to a whisper, he continued, "Anything I can get from him could help. Please."

The guards exchanged a concerned look and then whispered to each other. Finally, one said, "Make it quick. I don't see the harm in it, but I'd rather not face my commander's wrath for leaving him unattended."

"I won't be long," Arun assured them.

After the guards had gone up the stairs, Arun turned to Caedin, who was still mocking him. "If you think you're going to get me to tell you anything, I underestimated your idiocy," he said with a sneer.

"That was only for their benefit," Arun said darkly. "I know you still share your connection with your master; the Elves won't dare risk entering your mind again. I need to speak with him. And it will be I who will be his next host, not you!"

Arun yanked Caedin's head up by his hair and looked directly into his eyes. "Bälech, I have a proposition for you."

* * * * * * * * * *

When he was finished, Arun let Caedin's head go and the man slumped on the ground. Arun quickly checked his breathing and pulse. He was alive. *He won't betray me yet; he still needs me to come to him for the kind of victory he desires.*

"Guards!" Arun called. The two men came running down, as much to not be caught out of place as for concern for Arun. They stopped, stunned when they saw Caedin's body in a heap at Arun's feet. "I'm afraid his mind is still somehow linked with Bälech. He was about to say something when suddenly his breathing became labored and he passed out. He seems to be okay now, but I'd get a medic down here to just to make sure. I have to get ready to help defend the city; Caedin will not be able to help us, even if he wants to."

As Arun left the barracks, he fought a gnawing fear. *Could there be some other way?* If there was, he would need to find it fast.

CHAPTER XXII

Truth Hurts; Lies Destroy

By the next morning, all sounds of battle had ceased. Whispers of confusion ran up and down the Savanir line. What was going on? Why had The Dawn stopped their advances? No one knew or could even come up with an idea. One thing they did know: they did not like the grins of the enemy staring at them.

Inoch and Arun were preparing to go to the front. "You gave the Council the message?" Arun asked.

Inoch affirmed he did. "You sure you want to go through with this? I doubt it ends well for you."

Arun nodded. "I'm sure. And I talked to Baran, so your concern has been addressed."

Arun grabbed his fauchard and began making his way toward the front. Inoch handed a letter to the guard. It read:

Arun is going to try to live up to what I foresaw in him years ago and engage our Enemy in a duel for the lives of all the Savanir. Let them pass. However, I fear that potential future has already faded. Be prepared for his death. Let none pass after him until you hear from me.

-Vera"

The guard looked at Arun with a mixture of doubt and pity as he stepped aside. *At least that insane vision is finally of some use,* Arun thought to himself. Picking their way through the ranks of soldiers, they saw Baran had joined them, though he did not say a word. When they reached the frontline, Baran stopped and Inoch and Arun continued on until they were at the center of the clearing between the two opposing armies.

Inoch cleared his voice. "The champion of the Savanir stands ready for the duel as agreed." The soldiers in The Dawn chuckled as those in the center parted. Soon, Arun and Inoch could see a Warden making their way toward them. But something seemed different. His lips bore a smirk, not the grim or violent faces shared by most Wardens. But it certainly was not a smile of happiness. It was an impish grin, as if he was privy to some inside joke. His stride was easy, almost casual. Arun felt like this particular Warden viewed all of this as the game of mere children and that he had condescended to engage them at their level. Then he saw them. The eyes. They were an unnatural orange. Around his dark pupils, the irises glowed like molten rock. Arun felt terror grip him as he remembered seeing something eerily similar, but nowhere near as powerful, in the eyes of the Watcher who had tortured him. He stopped about ten paces after crossing the front of his army. "The Emperor of The Dawn stands ready," he said, almost lazily. "To receive the next Son of Bälech."

Yells of confusion swept over the Savanir as Inoch turned to Arun. "What does he mean?" Panic filled his voice.

"It's quite simple, really," Arun replied. "I had you tell Vera I intended to duel him to live up to her vision to get out here. But I've told you over and over I'm not your deliverer, and that plan you concocted at your house didn't have a chance of working. I didn't want this, but I'd rather live with him in my mind than suffer by his hand." Arun tossed his fauchard aside. "You'll be spared, Inoch, along with Kruthos and a few others. I negotiated that before I agreed to this."

"You can't do this!" Inoch screamed. "He'll never keep his word! And he'll have you wish for death in mere moments, but you won't find it … not until he gets tired of you!" Suddenly, Inoch pulled a dagger out from under his armor. "I won't let you do this!" he yelled as he went toward Arun's heart. Arun ducked, but the dagger still found his shoulder. Yelling in agony, he grabbed the handle with his hand as he collapsed to the ground.

"Enough!" Bälech said. "Seize them!" Those in the frontline of The Dawn ran forward and grabbed them as some of the Savanir attempted stop them. But it was no use, they quickly swarmed over Arun and Inoch and brought them to the Emperor. Arun was still grabbing at the hilt, gasping in agony when Bälech reached down and grabbed his chin to look him in the eyes.

The Tales of Lugon

"The boy was right, you know," he said in a malicious whisper. "You would be better off dead than my host. But … live and learn, right?" He laughed at his own joke as he turned to Inoch. "The last thing you'll see will be my new body striking you down - the image of your deliverance will instead be your doom."

"Damn you, Bälech!" Inoch screamed as he struggled against those holding him down. Arun tried to pull away. Those eyes were causing flashbacks, but he knew what was coming would be worse. Using both hands to steady his next victim, Bälech finally forced Arun's face in place while using his thumbs to hold Arun's eyes open. The next thing Arun knew, a Divine command was being issued. *Eg Bälech Daephas Do'ul Volencupen!*

The next minute seemed to last an eternity to Arun. He felt Bälech's presence overwhelming his mind. *Don't let go of that hilt! Whatever you do, keep those fingers closed!* he repeated to himself over and over. Then he heard Bälech's voice in his mind. "What is this?" Then the voice began to scream in terror. "Treachery! Treachery! Kill this fool!" But the only sound that escaped from Arun's mouth was screaming and gasping. Bälech had not been able to gain control over Arun's body before the effects of the Silent Stone began to take hold. "Curse you!" Bälech screamed at Arun. Between the agony of fighting for his mind and putting all of his focus on the dagger hilt in his shoulder, Arun could neither say nor do anything. He clung to the dagger hilt, no longer even remembering why it was important. All he could remember was that he could never let go.

"You, at least," Bälech's spirit boomed in unrestrained rage that echoed throughout Arun's mind, "I will undo before I am gone!" Suddenly, Arun's memories rushed to the forefront of his mind. But even before they were fully formed, Bälech distorted them. Descia had loved him, but Baran had seduced her. Athaz beat him mercilessly every time he had failed in his practices. He had been Head Keeper before The Bewildered kidnapped him and tortured him. Such were the warped memories Bälech implanted, but through it all, even though he no longer knew why, Arun screamed to himself: *Don't let go! Don't let go!* At last the rage seemed to be leaving him. Mental exhaustion and anguish converged upon Arun, and he finally relaxed as darkness took him, oblivious to all that was around him.

All this time, Arun was surrounded by mass confusion. Wardens and Healers mirrored Arun's writhing and screaming as they felt there very essences being ripped apart. With the source of their Divine Nature being absorbed into the Silent Stone, a mass Sundering of the thousands of Healers, Wardens, as well as the Watchers throughout Lugon, took place at once. In the confusion, Inoch was able to wrench himself free of his captors and made his way to Arun. Baran immediately ran out in front, turning to face the Savanir, telling them to wait. Eventually, Vera sent a messenger to ask Baran to explain what he knew. He wrote back as quick an explanation as he could.

Inoch and Arun laid a trap. They stole the Silent Stone and crafted a dagger hilt, the handle of the dagger that Inoch stabbed Arun with. Arun offered himself to Bälech through Caedin, pretending to all the Savanir, except Inoch and myself, that he planned to duel him.

Some of the commanders had also approach him by now. When they realized what was going on, they realized their opportunity. "Send them running!" they commanded their men.

Sure enough, with no one left to command them, most of The Dawn's army ran like wild men for the exit. But there was confusion, as many in the back, though they saw Wardens and Healers collapsing in agony, did not realize their Emperor was no more or that all their leadership was dead or dying. Many were trampled as their frightened comrades fled before the Savanir. But, eventually, the general madness took all of them, and they ran for their lives back to the outside world. When the Savanir reached the gate, they stopped their pursuit and resealed the mountain. The Battle for Menigar was over.

Medics were already tending to Arun. Inoch made sure that the one who removed the dagger had no connection with the Divine and took it from the medic's hand to keep it safe. The wound the dagger caused wasn't serious. However, nobody knew if Arun would survive his own Sundering. They carefully lifted him and bore him to the house of the nearest medic, accompanied by Baran, Kruthos, and Inoch. Shortly afterwards, Descia came rushing in. "Is he alright?" she asked breathlessly. The sounds of celebration in the street was a stark contrast to the tone of her voice and the mood of the room, and Baran was eager for the door to shut.

"Don't know … He hasn't stirred since we brought him in," Inoch said anxiously.

After an hour, Vera and Lady Lyr made their way down. Descia and Baran glared at them. The fact that Arun had acted of his own free will, even deceiving the council, did not matter to them. This had been their plot all along. Vera stepped up to Arun's bed and placed her hand on his head as she spoke the command to see into his mind. After only a few seconds, she withdrew.

"What did you see?" Baran asked.

Vera ignored him and went to Lady Lyr and whispered something in her ear before they began making their way toward the exit.

"Oh, no you don't," Baran growled as he stood up from his chair. He made a dash at Vera, grabbing her and pinning her against the wall, holding his sword out for any that tried to interfere. "You got what you wanted all this time. You *will* tell me what you saw."

Vera looked down at Baran, her eyes filled with pity. "He will live," she said. "But he will not be the same. His memories have been polluted. When he wakes, he will see all of us, especially you, Baran, as his enemies."

Baran let go of her in shock. "The Silent Stone did not do that to Athaz," he said.

Vera shook her head. "This was not the work of the Stone. I cannot say for certain, but I believe this was Bälech's final, spiteful act of hate. The only vengeance he could salvage against the one that ended him."

At that moment, Arun began to stir. He swung his legs over the bed. "Where …" But upon seeing Baran, a hatred that blinded him to everything else overtook him. He leapt for Baran, hands outstretched, anger overpowering the pain emanating from his shoulder. He meant to strangle Baran, and he meant to do it now, but several hands reached out and caught him. "Curse you!" he screamed so hard spit flew from his lips. Baran was too stunned to react as Arun turned his attention to Descia. "How could you leave me for *him*?" he screamed, tears beginning to roll down his face.

Vera immediately came up and replaced her hand on Arun's brow. "Witch!" he screamed. "I'll—"

At that moment he was silenced and went limp, his mind stunned by Vera's Divine command. "We will discuss this in a moment. For now, there is one more matter I must attend to."

To everyone else, Vera looked as serene as ever. Only Elves would have seen the pain in her eyes. This isn't how she had wanted it. Everything still seemed like such a mess, but she had one more thing to do before she could stop the torture going on in Arun's mind. She would heal Caedin. That's what Arun would have wanted if he was in his right mind. Then, she would meet with Arun's friends. "Not that I'll be able to give them what they want," she thought to herself. The Arun they had known was gone. After that? She shuddered. After that she would touch the Silent Stone, the penalty for her childish arrogance and disregard for the mind of the young boy she met all those years ago. *I won't be myself any more either*. She could not honestly say she regretted her choice, not yet, but she wished she could find a way to purify Arun's mind and avoid her fate.

Arun was still comatose when Vera came back to the medic's house. She did not enter. "Bring Arun to the Chamber of Council," she told the medics that were treating him. She turned to Baran. "Follow me." Baran and Descia made to obey her when she clarified, "Just you, Baran."

As they walked along, Vera spoke to Baran about the situation. "I know that you'll never believe me, but this is not what I wanted," she said. Baran did not respond. "Had Arun and Inoch told me the true plan, I would have stopped it. Getting Bälech to touch the Silent Stone was a brilliant idea, but there might have been other ways to coax him to do so. Though…" she paused briefly "…I have yet to think of a better plan myself. Still, I would not have had Arun risk himself in such an attempt that was so unlikely to succeed and with such a high likelihood to destroy him, as it has."

"Is there a particular reason you are telling me all this?" Baran asked. Vera thought for a moment before laughing reproachfully at herself. "I guess I just was hoping for a bit of understanding. But that's not why I asked you to follow me." She stopped and turned to face him. "I am asking for you to tell me what Arun would have wanted." Baran was confused. Why would she ask him such a thing? "I cannot restore his mind to what it was before. There are so many false memories so well-woven that I cannot possibly hope to sort them all and correct them. We have two options. You won't like either of them, but I am hoping you will be able to tell me which he would choose if he could speak to me." Vera waited for a response, but Baran just silently waited for her to continue.

"First, we keep him asleep and manipulate his dreams to give a life of peace and bliss. Elves would stay at his side and keep him in a perpetual state of enchantment. It would be an honor my people would gladly accept for his sacrifice for the Savanir."

"And the second choice?" Baran asked reluctantly. Vera hesitated for a moment before she began. "Remove his personal memories entirely. I can implant an accurate set of events in his mind, but he will have no personal memory of being involved in any of it. It will be the same as if he read a biography of someone and then found himself living that person's life, with no memory of his own before it. It will be a hard life, filled with doubt and confusion, but he'll be awake and free to act with the world as it really is."

Baran was shocked at how quickly he responded. "The second option." But though he instantly knew it, and why, his voice still cracked as he explained. "Arun would never want to live a lie. As upset as he was with you and everyone else in the Savanir, he was glad that he had learned of another world, and that it not only survived but thrived. You robbed him of his ambitions. You placed him in the middle of a war that he wanted no part in. But you revealed the lies of our home for what they were. Whatever you do, don't give him a life of lies."

Truth Unearthed

Vera smiled. "I won't. As an Elf, let me offer this small piece of comfort. Your friend's spirit that let you become like brothers will still be there. The value of Truth is intrinsic from circumstance. If you are right and Arun would have wanted this before, you will find he still feels that way after. Perhaps, in time, you might be able to form a new friendship."

CHAPTER XXIII

Consequences

"Try to bring all your memories with Arun to the forefront of your mind," Vera told Inoch, her voice weak from exhaustion. It had been five days since Inoch had defeated Bälech by stabbing Arun's shoulder with the dagger embedded into the hilt he had fashioned from the Silent Stone. He was hailed as a hero everywhere he went, but he wasn't enjoying himself as he ought. As Vera's Divine command began, Inoch tried to force himself to remember all of his dealings with Arun. But the last words his friend spoke to him the night before the confrontation continued to demand his full attention.

* * * * * * * * * *

"I always said I was not the savior of the Savanir," Arun had said when Inoch revealed his idea to craft a hilt from the Silent Stone.

Inoch had wanted Arun to duel Bälech. If he could just stab him anywhere on his body, no matter how superficial the wound was, all they need was Bälech to grab the hilt.

"It has to be you," Inoch said. "He won't accept a challenge from anyone else."

"Oh, I know full well I have to challenge him," Arun replied. "But I could never defeat him. I would not be able to defeat a trained soldier, much less an Emperor who wields the Divine in its entirety as a weapon."

"Then why are you acting like I've found the solution?" Inoch asked.

"Because all we need is for the host to touch the hilt, not for me to defeat him." Inoch continued to stare at him in confusion, so he rephrased it. "We don't need Bälech to touch the hilt. Just his host

… who that is doesn't matter."

For a moment, Inoch stood at a loss for words. It seemed like Arun was arguing semantics. But as Inoch looked into his friend's grave eyes and resigned smile, he began to put the pieces together. "NO!" Inoch yelled in disbelief.

"It's the only way," Arun said with a dark laugh. "You'll be the hero as you ought to be. I'm just going to be a pin cushion."

"You'll die … or worse!" Inoch said, his voice reaching new heights in alarm.

"That's going to happen regardless," Arun answered. "My fate was sealed the day Vera decided to try to make me into something I'm not. The Emperor would never stop hunting me once he learned who you believed I was. And here, in Menigar, the lucky ones will be those killed in its fall. But do you think he would let the hope of the Savanir off that easy?"

After that, it hadn't taken Arun long to convince Inoch of his change to the plan. Acting as though he would challenge Bälech, he would instead offer himself up as his next host. Only Inoch and Baran would be aware of the trap. Inoch would feign surprise and stab Arun to stop him, and Arun would hold onto the hilt and hope that Bälech would be so eager to accept this ironic victory that he would enter Arun before healing the wound.

It worked. And Inoch had hated himself for it. He had wanted to only aid Arun in his role of saving the Savanir, a footnote in the history books that would focus on Arun. Instead, he was now being hailed as natural savior of the Savanir. Yes, they had considered Arun a hero too, but with one of their own having actually come up with the original idea, fashioning the hilt and actually dealing the blow, many of the Savanir were all too eager now to accept Arun's claim that he was no savior. He was a brave young man who made a heroic sacrifice, and one they would always remember. But that was all.

"I won't deny that I'm happy your people will be free, and that I'll be a part of that … even if I doubt the future holds what you hope." Arun had said when they finished their planning. "And I would like to think that I would make such a sacrifice for you and the Savanir if I had come up with a plan on my own and been able to pull it off. Quite frankly, the only people I'm upset with are the Elves, especially Vera. Still …" Arun paused, his brow furrowing. Placing his head in his hands, he continued. "No people ever stop trying to survive, and the Savanir and the Dawn are mutually exclusive. When you first rescued us, I tried to hide behind the security that The Dawn had afforded me and others like me. But after seeing the state of most of this world, the battle at Lacris, and especially what I experienced at the hands of the Watchers, which doesn't even begin to compare to what others have endured, I understand them."

Inoch smiled. Arun shook his head. "Don't get me wrong. I'm still pissed. They had no right, even if I could have saved them as they thought. But if there is an afterlife, I won't regret this even if it doesn't work." Inoch nearly jumped as Arun broke into an unexpected laugh. "And who knows? I survived once by hurling a knife blindly at an Orc. Who's to say—"

* * * * * * * * * * * *

Inoch was thrown out of his memory as Vera removed her hands from his face and broke her connection with his mind. He looked into her face and saw tears in her eyes. It unsettled him. Sure, he had seen her cry at her brother's funeral, but that was in mourning. Her dark blue eyes now trembled in agony brought on by guilt.

"Thank you, Inoch," she said after a moment, turning her back to Inoch and facing Arun. "You may go now. I found all your memories with Arun."

"Yes, milady." Inoch bowed.

"One moment," she said, bringing him back, though she still did not face him. "Do you still intend to do as you said? To resign your post and follow Arun, wherever that might lead you?"

"Yes, milady," Inoch said again. "The Savanir owe him that much, and I personally could never let him face what is coming alone."

"Very well," Vera replied. Inoch bowed and left the chamber.

"Very, very well," she said again under her breath, now letting her tears flow more freely now that she was alone. She looked at the young man before her, his face a blank slate in his charmed sleep. She felt like a fool. She had started out naive enough. She had been young when she met the little boy near his Yeoman hut near Simpat after sneaking out of the Savanir camp. She had only just begun receiving visions from the Sea and learning to interpret them. Her heart was light and guiltless in what she had done then. Indeed, it still would be, if she had let it be. At the time, she heard the warning spoken to her as being a question of willingness to pay a price to free her people. But now she knew what Lyr had told her was true: that it wasn't a warning at all. The Sea had been trying to dissuade her from trying to force her vision to play out. It wasn't a warning. It was a threat.

In truth, Vera knew it long before, though she always kept blinding herself to it. No until that day that Arun revealed his fragmented memory of that night that her grandmother broke down the delusions of grandeur did she feel any guilt about it. Even then, she was so caught off guard by Lady Lyr's fury that, though she admitted she acted foolishly, she still refused to fully accept she had behaved reprehensibly. In time, though, doubts plagued her, and she began to wonder. Now she knew beyond all doubt that her grandmother had been right.

As if on cue, she felt Lady Lyr walk into the room. "I'm almost finished," she said. "I'm not trying to stall."

The old, tired Elf paused for a moment. "I never accused you of stalling," she said. "No, I came here because I could feel your conflict from every corner of the city, and I will not be able to offer much comfort in the future."

"You are no longer angry?"

"Oh, Vera," her grandmother responded with a small laugh as she came up behind her granddaughter and placed her hands on the young Elf maiden's shoulders. "Even at your age, you should have learned by now that anger and love are easily entwined; indeed, those we love the most can cause more anger than any enemy."

"I didn't think it would end this way, not at first."

"But you knew better than to alter someone's mind against their knowledge. And years ago you realized you should stop manipulating his course."

"Yes."

"And it worked. Do you know what the natural consequence of that will be?"

"Yes. There will be some that view this as a necessary, even our rightful place."

"Indeed," her grandmother confirmed. So far, this was not comforting. "But," she continued, "in the end, Arun chose to make a sacrifice he did not have to. He could have run. He did not. When running was no longer an option, he could have ended his own life, and no one would be able to fault him. He did not. Twice, he had the chance to ease his own suffering and leave us to ours. And when Inoch revealed his plan, it was Arun's own decision to face most likely a fate worse than death. The same soul will reside in him. His new life will be much harder than even the last several months of the one lost. He may never forgive you for it, but if he does, you can rest assured he always would have. Only he can set you free for the crime of stealing what was his alone to give. Only time will tell if he will."

The seer paused for a moment before continuing. "And that really should be your only concern. Much harm will come from your decision. But this is where I can offer you some measure of comfort. Your life, Vera, will be difficult. The most difficult of any of our people in eons. You must accept it. And to help you with that is why I have come. For when you are no longer able to sense the Sea, I would have you be able to recall this memory. Leave your task for a while and follow me."

Curious, Vera followed her grandmother back to the seer's chambers. Unlike most homes, even for the Elves, this one had running water that collected in a pool before slowly draining back into the underground river that ran below the mountains. This was a special feature in the home of the current seer of Menigar to allow them to commune with the Sea whenever they felt the need.

Truth Unearthed

"I have never attempted what I am about to do," Lady Lyr said quietly. "It took me most of my years to be able to wade in the Sea at will, to find in our memories the wisdom to deal with today. Even so, I rarely do it; it drains me of all energy, and I never know how long it will take me to recover. Leading another through it ... let us hope I have the strength. It is a good thing you always were a quick learner in this," she said with a rueful smile. "I imagine after the first jump, you'll just need me to lead you in the right direction and you'll be able to take on most of the work yourself." Taking Vera's hand in her left, Lady Lyr sat them both down on the edge of the pool and stuck her right hand into the water.

Suddenly, Vera was yanked into an ancient memory. A Dwarf ... Vera realized with horror it was the first time her people had witnessed the atrocity of a golem — an empty body of rock built by twisted Dwarven Divine commands. She could hear its empty voice, and she felt the crushing death blow an Elven ancestor suffered in battle from it. But before she could even fully recover from that shock, she felt her grandmother leading her to another one. It was of Bälech's armies as they swept across Lugon. The remnants of the Kingdom of Kelbragh were on the run. Bälech could have wiped them out if he wanted to, but believing the refugees were no longer a threat, he turned his attention toward the Dark Dwarf kingdom of Goldún. Kelbragh had fallen after three years. Goldún lasted nearly a decade before its golem armies, in its deathtrap-riddled fortress, was overrun by Bälech's combined might of Savage Races and early human followers. In that time, the Dwarves of Kelbragh had formed a city under the foothills just south of their old kingdom, thinking the last place Bälech would look for them would be their old stomping grounds. In time, that underground refugee camp became Menigar, the city of Hope for all races that would be known as the Savanir.

Vera now knew what to expect and did her best to aid her grandmother as she took them deeper into the Sea. Memory after memory flooded their minds. Eventually, Vera realized a pattern. Throughout the history of Lugon, that which was done in evil had been used for the benefit of the good. Lady Lyr must have sensed Vera's clarity in mind, for suddenly she found herself being brought out of the Sea.

"That was the last comfort I will be able to give you," Lady Lyr said breathless. "It does not excuse what you have done. It does not lessen your guilt or the life you must face for it. But your crime was committed in arrogance. Do not let arrogance also lead to despair. Take comfort in the humility of knowing that though you might alter a river's course, you cannot change that all waters flow into the sea. Lugon, even Arun, will reach their ultimate destinies regardless of what you or I do here. Ultimately, the only power we have is how easy or painful we make the journey, both for ourselves and for others."

Vera did what she had not since she was a little girl. She leapt into her grandmother's arms, wrapping her in a hug around her neck. "Thank you, *Valima*," she said, using the term of endearment that had no longer been considered appropriate when she came of age. She kissed her grandmother's cheek before quickly making her way back to Arun.

With new resolve and determination, she continued her work of giving the Man before her the starting point he would need to begin his new life. It wasn't enough. Nothing would be enough. Her actions may not be able to restore Arun to what she owed him, but they would do more than her shame.

CHAPTER XXIV

A New Reality

Arun awoke in a short bed. His legs would have spilled over the edge of it had they not been tucked so close to his body. "Where am I?" he thought aloud to himself. He tried to think back to what he had been doing before he went to bed and why he had chosen such a small one. Panic overtook him. He couldn't remember! He jumped off the bed and was pacing quickly as the fear of not being able to remember became stronger and stronger when a knock at the door stopped him in his tracks.

"Arun?" a voice called out from the other side. "Can I come in?"

"Who are you?" Arun answered.

There was silence for a moment. "Baran," the answer finally came as the door opened. When he entered the room, they looked at each other in silence. Arun's face was one of fear, but he fought to contain it, while Baran's was one of trepidation. "I guess you really don't remember, do you?"

Arun's head began to ache. "I know I should. I know who you are, but I don't remember actually doing anything we've done together. What's happened to me? Why can't I remember anything?"

"What is the last thing you know to have happened?" Baran asked.

"I ... I trapped Bälech in the Silent Stone, but I don't actually remember doing that either!"

"Yes, that was almost a week ago. Bälech scrambled your mind. You saw me as a friend that betrayed you ... and worse. Vera could not restore your memories correctly, so she removed all of it. She looked into my mind, as well as Descia's, Inoch's, and everyone else she could find, to give your mind a narrative to work from. I'm afraid it's all we could do."

Arun's eyes were facing Baran's direction but were actually

looking far past him, trying to process what he was being told. "And how do I know you implanted the right narrative?"

Baran paused before giving the answer. "You don't" he said at last. "You will never have the certainty you ought. The only thing I can say to offer you some comfort is to be honest now. Vera offered to have the Elves keep you in a never-ending dream of bliss for the rest of your life. I told her you would never choose to live a lie. Did I choose wrong? You can go back to sleep if you want."

Arun's eyes refocused on the young man in front of him, the man his brain was telling him was his best friend but his heart no longer felt it had any relationship with him. But with that revelation, a small feeling of familiarity awoke. It was not much. Though a part of him was seduced by the idea of a life of bliss, his soul recoiled at the thought of such a living death. "No. No, you chose correctly." He may not know Baran, but there was just the tiniest bit of comfort that Baran seemed to have genuinely known at least that much about him.

They sat for many minutes, both wanting to say so much, but neither saying anything. What could be said? Baran watched his friend in silence just as Arun watched the people of Menigar through a window. There were many that were short. *Dwarves*, Arun's brain told him. He also knew he had stayed with a Dwarf when he first arrived. It was as if everything about his life, he was seeing through the eyes of another. An empty identity.

"I guess I'm in the same Dwarf's house as before?" Arun asked at last. Baran confirmed that with a nod of his head. "I'm sorry," Arun said. "I know you want to help, and I can't imagine the pain of your best friend not knowing you, but I think I want to be alone."

Baran couldn't help but wince, but it was mostly at the "I can't imagine" phrase. Arun's memories were truly gone. "Alright. But if you need anything…"

"You'll be the first I ask," Arun said, forcing a smile. It was a cordial smile but without warmth. At the moment, it was all he could give.

"Right," Baran said with a nervous laugh. They awkwardly waved as Baran left the room.

Truth Unearthea

As soon as the door shut, tears of helplessness ran down Baran's face. Descia looked at Baran as he entered the room, and he simply shook his head. "He wants to be alone for now. Let's go." And with that, the friends, minus Kruthos who stayed behind to watch Arun, went back to Inoch's house.

Arun lay on the bed, curled up. He couldn't even begin to describe the sense of loneliness weighing on him. Perhaps this was all a bad dream, and if he went to sleep, he would wake up able to remember. Eventually, he did doze, but each time he awoke, he could only truly remember his most recent conversation with Baran. He felt like a lost child. At last, his hunger forced him out of his isolation. When he opened the door, Kruthos looked up from his chair at the table.

"I take it you're hungry?"

"Yeah," was all Arun managed to say in response.

"Alright, I'll whip up something quick as lightning."

"Thanks … Kruthos ….?" The name sounded strange on his tongue.

The Dwarf nodded. "That's right, lad." As he cooked, he talked to Arun about all the events that had gone on since Bälech's fall. The gates of Menigar were open, the Dawn was in a complete state of disarray, and emissaries had been sent to Hilae, Mizcur, and all the other cities to explain to the populace what had happened. "Of course, most think they're crazy. The highest-ranking military officials that were not Wardens have taken over their local towns. Trade has almost come to a standstill. There are dark days ahead for them, but here the city is still in a state of jubilation. I know you may not feel much like celebrating, but I would recommend you still get out and not stew all day. I'm a bit more familiar with Elves' abilities than Baran. I'm sorry to say that I am fully aware that your memories won't be coming back. Vera's abilities as a mature Elf were only surpassed by the Lady Lyr. But you'll drive yourself crazy if you just try to force yourself to remember. You should get out. Any place you want to go, you can."

Arun ate in silence, and Kruthos respected it. After he was finished, he thanked his host and walked out. He gasped again at the beauty of the stonework, the streets and giant lamps. "Well," he said out loud to himself, "I guess the only thing to do is to start making memories."

He walked the city's perimeter. As he took in the sights again, he found it was helping him sort the history in his head. He was able to picture the past events in his mind a little clearer, even if he still felt distant from them. Maybe if he went and visited all the places from his life before, he would be able anchor himself a little more firmly. Most of that was far away, in Hilae, where he imagined everything was descending into chaos. What could he do until then? There was so much to learn, to relearn. "I think ... I think I'll go to the Library," and with that he set off toward the heart of the Elven District.

* * * * * * * * *

After many long hours in the library, Arun eventually returned to Kruthos' house. The Dwarf was already asleep. *Good*, Arun thought. He didn't want to have to talk to him. He had spent the entire day reading of other peoples and their cultures, loving every minute of it. But every time he stopped, his situation bore down heavily on him. He wouldn't be able to just lose himself in books. That was no different than the dream life offered to him by the Elves.

With a sigh, he threw himself on the short bed in Kruthos' guest room, facing the ceiling. When he did, he heard a something give a slight crunch, and he could feel something in between him and the bed sheets. Reaching under his back, he pulled out a piece of parchment. It was a letter, addressed to him from Athaz. As he read over it, he realized he had no memory of this because he was the only one to have seen it, and therefore no one else's memory could be used to put this missing piece into the narrative. How many more parts of his life like this were there, he wondered. Shaking that thought from his mind, he read the letter for what felt like the first time.

The effect the letter produced was immediate and complex.

Tears welled up in his eyes. This letter was giving him a more real connection to his past than any of the things about him that Vera had planted in his mind. He had no doubt that Athaz would have been able to help him find his way back if he was still here. But he wasn't. Arun reread the letter a second time.

Suddenly, Arun knew exactly what he must do. He jumped out of the bed and woke up Kruthos. "Where is Caedin? What happened to him?" he asked.

"He's staying with a medic. Vera wiped his mind too because of what Bälech had done to him. Not entirely!" he quickly said, seeing Arun's alarm. "Only since he was taken to The Tennebron. He's getting ready to leave in the morning."

"Take me to him," Arun said. "I need to speak to him on matters that concern both of us."

They went first thing in the morning. Caedin was preparing to depart; he wouldn't stay with the Savanir.

"What do you plan to do?" Arun asked him after he explained the situation.

"Work as a mercenary. I have some training as a soldier, and if I die from the work, so much the better."

Arun grimaced. He wished he had died in The Sundering, but he was determined to find a new purpose. Caedin sought sleep. "Travel with me," he said at last.

Caedin's face and tone mocked Arun's offer. "Oh, sure, let you save me just as you saved the Savanir because you feel like you owe my pathetic excuse for a father something."

"Not for him, for me," Arun replied. "I need companions, particularly ones who are not loyal to the Savanir nor desire to resurrect the Dawn. You were trained as a soldier. I desire to learn to defend myself. I have no home. You have no home. We are far more likely to survive by depending on each other, especially since we don't want the aid of the powers vying for control of Lugon in this upheaval."

"And the fact that I don't want to live?" Caedin asked.

"May change in time with companions and a reason to live," Arun replied.

The Tales of Lugon

"And what reason do you have, Arun?" Caedin asked genuinely. "Your life from before is gone, you have no hope of reclaiming your dreams as a Keeper with the Dawn, and you hold the Savanir in contempt for what they did to you. What will you measure your life by?"

"To find the Truth with my own eyes. And when I can, help others as should be done … with no strings attached. Perhaps we could even fit mercenary work in that philosophy?" Arun finished, holding out his hand. "It can't end worse than living a life where you seek death," he added.

Caedin paused for a moment. "Alright. I'll travel with you, but no commitment for how long."

"I wouldn't have it any other way." Arun smiled.

* * * * * * * * * *

Baran and Descia had finished their dinner long ago, but they were still staring over their empty plates, deep in thought. Arun had told Baran of his plan. First, he would travel to Hilae. After that, he would be journeying all over Lugon, doing work as needed to pay for food and lodging and living the life of a wanderer. "You're free to come," Arun had told him. "But only do so if you wish; the Savanir could certainly use the help fighting the Savage Races if that is still your intent. And, it's an honorable way to live. Probably better for you and your soon-to-be bride. But, even if I can't remember anything, I knew it would be cruel not to at least let you know my plans."

Baran told Descia about it as they ate. "I think I have to let him go," Baran said at last. "Nothing I do will bring back the friendship Arun and I once shared. Even so, he wouldn't ask me to leave you."

"Who said anything about leaving me?" Descia retorted. "Men and their foolish notions of self-sacrifice! Do you honestly think I want to live with you sulking and worrying about your friend … for your friend he is whether or not he remembers it, wondering if you were blaming me?!"

"But Descia, we can't—"

Truth Unearthed

"Can't what? Live our lives in the past, trying to reclaim what is lost?"

Baran nodded.

"We won't be. Did it ever occur to you that Arun's idea intrigues me? For crying out loud, he is essentially starting the same task as he did with you in Hilae, and I wanted to go on that one too!"

Baran looked at her, unexpected happiness in his eyes. He walked around the table, picked her up, and kissed her before setting her down again.

"You really want to travel with him?" Baran asked her.

"Certainly, at least to Hilae," she said. "After that, who knows? But as long as we are going to travel with him, there is one thing I'm going to demand of you ..." She paused with an icy stare. "You are going to teach me how to wield a weapon. You aren't ever leaving me behind again like some lady that just keeps the house while the man dreams of coming home. Are you prepared for me to adventure with you? Because if you are looking for a woman to come home to, you need to keep looking," Descia finished. Her tone was resolute, but Baran could see in her eyes she hoped he was done looking.

Baran remained quiet for a long time, and Descia waited. This was no small thing she was asking, and it went against Baran's nature of protector, and she knew it. At long last, his features relaxed. "If you can survive training with me, I'll ensure you're able to survive anything I can," he said finally.

This time it was she that brought him down and kissed him passionately.

Vera was staring into the pool for hours. It had been six weeks since she had touched the Silent Stone, since she had lost her connection with the Sea and her people. With bitterness, she remembered the first time she had come here after she had been released from her bed as she recovered from touching the dagger hilt Inoch had shaped from the Silent Stone. It had been bad enough for her to stay in bed, unable to sense the presence of other Elves. And when her grandmother came to visit her, she thought it couldn't get any worse. The Lady Lyr's expression, though sorrowful, was as serene as always. Unable to sense her grandmother's pain, something she had always been able to do, made her feel cold and uncaring. Was this how Men and Dwarves had always seen them?

All too clearly now, she was able to see so many things that had always puzzled her about the other races, but on that day, in a single hour, she had been given years of lessons that she was still unpacking. She finally understood why the Men and Dwarves thought her people unfeeling. With embarrassment, she remembered her disdain for the violent emotional displays in the other Noble Races, only to in that hour act in that same manner with the intensity more befitting to their young children, not a mature woman. Never before had she realized how much of her peace had been rooted in the knowledge and connection she had shared with her people.

But it all paled in comparison to that first day she went back to the pool. She had been clinging to the hope that in the physical presence of the water, where the Sea and all its people's thoughts and memories were so strong that Elvish children could only be near it for moments before being overwhelmed, she would at least feel some shred of her Elvenhood. But there was nothing. When she dipped her hand, all she felt was a bitter coldness.

She had screamed until her grandmother arrived and forced her into a deep sleep to carry her back to bed. Today was the first day she had been back to the pool since that waking nightmare. The bitterness wasn't any less. Every now and then, a tear would work its way down her face, eventually dripping from her cheek into the spring to be carried out to the Sea, a place where she longed to go herself. Killing herself would not ease the pain. The spirits of Elves who ended their own lives were doomed to roam in misery and pain until the allotted five hundred years for their fading was completed.

"Five hundred years," she thought, as another wave of pain washed over her. She still had well more than four hundred to go. She was still young for an Elf, another thing that was pressing on her now. In the loss of all things that had connected her with her people, combined with her newfound emotional state, she felt as though she truly was a young human only her twenties. If only her body would age as fast as theirs! But this would not happen. She would be a stranger among her own people. As the Sea had prophesied, the only thing it had truly promised to her on that night, so it had become. She was a lone drop of rain, separated from all other waters. The bodies of her people being so near only reinforced the uncrossable gap that now stood between their minds. She had even considered leaving, living in exile until she at last could fade back into the Sea.

Suddenly, a thought came to her, a blissful hope that she almost forced back down to keep from feeling the pain she felt would soon follow if she let it grow. But grow it did. Though she could no longer sense the minds of her people, nor they hers, still they comforted her as they could. She tried to stop herself, so sure it would only cause more heartache. But she couldn't. "Show me!" she begged in a hoarse cry. "Show me anything! Pain, hope, a path, anything!" Anxiously she waited. After a few seconds, she knew what she had feared all along. Silence. How could there be anything else? The voices she had heard in the past were not of the drops contained in the pool, and neither could the visions have been. With a final bitter tear falling, she turned away from the pool as the ripples distorted her reflection.

"Vera," a voice suddenly called to her, yanking her mind back to what was in front of her.

Arun stood in front of her. She hadn't seen him since removing his memories. The guilt had been too much. And now he had found her lost in her own pain.

"I'm sorry, Arun," she said quickly trying to remove the tear stains from her face.

"For what?" he asked.

She realized he was sincere. And that was fair. "All of it," she said at last. She could feel his eyes examining her, as if he was weighing her sincerity.

"Good," he said at last. The response jarred Vera. It wasn't an acceptance of her apology, but he didn't say it like he was mocking her.

"I depart tomorrow. Caedin, Inoch, Baran, and Descia are going with me. First, we go to Hilae. The memories of my former life, though they never feel … present … with me like memories since I woke up, are still more firmly grounded when I go and experience the places where they happened. And…" he paused and looked directly at Vera "…I am going to try to help people. *Anyone* I can. Human, Elf, Dwarf … Savanir or Dawn. It helps me forget my own pain. We do not view ourselves as beholden the Savanir. Do you understand?"

Suddenly, Vera didn't feel meek. Though she couldn't blame Arun for being angry at her, she didn't think he was being entirely fair. "Can you honestly blame me so harshly?" she said as her anger rose to the surface. "You are not the only one who has lost much!"

"Yes, I can," Arun said in a flat, cool voice. "You chose your sacrifice. I did not. I can also see your arrogance in which you were so convinced of the vision the Sea brought you. The Sea showed me walking with your people freely. And, indeed, I have no doubt had you succeeded, I would have wanted to learn all about your people without me playing any role in it. But I never was able to deliver you. Inoch played a much more important role than I did. It was his idea. It was his hands that formed the hilt from the Silent Stone. The only role I played was to get stabbed, and the only reason I had to be the one to play that role was because Bälech believed all the garbage he heard about me being some sort of chosen one — a load of feces that you could have made up about anyone in your own kingdom and served just as well."

"Much of what you say is true," Vera admitted. "But not all of it. You did choose to act. You chose to stay when we begged you to flee. Your mind had been tortured by Watchers, and knowing that letting Bälech enter you would likely be far worse, you chose to do so anyway rather than ending your own life or trying to get yourself killed in battle. The full Truth, Arun, is you understand me. Or you did. But I guess I can only blame myself for you not doing so now. Though…" she paused for a moment "…you always made your ill feelings concerning my decision known."

Truth Unearthed

"It still doesn't change the fact that anyone could have served my role," Arun said hotly.

"Not anyone could have," Vera corrected him again. "Many — nay, most — would have flown when we asked. Most of those that did not would have tried to die in battle. Arun, from the time I first met you as a young boy, your biggest strength has always been your compassion for others. Though not courageous by nature like Baran, your desire to help others leads you to act with reckless abandon for your own safety. Even if you detested me, the one who endangered your life and robbed you of everything you held dear, you pitied my people's plight against Bälech. And, unless I misguess, this is as much to help Caedin as anyone else."

Arun opened his mouth before closing it again. He didn't want to give her this. But before he could say anything, she gave up waiting for him to speak and continued, "I do not say this to justify what I have done. Much like Athaz when he was before my grandmother, I must ask you for mercy, for I cannot atone for my actions, but neither did I feel I had a choice at the time. Of course, I did. We always do. But even Men often err when they believe they have an understanding of what will unfold in the future based on their immediate actions. It is an ever-present temptation for an Elf whose visions from the Sea grant them glimpses into potential futures." She paused for a moment. "My grandmother will bless your departure. You will be free to go, and we will hold no claim on you or those that go with you. But I beg of you, do not cut off all communication with me." The request was unexpected, and Arun's face made words unnecessary to show his doubt. "If you truly seek to aid any, truly regardless of their faction or origin, then I beg you to hold true to that. I will never again ask you to aid the cause of the Savanir. But, in my position, I will know of many people that could use help. Will you at least hear any request I send you? You will of course be free to refuse."

Arun bit his tongue. "My own words strike back at me." He took a seat nearby at the pool to think things over. "I won't deny I want to refuse this. I won't deny it also crosses my mind that you are manipulating me again with my own words, but I believe you were truly sincere when you apologized a moment ago." He continued thinking for a while, and at last he answered. "Any I can aid that does not benefit your place of power, I will consider accepting on one condition," he said.

"Name it," she replied.

"That they never know you or the Savanir requested our help," he answered. "You will not use me to enhance your position in Lugon."

"I swear it."

He got up and left her without looking back. Vera watched him leave, a mix of guilt, pity, but also relief in her face. She did not need the Sea to tell her that their lives were still entwined and that both would play major roles in the reshaping of Lugon—or they would die trying.

THE TALES OF LUGON CONTINUE...

FOR MORE INFORMATION ON LORE, UPCOMING BOOKS, AND CONVERSATION WITH FELLOW READERS, VISIT WWW.TALESOFLUGON.COM

Brakon awoke, hardly daring to move. He didn't even open his eyes. Nothing was wrong, and that meant something was amiss. He could think clearly. He felt control of his glorious wings, his terrifying claws, and his powerful armored ruby-colored body. What he could not feel was *him*. That blasted Nochane that had both given him this body and then imprisoned him in it. The fire in his belly grew with his rage as he thought about his hated enemy. Losing control of his restraint and no longer caring if he brought attention on himself, flames hot enough to incinerate flesh and bone shot forth from his maw as he shouted the hated name: "**Bälech!**"

Well, that will certainly get his attention, Brakon reasoned as he prepared both his mind and body for the battle to come. Only it never did. His eyes were open now, scanning his prison den, lit only by the small flame he let through his nostrils to light up the darkness. The cursed wretch was nowhere to be seen. Unsure how long this unexpected freedom would be left unhindered, he unfolded his massive wings out to their full span and beat the air around him. He stretched his enormous, muscular body (twenty-eight feet plus an additional six feet for the tail) out to its full length before tensing every muscle in his body and letting loose an unbridled roar, the echoes of which shaking the chamber as debris fell from the ceiling under Bälech's palace in Hilae.

Still nothing. A faint hope sprang to life from long since cold ashes. Though no longer a Divine creature unchained by flesh and bone, the alchemic process Bälech had used had an unintended side-effect: he could sense other Divine beings other than his own kind, something not even Bälech could do. He focused his mind and searched for his enemy. He was not there in the palace. Now he began his search through the city. At first nothing, but then something ... something weaker than he himself had been when only a Divine Pensi. It wasn't wholly foreign but nothing in his former realm had been so weak. Then he heard it. A command, a shaping command, and he remembered it instantly. *A Dwarf! In Hilae*?!

Brakon himself had devoured thousands of them with Bälech's blessing, back when he still willingly served the fledgling emperor in exchange for the magnificent body and power he now possessed. A time when dragons were still needed; a time before he kept them permanently enchanted, a trap hidden in their bodies for when their risks outweighed their uses. The Dwarves were nigh extinct last time Brakon roamed the outside world, and regardless, he knew that they would never have served Bälech, who likewise would never let them walk freely in his capital.

It could only mean one thing: he was free. Free to feed himself. Free to fly. Free to rule. Yes, lordship was what he and the others had been promised in exchange for their service, only to be betrayed and kept asleep until such a time as their charmed services were needed again. Taking a deep breath, he lit the torches through the room so he could see clearly. There, in the center of the far wall was the door, invisible to most but not him. Bälech kept the portal Divinely sealed. Still cautious, Brakon readied his flame breath as his tail inched toward the door and gave it a slight push. Emptiness. The dragon roared again in laughter as he easily made his way out. Divine spells had been the only defense; none other had been necessary, and Bälech wouldn't want to waste time opening up the exit for a dragon when needed. Brakon only felt a twinge of regret that he had not been the one to snuff out the flame of his accursed master. But the sense of freedom was still so fresh that nothing could lessen his mirth. At last he saw the sky; the stars were out on a cloudless night, and Bälech's palace still stood, casting a shadow over the hole where he would issue forth in mere seconds.

All his hatred for his master returned at the sight of the glorious dwelling place Bälech had built on the backs of him and his brethren. They had been promised kingdoms of their own, not pits in the ground. With a roar, he leapt into the sky as he sped toward the palace. He could not kill Bälech, but Brakon would have his revenge. He would destroy the home of his master. He would raze Hilae to the ground!

Glossary of People, Places and Terms

(Note: This List is not exhaustive. For all lore regarding Lugon, please visit www. talesoflugon.com)

People

Aldo (al•dō): Savanir soldier and spy under Blake's command.

Arnost (är•näst): A member of Brasan's crew.

Arun (ā'•roon): Born a Yeoman child, Arun was declared gifted by the Dawn's Watchers as a young child and taken to Hilae to study at the Academy. Childhood friend of Baran.

Aster ('as•tər): Innkeeper and spy for the Savanir in Mizcur.

Athaz (ā'•θaz): A Yeoman that joined the military to provide a better life for his family and protect his homeland. Became a Warden after the Rebellion of Setenbor; Arun and Baran's chaperone for their Graduate Task.

Bälech (bä•lək): A being whose existence is tied to the Divine; the sole surviving of his race, the Nochane. Founding Emperor of the Dawn. Worshipped as a deceased demi-god by the people of The Dawn.

Baran (ber-in): A young man who grew up in the Court and desires to become a Warden. Childhood friend of Arun.

Blake (blāk): Leader of a Savanir cell of spies in Mizcur

Brasan (bras•ən): Captain of The River Daughter.

Caedin (kā•dən): Athaz's son.

Damon (dā•mən): A member of Brasan's crew.

Descia (des•kī•ə): Young Keeper of the Chronicle; takes over Arun and Baran's Graduate Task of beginning an excavation at the Ruins of Lacris.

Garren (ger•ən): Savanir soldier and spy under Blake's command.

Geown (gī•ou•n): Elderly Keeper of the Chronicle that accompanies the expedition to Lacris.

Inoch (ē•näk): Young Savanir military leader. Leads young troops against the Savage Races.

Kruthos (kroo-θōs): Dwarven mason who serves as Arun's host when he arrives in Menigar.

Lilleth ('li•'ləθ): Athaz's wife.

(Lady) Lyr (lir): Elderly Elven Seer of Menigar; Grandmother to Vera and Therran.

Nihil (nīl): A senior-ranking Keeper of the Chronicle that accompanies the expedition to Lacris

Paleon (pā•lī•än): Descia's father.

Sylphia (silf•ī•ə): A Keeper of the Chronicle that accompanies the expedition to Lacris.

Therran (θer-rin): Elven general of all military forces at Menigar.

Vera (ver•ə): Elf-maiden who meets Arun at a young age; granddaughter of Lyr.

Waren (wôr•in): A member of Brasan's crew.

Xiarch (zī•ärk): The Deity worshipped by the Savanir, Creator of Lugon and the Divine Tongue.

Places

Abscos (əb•skōs): Small town on the northern banks for the Argom River, just south of The Meros Wood. Place where Paleon lives in Retirement.

The Argom (är•gäm) *River*: The largest river in Lugon.

The Briar Patch Mountains: The ruins of the ancient home of the Cruach Dwarves (Kelbragh)

Desip (de•sip): A small town on the northwestern bank of the Grigor River between Hilae and Mizcur.

The Forest of Orus (ôr•roos): A dense forest west of the Makrin Mountains and north of the Green Peaks.

The Grigor (grī•gôr) *River*: The river that runs west of the Briar Patch Mountains until it joins the Argom River.

Hilae (hi•lā): Capitol of the Dawn.

(The Ruins of) Lacris (la•krē): The place of the final stand of the United Kingdoms against Bälech.

Lamphine (lam•fīn): A small Yeoman town on the northern banks of the Argom River, in-between Mizcur and Abscos.

Menigar (min•i•gär): Capitol of the Savanir, built by the Cruach Dwarves after fleeing from Kelbragh.

The Meros (mer•rōs) *Wood*: A rich forest north of the Argom River.

Mizcur (miz•kər): Economic hub of The Dawn. Situated where The Argom River and Grigor River merge.

The Mossy Plain: The flat, mossy lands surrounding Hilae in all directions except to the southeast (where the Grigor River flows).

Simpat (sim•pat): A small, poor town in the eastern banks of the Argom River, near the Tikus Foothills.

The Tennebron (ten•ə•brän): Ancient home to the Dark Dwarves, it was converted into a prison of torture by Bälech; now run by Orcs.

The Tikus (tī•kʊs) *Foothills*: The hilly lands south of the Briar Patch Mountains and north of the Ruins of Lacris.

The Tower: The library where all official knowledge and records of The Dawn are kept. Run by the Keepers.

Terms

The Bewildered: The name given to the men of the Savanir by the Dawn; Elves and Dwarves are, officially on record, extinct.

Cloud Silk: A light, strong fabric manufactured by the people of Menigar

The Court: The upperclass/nobility of The Dawn. Very unstable.

(The) Divine Tongue - The original tongue of Power that Xiarch used to create Lugon; it still carries Power in for his creations in the aspects that he blessed them with. Often abbreviated to "The Divine" or even "Divine".

Healers: Men that Bälech has infused with the Divine for the purpose of healing wounds and curing poisons.

Keepers of the Chronicle: The historians and sociologist of The Dawn, often shortened to "Keepers".

The Savanir (sa•və•nir): The Elves, Dwarves, and Men that resist Bälech's control of Lugon. Live mostly in hiding. They have three true strongholds, the chief being Menigar.

Son of Bälech: The title that the people of Dawn use to address their Emperor.

Wardens: Men that Bälech has infused with the Divine for the purposes of combat. Serve both as his personal guard and field generals.

Watchers: Men that Bälech has infused with the Divine for the purpose of intelligence gathering. Serve as both his secret police and interrogators.

Yeomen: The serfs of the Dawn; make up the overwhelming majority of the population.